Burning Notes

CAPTIVE WRITINGS
BOOK FOUR

M.L. PHILPITT

Playlist

"lovely" by Billie Eilish ft. Khalid
"Nightmare" by Veracity
"Cut" by Plumb
"Scars" by Boy Epic
"Memories" by EarlyRise
"I Scare Myself" by Beth Crowley
"Monsters" by Katie Sky
"Journey (Ready To Fly)" by Natasha Blume
"Still Here" by Digital Daggers
"Love Me Like You Do" by Ellie Goulding
"Let You Down" by The Material
"My Escape" by Ravenscode
"Middle Finger" by Bohnes
"Venom" by Eminem
"Heart By Heart" by Demi Lavato
"Wicked Games" by The Weeknd
"Angel With A Shotgun" by The Cab
"Where Butterflies Never Die" by Broken Iris
"Angel By The Wings" by Sia
"the lonely" by Christina Perri
"Lost My Mind" by Alice Kristiansen
"Can You Hold Me" by NF, Britt Nicole
"NVM" by Faith Marie
"Shattered" by Trading Yesterday
"Glass Heart" by Tommee Profitt, Sam Tinnesz
"Don't Deserve You" by Plumb

Author's Note

Burning Notes is the fourth and final book in the Captive Writings series, which must be read in order. Start the series with Ruthless Letters.

Timeline: Burning Notes starts in the middle of Vicious Texts and takes place during that time when Teagan was in the hospital. This will make sense once you read chapter one.

Burning Notes is a dark romance with content some readers may find triggering. Since some retailers don't like to see warnings on the purchase page or even within the initial pages of the book's file, if you are concerned about triggers, please visit my website for a list or contact me. Due to the nature of the book, I encourage you to look at the list, especially if on-page SA/non-con is triggering (not done by H).

For all those still pushing through.
Don't be normal. Be you.

He ensured I was safe, even if it meant battling my personal devil. There was never a moment I felt alone, in having to overcome what I endured. Through a series of notes, he opened up his own previous wounds and shared the most intimate and scarred parts of himself with me, all to show me the light on the other side of darkness. To help me to understand that every time threatening shadows emerge to play their twisted games, there's always a way to banish them, to send them back from where they came. It may not happen right away; it most likely could take years, but it will eventually be expelled, and when it is, there's nothing better than the feeling of conquering them.

He brought me into the light. He *became* my light.

It started like any other day in my own personal Hell, crafted for a select chosen few. I awoke alone, shivering in the cold basement, and stared out of my glass cage, aware that when the devil seized me, I had no one who cared enough to search for me.

Then *he* came.

After that, everything changed.

He cared for me—cared *about* me. Maybe it's ill-advised

I trusted him so easily. Maybe I got away from the devil, only to end up in a demon's clutches. But his ice-blue eyes told me all I needed to know, so I willingly put myself in his control and found something else instead—something I never thought I'd be able to recover.

Myself.

He gave me back the parts of me the devil stole.

And in return, I gave him my heart.

One

WILLOW

Whenever I manage to sleep—when my exhausted and wrought-out body finally succumbs to slumber and I succeed in escaping from the present for a short time—my mind repeatedly brings me back to the moment I applied for a job with Miller Inc. The worst decision I ever made; my biggest regret in life, which may very well be my final one because I've been in this basement, cut off from the outside world, for nearly six months.

Almost but not quite. My skin only shows five scars—five ticks as he uses my thigh as a monthly countdown. I'm sure it's meant to torture me, but instead, it eases my mind, knowing I'm getting closer to the end.

He doesn't keep women longer than six months. It's a fact he continuously reminds me of, claiming after that amount of time, a particular woman's screams tire him, and he craves something different. Some*one* different.

I don't scream. Not anymore. Not after realizing he gets off on the noises. He claims all the other women cry right up until the last second, so some level of determination compelled me to shut up and not allow him to win. Maybe it's because he won't listen to me, so there's no point in begging. Maybe it's the fraction of defiance I've retained in my broken, shattered mind. Maybe it's because he's broken me so badly, so completely, my voice no longer works.

By the second month, I stopped begging. Stopped questioning his actions, for the very reason I resist screaming. He doesn't listen or respond, so there's little point in wasting breath and energy, I've come to realize, I'll need.

Screaming, begging, crying, and everything in between strengthens his power because when I do that, he wins. He has too much of it as is, so I won't allow him to seize more.

As the days turned into weeks, and the weeks into months, I ask myself what the point is in all of this. If I beg, perhaps he'll kill me sooner. Maybe he'll get so excited by my cries, he'll go rougher than he means to, and it'll finally be over. I'm holding onto reaching the inevitable end and…why should I?

Down here, down in Hell, I've lived through experiences one wouldn't even imagine being possible. The blood, the cuts, the whips… No amount is ever enough for him. The screams, the begging, the crying—he wants all of it. Begs *me* to make agonized noises to appease his own proclivities.

A tiny part of me continues to hold onto life, even maintaining some level of lucidity on the slim, impossible chance I'll be rescued. That someone, some angel from Heaven above, will learn of my presence and will come for me. A far-fetched dream, I know, and one I *should* have long put aside, but it's a hope I enjoy pretending could be a possibility.

Even if the possibility is impossible. Even if it's nothing but my broken, wrecked brain playing games and tricks on me, hoping that someone would—*could*—actually save me. It's humorous at best because *he* won't free me for anything. I know because he's told me that before. Death is the only thing that will free me.

There's no hero to rescue me. There never will be.

But I'm only human. And humans have fantastical wishes.

As if to reinforce my dire thoughts, a loud clinking sound can be heard from the hallway, but it's not my imaginary hero. It's the villain of my story.

The monster. The Devil.

Pick any evil name to call him, but none truly convey what Alex Miller truly is.

Fairy tales are all about discovering the fraction of goodness that is buried inside the monster, which usually requires a single heroic act or a kind woman to return its humanity. But I firmly believe Alex has no humanity, and never has; therefore, no act or woman will be able to reveal the good within him. It doesn't exist.

My arms tense around my knees, curling my body into a tighter ball as I listen to the clicking of his shiny shoes—they're *always* expensive, gleaming shoes—as he approaches the cage. I shut my eyes, since he doesn't like me regarding him until he demands it. When I don't obey, the hits are harder, the hate more vicious.

"Good day."

It's always "good day." He never indicates morning, afternoon, or night, and with the windowless basement I'm trapped inside, I know it's to drive me further into madness. There's never any indication of time down here, or of how long it's been since his previous visit, or of the number of days that have passed.

The door to my glass cage unlatches and fresh—fresher, at least—air enters alongside him. The basement's scent of death and torture isn't much better than the stuffiness of despair inside my cage, but at least it's a slight refresher.

"Oh, my pet. Is that how you say hello?"

This is how you like me. Scared and timid of your approach.

Yet, he consistently comments on me not greeting him as though he's the king he believes he is.

My arms, frozen because it's so cold in the basement, unlock from my body, and I roll onto my knees, immediately bowing my head so low, it nearly touches the floor in front of me, an inch from where he waits.

I stare at the shiny shoes, knowing he'll splatter them with my blood, and somehow, it'll be my fault for bleeding too messily. Alex's game is to make everything my fault, because then he has reason to extract more pain from me.

"That's better."

Even with his pleased comment, I don't lift my head. The first time I did so, without his permission, was the first time he nearly broke my nose.

"Stand up."

I do, my legs shaking and knees creaking from lack of proper use, while my eyes remain pinned on his feet. My matted, blonde hair falls on either side of my face. It's beyond greasy, considering it sees water once a week, when Alex finds it in him to allow me a bath. It's never a gift from kindness though, but rather a necessity, so he doesn't grow hateful of my scent, and so my wounds don't become too infected to the point I'll be useless. It's never warm water, and I only have access to a plain bar of soap. With the short time he grants me, I start with my body first, and then attempt to wash my hair the best I can before he yanks me from the tub, but it's never enough time.

Alex's hand moves, coming toward my face. A finger hooks under my chin and he forces my head up. I don't fight the movement, and my eyes lift too, landing on his chest.

"Look at me."

People claim a person's eyes can indicate a lot about their personality, and I realized after an only a day here, how true that claim is. When Alex hired me, he was masked, his true nature hidden, but once he got me down here, the mask came off. So, when I sleep and dream about the moment I got hired to work for him, I question how I missed what was so obviously in front of me.

A damned madman.

A psychopath, even if it's not the official clinical term.

Back when I was free, which seems like a lifetime ago, I checked out any available psychology books from the public library. Having an interest in the field, but being unable to afford formal education and get a degree sucks, but I vowed I would at least teach myself what I could.

Not that I've memorized the diagnostic criteria of every diagnosis, but I'm positive Alex is an actual psychopath. Modernity may have done away with the term, recoining it as antisocial personality disorder, but I much prefer calling him a psychopath. It has a better ring.

He aligns with so much of the criteria—disregarding and violating other's rights without care, hearing himself talk as he consistently recounts his previous experiences with the women who came before me, and lacking remorse for his actions.

Some would argue there are negative connotations attached to the term psychopath because it implies being deranged and dangerous, but there's no better description for Alex Miller.

The darkness in his eyes flares alongside his nostrils as he scans my naked body. Naked, not by choice, but because he doesn't provide me clothing.

His hand drops from my chin and buries between my legs. Trained on his expectations, my feet shuffle apart, granting him a better path to my pussy. He rubs my clit, but it burns with dryness.

I used to trick myself into arousal by pretending I desired his touch, but after so long, even my fake fantasies have become useless.

He flicks my clit, and his free hand shifts to my thigh, where he roughly grabs hold of the skin there, lifting my leg until I'm angled in a way that gives him better access. The new position forces me onto one leg, and I stagger, my hands immediately grabbing hold of his bare arms, right under where his sleeves are rolled up. Falling is better than relying on his assistance, but the landing will only injure me.

Even before his finger sinks inside me, I know it's coming. He pushes through the dryness, and I wince, continuing to stare at his shirt.

Body, get wet.

Unfortunately, it's never that easy.

"Always so tight for me. Just for me."

If he was another man, those words may elicit something, but Alex's possessiveness isn't cute or romantic. It's cruel and abhorrent.

His finger probes my insides, searching for my arousal, and I have to bite down on the flinch working its way through my body. He'll want me to flinch, aware he's prevailing over my pain, and I don't wish to give him the slightest satisfaction.

After another minute, he curses and pulls his hand away. My insides cry with joy, but the burn still flickers at my core. "Fucking bitch. I'm trying to care for you."

Alex's care is evil. I don't want it. I prefer his hate because it's predictable.

Alex "cares" for one other woman—his girlfriend, Teagan. I've witnessed the price she pays for his love. Recently, I had the unfortunate and heartbreaking experience of staring at her as he raped her against the glass of my cage. In that one moment, we were two condemned souls, bound together in misery and comradeship.

"I'm sorry," I mutter, dropping my eyes to the floor.

"No matter. I'm here for another reason. Do you

know what day it is?"

That day already. Breath halts in my throat, choking me in near-excitement because this will be over soon.

Alex only asks that question once a month.

My attention drops to the thigh he's still gipping—to the scars scratched along the skin there. Five months is an endless length of time when they're tallied upon my skin.

Five months.

Five cuts.

Always deep enough to leave a lasting scar.

But he'll be adding the sixth. Six means this is *it*. This is where it ends. Today, tomorrow, *soon*. There will never be a seventh slice because, instead, he'll do unspeakable things to my dead body, but at that point, I won't care. The moment my eyes shut forever is the very second I'll find peace.

My teeth sink into my lip to prevent from appearing too excited.

Alex drops my leg without care and backs away, out of the cage, while leaving the door wide open. I've long learned not to even bother trying to escape because I won't get anywhere. Instead, my vision blurs over as he heads for his wall of hellish items. Knives, ropes, cuffs, tape, chains, whips… the list goes on far too long.

I don't need to watch to know what he's grabbing. It'll be his "preferred" blade, as he refers to it. A dull blade, due to the number of times he's used it. It'll always be sharp enough to slice my skin because he makes it so by shoving it deep, but never sharp enough to create a quick and easy cut. He revels in the hard drag it takes to pierce my skin, aware it increases the pain.

Before he makes it back to my side, I turn around and press my front to the glass wall behind me. It's the position he prefers me in for this. The cage's wall should be numbingly cold, but the benefit of my life down here is that over time, minor nuisances are no longer a bother.

Through the glass and across the basement, I stare at my reflection in the large mirror he's hung there. It's why he wants me on this particular cage wall, because it gives way for me to stare at myself as he cuts me. I spot a woman with familiar features to mine, but the reflection is a shell of my old self. She's not me. She's what Alex Miller has forced me to become.

I watch him approach, watch as his handsome face breaks into an easy, sinister smile with my obedience. His hand—the one not clutching his blood-stained knife—lowers, and he unzips his trousers before pulling out his cock.

Good.

If he's taking me himself, it means he won't be using any other paraphernalia. Too many items have been inside my body for his sick pleasure, and his cock is the easiest to handle because I can at least try to pretend what he's about to do is normal.

He strokes it a few times while maintaining eye contact. His lips curl in a satisfied smirk, but it doesn't affect me as he believes it does.

His lips skirt the side of my neck and his next words are murmured into my skin. "For your six-month anniversary, you choose, my pet." His fingers push between my ass cheeks and briefly touch the hole there. "Here or your delicious cunt? Which hole of yours is crying for my cock?"

His head lifts from my neck and his form straightens, the smooth material of his suit brushing my bare skin. It's a sensation I've become numb to.

"You better pick before I do."

And he'll choose the one that brings me the greatest pain.

"My cunt," I whisper, despising the dirty term he makes me use. Between the two options, it'll hurt less.

And then I shut my eyes and drift. Drift and drown in

the sea of trauma he's forced me to weather. Yes, trauma. I'm self-aware enough to recall the psychology books and the descriptions and symptoms of what trauma looks like. What it's described as *feeling* like. Alex robs me of stability every time he's down here, and it's amazing I haven't lost my mind yet. I wish he broke me faster and harder, simply to end the sadistic, twisted kinks he imposes on me. If I could be numb to it all, perhaps it would be a fraction better.

I embrace the darkness, because with my brain floating outside my body, it's easy to pretend he finishes quickly, rather than dragging it out.

It's in this blackness, I don't allow myself to feel his feet kicking my legs farther apart, his fingers probing my core, as if expecting to find me suddenly wet, and of his hands fisting the skin of my ass as he grabs hold.

His cock bounces against my core, but I don't resist. No longer. My insides have shut the sensation off; of fighting his entry. Instead, I drown in the sea, willing it to take me away to nothingness.

This is nearly over. The final month…

It's in this blackness, I block out him dragging his cock against my core, until he—

—Breaks me.

Splits me. The pain is so much worse than usual, since I wasn't expecting him to have pushed inside my ass, forcing past its protective barrier. I bite down on the instinctual scream, sinking my teeth into my tongue, not giving him that much, but it can't completely be held in and it releases as a loud moan. My eyes fly open, landing on his crazed, excited ones through the reflection.

"It's fucking adorable you assumed you had a choice. You are *nothing.* You're *mine.* Mine to take how I goddamn please."

He fucks me harder, rougher, and my broken nails

scrape uselessly against the glass as I take it. His teeth clamp down on my shoulder, his bite hard, breaking the skin. I flinch as I release yet another traitorous wail. After a moment, his head lifts again; I don't need to look in the mirror to feel the hot, wet liquid sliding down the side of my neck and onto my breasts.

Blood.

His tongue flicks at my skin, lapping it up. His mouth yanks and sucks at the cut, but the sensations are soon pushed aside for the new and expected one—the blade against my thigh. I watch in the mirror as he angles it partway down the upper part of my leg, at the bottom of the column already cut into my skin.

He pauses, his dark eyes clashing with mine in the mirror, and his lips curl at the same time he pushes so hard inside me, my hips bounce against the glass.

"Happy six months. Can't wait for six more."

What? The moment the word shoves its way into my mind, the slice happens. The dulled knife cuts jagged against my skin, and I hiss with the slice, the cool air hitting the fresh wound. More blood drips from my body, slipping down my leg.

His hands clamp on my hips and he pulls me from the wall, keeping me tight to his own body, so he can pound into me harder and rougher, until I feel as though he'll shatter the rest of me.

"I normally tire of a woman by now, but I'm still quite fascinated with you, so why should I end this, when we're enjoying each other so much?"

"Why?" I whisper, allowing myself to speak out of turn. Even if he punishes me, I *need* to know. Need to understand why he believes I'm not broken enough yet—why he wishes to drag my life on longer.

Alex moves the cold knife to my core, the edge of it pressing right against my pussy lips. One slip, and he'll slice my clit. My leg muscles lock, working to prevent any movement that could make this possible, but his hips jerk harder, slamming my front against the knife. He moves it away at the last second, amusement sparking in his psychotic, black eyes.

"Because of this." The knife drags along my thigh and up my stomach, following the curve of my body. "Every other woman breaks around the one-month mark, but you…" His eyes meet mine in the mirror as the knife stops at a nipple, digging into the sensitive skin around it. "There's still a fire I haven't been able to completely extinguish. You've dimmed, but I'm not satisfied with that."

"No," I murmur, shaking my head slightly. I'm broken. I'm craving death. "Just end me. Kill me, Alex."

His eyes narrow, his pumps slowing as he studies my begging expression in the mirror. A strange emotion passes over his face before being interrupted with a mocking look. "And provide you the escape you crave? I don't think so." The edge of the knife knicks my nipple, but this time, my noises remain silent and hidden.

"Please," I beg, despite my claims to never plead again. "Please, Alex. You've gotten what you wanted from me."

"Not a chance. The very fact you're begging for escape indicates this," his finger stabs into my right temple, "still works. I *will* have you screaming before I kill you, Willow. You think I haven't noticed how you remain silent when I hurt you." To enforce his words, his hips slam again. "You're defiant, and I won't have that."

Alex's pace increases, a blinding pain soon following, and my body goes weak, blood dripping from multiple parts of it. When the knife falls from his hand and clangs at our feet, relief loosens my senses for the briefest of seconds, enough time to return to my void.

When he finally rips from my body, I crave to curl up

and die. Maybe today will be the day he'll bleed me dry, but even while wishing it, I know it won't happen because this time is nowhere near the worst of them.

The second he releases me, I lower to my knees because it's the position Alex prefers me in after every round of torture.

He palms his softening erection, and his eyes sparkle, landing on the blood streaming from my shoulder and leg. His hand wraps tighter around himself, and I know that look on his face means he's excited and wants another round.

"Pet, take me in your——"

The shrill sound of a doorbell shrieks throughout the basement, prompting Alex to scowl. From his pocket, he whips out his cell phone.

He clicks a few buttons before grunting. "Fuck, I forgot. Well," his attention falls back to me, "I guess you're free. For now." He zips his pants and exits the cage right away. Once the door is sealed and locked, he strides away from the basement without looking back at me.

With his exit, my body loses any strength it was clinging too, and I loll, my head thumping lightly against the cage's floor. My arms go around my knees, and I adopt the same position I was in before Alex arrived.

My eyes land on the fresh mark on my thigh. Six months. And counting, according to him. He wants me shattered. He doesn't want a survivor.

For him to kill me, it seems as though I need to let go. Let go, and fall into complete and utter madness.

Two

WILLOW

Six Months Ago

"Willow?"

Concentrating on the multitude of emails and appointment requests, I missed Alex—Mr. Miller, I mean—positioning himself at his office's doorway. His hands rest lazily inside his pockets, his ankles crossed as he leisurely leans on the frame. His chocolate-coloured hair is messy and sticking up from where he ran his hand through it multiple times.

I paint on a polite smile and push away from my desk to address him directly. "Sir."

His responding, bright smile has me wanting to wipe my palms on my fitted skirt, but I resist and remain still. Even as he pushes off the frame and approaches, I don't move, trapped by his influential gaze.

"Willow, over the past six months of your employment, you've far exceeded my expectations, and I'd like to show my gratitude. Would you be interested in getting a drink with me later?"

A drink? As in… he's asking me out? My stomach flips, hands sliding from my lap in shock. "Um." I swallow, licking my damp lips before trying again, "Um, yeah. Sure.

Thanks."

As though he's nervous too—which I realize is an idiotic notion—he straightens his already perfect tie. "Wonderful. Six work for you? I can send my driver, and he'll bring you to my home."

Oh. He means drinks at his place. Even more intimate, but despite all the reasons **HR** drilled into me upon being hired as to why any form of intimacy with Mr. Miller would be a bad idea, I nod, unable to resist the offer. After all, this may simply be professional. No doubt, he has plenty of meetings at his house, and inviting me over for a drink is one in many.

"That'd be nice. Thank you, Mr. Miller. I look forward to it."

"Please, after today, it's Alex."

"Alex." I test the word—the familiarity of his name, and I quite enjoy it.

He smiles again before twisting back inside his office and shutting the door. I don't mind though, because it means I won't have to fight to hide my unabashed grin.

His driver drops me off at the largest mansion I've ever seen. The brick stands sky high, with pillars lining the huge front doors. It's like something out of a fairy tale, and as I step toward the front entrance, I can't believe I work for this man. I've been privy to everything his company does, but to witness where he resides when he's not at the office, makes Alex seem even more magical and unreal.

"You may enter," his driver announces, gesturing to the front door and yanking me from my thoughts.

Despite the anxiety coursing through my veins, making the muscles at the back of my neck knot, I breathe in the fresh air and stride up the wide staircase toward those large doors. The wrought-iron handles taunt me with the strength and effort they appear to require.

I'm considering the possibility of coming off as a weakling as I struggle to open the doors when one opens, Mr. Miller filling the doorway.

My mouth goes dry at his casual outfit. I mean, by other people's standards, he's still quite dressed-up, but his rolled-cuff sleeves, lack of suit jacket, and dark jeans are quite something.

"H-hello. Thanks for having me."

Mr. Miller—Alex steps aside, his arm sweeping in an arc. "Pleasure's all mine. Come in."

Stepping into the foyer has some definite Cinderella-y vibes, which means I shouldn't be here. A vestibule such as this one is meant to be graced solely with rich people, and not some low-income twenty-four-year-old who never attended college and dresses in second-hand clothing since it's the cheapest way to follow Miller Inc.'s dress code.

He strides away the entrance, leaving me to follow him down the long hallway. I can't help but gawk around his house. I mean, this is where he *lives. Like, what?*

Alex leads me all the way to the end of the hallway, turns, and strides down another short one, which leads into a wide opening, revealing a restaurant-style kitchen, easily larger than my entire apartment.

Long marble counters gleam under the bright lights that Alex flicks on, which bounce off the shiny stainless steel of the chef-quality appliances. Along one counter, at least two dozen different spices wait in jars to be used. Spices, I'm likely unaware the names of half of them, let alone how to use them.

He leads me toward one end of the island, pulling out a bench as he goes. "Take a seat."

I do so, watching as he continues toward the fridge

and removes a half-empty wine bottle before finding two wine glasses, in which he pours the pale liquid. He slides one glass across the countertop, which I take, immediately bringing it to my lips.

"Mr. Miller—"

"Alex, please," he interrupts. "I've told you that already. There's no reason to be formal."

The glass freezes against my lips as I quirk my brows. "No?"

"Not at all." His easy smile sends flutters to my stomach, making me feel like someone else. Maybe, Cinderella, since, after all, I'm in the castle with Prince Charming.

"Well, okay then." I take a large gulp—large enough that the crushed, sour grapes scrape at my throat as they go down. "Thanks for the invite."

"You're welcome." He takes another sip of the wine and I watch as his throat bobs, swallowing the alcohol. Alex bends over, positioning his arms on the counter, and I swear something inside me turns on for the first time in forever.

Literally the first time. As in, I've never had sex.

"Tell me about yourself, Willow. Family, friends, activities you enjoy."

Hot millionaire boss wants to learn about me? Um, okay. "Well, I don't really talk to my family anymore. I'm fairly new to the area, so I haven't made friends yet. And as for activities… watching movies, I guess."

Alex's lips pull into a smirk, and even that makes my palms go damp.

Stop. This is a friendly interaction.

"Why don't you talk to your family anymore?"

I shrug, my attention falling to the single sip I have left. After this, I hope he's planning on bringing out another bottle, because it's quite tasty compared to the cheap stuff I buy.

"There's not that much to talk about. My parents were super strict, and when I finally moved away at eighteen, it was nice to have the break. And then… I don't know. I stopped calling home so often, and finally, stopped calling altogether. Now, I easily go six months at a time without contacting them. I think it's been over a year since I spoke with them."

"Huh." He takes his final sip too, his attention drifting to the hallway we came from. "Don't you miss them?"

"Sometimes. At this point though, I doubt they'd even question it if we never spoke again." I chuckle weakly at the absurdity.

Alex smiles, but it doesn't reach his eyes. "Well, that's sad, no?"

I shrug again, fingers twirling the glass between them. "I guess I'm used to it by now."

His lips purse. "More wine?"

"Please. Then I want to know about you."

Oh, God, one glass and I'm bothering a millionaire to tell me personal things about him.

Alex smiles and pushes off the granite countertop. "Works for me. Come for the walk? I'll show you the wine cellar."

A wine cellar. Of course he has a wine cellar. Because who doesn't have one of those in their house? It's totally normal—not.

I abandon my glass and follow him through the hallway. A short ways away, he stops at another door. This one he pushes open and takes the lead, flipping on a light before striding down the stairs.

I've watched enough movies to know wine cellars are, well, a vault on a lower-level, therefore nothing exciting to see. Still, his is likely larger than my entire apartment, so with that thought, I blindly follow Alex into his basement.

The place where he twists a pleasant interaction into the beginning of my end.

Three

WILLOW

Whoever was at the door must be important since Alex doesn't return, leaving me inside Hell to stare blindly at the ceiling and pretend my life has already ended. That the slice on my leg, still stinging from the basement's chill, was the exact cut that destroyed my life.

Often, when I zone out and stare off at the ceiling, I enjoy visualizing that I didn't meet Satan. That I didn't stupidly follow him down the stairs and straight into his trap.

That first night—that first rape—I had already realized what an idiot I was. How Alex had every moment planned out, from the invitation to his questions about family and friends—people who could search for me.

A set-up I soon learned he perfected when he showed me the images of the girls before me. My predecessors, both here and at work. His other victims, those he used to hone his planning.

I'm not his first.

Men like Alex Miller—rich, powerful, and admired by everyone—are invincible. Nothing can stop them because no one bothers to examine what's underneath their beautiful surface. And those who are aware of the gory and sordid details are exactly like him.

I wish I could say Alex was the only sexual encounter I've ever had, but that's not the case.

Five different men forced upon me.

Five different instances.

Despite the agonizing hate I felt each time, they also brought me a fragment of hope. Hope that one of these men would report him, should they see what Alex is truly doing. I've never learned who they are or where they come from.

Alex is smart though. He knows the risks. Slavery is one thing; torture is another, so his dungeon of pain is for him and him alone. When Alex brings in someone to try me out, I go to him, never the other way around.

I tried to run away once. The moment Alex led me upstairs and tossed me toward the other man, I sprinted. It was a hopeless attempt, since if I made it outside, I'd need to make it to the main highway, naked, and hope someone would stop and help me before Alex caught up. Except, I barely made it from the room before they stopped me. After his friend left, I thought he'd kill me that day.

That was the first time. The two other times, I never bothered to try and escape. Not before, or during, when the man shoved himself in whatever hole of mine he craved, or after he left me limp on the floor, staring at nothing while Alex and the stranger celebrated with a drink.

The basement's door unlocks, and my arms tighten around my body. Twice in one day? I suppose he's returned to finish what he wanted earlier.

Feet scrape down the connected short hall, hinting to Alex's impending arrival. To agony bound to come, and to more blood that he'll shed. More hate. More cruelty.

What I don't expect is a small crowd of people to enter the room.

Alex has done it. He's discovered new ways to break

me. A fucking *group* of people to what—watch? Or to participate and take turns? A group down *here*, the place he allows no one.

People are down here.

As the thought registers, so does the shock on the strangers' faces. Four men and two woman, all except one wear identical expressions of horror. Between them, one of the guys is gripping onto Alex's upper arms. Blood streams from Alex's nose, and I blink, shock clearing the way for me to see the gun pointed at him.

A gun. A weapon is pointed at my villain.

I laugh to myself. A soft chuckle for only me: my first laugh in months. It's funny because my brain has officially, thankfully, done it. I'm gone. I've floated down the path of darkness, going so deep my imagination has dreamed up the ultimate fantasy. That people have found me, have come to rescue me, and that Alex doesn't win.

For now, I peer at the group, scanning each of them. If my brain wants to experience this dream, so be it. I'll allow it the peace it's clearly craving.

A black-haired guy comes forward, holding something up in his hand. By the time my eyes register the item, I'm blinded with the quick flash of the cell phone.

From the side, a figure moves, approaching the cage, a strange expression on her face, as if she's uncertain what she should be feeling. Her brows dip, confused.

Teagan.

It's clear I'm dreaming now. Teagan and me, we're one and the same. Comrades in arms, but she wouldn't risk Alex's wrath to help me. Not that I blame her. Had I been in her position, I'm uncertain I could either. In some ways, I'm pleased I'm the one locked up because it's Teagan who experiences "normality" with him—whatever that looks like.

One of the guy glances at her. "How do we get in?"

"Go ahead and show them. Unlock it, babe," Alex order Teagan.

She murmurs something I don't catch and strides toward the cage's door. Her hand lifts to the number pad and she punches in the code—one I never realized she knows. The door unlocks and she opens it, stepping inside, her pitying gaze landing on my form. Her hand stretches toward me.

"Willow."

Still, I don't move, don't dare wake from this strange dream.

"Teagan," Alex purrs. "Babe, look at me."

He's speaking to her in the 'pretty' tone he used on her just the other day. The controlling one, in which his voice goes deep and he speaks with a smile in his tone.

"Kill her."

Thank you, Alex. This is it—the moment I've been both fighting and craving. He's opted not to keep me after all and handed the task off.

This is a dream, my inner voice reminds.

Right. Well, in my dream, people have found me, and this will end. This is the greatest thing my imagination has ever thought up.

In movies, people always mention how they have a final thought about a person or things they've done throughout their life before dying. Final regrets, final wishes. I have nothing and no one to think about. Instead…

Peace.

I did it. I survived Alex's hands, only to die by his verbal command.

I'm okay with that. Even if it's only in my mind, I'll pretend this is reality.

Her slim hands wrap around my throat, the grip tightening bit by bit. I shut my eyes to fall into death…

Her hands disappear, and my eyes reopen, spotting

two figures hovering over her. One yanks Teagan's arms behind her back, wrenching her crazed self away from me. The other kneels by my side.

I should be livid they prevented my death—my freedom—but instead, for half a second, I'm pleased. Death wouldn't have allowed me to look upon the angel in front of me. There's no way my brain could create such a beautiful man.

Sweat-dampened black hair is plastered to his forehead. On an average day, I'm sure it'd be free flowing and hang in his eyes. *Why, brain, why not give me that version?* What my mind *does* invent is the craziest blue to ever exist in a person's eyes. They scan my naked body, pausing on every cut and blemish on my form, spending an extra amount of time on my freshly injured shoulder. There's a lot of damage done to me, so by the time he reaches my feet, I'm sure an entire moment has passed. A curious hardness ices over his eyes.

For the first time in six months, my heart beats.

What a strange dream.

"Bella ragazza." His words are murmured, a near-whisper, in a language unknown to me.

His hand stretches toward me slowly. I should probably rear away from the unknown stranger, but in my dream, there's no one who'll harm me, right? I study the tattoos decorating his arms, disappearing inside the sleeves of his T-shirt and peeking out from the neck hole. Piercings embellish his face—his brow, his nose, and his lip.

In my previous life, he would be someone I would run away from, but after six months, I've learned one very important lesson: beauty is a notion. But it's also a falsity. Beauty doesn't necessarily mean good. Exactly how scary doesn't necessarily mean evil. Alex Miller is a beautiful man. He's handsome, with a great smile, and pleasant features in all the correct places.

For that reason, I take the guy's hand. He brings me closer to his body, nudging my arms around his shoulders. I place one there, and his arms come up under my legs and he stands with me.

In a barely audible tone, he whispers, "We're here to save you. Trust me."

I shouldn't. The last time I trusted a man, I ended up in here.

But this is a dream. A dream wouldn't invent someone kind, only to make my life worse, right?

His thumb rubs at the base of my spine, and it ignites my soul, imprinting on my skin, and I drop my head into the curve of his neck, inhaling his sweet scent as it consumes the remainder of my mental capacity.

Any touch I've ever gotten has been a vile, lustful one, and never for my own pleasure, but my dark, nameless angel's touch does something else. I shut my eyes, welcoming the place my splintered mind has ended up. No way can *any* of this be real, but especially him.

When I hear a screeching, "No!" I don't raise my eyes. The dream is ending; therefore, my mind created an out, and Alex is finally fighting back. He'll kill them all, including my angel, and I'll wake up in my cage, reminded of how freedom is a mere dozen steps away.

Fourteen, to be exact.

Fourteen steps until reaching the door to the cellar. Every time he takes me from the basement, I count them with the fragment of hope I'll one day be able to walk them as a free woman—before I knew how impossible that was.

Alex's next words cut through my thoughts. "Out here where I can watch you both."

He's speaking to my dream-saviour.

I feel the rocking of his strides, taking us from the cage. We'll leave it, Alex will kill them, and reality will return.

My angel's chest rumbles with speech as he whispers to the other guy, "Reach into my back pocket. Click send."

Oh, they think they can bring in help. Okay. Right.

More commotion—yelling, mainly—fills the background, but I tune it all out to focus solely on my angel's scent. If I'm lucky, my senses will be able to retain his aroma even after I awake.

A gunshot bellows and I flinch on behalf of the group Alex is currently killing.

But then *he* cries out.

Oh, fuck brain, you're truly gone. At this point, Alex could be slicing into my skin, and I'm positive my mind wouldn't know any better. He's dying in my imagination, suggesting I'm gone. My mind is no longer sane. He'll never die, even in my dreams, because my common sense knows better.

"You're free."

Of course my dream-saviour would claim that.

There's more commotion for a while, but my dream blocks out the conversation until I, once again, feel the rocking of his body beneath mine. Based on the scene behind me, we're walking away from Hell—from the glass cage that's been my home for so many months, and from Alex gasping on the floor, clutching at a wound on his lower leg as more people stream into the room around us.

Thank you, brain. Next time, make the bullet hit his heart please.

We reach the start of the hallway leading out of the basement.

One step.

Two.

I squeeze my eyes shut. Fourteen steps in total, and that's when this dream will end. My psyche isn't that creative or cruel to create *that* tease.

Three steps.

Four.

My angel's thumb strokes my back again, his whispered words a low hum in my ear, "You're safe now. That fucker won't hurt you any longer, I promise."

He can't make such a promise.

Five steps.

Six.

Other voices arise behind me. Teagan's dismayed whimper. Another girl muttering about betrayal.

Seven steps.

Eight.

Alex screaming in the background. *Good.* It's his turn to scream.

Nine steps.

Ten.

Alex's screams remind me how, in four more steps, this fantasy is over, and I'll wake up.

Eleven steps.

Twelve.

"Willow," my angel whispers. His warm breath blows over my face, accompanying the heat his next words jolt in my heart. "You're a damn survivor, sweet girl, and he won't touch you again. I have you. You're safe."

Oh, how I wish those words could be true.

Thirteen steps.

My arms tighten around his neck, knowing in one more step, this is over.

Fourteen.

And done. I'm back in Hell.

Fifteen.

Sixteen.

Seventeen.

Wait—What?

Eighteen.

Nineteen.

How is this possible?

And then the air changes, and from over my saviour's shoulders, I spot the cases and racks of wine bottles, taunting me with the trick that lured me down here in the first place. But it's more than simply a sign of teasing: it's a symbol of freedom. The rack means we've made it to the basement stairs.

I hear the thud of his shoes as he begins to climb them. Feel the air becoming warmer and lighter with every step.

It smells like freedom.

Is my dream reality or have I become that broken?

I think… I think it might be real.

Trauma.

A nasty word used by therapists and doctors to rationalize an act so horrible, it fucks with the brain and one's ability to function. Little things become triggering; nightmares become frequent, and memories deteriorate one's mental well-being. But it's more than something to live with—more than a term in a medical book.

It's a fucking lifestyle, and one I've been living since I was a child. One Teagan is about to experience when she comprehends everything Miller has done to her. Witnessing her nearly murder Willow on his command confirmed what we've all been suspecting. Alex fucked with her sanity, and she doesn't even realize it.

If he fucked with Teagan's mind, no doubt he used Willow's as a playground.

Willow.

Willow.

No matter how many times I repeat the name, it doesn't lessen the imprint it has on me.

The moment our skin touched and she glanced up through dull, lifeless eyes, something inside me shifted. A piece of my heart broke off, floated out of my chest, and right into hers, linking the two of us together.

It's fucked, but I don't care in the slightest.

She's a survivor. Coming from someone who's experienced a fraction of what she has, she sure won't feel as though she is, so it'll be up to me to remind her.

The moment I lifted her in my arms and her head found the crook of my neck, she claimed me. It's as though everything I'd been working toward wasn't for Teagan or any of the others; it's been for her, completely and solely for the woman whose heart I felt beating in sync with my own.

And I claimed her too.

I *want* her.

I want to hold her, to learn about her, to listen to her horror-filled tale. It's her small whimpers, the blood stains all over her skin, and the lifeless look in her eyes that have my feet continuing toward the basement stairs, rather than turning around to kill Miller.

For years, I've been hunting the bastard, fighting to bring light to his treachery. It led me to Ryker, who has his own issues with the guy; Tristan, who now has a reason to hate the guy; and Brent, who probably has the largest reason for wanting the scum bag dead. Now, I've joined them, and in more ways than one.

My arms tighten around her as I ascend the staircase, paying no attention to how her eyes flash to the cellar behind me, widening, when we leave it behind. As I stride down the opulent hallway, my stomach knots, wondering when she last left this hellish basement.

That place is his personal hellscape; a playground for his evil soul to play in. How anyone could fathom doing what he has is beyond me, and in my profession, I've witnessed multiple forms of evil, but Alex Miller is on a whole other level.

"I have you," I whisper, stepping out onto Miller's front steps.

The cool evening air, not stagnant like the basement, blasts our faces the moment we step from the house, and I curl her naked body closer to mine, willing some of my heat to penetrate her skin.

Everyone follows behind with Royal Canadian Mounted Police—a favour I called in—pushing Miller through the entry.

It's over. Years of work is coming to a head, yet at the same time, it's all just beginning. After this, I'll have the court battle of my life to convict Miller and free Teagan. She'll be charged as an accomplice, but once the doctors check her out and write their report, I know the charges will be dropped; it'll just be a matter of finalizing the paperwork. Then, I'll be working on ensuring that Natalie receives her inheritance, which I'm nearly one hundred percent sure Alex kept from her.

RCMP cars and armoured trucks as well as a few ambulances litter the massive circular drive. I tighten my hold on Willow, unwilling to hand her over to strangers yet. Only a medical professional will be looking upon her naked, tormented form.

Ryker heads by me, his arm thrown over the shoulder of an officer who assists in lessening his limp as they head for an ambulance. Poor fucker got stabbed in the leg by Alex.

Next, Tristan walks by, his arm clutched around Natalie's waist as he also ushers her to an available ambulance. Once Alex held a blade to her throat, that was all Tristan's sanity was able to handle.

Brent, holding Teagan, who walks with a blank expression, in his arms, steps up beside me. "We fucking did it."

"We did," I respond low enough that only Willow can

hear me. "*You* did it, Willow. You survived."

WILLOW

"You did it, Willow. You survived."

Did I? I certainly don't feel like I have. Rather, my brain snapped, leaving me with no clue as to what reality is and isn't anymore.

I open my eyes, looking past the others, who walk behind my angel, and up the side of the mansion's exterior. The massive doors I once revelled in entering are propped open as officers stream in and out.

Alex's face fills my vision then, as he's dragged from his house. I lift my head from my angel's neck, curious of the strange sight—the sight of people *helping*—saving—me as they remove Alex from his own home.

An officer has Alex's hands bound behind his back in cuffs, while another maneuvers him by us.

This is real… The stranger holding me has been telling me the truth the entire time. Because if this was really a dream, I would have woken up by now. I wouldn't be immersed in the flurry of sounds and colours, or surrounded by a multitude of people, some staring at me as they work to imagine the horrors I've experienced.

Horrors they can't dream up.

Alex's eyes meet mine over my angel's shoulders, and rather than fury, he smiles easily. He's not fighting their hold as the officers push him past us. His shoulders are slumped and relaxed, as though this is a good thing.

"Willow, your freedom is brief. Don't get used to it."

Right. Of course he feels at ease. Because none of this is forever. His capture, my freedom, my angel. In a snap of a finger, Alex will have his fancy lawyers break him free from these new chains. He's rich and influential, and these past six months have shown me the freedom that money can buy, giving someone the ability to hide from the law.

It'll be days at most before he shoves me back down in his basement, and then he'll do what he promised earlier today, forcing me to remain a caged prisoner for another six months.

I'll die before I return. If it takes me killing myself, so be it, but he's not getting me back.

Sometime during my runaway thoughts, the stranger's touch breaks through to me. His thumb strokes the small patch of skin on my back, pushing through the truth that'll eventually find me again. But, for now, I watch Alex being shoved inside a nearby vehicle, and when the door shuts, I avert my eyes, pretending it's truly over. I'll enjoy this newfound freedom while I have it.

Two officers approach then, and I feel the arms around me tense. For some reason, it makes my heart beat slower. This guy—this total stranger—isn't ridding himself of me at the first opportunity.

"I need to get you to an ambulance."

But then people will touch me. They'll want me to talk about what happened: to recount every second of the last six months.

No. I can't.

I don't know why, but my hand goes straight for his shirt, to the space over his heart, and my fingers curl in the cloth there. For the first time since he approached me in the cage, my eyes lift and connect with his. I hope he can see my plea to not let me go. Letting me go means other people will touch me, and… *No.*

"I'll be there with you, I promise."

His steps begin bouncing, and I glance behind us, watching distance grow between us and the mansion. My hand in his shirt tightens—my minor, pathetic act of resisting others from interacting with me.

"You need medical help, Willow. I can't be the one to give it. I'm sorry."

Other people will want to know the truth. Other people haven't *seen* what I was living in, which means they'll need me to describe it to them. To describe *how* Alex touched me. To detail how his knives felt when he fucked me with them, and how they felt flaying my skin. How he beat me, strangled me, starved me, degraded me…

"Willow," the stranger's voice cuts in, "it's okay. You're *okay.*"

He identified my feelings. *Felt* the fear creeping in. *Sensed* my racing heart. Perhaps even caught the scent of the blood roaring in my ears.

My fingers uncurl and I rest my hand flat over his heart, keeping my eyes on his. With every step he takes, every rock of my body, something between us shifts.

It's moronic. Foolish. I'm sure it's simply my imagination playing tricks on me—of inventing something positive after months of hate, but for now, I'll take it.

Don't leave me.

The words dance on my tongue, wanting to be said aloud. I *want* to give this stranger my voice—to give him that piece of me, but they don't come. I remain silent.

"We'll take her from here."

Take her.

"No." The grip on me tightens again. "Tell me where

to put her, and I'll do it."

I don't look to see who he's speaking with, but they must gesture to go ahead or something, because then there's more rocking and one arm leaves my body at the same time his other tightens. There's jostling, and I watch the scene beyond his shoulder distort as he hoists us up into the ambulance.

Cushion meets my back, and though the stretcher is probably shitty for an average person, it's everything for me. After sleeping on the glass cage's bottom, with only a blanket on the nights Alex took pity on me, this is comparable to a five-star hotel. If I died right here, on this bed, with my hand still clutching the angel's shirt, I'd be okay with it.

His free hand finds mine and lightly pushes at it until I'm forced to unlink my stiff fingers from his shirt.

"It's okay. She's here to help."

She?

A figure moves in the corner, a woman with a tight bun and white scrubs. She closes the door, and thankfully, shuts off the world and the commotion beyond.

"Hello. Your name is?"

A gasp of breath stalls in my throat. *She wants—*

"Willow," my stranger answers for me instead. He remains by my side, his arms relaxed, but even with only knowing him for a short time, the tension around his eyes and the lock of his jaw tells me he's not relaxed. He's angry.

That volatile emotion means I get injured.

Then his bright eyes flash down to mine, and the skin around them smooths, and my heart slows from its rapid beat to something more manageable, allowing me to breathe once more.

The doctor narrows her eyes at him and repeats, "I asked *you* for your name. Can you tell me please?"

Willow.

After a short stare down, the medic nods, keeping her impassive face blank from emotion. "Okay." Her eyes study my body, and I see the moment she notices the cuts, the blood, the caked-on dirt from the many days it's been since my last bath.

While she examines me, I study my guardian angel, discovering he's also examining me. Though he already saw me in the basement, I want a blanket. Not for warmth, but for coverage from his probing gaze. The ambulance's lights are unforgiving and hide nothing.

For Alex and his friends, I've been a body. A toy to find pleasure with. To torture.

For the paramedic, I'm a patient. A project to study. To fix.

For this stranger, I'm *someone*. A person to help. To see.

His eyes flicker, a blue flame igniting in their depths.

What is it they say about blue flames? That they're the hottest type; the kind to burn through your skin instantly.

Both sets of eyes dart away at a loud yell from beyond the closed doors, and the guy's chest huffs with an exhausted breath. It's obvious he recognizes the noise.

"I'll be back," he speaks low, before glancing toward the woman and back, "I promise. Right as soon as I take care of this."

With the little strength I have, I manage to lift my hand toward him, but he turns away, not seeing me in time, as he quickly opens the doors and jumps down from the truck, soon shutting them again. With his leave, the air feels different. Colder.

The paramedic returns to studying me, but this time, her eyes land on my face. "Do you want him here?"

I nod because I never wanted him to leave.

"Can you speak?"

Again, I nod.

She pauses for a few seconds before her mouth turns

down into a frown. "*Will* you speak?"

I shake my head. *Speaking means you'll want things from me.*

Her frown deepens and she jots something on the notepad in her hand.

"Can I place a blanket over you?"

With a small smile splitting my mouth, it grants her the permission she seeks. She reaches toward a container at her feet and whips out a blanket, lowering it and wrapping it around me. The cotton is rough and woolly, but it's the warmest and most comfortable item I've felt in a long time.

"There. That should help regulate your body temperature."

Thankfully, the doors open again and the strange guy from earlier slips inside, his gaze immediately finding mine. His hand brushes the top of his hair, a look of exhaustion replacing his relief. He's tired, and I wonder how long he's been at this.

And what *this* is. Why did he and his friends find me? *How* did they find me?

Did Teagan turn on Alex?

He'll kill her once he pays off the officers. He'll murder her for trying to better the world and then he'll put me back into his box.

He'll be so angry.

He'll use me, show me what true anger feels like. He'll reap vengeance by extending my pain, but not to the point of death; he'll force me to continue to outlive his agony.

Then he'll target all those other people who were in the basement. He'll find my dark angel and will sever his wings, so he's unable to fly back to my side.

He'll find me again and—

"She's hyperventilating." The woman's face interrupts my view, her lowered brow and frantic eyes scanning me before she retrieves something from behind me. I can't make out what she grabs, but her hand goes to my wrist, her thumb touching the skin there.

She's cold.

Alex was always cold to me.

She grips tightly, similar to how Alex would grasp my wrist to drag me into his desired position.

But she's not Alex. At least with Alex, I knew what to expect, but this stranger…

My arms fly out, the blanket tangling with my body as I push into a sitting position. The touch on my wrist disappears as her two hands grip my shoulders instead, forcing me back down. My heart rate spikes, and for the first time since Alex's initial raping, I feel fear. Fear of the unknown. Fear of another person.

I'm *not* numb.

"Willow!" My angel's voice cuts through. The hands at my shoulders are knocked away, replaced by his soft pressure, his thumbs stroking away the woman's touch.

When my body relaxes into the stretcher again—when I allow him to ease me—the edges of his face go fuzzy, fading, and the world goes black.

Six

WILLOW

Beep… Beep… Beep.

The noise is close by. This much I catch as my body slowly rises to the top, awareness settling in. At least my hearing works still, that's something at least, even if I can't move yet.

With the thought, the weight lifts off my chest, refilling my lungs with a fresh burst of air. The sensation of being able to feel once more returns, and my fingers curl, fisting the blanket they rest over. It draws realization to the rest of my body. The mattress beneath me is softer than the stretcher, and better yet, my head rests on a spongy pillow. The air is warmer than anything I've felt in a long time. My hand, curled around the blanket, makes the tape taut.

Tape?

Then my eyes open. Dim light trickles through the opening of my eyelids, until I'm blinking into the unfamiliar room.

Lifting my head, I scan the space, noting the plain walls, the white bedspread, and the two windows—one to my left, covered with a curtain while sunlight plays at its edges. The other is to my right, showing the hallway beyond. Across from me, I see a bathroom through the open door. My scan concludes at the room's main door. This one is shut with a figure leaning against it, his arms crossed while ice eyes watch me.

I'm in a hospital. And my unknown saviour is here.

Even as I awake, he doesn't move, tipping his head to the side. My mouth opens to say something to him—*anything*—but nothing comes out. Instead, I continue my self-examination, scanning every part of me.

For the first time in six months, I'm clean. As in, scrubbed spotless to the point I know what shade my pale skin is again. Needles are jabbed into the back of my hand, giving reason for the tape, and a hospital gown is draped over my form. It's the most clothing I've worn since Alex took mine from me. Others may think a hospital gown isn't comfortable or anything special, but for me, it's everything.

For months, my body has undergone extreme pain, and while it's felt every ache ever executed on me, somehow the pain is more sensitive now. Perhaps, it's because my body is finally comfortable enough to allow itself to heal, or maybe it's simply the fact I'm not in that basement—not forced to hold in the cries. Bracing my arms, I shift, and every muscle screeches in response. Muscles that were pulled on and stretched as I would hang from chains. Insides throb and ache, compelling me to understand all that his brutality has done to me internally.

I'm hungry. That's the other pain. A discomfort I've long shoved aside because when one is using all their energy to remain alive, simple things such as nutrition become less important. Being fed once a day is all I need—all I want—when prior to *him*, I would eat three full meals a day without a second thought. It seems so imprudent now; all the food I consumed back then and took for granted.

In the midst of my body scan, something moves in my peripheral vision, and I jerk up to spot my angel approaching. His blank expression and slow walk are agony, until he finally reaches my bedside. His hands shove into the front pockets of his jeans and his shoulders slouch, adopting a position that appears relaxed, but after a closer examination, I don't believe it is. Having him up close shows the black marks beneath his eyes—the sign of exhaustion.

"Welcome back." After a beat, he adds, "You're safe now, Willow."

He keeps saying that, but he isn't the one to make that decision. Alex is. Alex will obviously return, and I won't be safe.

"You were sedated because you were panicking." His tongue flicks out and he pulls his lip ring into his mouth while he considers his next words. "That was nearly four days ago. They believe once the sedation hit, your body went into a deep sleep because it needs it."

Four days? He's claims it's been almost *four* days since he broke down the doors of Hell and got me out of there. Four days since Alex was arrested.

I open my mouth again. For him, I want to speak. I want to give him my voice because it's the least he deserves for battling the devil. I want to speak because he doesn't have rules on when I can and cannot talk.

"Thank you."

His body does this jolting thing as his mouth falls slack.

"You speak."

I nod.

"They weren't sure. The paramedic said…" He shakes his head, instead muttering, "Never mind. I'm glad."

"You saved me," I explain simply. A pointless endeavour. If four days have already passed, then we're only getting closer to Alex's return. Four days is more than his lawyers require, I'm sure.

"Willow, officers want to speak with you. They want

a statement."

"There's no point," I murmur, shaking my head slowly. "Anything I reveal won't matter. He'll return because your *officers*," the word brandishes harshly from my throat, "will be unable to fight his legal team."

The skin between his brows furrow. "I understand why you believe that, but I'm doing everything I can to ensure it doesn't happen."

But you don't have enough power to win.

"Giving a statement will help the process. The RCMP has him in holding based on the obvious evidence they saw, but they prefer it when witnesses also speak to them, to give them details." His hands come up, hovering somewhere by the bed railing. They pull my attention away from his piercing eyes, so for that, I'm grateful. "I don't like this, Willow, I truly don't, but I know the legal system. This will be good, I swear. I'll tell them you'll do a written one instead, so you don't need to speak to anyone you don't want to."

For that, he has my attention once more. Because, for once, someone is paying attention to me.

I always dreamed that one day I'd make it out alive, but it meant I'd simply crawl to whatever home I had and live out the rest of my days, hiding beneath a blanket. There'd be no officers, no doctors… no angel. He's abnormal, because no normal person would break into a rich man's house, rescue a stranger, and then remain by her bedside days later. Even without my grasp of reality, I get that.

"Who are you?"

"Hawke."

Hawke. I roll the name around in my mouth, digesting its uniqueness.

"You saved me."

He nods once, more of a jerk of his head than anything.

"Thank you."

In that moment, the door opens, interrupting whatever Hawke would have next said. A woman in pink scrubs rushes in, her messy hair tied in a bun, but the smile she gives me is blindingly polite.

I push into the pillows at my back. Polite smiles usually mean something worse is coming. Alex was polite once; when he walked by my desk at work, he'd grant me a smile and a cheery greeting. Look how that ended.

Hawke approaches, as if he senses something. He glances down at me, and the small fire burning in his eyes has me shrinking into my pillow for an entirely different reason. Passion. Protectiveness. Treatment I've *never* gotten, even as a child.

…And I'm the person he's giving his attention to.

Why?

"Oh, good, you're awake!" The bubbly nurse steps closer, not noticing, or simply not caring, how I'm trying to shrink into the bed.

This is too much…

Too much because she'll want to know what happened and how I feel. She'll want me to *analyze* what I lived through with the belief that *she'll*, somehow, make it all go away. I won't be better though. Alex ensured I'll forever be unfixable. The scars he scored into my body, physically, emotionally, and mentally, won't fade.

He'll be my constant shadow. Even *if* Hawke is correct in that Alex isn't coming for me, what do I do now? Find a new job, to what—be captured by that boss as well? No one has ever been a permanent fixture in my life. I'm not a girl with lifelong friends or a caring family. No one missed me when I disappeared six months ago. Perhaps if my parents had noticed me gone at all, they would have contacted authorities. Therefore, I don't have anyone to help me make sense of this.

I'll be alone.

I *am* alone.

A nurse won't understand that. She'll want my words, but speaking won't change anything. Not now. They can't wipe away six months of agony. There's no point in allowing myself to open my mouth and attempt to heal what the past has brought forth.

"How do you feel?"

I remain silent, letting her guess my emotions.

The nurse's gentle smile falters ever so slightly. "Oh, okay. Willow… Can you state your name for me? Your birthday? A fact, if you will, please."

Unable to help myself, my eyes find Hawke's again. He reads me correctly, for his responding murmur is, "Her name is Willow."

The nurse's brows lift, her eyes narrowing on him. "Mr. Blackwood, I have asked *my* patient for a response. Please allow her to respond."

"She's not yours," he snaps back. "As you can see, ma'am, she doesn't wish to talk."

My stomach flips, in a good way. Someone is *protecting* me. He's read me, recognized my feelings, and validated them.

The nurse crosses her arms, attitude lining her mouth. "Mr. Blackwood, please remember how many rules we are breaking for you right now. Keep that in mind as we do our jobs."

Not even a breath later, Hawke shoots back, "And you'd best remember who my family is or I'll have you fired for frightening her."

She scowls, and before exiting as quickly as she breezed in, she comments, "I'll let the doctor know you're awake and she'll be in to debrief you. I'll also get food sent in." When the door is shut behind her, my breathing becomes less staggered, my anxiety lifting.

The moment we're alone, Hawke twists to face me. "She wants to ensure you're actually present. Being awake isn't enough for them. You won't talk to her?"

"There's no point. The moment I confirm a name, they'll want me to tell my story, but they're not going to do anything."

Hawke's shoulders slump and I catch the flash of annoyance, even if he hides it well. "Not the nurse, Willow. For now, they need to know how you physically feel."

I *think* he's fighting with me, though I can't completely tell. Nor do I want to argue the case.

"You speak to me," he continues.

Something flips in the air between us, something that turns it electric, and I wish there was a reason for it. I wish I knew *why* I'm feeling what I am. Why my nerves are warming, and my heart feels as though it's beating for the first time in months. Why my body is finally feeling something other than fear.

"Because you deserve it," I finally respond.

Hawke's mouth opens, words nearly coming out, but we're interrupted by another person—another woman, this one in a white lab coat. As she enters, her eyes scan the clipboard in her hand.

"We're glad you're awake." This doctor doesn't smile, and strangely, it makes me feel more at ease because she's not pretending. She approaches the bedside, but her attention is solely on the beeping machines by my side. "Your heart sounds normal again," she comments. "You're relaxed, and that's good. Any pain?"

I shake my head, responding to her in the way that will lessen the attention she gives.

Understanding passes through her gaze and she glances at Hawke then back so quickly. "Do you want him here?"

I nod.

Her lips purse, debate settling upon her expression before she blinks and looks down at her papers again. "All right then. Well, Willow, I won't beat around the bush. You were examined while you were asleep, as we believed it safer for both you and us. We took blood samples and tested you for diseases and pregnancy. Both tests came back negative. You are heavily scarred. There are old marks on your legs, which based on the age of some of them, I'm sure you're familiar with. For now, it's a matter of rest, relaxation, and—" she pauses, "and what happens next."

From the corner of my eye, I spot the muscles in Hawke's arms flex, and he crosses them over his broad chest. Instincts scream at me to get out of bed and rush from the room.

Over the past six months, I've learned to read emotions well, and I know when men are angry. It's in the way their jaw ticks, and their legs spread to take up more space, an alpha energy emits from them. Those little hints are precursors to the blows.

But then Hawke sighs and munches on his lip ring again, and it reminds me who he *isn't*. Alex or anyone from his circles would not wear body jewellery. It'd clash with their suits and flawless, lying grins.

Hawke isn't Alex. He won't hurt me. My gut deems so. He's irritated with the doctor's words, and that explains the reaction he's having.

The doctor glances down at her hands and back, a woman who's clearly had to deliver news like this before. "We'd like to keep you for observation and rest, and I am referring you to a psychologist because, at this point..." Her mouth twists. "I'm sorry, at this point, it is your mental well-being we need to worry most about."

I touch my head. My mental well-being. Is there even such a thing? Well-being is for women who weren't tortured, tied-up, and raped over and over. It's for women who have had stressful days at work but then go home to relax in a hot bath.

No. Mental well-being isn't something women who have had their minds yanked from them are capable of procuring. I have no mind left to heal.

"I'm going to send one of the hospital's counsellors in later, okay?" Her brows lift with her question, and only relax when I nod. "They'll ask you a few questions and give you suggestions, but do not feel pressured to talk, okay?"

When I nod again, she smiles for the final time and backs away. "All right, I'll be back in a moment. I have some medication set aside for you—pain meds—to help ease your aches. Unless you're opposed to them?"

Medication sounds really fucking good actually. I shake my head, so she leaves the room, the door remaining open, foreshadowing her impending return.

While she's gone, I look to Hawke, who simply watches me.

The doctor returns with a small medication cup and a paper cup, filled halfway with water. She hands me both. I barely glance at the white pills before downing them, chasing them with fresh, cold water.

"I'll leave you be for now," she says after collecting the cups. "Press the button on your bedside if you need assistance. And, um—" This time her throat bobs and her feet shift as she gives her attention to Hawke. "RCMP officers are still outside, waiting."

I'm still working on why she's speaking to Hawke about such things, but then he responds with, "Tell them her lawyer said she'll speak to them another day. If they have an issue with that, they know who to contact."

Lawyer? My angel is a goddamn *lawyer*? What does this—*could* this—mean for me?

The doctor takes another step away, one hand lifting in a calming gesture. "I'll let them know." Her gaze finds me again. "We're so happy you're here, Willow. Please let us know if we can call anyone on your behalf."

Then she's gone, leaving me with my strange angel and a new round of questions I have for him. So, instead of shriveling back into the bed, I sit straighter, meeting his scrutiny head on.

"You're a lawyer."

"I am," he replies, expression guarded.

"Why are you here?"

"I want to be."

Wants to be. My face scrunches with disbelief. "Why?"

Hawke falls silent, and then the skin between his eyes wrinkles and his mouth twists into a question, as though he's wondering the same thing.

There's nothing but edgy silence for a while. So long, exhaustion creeps up and my eyes get heavy. After another moment, I fall back into the pillows, head lolling to the side. No doubt, my body is soaking up as much sleep as I can.

"It makes no sense for you to be here."

I wish I could remain alert for his response, but whatever cruel game my body continues to play, or the medication, beats my determination, and I can't keep my eyes open any longer. A wave encompasses my shattered mind, yanking the pieces into the cool drift.

But before they're too far away in the ocean, dragged beneath the black current, I hear a murmured, "I wish I knew, Willow, but I just am."

Seven

WILLOW

When I open my eyes again, sunlight peeps between the edging of the curtain, indicating I didn't sleep for long. Clearly, a short nap is all my body required. Blinking into the brightness, I sit up, the blanket falling to pool at my waist.

This time, my hand doesn't have needles jabbed into it and there's no beeping machine at my side. They've obviously decided I'm well enough.

With alertness comes the realization of a full bladder. Earlier when I awoke, Hawke mentioned being asleep for four days, so it's no wonder my body is yelling at me to give it the things it needs, like release.

I scan the eerily silent room, seeking Hawke, while my mind suggests, *your reminder of his presence earlier likely spooked him away.* But no—because there he is, slumped in a plastic chair by the door, as if guarding it from intruders. His head is tipped back, resting on the wall behind him, and his eyes are shut. His ripped jean-clad legs are spread wide, feet braced to hold him in the chair. Beneath the large sweater he wears, his chest rises up and down slowly.

He's asleep.

I watch the stranger who feels compelled to remain by my side. Maybe it's a hero complex, and if I had the slightest bit of rationality, I'd send him away, but thanks to Alex, any ounce of reason has long been beaten away. Alex, and the fact that something prevents me from uttering those words.

Leave.

Perhaps because he's the first person who touched me without meaning to harm my body or mind, he's who I've latched onto. Maybe because he's a literal angel who rescued me. Either way, I *want* him here. I shouldn't. I should send him away for his own safety and my own. Who knows what Alex will do upon learning another man sat by my bedside?

I can't do it. So for now, I'm being selfish. Therefore, the very words I *should* scream at him remain trapped in my confused mind and lost heart. Lost, because it can't choose an emotion, can't figure out how to rationalize all this.

Continuing to study him, my eyes pass over his visible piercings, the tattoos edging his collar, and his ridiculously beautiful face. With his pale skin and long black hair, he reminds me of the goths back when I attended high school, but he's no skinny kid. I've felt the muscles beneath my back, have heard the intensity in his voice when he's fighting *for me*. He's different.

Unique. Even without truly knowing him, I sense that about him.

As though he feels my scrutiny, he shifts slightly, lifting his head and blinking into the afternoon sunlight. His shoulders roll as his eyes continue to flutter, waking up, and he stretches his back, finally peeking at me. Catching me awake and watching, his own eyes widen and a small smile stretches his mouth.

"Morning," he murmurs, voice rough with sleep.

"Morning?"

"You've been asleep for almost," he glances at his phone which he pulls from his sweater's pocket, "a day."

"Huh." My eyes slide to the window to the outdoors again, to the sunlight. *Most definitely wasn't a quick nap then.*

"It's good," he comments. "You needed the rest."

In the midst of him talking, my bladder pokes at my insides again, reminding me what I was about to do. Pushing the blanket off my body, I slide to the edge of the bed, ready to stand for the first time in days. By the time my bare feet touch the chilly tile, Hawke is right there, his hand poised to help.

After a brief pause, in which I remind myself to breathe, I give him my hand, letting him help me to my feet. I shouldn't enjoy his touch as much as I do, but the warm zing unlocks something inside me—something Alex long rid me of.

Desire.

A stupid, pointless emotion. After all, Alex will be back soon. I'm surprised he isn't here already.

"You must be so hungry. I'll find the nurse and have her bring you food. You need to eat. You need to—" He stops, pressing his lips together. "*I* need to see you eat, Willow."

That desire from earlier returns, sending fire up the length of my body. For a long moment, I don't release his hand. Too busy staring at him and attempting to decipher his words. Finally, I manage to step away, continuing to the bathroom.

The flooring is chilly on my feet and old aches prevent me from moving too quickly. It's almost as though resting is making me sorer than if I had remained trapped. In the bathroom, I'd like to lift the gown and examine my body, seeing how the bruises Alex enjoyed decorating my body with have been faring.

As I step away, Hawke speaks again, "I got the police

to leave finally. The right to remain silent is a Charter right of yours, and until you wish to make a statement, you can be silent. If you wish."

I nod my head, so he can see my agreeance, but say nothing. When I'm in the safety of no longer being in his gaze, I allow myself to smile. Once upon a time, I never believed I'd want a man to save me in the way Hawke continues to, going as far as to understand my fears.

Instead of making it to the bathroom, the room's door swings open and a head pokes in. I recognize her to be the doctor from earlier—yesterday actually, I suppose.

"Oh, lovely you're awake."

At this rate, I'll never pee.

The doctor enters, scanning me once. "You look good, Willow. We're happy you are getting the rest you require. Dr. Abbott, the hospital's counsellor, has been waiting to speak with you, and if you're okay with it, I'll send her right in."

The urge to glance at Hawke, for him to determine the safety in this, is so strong, but instead, I nod weakly. The more I play along, the less questions that will be asked.

With my agreement, the doctor backs away, smiling. The moment the door shuts, it opens again, a different woman stepping through. This one isn't in scrubs, but rather an immaculate light pink pantsuit. She approaches, her hand held out, expertly manicured nails a teasing comparison to my chipped, broken ones. Her entire appearance, in fact, is flawless and jealousy instantly burns in my stomach.

I recall wearing a similar outfit to Miller Inc. one day for work. Only six months ago, yet, it feels like an entirely other life. I suppose, it was. A life in which I was pleased to have a steady full-time job with adequate pay and benefits. A life in which I was a single woman, trucking along until a decent relationship presented itself. A life I was happy to have. A free life.

"Hello, Willow." The woman's greeting forces my mind back to the present. "My name is Dr. Abbott. I am the psychologist here with the hospital. Normally, given your circumstances, we prefer to speak with patients alone." Quickly, she glances toward Hawke, who's reclaimed his defensive stance. At some point, he's moved closer to me than where I left him earlier after getting out of bed. "But your doctor has debriefed me on your situation, and as long as you'd like him here, then it won't be an issue."

I nod, hoping she understand that as permission for Hawke to remain.

"Perfect." She smiles softly. "I'll talk and be sure to ask any questions you wish to. Should you want to remain silent, that is also fine." After the briefest of pauses, she starts again, "This is an information-only briefing. I'm not here to conduct any assessments on you. Have you ever heard of the term Post-Traumatic Stress Disorder? More often referred to as PTSD."

It came up in the many psychology textbooks I once read. I nod.

"We haven't officially assessed and diagnosed you, of course, but given your experiences, the prevalence rates are extremely high that you may experience it. It could be triggered by anything, anyone… the most minor of objects. A flicker of light. A sound. You may experience flashbacks, often in the form of dreams. You may find yourself detaching from the world around you and wanting to be alone. Concentration difficulties can occur. The list can go on for much longer, but whatever happens next, I want you to know you are safe and help is readily available."

She pauses to hand over a slip of paper. "These are a list of clinics that offer counselling and other treatments for PTSD. Most of them use a sliding scale model for their fees, so please do not concern yourself about the costs associated. My contact information is also on the back of the paper—"

I flip it over, spotting her name, email, and number.

"—if you wish to speak with me again, I am available. Should you experience these symptoms and wish for medication to help control them, we can also provide it." She stops talking and her shoulders lift and release a heavy sigh, followed by a deep breath. "Willow, you are safe now. No matter how many times he blamed you for anything, nothing that occurred was your fault. You need to fight to make sure he remains out of your head."

As if it can be that easy.

I scan the paper once, twice, three times, until the words blur. Until the names of the clinics mean nothing to me because therapy is for people who need it. I don't need it, because once Alex comes for me again, there's nothing counselling will help me get over that will lessen the effects of his next round. Mental health supports are for people with issues like depression and anxiety, not for those whose minds were used as a psychological playground for a sadistic villain.

I think I'm shaking. I feel like I am. The longer I stare at the words, the more my muscles fight to maintain their grip on the paper, resulting in the quivering feeling rushing up and down my forearm. Maybe it's stable, maybe it's not. I can't tell at this point.

So to end this sooner and get Dr. Abbot out of my room, I nod again, even forcing a small smile to represent gratefulness. I believe I am, but I won't be using her list, so there's little point in this entire charade.

My response seemingly satisfies Dr. Abbott. "Okay, Willow, final point then. The hospital has been searching through records for your family but cannot find mention of anyone. Is there someone we can contact for you, to come and get you upon your release?"

A truck hitting me straight on would have been a

more pleasant feeling than the effect her seemingly caring, innocent and *normal* question has on me. My heart skips a beat while my hands instantly go damp. My feet inch to the right, toward Hawke, only so he can take me from this place, the same he did Alex's basement.

My parents and I always had a rough relationship, that with time, only grew weaker. What I told Alex six months ago was the truth—that I could go a year without talking to them and they wouldn't notice.

Close enough.

Given their nomadic lifestyle, I can't even say for certain where they presently are or what the last contact number I have for them is. The family I grew up with isn't the family I have. They're gone, just like the old version of me.

Everything of the ex-Willow Avery is gone. Alex stole her away. I'm not her any longer. The new me doesn't have a family, a home, a job, or even the fucking ability to speak to strangers.

Therefore, even *if* the hospital reached out to them, and even *if* they cared enough to realize we hadn't been in contact for months and I need their help, they won't be seeing their daughter again. No. She's long gone, buried beneath blood, sweat, tears, and heartbreak.

No. My lips even form the words, the temptation to speak them so strongly. I shake my head for good measure, focusing only on Dr. Abbott. Hawke's eyes burn into me, singeing my neck, right where the edge of the gown is, but I don't dare look at him. Eventually, it'll hit him that I'm such a mess, there was nearly no point in saving me.

Dr. Abbott frowns, checking a final time. "No one at all? Not even an old friend?"

What friends?

Again, I shake my head.

"Okay." Her tone implies my responses are not *okay*, but she continues, "I wish you all the best, Willow. Please reach out if you have any questions."

Then she leaves, without glancing at Hawke, so I rush to the bathroom, *finally* making it there. But instead of emptying my bladder as my body was previously dying to do, my legs give out just as I shut the door. I lean against it, bringing my knees up as the sob hits.

It hits and hits strong, causing me to gag on my own tears, determined to remain silent. I form a fist, shoving a part of it in my mouth for me to bite down on, to avoid from crying out. Hawke doesn't need to hear my breakdown.

Not sure if it's Alex's torture, or the care I've been receiving, or the mere mention of the family I once had. Or maybe, it's the sudden realization the girl they believe me to be and the one I currently am are so different from one another, it's ridiculous.

I've lost so much. Everything but my life, except the moment Alex is freed by his lawyers, he'll come for me. Maybe then, he'll finally end my life. Maybe this time, I'll welcome him with open arms as he delivers slice after slice on my body.

Death will surely be more welcoming than the life I'm thrusted back into.

But for now, I cry.

Eight

HAWKE

She's trying—and failing—at holding in her tears. The moment the sob breaks, I'm by the bathroom door, hand on the fragile knob, readying to burst in.

She shouldn't be experiencing her pain alone. That's what I'm here for. To take away the pain so she can live a happier life. No one was around for me, but fuck if I'll allow her to go through it alone.

Instead of turning the knob though, my forehead falls onto the door and I breathe in a deep gulp of air, using it to clear the insanity from my mind. Because I'm fucking mental to want to hold her, to care for her, to wipe away the tears presumably pouring from her eyes. She's too fucking innocent for the likes of Alex, and every tear she sheds because of what he's done will be another pound of flesh I take from him.

Originally speaking, metaphorically. But as the minutes tick on, I'm considering my brother's offer more and more.

"The officers can bring him here. We'll take care of him. Hell, if you want to join, be my fucking guest."

"No, I'm going about this legally. Take a page from my book

sometimes."

"And yet… it's I you reached out to, Hawke. Careful how you speak about us."

Contacting him was the worst fucking idea I've ever had, and I've had some shit ones in the past. It was a while ago when I realized the kind of maniac Alex is would require a much stronger force at my side. I learned early on he had all local police under his control, so I went to the federal level. Alex may be cunning, but the RCMP listens to only one outside force—my family.

So while calling my brother and speaking with him, for the first time since I was fifteen-years-old and left home was a nightmare to even consider, I needed to. For Willow, for Teagan, for the girls past and future, and if I'm being completely honest, for myself. I refused to come so far only to fail against the likes of Alex Miller.

My family has the connection to the RCMP I no longer have. One call from my brother, and I knew I'd have them on hand. It was as simple as calling them in the day we decided to go to Alex's house, after Teagan revealed all. They remained outside the house until I sent the text. Or, in the case of how it went down, when Brent sent the text message.

My family doesn't do anything unless it benefits them in some way, and while they gained nothing from Alex's arrest, they gained a conversation with me. That's more than I've given them for years.

The moment Willow sobs again, my hand twists at the knob, ready to force myself in, if only to hold her.

But I don't. I pause instead, taking in a deep breath. I remember being in her situation once and the only thing I wanted was to be left alone to cry. The moment a tear was shed, doctors and counsellors rushed into the room, and it was only at night time when I hid beneath the blankets that I managed to get it out.

For that reason, I release the knob and back away. This is Willow's moment to cry it out, and I'll give her that for however long it takes.

To ensure she hears this decision, even without me blatantly stating it, I continue out of the room entirely and shut the door, pulling it closed a bit louder than I would normally. Should she wish to come out and continue crying in the safety of the empty room, she can.

Besides, it's been an entire day since I've heard anything about Teagan, and knowing she's only down the hall and around the corner, I head there. After Teagan was taken away in an ambulance, no one managed to get in to see her. The doctors have her locked down, partly because Alex already gave his statement which aimed to place much of the crimes on her—*dickbag*—and partly for her own well-being. The benefits of being her lawyer, though, definitely have their perks.

On my way down the hall, I pass the department's waiting room, where a few familiar faces stare at me. Ryker from his spot in the far corner, Tristan beside him, and Natalie beside Tristan, all watch me with sorrowful eyes. The only one not watching me is Elena, who paces back and forth across the waiting room.

Back and forth.

Three times until I finally speak up. "Keep doing that and you'll wear a hole in the carpet."

Elena jumps, her head whipping in my direction, and she stops pacing to stalk toward me, a fierceness in her heavy steps. "They won't tell us anything!" she exclaims. Raising her voice, she adds, "The *assholes* won't listen when I say she has *no one*. No one, Hawke, and you know that. *We're* her people and I need to be in there with her."

Grief is funny. The five stages psychology claims we go through—denial, anger, bargaining, depression, and acceptance—aren't linear. Elena is clearly in the anger stage, but as she waits for me to speak, her expression breaks. Her brows go low, her shoulders cave in, and she just appears so devastated.

Flicking my chin toward Ryker, I indicate she needs him. For the moment though, I rest my hands on her shoulders, staring her in the eyes.

"I'm going to look in on her, I swear, and I will pull every string I can to get you into her room."

When she breathily responds with, "Thank you," I release her in time for Ryker to come up beside her. He leans in slightly, providing his warmth. From the way Elena doesn't react, you'd think she doesn't feel him.

"Brent's currently fighting with the nurses. You may need to go save them," Ryker tells me.

"For the right reasons," Elena cuts in. "At least someone's doing something."

I sigh. The day after Teagan was taken away from the Miller mansion, Brent annoyed some elderly nurse, only to be turned away. All that did was result in a very enraged phone call to me. Even I only have so much influence. My name may have gotten me into Willow's room while she slept the days away, but doctors report Teagan being a different case. Nearly killing another human does that. She's not stable, which is exactly what I told Brent the day we rescued them.

Every day since, Tristan brings Brent by. Usually the trip is short, in which he returns home. Today, however, the entire group is here. I do recall a text earlier mentioning Brent was refusing to leave until he saw her, and I suppose he brought back-up.

"I'll handle it."

Natalie stands, approaching us. "And Willow? How is she doing?" Natalie bites down on her bottom lip while her eyes express it all—guilt. She's fighting it, simply due to her brother's monstrous acts. Not her fault at all.

"She's all right," I supply, determining it to be the most reasonable response, since *fine* can mean a variety of feelings. "She woke up yesterday for the first time. A nurse and doctor managed to speak with her a bit before she fell asleep again. Just woke again not long ago."

"Surprised you left her side." Tristan waggles his brows as he approaches, giving me a knowing look.

"She needed a moment." As if being compelled, I glance over my shoulder, in the direction of her room. I left to provide her that safe moment and check on Teagan, and I've been spending my entire time out in this waiting room. "On that note though, I need to go."

I back away. Farther down the hallway, halfway between Teagan and Willow's room is the nurses' station. As Ryker mentioned, Brent is there, leaning over it, being glared at by two clearly annoyed nurses. One is that pink scrub-wearing one from yesterday.

I clap his shoulders, causing him to jump in surprise. "Brent, stop."

He shoots me the same glare he had the other day. In fact, not much of his appearance is different. His clothes are, but they also show signs of being days' old. Black marks decorate the skin beneath his eyes, and he looks as high-strung and pissed-off as he did the day the ambulance drove Teagan away.

"Fuck off, Hawke."

Willow's pink scrub nurse glances at me. "If you don't get him out of here, we're calling security and escorting him and his friends away. For the millionth time, she isn't on this floor anymore."

Surprise doesn't even register. Teagan's situation is, in many ways, worse than Willow's, and her treatment will look very different. It's something a doctor warned me of that first day. She's in the mental health department, where they'll help her more than anything we could do.

"You're lying!" Brent hisses, nearly throwing himself over the counter again.

"*Okay*, buddy." I loop my arm around his chest and yank him away from the counter. "Leave them alone. They have no reason to lie to you. Remember what I said to you the other day about what we need to do for Teagan at this point?"

"You had to have known it isn't that easy, Hawke. She *needs* me. I have to be by her side. You know that as well as anyone," his eyes flick to the hall behind us, "or is it only right for you to be in the room?"

"It's different," I mumble, voice lowering, so only he could hear me. "They don't believe Willow will require the same support."

Brent huffs, crossing his arms, but he backs away from the nurses' station, heading toward the waiting room. I give a quick nod of thanks to the nurses before trailing behind him. Instead of stopping though, he immediately stalks by them and toward the elevator.

Elena practically squeaks before rushing after him, and Natalie quickly follows her. Tristan and Ryker take up the rear, walking slower to fall into step with me.

"No luck?" Ryker asks.

"She's been moved. They're going to work on her mental state is my guess. Careful with him." I jerk my chin toward Brent, who's far out of sight now.

"You know he'll be back tomorrow, right? And I'll be the sucker to drive him?" Tristan rolls his eyes. "I do it because I feel for him. If Natalie was in her place, I'd be doing everything I could to get in."

"Or Elena." Ryker voices his agreement.

"I know," I murmur. "Just be careful. I suspect he's one more demand away from getting banned." The elevator comes into view, so before I'm much farther away from Willow's room, I wave goodbye and turn away. "I'll talk to you guys another time."

By now, she's had her time, and I need to see her again to satisfy the feeling in my chest which is slightly worrisome but completely welcoming.

Nine

WILLOW

Even though Hawke left a while ago, I don't come out until I hear the door open again. He probably thinks I'm ridiculous, but at some point, I'll have to face him, so I may as well do it now and get it over with.

Trudging slowly from the bathroom, I push my hair away from my face to get a better look as he shuts the door, pressing his back against it and keeping everyone on the other side out. I appreciate that. If only he could have done that for me six months ago.

"Hi," I whisper. "You left."

"To give you space." He licks his lips and I watch as his tongue flicks at the metal ring in. Through darkening eyes, he asks, "The moment has passed?"

He doesn't ask the typical 'Are you okay?' and I find that interesting. As though he knows I'm not. *Okay* is such an unfathomable feeling to have at this point, and he knows I'm just not there. Will I ever be?

"Yeah," I reply, voice dry. I need water, and my stomach is still grumbling because food has yet to come.

For now, I return to bed, pulling the blanket over my lap. When I'm covered again, Hawke leaves the door and reclaims his chair by my bedside. He drags it even closer, the metal legs screeching on the shiny tile.

"Something hit, I guess," I continue.

"I'd be worried if it didn't."

Looking into his eyes, I believe his words. In Hawke's mind, breaking down *is* my normal.

"Breaking down means you're still feeling, Willow, and that means Alex didn't shatter your mind. It's when you don't cry, don't think or feel your past, your pain, that it becomes worrisome, as that'd mean you're numb."

I can't imagine anyone being numb from what I lived through. "Isn't that impossible?"

"No," he responds, gravely. "It all hits us differently, and I know someone who can recount their past, even the most recent events, all without a tear."

"Wh—" I cut off my question, leaving it unfinished because, even as I ask it, I realize who he means.

Teagan. Teagan who had to shut it all off, if only to remain sane through the years. I think if I had to survive years, I'd be silent too, but I understand what Hawke means. It's because I'm *not* her, that I still feel.

I don't want to feel. I don't want to feel like *this*—this mess. A person who the doctors felt required a therapist because I'm too far gone to even fix myself.

"I don't know anymore," I finally whisper. "I dreamed of one day escaping, but I never imagined the after. The possibility of one seems too far away and yet… it's here." I drag my gaze from my hands to him. To the complete stranger who's still by my bedside after all this. Soon though, he'll leave me alone again and will return to his likely impeccable life. And I'll just… be.

I'll be. I'll be stuck in this in-between, fighting between life and death. Sanity and trauma. Fighting to make it through each day until Alex finds me again and restarts the process, which will lead to my eventual death.

Lost in my head, I don't notice Hawke's hand creeping closer to mine. It rests on the bed, pressing against my leg, but the weight is welcome. Real. A reminder of my presence.

He slowly moves it again until the tip of his pinky brushes my hand. It's enough for my insides to thaw. The slight brushing feels soft and welcoming: an invitation.

"I want you to come home with me, Willow."

I yank my hand away from his touch, leaning as far away as the bed will allow me, as panic claws at my throat. I do nothing but stare at him with wide eyes, waiting for the punchline in his statement.

Is this all some sort of game? Did Alex hire him and his friends to "rescue" me, to make me feel safe and free, only to rip it out from under me and force me into a hell worse than before? Worse, because I had a taste of freedom?

Has yet another man fooled me? I'll never learn. Is this why I'm still in the hospital? He's simply keeping me here until Alex barges into the room?

"N-no."

No.

If Alex wants me, he can come for me himself. I refuse to be tricked into another man's home, just for him to collect me there. The bastard can face me here and now.

Alex—

No—

Hawke moves, rising to his feet. His hand is still by the bed, the same arm lifting a fraction, as if going to reach for me, before he wisely pulls back. He watches me, studying me as though I'm crazy.

Maybe I am. Because beneath the cautious look is concern. The same concern he first looked at me with when he lifted me into his arms and carried me from Alex's basement. The same place where Alex was arrested by federal police. Could that be faked? Unlikely, but I'm sure Alex has the means to pull it off.

"You're fooling me."

Has my angel become a dark angel, one working with the devil? A demon who only serves the master of Hell?

But no. Beneath the eerily bright blues of his eyes, I don't see evil. Darkness, yes, but I believe that everyone has a bit of darkness in them—some more than others—but Hawke *isn't* Alex.

He. Isn't. Alex.

Pressure on my head explodes, but then I realize I'm the cause. Somewhere in my fucked-up thoughts, my hands began pressing into my temples. I bend my legs, folding my entire body to block out any view of Hawke, not wishing to see him watch whatever's happening to me.

I've read the books in the past. I know the symptoms. Trauma can bring on a lot of confusion as to what's real and what's from the past, or in my case, who's good and who's evil.

I *know* Hawke isn't a bad guy. Even if I have no con-create proof, other than him rescuing me, I feel it inside me. After six months with Alex and the five men he introduced me to, I recognize evil. I've breathed it for so long, was forced to taste it as a heavy hand would press into the back of my head, felt every hit they'd send my way, so I know what is and isn't evil.

But my confused, broken mind is lumping Hawke into that same category as the other men.

Large hands wrap around my wrists and gently tug them away from my head. For some reason, I allow him to do it. Perhaps, it's the re-realization that Hawke isn't Alex. He's not here to trap me or to return me to the devil. He's not a demon or even a dark angel.

Simply a regular angel with only goodness in his heart.

I hate myself. This feeling. This lack of control. It's too much…

Hawke lowers my arms back to the bed and immediately releases me, but the branding left on my arm remains. I can nearly see where his fingers rested a moment ago, the impact of them so much stronger than any hit Alex ever gave my skin.

And yet… I feel no fear.

"Look at me," he demands gently.

I want to. I want to so badly, but all he'll do is remind me of what I accused him of being.

"Willow," he prompts again.

After another moment, his hand comes up beneath my chin and he tips my head up, all without gripping me, just gentle nudges upward. Unable to avoid looking, I finally do, silently gasping with his nearness.

Again, instead of jumping away, his closeness doesn't frighten me. Rather, his addictive heat drags my body forward an inch, leaning into him.

"I get it, Willow, but I will *not* hurt you. I will *never* raise a hand to you. I want to protect you, and the only way I know how to is to not let you out of my sight. I want you to come home with me because I'm a selfish bastard who refuses to watch you walk out of this room and go somewhere else. You'll have access to my entire house, but you can sleep in my room. There's a lock installed on the door, and if locking it is what makes you feel at ease, then fucking go for it. *I'm* your person right now. *I'm* here for you because I want to be."

He's insane.

And maybe I am too, because as I stare into his ice eyes, I want to believe him. I'll trust him for now, and in two months, when he's forcing himself upon me, I can reflect on this moment with humour and laugh at just how dumb I am that I did it again.

That's not him.

"You don't even know me," I murmur. "I'm simply the half-dead girl you found in a basement."

"I know who you are," he counters right away. "You're a strong girl who found herself in a bad place. You're a survivor who deserves the world. You weren't half-dead when I found you because you were still so alive, hanging onto your own life for all it's worth, and I'm so fucking happy you did or else I wouldn't have gotten to know you."

I wish I could identify why my heart stutters.

"I know you believe you're broken, but I'm taking up the task of being your protector, if only to show you how you can heal your own wounds. It'll take time, but it's doable."

"Okay." What else could I say to him after all that?

Even with that conversation finished, Hawke doesn't move away. Eventually, his hand lowers away from my face, and I miss the contact, the feeling of gentle caring, of a man touching me with care rather than malicious intent.

"You win."

"I'll warn you now, Willow, I always do."

Then his eyes flick toward my lips. He bites down on his own, taking his lip ring into his mouth and his eyes grow hazy with wonder.

How would it feel to kiss someone with a lip ring?

Whoa. I shake my head, panic growing at my own dangerous thoughts. What is wrong with me to even be considering something like that, with him—with anyone?

I lean against the pillows, breaking the spell over us. Hawke blinks and pulls back too, standing and reclaiming his chair by the bed. The heated atmosphere doesn't extinguish for a long moment.

"He's going to jail," Hawke announces after another minute, his words so certain.

He thinks so, and I let him believe it. Let him tell me how I'll be safe… that I will never again feel a blade slice my skin or be raped by strangers; I will never again have my wrists bound as I lie there, unable to move on the cold, dirty ground.

Every story has an ending, and in my experience, it's never a happy one like books and movies trick us into believing we'll get. Mine won't be any different. Alex won't be gone for long, so this small taste of freedom—this hint of a happy ending—will soon be overtaken by the dark reality of life.

Remaining firm in my decision to allow Hawke to believe his own words, I reply with, "Thanks."

One way or another, my end will be painful because a happily-ever-after isn't in my cards.

Ten

WILLOW

The door opens and shuts and the bubbly nurse from before enters, a tray of food in hand. Even without knowing what's on it, my stomach twists with a painful need.

Food. Real food. Not bread delivered once daily with a small glass of water.

The quality of hospital food has been a long-time joke, but right now, I know it'll be a gourmet meal I can't wait to sink my teeth into.

Hawke moves aside, watching as the nurse drags over the table and sets the tray on it before positioning it over my lap. She smiles sweetly. "There you go, Willow. I'm sure you're starving, considering you've been asleep much of your time here."

I'm starving because I haven't had a full meal in six months.

I try to push my lips into a smile, showing how grateful I am to her. In truth, she could work for Alex and I'd still be smiling, simply for the fact that she's feeding me.

She seems to accept my gratitude and then backs away after glowering at Hawke. I wish I knew what was going on there, because it's clear, she hates him. In fact, so far, all the staff seem to be cautious around him.

Once the nurse is gone, he returns to his spot by my bedside and watches me expectantly. My hand quivers as I lift the plastic tray covering and set it aside, despising how food has me acting like I'm a child who needs assistance with even basic tasks. This isn't at all worthy of the woman he believes he's saved, which is why, even as my neck heats, red creeping up my cheeks, I don't look at him.

Beneath the cover is what's likely the grossest combination of ham and powdered potatoes, paired with a cherry-flavoured Jell-O and a plain granola bar. I scan every item, the fork and knife beside the plate, and the small bottle of water they've provided.

How does one eat after being deprived of basic human rights? How can I just lift the fork and continue as though this is normal?

"Eat, Willow."

That's how. With a command. In shaky fingers, I lift the fork. It feels heavy and unnatural in my grip and no matter how many times I reposition it, it doesn't feel any more normal.

Hawke leans in closer. "Eat, Willow. Or I'll feed you myself."

Why did that statement make my insides clench, and not in fear? There's something about that offer that nearly has me dropping the fork altogether and calling his bluff— but no. I don't. There's also a lot to be said about feeding oneself for the first time in months.

Holding the fork in my tight grip, I stab it into the meat until I get a small piece and shove it in my mouth.

The tastes explode. The juiciness of the ham fills every inch of my mouth, and I shut my eyes, just to savour. Not to chew yet but to hold the taste in my mouth. Ham was never one of my preferred meal choices, but right now, it's everything. It could be undercooked and I'd still enjoy the way it grants me more energy than I've had in months.

And I realize it's impossible to gain energy after only one bite, but it's what it feels like anyway.

My teeth move, tender from lack of use, chewing the piece, activating more of the flavour before I swallow it down with a lone, dragged-out moan.

You're being watched.

The moment my throat takes the meat, my gaze whips to Hawke, my cheeks somehow get even warmer. He probably thinks I'm a moron for acting harebrained over something so simple as food.

But his bright eyes express something else. Something that doesn't make me feel embarrassed at all.

His throat moves with his swallow and through a dry throat, he asks, "Tasty?"

"Delicious."

"Good. I'll admit I'm a bit disappointed I don't get to feed you though."

Is he flirting? *Can* someone like him flirt with someone like *me* during such a time? Instead of responding, I chuckle, forcing it out before going for another bite.

And then a sip of water—which turns into a chug.

And then, I'm attacking the powdered potatoes that taste as though a Michelin-starred chef whipped them up.

When I finish everything on the food tray, I wonder if it'd be unladylike to lick the plate, and if he'd even care.

Instead, I set it aside and nudge the table away from the bed, laughing lightly. "If that tasted good, I wonder what a burger would be like."

"Want one?" Hawke lifts up his phone. "I have a few friends who continue to hover around the hospital. I can have them get you one within minutes. Just say the word."

Such a strange guy. "No," I tell him, tilting my head in wonder at how such a person could exist, "but thanks. I should probably take a break."

"Probably smart," he agrees, slipping the phone into

his pocket. "Don't want you to get sick from overeating."

"Exactly." With the meal over, there's nothing more to do but watch each other.

I study the room, and then the door leading to the hallway beyond, where doctors flit back and forth. They've already asked about my family, already looking to the future where they expect me to leave here. Because that's how hospitals work; people come in for care and then leave when they're better.

I'll never be better; therefore, I'll never be leaving.

Makes it easy for Alex to find me.

If he hasn't already. He's likely watching you, preparing to take you again.

The nurses… the doctors… so many people he can pay off. So many people who can turn their backs away from their career, their oaths to protect and heal, all so he can steal me. And they'd do it, because it's that kind of charisma Alex has.

My throat gets tight, fear creeping up fast until my heart pounds in my chest and my hands find the bedrails, clenching them tightly. If Alex wants to come for me, he'll need to physically break my hands before I release my grip from this bed.

"How long must I be here?"

Hawke stands, his attention going to my hands, and then my face. His own gets tight with before he asks, "What's wrong, Willow?"

"They'll keep me until I'm better. I'll never be better!" I actually do let go of the rails, to rip at the blanket, yanking it off me, uncaring I'm sharing my body with yet another man. "Look!" I gesture to the white scars on my thighs from his monthly tally, as well as the newest one that is still red but now healed shut, never deep enough I'd bleed out. Then I point to the other various bruises on my legs—some old and some new—but all *there*. Black, blue, purple, and yellow, depending on what stage of the healing process they're in.

"Willow," he whispers, his eyes cataloguing every mark on my leg.

"These don't heal overnight, Hawke. And what about the rest of me?" I gesture to my torso, where I know there's more cuts and bruises. My thin form that needs more nutrition. "*This* doesn't go away quickly, and they'll want to keep me here."

His lips purse as he grasps the blanket and recovers my legs without touching me. Backing away, he murmurs, "Give me a minute."

The door opens and closes and he's gone, leaving me to suck in deep gulps of air as I attempt to breathe through the inevitable anxiety.

When the door opens again, an entire hour has passed, according to the clock on the wall. This can only mean negative things, like the doctors told him no. Called him an idiot for even asking such a thing. I mean, Alex is all over them, right, so of course I'm not free. Not even here.

"They want you here until tomorrow because they want to check—" He stops, his fingers tugging on his lip ring before starting again, "They just want to make sure of one thing, and I agree, it's a good idea. They said they'll let you go home tomorrow, so long as they can provide you pain medications to take at home, as needed, if the pain worsens."

A million pounds lift from my chest. "Seriously? Just like that?" A large smile breaks out on my face, unwilling to be held back because, for once in my life, *I* was listened to, what I said mattered.

Hawke's nose scrunches and he shakes his head, but he's grinning regardless. "Oh, no, not 'just like that,' but I have my way of convincing people to do as I say."

My smile falters because that doesn't sound good. "Um…"

He waves his hand in the air before retaking his seat from earlier. "No worries, Willow. I simply reminded them that by law, you're not required to stay here if you do not wish to. Legally, you are allowed to turn away medical assistance and they are not able to force it upon you, so if you feel ready to leave, despite your still-weakened body, then they can't stop you."

"Useful having a lawyer around."

He laughs, and it's a beautiful, musical sound that makes my mind go blank for a moment.

"I've been told that a few times," he replies.

"Thank you. Yet again, you've come to my rescue."

His grin slips away and he leans forward, resting his hand on the bed by my side, but not quite touching me. "I've said it before, Willow, I'm not going anywhere. If it's a rescue you need, I'll be here for you."

"Which leaves me with nothing to do but say thank you."

His full lips move with his responding, "You're welcome," capturing my attention and holding it there. The lip ring catches in the room's florescent lighting and I desperately crave to reach for him, to touch it.

He'll let you.

He might, but I'm not… I'm not *good* enough for that.

So I continue fisting the blanket by my side and count the seconds down until I can get out of this place.

The middle of next day, the doctor releases me with well wishes, medication, and a reminder of previous conversations. From what I see, they don't put up a fight when discharging me into Hawke's care. Maybe it's completely normal for the kidnapped girl to be taken home by the lawyer-stranger turned saviour, or there was more to his conversation yesterday than he let on.

Walking the hallway makes me feel like a celebrity, but for all the wrong reasons. Nurses actually pause their work to watch as I go by. I stare at my Crocs-covered feet, but the sorrow they send my way prickles my spine and sends an unwelcome consciousness through me, making me pleased I rejected the wheelchair they offered. For the sake of my pride, I'll walk out of here on my own two feet. Shaking my head slightly, my hair falls around my face, blocking more of me from their penetrating stares.

From beneath the strands, I see Hawke move, slowing so he is walking in line with me, attempting to shield me from all of the prying eyes. It's impossible to completely hide from them, though, with all they know about what happened to me.

Inside the elevator, there's a reprieve from the heavy stares, and although I feel Hawke watching me, I still keep my gaze on my feet. The elevator doors open and I rush from the small confined box into the hospital lobby.

It's busier than the floor I was on, but with my head down and Hawke leading the way, we're at the main doors in no time. They slide open with Hawke's nearness and he goes through.

I stop. The doors shut, not even picking up the fact I'm right here. It's fine though because for a second, staring at the outdoors is enough for me.

For the first time in six months, I'll be outside, able to do what I want and go where I want.

I can't.

Once, I was a normal human being, and visiting the hospital would have been so simple, so easy to leave; I would never have thought twice about it. So curious how a single event—a single meeting—can change that. Leaving the confines of the hospital and entering the real world again isn't simple, isn't easy. It's a lot. It's overwhelming.

Of course, Hawke doesn't make it far before he twists to find me. My lungs constrict with heavy emotion at the fact he doesn't look surprised by my distance. Like he was expecting me to falter when it mattered most.

His earlier words echo through my mind. *"You're a survivor who deserves the world."*

Do I? It's debatable; Alex certainly didn't believe it.

Maybe I don't deserve the world, but I do deserve the fresh air I'm about to breathe in. I'll take it now, that way when Alex comes for me, I'll have had a taste. Perhaps it'll be enough to get me through the next six months he's planning.

When I move, the motion detector catches me and the doors slide open smoothly, giving way for the gust of air that comes straight for me. Sucking it in and trapping it in my lungs, I walk forward, head held high, stopping by Hawke's side.

He doesn't comment on what just happened, but rather points to a vehicle parked a little ways in front of us; a minute walk. "That's my car."

"Parked this close to the hospital the entire time?" The fee that must have incurred would be so high.

"I had a friend move it over from the lot earlier."

I wonder who but decide it's not worth asking because while I feels so alive with the breeze coasting over my skin, it reminds me of one thing and one thing only—I'm out in the open.

If the wind can touch me, then so can Alex, even if it's through other people. A shiver snakes down my spine and my insides turn rigid, stupid, infuriating paranoia getting the best of me.

"Come on." Hawke nods his head and steps off the curb.

I quickly rush after him, keeping close. Other people linger around the building. Some glance over at us, and while we're merely two people in a city of thousands, it feels like they can see right through me, directly into my mind, finding out exactly what has been taken from me and seeing me as abnormal, not like them. That life got the better of me in the worst ways it possibly can.

Hawke stops by the shiny black sedan. In some ways, it reminds me of the black town car that once picked me up and drove me to the Miller mansion. In other ways, though, it doesn't. For one, there is no stranger driving. And two, this car's driver opens up the passenger door, allowing me to sit beside him and fully see where we're headed.

The most important difference is the scent. Despite the fresh air around us, the scent that hits me once Hawke opens the door is so sweet, so *him*, it'd be impossible to believe this vehicle could be owned by anyone else.

I get in, granting Hawke a small smile once I'm settled, letting him know I'm all right. I pull my knees tightly together, the fabric of the grey sweatpants rubbing together. My sweater-covered arms cross tightly over my chest, keeping all of me intact. I'm thankful for the sweats because it conceals the scars and bruising on my body that Hawke hadn't already seen.

Hawke shuts the door behind me and climbs into the driver's seat, immediately pressing the vehicle's engine start button and pulling away from the curb. He doesn't linger, and for that, I'm grateful.

"Tristan offered to pick us up in his car, but I figured we should limit the number of strangers right now. I hope that was okay."

I grunt, barely glancing his way. I don't recall the name at all, but he's correct in me wanting to be alone. The more people that see me, the more people who'll demand my story, which means the more people Alex could hurt.

"Tristan was with me in the basement," he continues.

Ah, so he already knows all about me. Still, he'd stare at me, no doubt. Maybe he'd even want to make conversation, but I'm not even sure I recall *how* to make conversation with someone, like a normal person would.

For the remainder of the drive, he doesn't talk, and again, I'm grateful. The silence gives me time to ponder the chaos of my life.

The journey takes us out of the city, out of Cortville, and onto the long stretch of highway. So if Hawke's home isn't in the city, it must be nearby for him to be staying with me for as long as he has.

Cortville's exit sign has my attention for as long as it takes us to pass it. The city has been home to me for a long time, ever since I left my parents and went out on my own.

At the time, it held little meaning, other than being a large place I could eventually hope to secure a decent job. I did exactly that, even if the job had a terrifying ending.

Which is why, as we pass the sign and officially leave Cortville, this feels *right*. Not only did Hawke take me away from Alex's prison, but also his city. Ideally, he'll keep on driving and won't stop for a long, long time. Maybe until we get to the States. Or an airport that'll bring us to international lands.

Being in a different city won't stop him from finding you, the nagging inner skeptic reminds me. She's right, but I want pretend, for the length of this trip, that Hawke is driving me into a world where Alex no longer exists.

About an hour later, we pass the sign entering Bridgetown. I've been here only once before, very briefly. Even after moving to Cortville, when I was job hunting, I applied as far as here, willing to move again or buy a cheap car that'd get me the hour's drive away.

Hawke drives through the quaint town. It's not little enough for that small-town charm, but it's definitely less populated than Cortville. A small city, if I had to label it as something. He drives a few back roads until approaching a quiet neighbourhood. It's the kind of neighbourhood where houses have manicured lawns, children play in backyards or the local park, and residents lounge on their deck. A place where people's lives are average, and they enjoy their normality before returning to their nine-to-five jobs.

He stops in front of a two-story home with white-siding, a large bay window, complete with shutters, and a styled front entrance with bushes that line the pathway. It's such a basic-looking house, it doesn't fit a guy who looks as extraordinary as Hawke does.

"Home," Hawke announces, pulling into the two-car driveway.

Home for him, but not me, regardless of his offer to

remain here. This isn't my home because someone who has survived what I have doesn't live in average-looking houses like this one. Homes like this are for people who don't get kidnapped, raped, and beaten over and over.

Hawke opens his door and comes around to my side, pulling mine open as well. Instead of climbing out, I stare at the driveway behind him, realizing that once I step out, I'm *there*. Here. Here in suburbia.

His hand cuts into my vision, breaking my stare. But rather than take his hand, I study it. In the hospital, I hadn't paid enough attention to him to see specifics in the tattoos on his arm. By his wrist, a flame wrapping a black rose gives me pause.

I've never understood tattoos. While I don't have any, people have described them as being a sharp point scraping painfully across your skin until you're so numb you appreciate the artist for what they're doing. I find it stupid, really.

Alex fashioned himself to be an artist once, in which my blood was the paint, my body his canvas, me the model, and my scars the art. He unfortunately gave me tattoos, but they could never be considered as beautiful as Hawke's.

"It's okay."

Right. He thinks I'm hesitating because I'm scared, instead of just studying his tattoos. Or am I looking at his art to avoid getting out of the car?

Taking his hand means a new chapter will begin. A short chapter, more of an intermission than anything, to remind me of what freedom feels like before Alex returns.

For that freedom, I place my hand in the angel's palm.

He helps me to my feet and shuts the door, ushering me up the driveway and toward the plain, white door. Hawke pulls a key from his back pocket and unlocks the door, pushing it open before stepping aside and gesturing inside.

"Whenever you're ready, Willow."

No demands to enter. A simple statement that leaves entering his house entirely in my control. For a moment, I think it's dumb, because no length of time will give me the strength to make the step, but then I look into his bright eyes and see so much compassion, so much hope, it drives me forward, making the step that changes everything.

I enter Hawke's house.

His identifiable scent—the same one I breathed in when he lifted me from Alex's cage—consumes the entire space, sucking me into its vortex. It's everywhere, swirling around me, basking me in the scent of *him*.

I take another step, scanning anything I can see. An immaculate living room is to my right, while stairs leading up are immediately to my left, by the front door. Everything is so clean, so stark, as though he doesn't spend much time here. It's a thought that tugs my mouth down in a frown because if I had a house like this, I'd never leave. Not after knowing what evil exists in the world.

Hawke walks around me, gesturing into the room to my right. "Living room." He walks forward, past the stairs and down the short hallway. "Bathroom," he labels, pointing to a skinny door. "And kitchen."

The kitchen entranceway is wide open, showing a table in the centre of the room and near-bare granite countertops stretching the length of one side, leading to the fridge and stove.

"Please help yourself to anything you want."

My throat constricts. How could I take anything I want? How does one *do* that? Alex never gave me access to anything good; I haven't gotten things I've wanted in a long time. When I ate, it was meager and whatever Alex felt a shred of generosity to give me.

I nod, aware it's the response he desires, and when I give it, he grins as though he just won a prize.

"Are you hungry now? I can make you something."

I shake my head. I couldn't possibly start out this… this… whatever *this* is by consuming his food.

Hawke steps by me and leads me back down the hallway, passing the staircase again. I spot something I hadn't earlier and every nerve in my body ices over, all while screaming at me to get the fuck out.

There's small door, about my height, beneath the staircase, presumably leading to a basement.

Hawke isn't Alex. Maybe. I know this. But the door—

"Willow," his smooth voice interrupts the pending panic attack. "I promise you there's nothing down there. And more so, that isn't our destination."

I know. The words won't come out though, trapped in a still-tight throat, so I nod and continue following him, even if my eyes linger on the basement door.

At the top of the stairs is a single bathroom and two doors. One is open and I see a large desk through it. I recall what he said about his job title at the hospital, so I suppose as a lawyer, he takes his work home often. He continues past it and toward the other door, pushing open the half-shut door to reveal a bedroom.

Decluttered, of course, with only a made bed and a nightstand. A closet is across from the bed. It's simple and practical and very impersonal, exactly like the rest of the house.

Hawke goes to the closet by the door and grabs a small bag, which he begins stuffing with clothing. "I'll take clothes with me, so I won't need to bother you often. I'll be sleeping downstairs. You can come and go as you please, or…" His uncertainty warms my stomach. It's reassuring to know I'm not the only one hesitating over this strange situation. "Um, so, yeah. Whatever you want." He pauses and his throat moves with his gulp. "I'll get you clothing too."

I glance down at the grey sweats. In the past, I've worn nicer clothing, but after recent months, they're perfect. Better than having no clothes, which had been my reality for half a year.

"I-I'll leave you be." Hawke ducks his head, his eyes slamming to the ground as he exits out the doorway.

For the first time since the hospital, I speak. The need to respond to him is too strong to ignore. "Thank you, Hawke. For everything."

I step closer to him in the doorway, stopping when there's only a small space between us. My gaze dances up the length of his body, and I realize then, he's a full foot taller than I am. So much about him my mind blanked out while in the hospital, instead focusing on my strange new reality rather than the angel who made it possible. His head hangs, his hair over his forehead, just like the goth-style guys I once crushed on in high school

"Thank you," I repeat. "I-I just—I…" A sentence refuses to form, and I don't even know what I'm attempting to say.

Hawke's lips twitch with the start of a smile. "Believe me, Willow, this is for my pleasure too."

What does that mean? But as I examine his eyes, his lips, even the way his form bends toward me, I think I know.

So when he walks away, I almost believe him.

Twelve

HAWKE

It's been three days since Willow's come home with me, and I haven't seen her at all.

I'm not entirely surprised though. During the day, I hear her moving around the room. Often, it seems as though she's pacing around the small space. I wonder if it reminds her too much of the cage she was trapped inside, or if the familiarity is relieving.

Since she hasn't left the room, I bring up trays of food and leave them outside the door, and every time I bring up another, the previous one is empty and left outside the door again for me to collect. We don't talk—other than my announcement of food being available—but she's eating, so it's all that matters.

I'm hoping she's also changed her clothes and gotten out of the cheap hospital sweats and into something more fit for her. After the first day, I had Elena and Ryker drop off clothes, based on me estimating her sizes. When I later went up to deliver food, the bag of clothing was gone.

Each passing day, the urge to barge in and see her again grows stronger. There are times I debate ambushing her when she quickly leaves the room to use the bathroom, but in the end, I understand her pain.

I get it in a way I wish I didn't have to. I sympathize, empathize… and *know* her feelings. The fear of one's own shadow, of constantly being found, of never feeling completely safe. Even if she truly believes Alex is gone from her life, it's difficult to repair one's mind in the way that's required to move on.

Hands pin my wrists, a knife cutting into the base of my throat as I thrash against the man's tight hold. Another man approaches, a sick grin stretching his lips as he scans my naked, barely-teenage body. The moment his eyes land on my dick, they light up.

I kick out, aware of how useless it is against the chains tying me down. The man's hands land on my ankles before sliding up my leg and—

"Hawke!"

I'm jostled awake and away from the nightmare—the memory—of three days ago. It may not have been the first time the sick fuck touched me in that way, but each time was always as bad as the first.

With my eyes open, I see the nurse hovering over me, frowning, like she disapproves of the darkness my mind is stuck in.

"Are you okay?"

She's asking if I'm okay? A question that should be used for a broken hand or any other physical injury. Getting kidnapped and raped over and over isn't okay. *There's nothing remotely fine about it, so how the fuck does she want me to feel?*

I turn my head away, looking at the window past her. "It's whatever. Just a nightmare."

Her frown doesn't go away, but she twists toward the door. "Hawke, your parents are still waiting to see you."

Exactly as they've been waiting for the past couple days, ever since Dad rescued me, but I continue to send them away. No matter what they've paid the staff, I promised double to ensure they don't come through my door.

How many times have I told Dad I hate the lifestyle he forces on me? And this is why. The life is fucking disgusting and depraved and kids get dragged into the middle of the feuds.

I blink, turning away from that dark hole.

It takes months, years, even longer to be able to function as one used to. It takes even longer to trust people again, especially ones not previously known.

If I was wise, I would have dropped Willow off at a shelter for abused women, where there are trained professionals to help pull her from her shell. She can heal there, and when I need her for the next step in the fight against Miller, then I'd retrieve her.

But I know why I didn't, even if it's every selfish reason I shouldn't have. The future is unknown, but I want her here with me. I want to help her; to be the safe person she can rely on while she fights the demons threatening to yank her back into the soulless darkness.

I lean back on my leather couch, which has been doubling as my bed and office for the past couple days. I have an office upstairs near my bedroom, but chose not to use it in case it'd make her even less likely to leave the room. Working down here is a small sacrifice.

The document in my hand blurs with the length of time I've been working on it. It's one of many I've been sending to the judge, as part of the process to begin a trial. Between the photos I've taken and the RCMP's confiscated proof, there's more than enough physical evidence to begin the process. But nothing in the legal system is done without a mountain of paperwork attached to it.

This is step one. Step two is getting Teagan out of the hospital to testify. What she'll bring forth will make Miller unredeemable in the entire court's eyes, convicting him will be a snap.

Sorry, Brent. I told him Teagan would be fine, all while fully knowing she'd be charged. There's too much evidence of her out with him, posing as his girlfriend—which was exactly his plan. She's being seen presently as a possible accomplice, and every day that Alex spends in the system, he continues to pack their heads with more lies.

Medical reports alone having come back the past couple days will do what I need them to do and will clear her of any wrongdoing. As I've told Brent, the court won't charge a person who's been conditioned as she has been.

Miller's more of a psychopath than we ever believed. He's good, in the way a criminal can be *good*, meaning he had a well-thought-out plan. My eyes drift to the stairs, thinking about when he said the words, activating Teagan into his own little killing machine.

"Kill her."

The instant he gave the order, I saw a switch flick off in Teagan's eyes, and I realized what was so perfectly hidden from us. If only I could have spotted it a second earlier, Brent could have broken them up, and Willow wouldn't have the memory of nearly being strangled to death by a fellow captive.

I sigh, drawn-out and heavy, but it's not enough to lift the weight from my shoulders. Instead, I lower myself onto the couch, pressing even deeper into the cushion, glancing at the unread messages on my phone.

Me: *Running away won't help her.*

Me: *I get being frustrated, but we could also use you here. What happens when she's healed and released and you're not there for her?*

Me: *Brent, answer your phone.*

Exactly as the nurses warned him the other day, they banned him after he returned the next day and tried to get into the mental health department, which has a strict no-visitor rule. Tristan stupidly drove him to a car rental lot, where he rented a car and took off.

Not that I blame him. Multiple times, I've wished I could run away, and perhaps I would if it wasn't for having to end what I've started with Miller's case, and for the woman upstairs who needs me.

As if sensing me thinking about her, I hear her pace the room above me again. Each time I hear her walk, an excitement awakens in me, all before I remember she's not coming down. Not yet, but she will on her own. Hopefully.

So why do I feel the need to bring her out? Like *I* want to be the one to give her life again. Show her all the good there can be.

On the coffee table, I retrieve my notepad, flip to a fresh page, and jot a few words to her.

Just in case.

Thirteen

WILLOW

Hawke's footsteps approach the door then quickly leave. Only when he returns downstairs do I open the door. Not too quickly though, first I peek through a one-inch gap to check that I'm absolutely alone before opening it the rest of the way.

Coward, my inner voice scolds me.

Yep. I am, because although Hawke may have been fine in the hospital, we're back in the real world. It's easier to pretend being free from Alex's prison is now a reality, if I create my own self-imposed cage out of Hawke's bedroom.

Typically, when he comes to the door, it's to deliver food. The other day was women's clothing and toiletries. A year ago, I would never have believed I'd be crying over something as simple as a toothbrush, let alone the accompanying jeans and shirt. The moment I slipped on the kind of clothing I used to wear, freedom became real. Clothing that covers my entire body, clothes that are *mine…* It's the little things that make a difference, even if it is only for a short time.

This time though, it's not food or clothing I find, but a small scrap of orange paper. I bend to retrieve the sticky note, wondering why he could have possibly left it. After all, he could just speak to me through the door, like he's done the other times.

"I have food here, Willow."

"Willow, I want to help you."

"Are you in pain? I have your meds if you need them."

That was only the first and second day. After that, he seemed to comprehend I wasn't going to respond and he stopped announcing every time he delivered something.

Backing into the room again and shutting the door, I lean against it as I unfold the note, reading the messy scribbles he left there.

You've created another cage for yourself out of my room, but I understand. I recall doing the same once. I'm not asking you to open the door because I know you'll only do that when you're ready to, but I want you to know I'll be here for you when you choose to come out. You're not alone in this, even when you feel like you might be. I know something of what you went through, being forced into such things.

His understanding and acceptance of requiring space makes my cheeks burn, my dried lips stinging as they crack with a genuine smile. I read the words over and over, taking in specific ones: *I know something of what you went through, being forced into such things,* and the smile falters.

Does he? Can he truly?

My finger traces the words. Is he a survivor as well, and he's telling me so through indirect words?

Hawke's room may be sparse, but he's bound to have a pen around here somewhere I can use to respond. I imagine him sitting in bed, reading over texts and contracts and making notes before succumbing to sleep. I wander over to the nightstand, assuming the pen he'd use is there, tossing it in the drawer before switching off the light. I tug open the drawer, and, sure enough, it's exactly where I thought it would be.

I flip the note over to the blank side.

I wish I knew what that means but thank you. It's safer in your room. The world is on pause when I'm in here.

Just like it was 'on pause' when I was in Alex's basement. On pause for me, and yet, still turning for so many others.

Sometimes, that's what made it the so difficult. Pretending that I wasn't in Hell while the rest of society went on, continuing to work, going out in the evening, spending weekends at the movies, and living their best lives. Ignoring that one day I went to my desk at Miller Inc. and the next I was gone, never to show up again. I often wondered how Alex sold that off; how he managed to get my replacement in so quickly, as if he has a line of women waiting to fill the role the previous one left behind. Alex may have been vocal in letting me know how I'd die and how the women before me had, but he never admitted the intricacies of his planning.

Even now, the world continues for everyone outside this house. People get up, go to work, and return home for the night before doing it all over the next day. They have no clue that one house over is holding a shadow of what used to be a person—me. No clue of the true evil the world can create.

Blinking back the tears I feel forming, I shake off the dark thoughts, ignoring the lingering weight of them, and slip the note beneath the door. He'll find my response the next time he comes up here.

For now, I return to bed, getting beneath the blankets. If I believed the hospital bed was amazing, it's nothing compared to Hawke's pillow-top mattress. Over the past three days, I've wondered if it's exhaustion, depression, or simply enjoyment keeping me confined to his bed. I've remained here as long as I can, never tiring of lying down or the feel of being untouched for more than a few hours at a time. The warmth of his blankets, even if we're into the hotter time of spring, is everything I've missed, and I roll myself into them, catching up on months of freezing when I was naked and shivering on a cement floor.

More often than not, I doze. Even while my mind continues ravaging itself, I'm pleased my body has settled down. It's catching up on so much sleep and gaining back some strength before Alex finds me again. At least this time, I might make it another six months.

Settling into the bed, I wrap myself in Hawke. His scent is here in every thread of the blanket, and rather than being overwhelmed by it, I like it. It's… *enjoyable*. As though he's holding my sanity in his hand. The second night, I slept with my face in his pillow, trying to permanently imprint his scent in my mind, so I may take him back with me into Hell.

It doesn't keep the nightmares away though, no matter how hard I try.

Each night, Alex returns. His hands pin me down while his cock shoves into my body. When I resist, he slaps me and forces me down on my knees. If I fight, he returns with rope, or chains, or fire, or whatever he feels will best keep me still.

Each night, the nightmare forces me awake and it's a while before the shapes in the dark room become what they actually are—bedroom furniture—and not torture devices. Once I calm down, I can usually return to sleep.

Hawke claims Alex isn't coming back, but he is. He always does. Even Hawke and all his supposed lawyer abilities can't keep him from wrecking my mind further. But if I shove aside my beliefs and hear what he says, that Alex isn't *physically* returning, I still don't see how any of this ends.

It ends when I move on and create a new beginning, as if I don't have an unspeakable past. It ends when I find a new job and pretend I'm not terrified of my next boss being a psychopath. It ends when I attend social functions again and feign being normal.

It ends when I leave my self-imposed prison. The irony is humorous at best. I've gone from one cage right into another.

That's why this doesn't end. The endless torment will continue no matter where I am located in relation to Alex Miller.

Footsteps creak the floor beyond the door, momentarily distracting me and pushing aside my thoughts. As I listen, I imagine Hawke bending down to retrieve the note.

I sit up, pausing as I wait for his next move. After a moment, another orange note slips beneath the door.

Uncaring that he can hear me coming, I slip from bed and grasp the note, unfolding it to read his fresh words.

The room might be safe, but out here is as well because I'm here, and I'm fighting for you. We'll get you safe and happy again, I promise. You should know I always keep my promises.

Pen in hand, I respond right away: *Why?*

The moment I slide the paper beneath the door, he takes it away and I hear a rustling. The flooring cracks again and the shadow beneath the doorframe fills, as he presumably sits down. I do too, aware that a mere couple inches away, he's there.

A new orange sticky note slides beneath the door.

The response I want to give is that I don't know, but that'd be a lie, and I promise I'll never lie to you, Willow. I feel… protective of you. There are words I wish I could use, but you'll think I'm insane.

I read his odd note twice and a fluttering takes off inside my stomach. He feels protective of me. When was the last time anybody felt protective of me? There's no moment coming to mind.

What are the words? I write back. This time, I hesitate before my fingers release the note back to him. Do I truly want to know when he believes I'll think him crazy? Why am I tempting fate by possibly wrecking the only positive thing in a long time?

You never learn your lesson, my inner voice chides. I don't, and yet, I send the note back anyway.

There's a momentary pause before I hear Hawke's pen. This time, when the paper comes back, my arm feels so much more weighted as I retrieve it. The answer could be anything and I'm not sure how I feel about the endless possibilities.

What if it's something I don't want to know? But what if it is? What if it's something I don't realize I wish to know and it changes every tangible thread weaving between us?

It might be so dumb of me, but the moment we met, I felt something switch on. Something that has me wanting to claim you as mine. Not to trap, but to protect. To care for. To… You can fill in the blank.

Can I fill in the blank though, when the unknown offers too many options?

My fingers stroke over the impactful words *claim you as mine.* Words that, as he said before, should make me believe him to be insane. More so, they should make me want to crumple the note, toss it in the trash, and never speak with him again.

Yet, I don't want any of that. Rather, I want to clasp this note to my chest and reread the words over and over, until they're permanently tattooed on my heart, because someone wants *me.* Not to hurt me, but to protect me.

"Willow." The way he says my name is the way I imagine someone would speak before dying. Low and weighted, deep and wanting. He's asking me to respond, and oh, how I long to, to be *normal.*

After another moment, I hear a rustle and a flash of orange appears beneath the door. He's written another note.

I'm sorry.

And this time, there's no further chance to reply because I hear Hawke lift to his feet and his steps disappear down the stairs.

Wait. My hand presses against the door, imagining him still on the other side. *I'm sorry too.*

It's too late though. I'm always too late.

With both notes in hand, I return to bed, holding them tight to my chest as I allow the tide of misery to sweep me beneath the black current.

"Spread your fucking legs so I can see your cunt."

He wants to do more than look, but knowing what happens when I disobey, I follow his command and his hands immediately go between my legs, prodding at my dry core.

"Mm," Alex purrs in my ear. His other hand links with the strands of my hair and he yanks my head back, bowing my body backward in an awkward position. "Look at my pretty cunt, waiting for me to fuck it raw. You missed me, right? I hated having to leave you for the night."

He left town for a meeting, and they were the best twenty-four hours I've ever had since being trapped.

With his grip in my hair, he drags me from the cage and out into the main area. This isn't good. Being removed from the cage means he's doing more than just raping me.

"Alex," I grunt in protest, even knowing that it's useless. The past two months since being captured, I've learned he hates being addressed by his first name. Perhaps it reminds him of the human he should be.

I knew after day two in here, he's not human. A human would show me at least a shred of decency.

Alex wrenches me to the opposite side of the room, toward the handcuffs he has hanging from the ceiling. Panic rises inside me, bringing nausea up my throat. I cry out, shoving my heels into the cement floor, although my pitiful, weakened state is nothing compared to his strength.

"N-no. P-please." I hate those things. I'm to hang from the ceiling while he tortures me. The metal cuffs dig into my wrists, leaving bruises and cuts for days to come.

He yanks roughly, throwing my body a few feet in front of him. "You don't make fucking decisions. You haven't realized that by now?"

Positioning me, he straps the handcuffs on my wrists before pressing a button on the wall. A quiet buzzing fills the area, and the cuffs lift my arms over my head, continuing until my feet leave the cold ground and my arms are stretched at an uncomfortable angle, the weight of my body shoving my skin into the metal.

"A-Alex… please…" I beg, even knowing the uselessness in my words. Alex doesn't have a heart and won't listen to anything I say.

Alex peruses me, a grin spreading. "Delicious, Willow. Fucking delicious."

From his pocket, he pulls out a knife, and then his attention falls on my core, and I know what's next.

"Willow!"

Hands wrap my wrists and wrench them to my side.

Instinct drives me forward and I buck, thrashing against the hold, at the hands that continue to bind me from the ceiling for his sick games.

"Willow!"

But then the voice penetrates my thoughts and it's different than the one in my nightmares. I force my eyes open and rapidly blink the sleep from them to focus on the bright, blue eyes watching me with concern. No dark, evil eyes in sight.

Hawke.

For the first time in days, I speak. "What are you doing in here?" I ask my question before glancing at his hands holding mine down, waiting for the panic to kick in. I should thrash again—anything to be freed from him.

It never comes.

Hawke follows my gaze, noticing where I'm looking

before yanking his hands back. He doesn't move his body though, still remaining bent over me.

"Sorry," he murmurs. "You were screaming and hitting yourself."

Of course I was. Because Alex was about to cut at my body before taking me in every hole, all for him to leave me hanging there until the next day. I glance at my arms, still by my side, spotting the fading bruises and permanent scars those cuffs have given me.

"Nightmare," I supply. Words are dry in my throat, but I only need to satisfy his concern and then he'll leave me alone.

Hawke's lips press together once before he straightens. I follow, sitting up and pulling the comforter to my chest.

"They're not easy to get over," he murmurs. His eyes dart to the side of the room, unseeing wherever he's allowed his mind to go. "I'm sorry. I didn't want to come in but I had to make sure you were all right."

"It's okay," I reassure him. And it is. Hawke doesn't need to apologize for saving me from myself. I plaster a soft smile on my face, hoping he'll see I'm not upset. If anything, gratitude eases the tension in my shoulders.

"Well," Hawke backs away from the bed, "I'll be leaving then. Goodnight."

"Night."

The door shuts behind him. This time, being alone is much more noticeable. Much more... stifling.

Because when he was here with me, I felt a bit less lonely.

Even for the briefest second.

Fourteen

WILLOW

The next morning, I find a note on the floor.

Please let me know you're doing better. I stayed awake for the rest of night, keeping an ear out for any screaming, but you seemed to sleep through the night.

He stayed awake all night? Stayed awake for *me*? I read his words over and over, committing them to memory before writing on the other side and returning the note beneath the door.

I'm okay. Thank you. You didn't need to remain awake all night though. I'd be fine.

Within minutes, his feet come to the door, like he was listening and waiting for me to wake up. I drift toward the door, expecting a repeat of yesterday. But instead of paper coming back to me, he speaks.

"I wanted to, Willow. Sometimes the most difficult part is managing to sleep through the night, and after the months you've had, you deserve all the sleep you can get."

My head is in the middle of sorting through the wave of emotions his words drown me in when he continues.

"I've brought food up. It's out here. I also wanted to let you know I must go to my office, so I'll have to head out.

I've been trying not to, but there's stuff I need there."

Leaving? As in, leaving me *alone*? When he goes, I'll be easily accessible to Alex or whoever he sends for me. Sweat beads on the back of my neck and blood rushes to my ears, blocking anything good out. There's only room for fear, for panic, for—I grasp the door, readying to open it, if only to demand he remain here.

"I didn't want to leave you alone and feeling unprotected, so I've asked my friends, Ryker and Elena, to come over. Elena was the one who got you the clothing the other day, and Ryker was with me when we found you. They know you, but I've instructed them to not bother you. I'll only go when they arrive. Okay?"

He thought of me.

He remembered me.

He *cares* about me enough to convince his friends to come over and babysit me.

My hand rests on the wooden door, lightly touching it, aware he's on the other side. How easy it'd be to open the door and tell him thank you, without a barrier of my self-hate between us. How much he'd likely appreciate my effort too.

Instead, I whisper, "Thank you, Hawke."

All this because I'm too much of a coward to be alone.

I'm a stranger. He doesn't deserve any of what I'm bringing down upon him. More so, he deserves a lot more than a *thank you*. He deserves...

...Not to have me in his life. Because when Alex is freed and comes back, he'll tear down anyone in his way. Hawke's been great to me, and Alex will slaughter him as payback.

"It's my pleasure, Willow," Hawke murmurs. "I'll be back in a few hours, okay?"

"Okay," I whisper.

The wood cracks again as he walks away, and with

his departure, I breathe again. I breathe in my reality. I've spent days holed up here, hiding from real life, but the truth of my reality is that Alex will do more than just injure me. It'll be Hawke; it'll be his friends, and I can't stand by and watch as they all get hurt, simply because they happened upon me in his basement.

In the matter of seconds, more voices drift from downstairs, as his friends arrive. All they are though is more people who'll build a wall between Alex and me; a wall he'll revel in tearing down. They're more people who'll get killed. More death.

I *feel* when Hawke leaves the house. Electrifying energy exits too and the area becomes cold, almost uninviting. I stop breathing to hear the low voices speaking downstairs. While it was sweet of Hawke to leave guards here, how can he hope for me to rest until he's back?

Then, somehow, footsteps approach the door. I totally missed them even coming up the stairs. I back away, keeping my paces light and hoping whoever's on the other side won't hear me.

"Willow," a female voice tentatively calls out. "Hi. Um, my name's Elena. I'm one of Hawke's friends."

I remain silent.

"He asked me not to come up here, but I needed you to know that I'm here if you need anything. Anything at all. More clothes, or shampoo, whatever." She pauses, and I see a slip of paper appear on my side of the door. "That's my number so you may contact me whenever you want. Although," she scoffs, "I suppose you'd still need Hawke's phone, and he has my number, so… sorry, I guess that sheet of paper is pointless."

She's trying, which means it's not pointless.

I've never had close female friends. I was never one of those people who got off on hanging at the mall all evening and going to the movies, all to gossip about the next boy they were interested in. As a child, I was the poor kid no one wanted to be around. As a teenager, I was so busy working, in hopes my family would come to appreciate me for the money I brought into the house. As an adult, I was a loner, sludging through life.

Elena is trying for me and damn if it doesn't have my heart knotting and my mind returning to the dark place it was in recently. Elena's trying to be a decent person, but Alex will slaughter her for her kindness.

"Anyway," she continues, "sorry. But, yeah, I guess if you need anything, get him to reach out. I'll be here whenever you need me to be. And, um," she pauses, likely colleting herself because her next words hit in an entirely different way, "if you just wanted to talk—about *it* or anything else—or to… watch a movie, or something. Anything. Willow, I can't imagine what you've lived through or what you're feeling, and I won't pretend to know either. Just be aware that you're not alone in this. We're all thinking about you, and Hawke is working every day to make *him* go away forever." She steps back and her voice fades. "Sorry, that was a lot, so I'll leave you be. I just wanted you to have my number."

Humanity is such a strange phenomenon. We're all born with it, but it's us who ultimately determines to discard theirs or not. Alex, I'm sure, once had potential as a child, but his background, family, and own twisted mental health deemed his humanity useless for the games he came to prefer. People like Elena and Hawke use theirs to strengthen themselves and the world around them.

So, before she gets too far away and I miss my chance to remind myself I still have mine, I call out, "Thank you, Elena. For the clothes and for this conversation. You're very kind."

"My pleasure." Her response is perkier, and in the safety of Hawke's room, I smile, enjoying how my words made someone feel good.

Then she walks away and her absence twists at a deep, buried longing, as if I want to open the door and follow her down the stairs and spend the afternoon with her being normal. What's normal though? Normal is for people who don't have their villain returning to torture them.

Which is why instead of opening the door, I slide to the floor and lean on it. My knees bend and I lay my arms over them before I let the tears freely fall.

I cry.

I feel.

I *feel*.

I feel everything I've missed during the past six months. Feel how Alex created a monster within me: a place where disparity and hopelessness are strengthened and fed hourly. Feel how I'm a shell of who I used to be. Feel how he tried to strip me of humanity until that very last second when Hawke claimed me.

My humanity isn't gone, despite all his attempts, and I'll prove it to Alex. When he is out of jail and comes for me, it'll only be me he finds and no one else.

Fifteen

HAWKE

"Blackwood, you have so much to explain, it's not even funny." From across the conference table, Jason growls and crosses his arms.

He's aiming for intimidating, but it isn't working. He may have started this firm, but he's given me a fifty-percent partnership in this, and we're finishing this case whether he likes it or not.

"Alex-damned-Miller, Hawke. *Alex Miller.*"

A name that's sparked respect and fear for years. Jason always avoided Miller Inc. and any of their business handlings, aware that their team of lawyers would strip us of power if we lifted a finger against them.

Which is why, for years, ever since the first family first came to me, I've been fighting this ongoing battle alone. A battle I believed to be useless until learning about Ryker Ames.

"We have proof," I shoot back.

"It's the RCMP who found him," Jason points out, his hand gesturing to the side. "It's in their hands now. Let them deal with it and don't think about dragging our firm through the mud."

Beneath the glass table, my hands fist. "The RCMP was phoned in on a favour to *me*. They have no reason to take over local police jurisdiction. The deal was they'll hold him until the court sets a date, and then he'll be my problem again." It was less a deal, and more a demand.

Jason shakes his head, his clean-cut blond hair barely moving an inch, thanks to the product he uses to keep its shape. Jason and I couldn't be more opposite, but it's what makes us a formidable team. We each have our specialities and techniques, and when we work together for a client, we're unstoppable.

He holds up his hands, his head slowing. "I'm not helping you, Blackwood. This is all on you."

Good. I don't want his help. It won't be a long fight anyway. Between Willow—if I can get her to make a statement on the stand—and Teagan, plus the images I have and the evidence confiscated by the RCMP, and the doctors' reports about both girls, it'll be the easiest case ever. The most trying certainly, and hopefully, one that goes my way.

Jason huffs and sits forward, the leather in his chair cracking as he leans across the table. His eyes study me for a moment, narrowing when he asks, "Why do I get the sense this is personal for you?"

His instincts are always right and it's what makes him a good lawyer.

He doesn't know the truth about what happened to me, or who my family is. Jason and I met during law school, completed our internships together, creating a friendship along the way. When he contacted me about starting up a law firm, he offered me a partnership.

"Because it is." This time, I lean back in the chair, knowing the disagreement is finished. "What he's done… Yeah." I stop, leaving it there as my eyes drift to the door. "I'm doing it for Teagan and Willow. And for all the other women he trapped down there." *Who aren't here to tell their own story.*

Jason's dark eyes flicker and he glances at his hands and back, and I see the compassion he fought to show, instead burying it beneath his fear of Miller and the influence behind the name. He groans. "Fine, is there anything I can help with?"

I grin, and push my dark bangs away from my face as a chuckle seeps out. Of course I won, even after he denied wanting any part of it. Jason is a helper; he can't resist working a high-profile case. "Actually, I'm in the process of getting a hold of the late Mr. Miller's will. Can you look it over and dissect it?"

"Something I'm looking for in particular?"

"Who the beneficiary is. His sister, Natalie Miller, was recently found by Alex. He tried to become a family to her, claiming it was retribution for their father's neglectful actions, but all he was doing was luring her in. Something inside me senses Alex was lying about who that wealth truly belongs to."

"Done." He blows out a breath, his lips hitching on one side. "Fuck, man, quite the situation."

"Tell me about it." And he doesn't even know who's in my house, an act that goes against so many of our profession's ethics. If he learned the complete truth, he'd think I'm insane. Not that I don't completely trust him, but I still won't risk Willow's safety or our set-up because I'm not letting her go.

For how long?

Even when this is all over, I can't let her go. Not yet. Not—

The ringing of my cell interrupts our meeting. I murmur to Jason, "Sorry, give me a moment."

I pull my cell from my pocket and the name on my screen has my insides going cold with unknown fears. *Ryker.*

"What?" I bark, clicking the green button instantly.

"Man, she's gone. Don't even know how she snuck by us, but she's gone. Elena went up and your door was open and—"

I hang up on him, shoving away from the glass table. "I got to go."

Jason scrambles to his feet, the office chair smoothly gliding backwards in his rush. "What's wrong?"

But I'm already gone.

Sixteen

WILLOW

I'll admit, I didn't put much thought into running. Obviously, Elena and Ryker will eventually notice I'm gone and will contact Hawke. I didn't consider how I only have the clothes on my back, and don't even know where I'm headed.

I just took off, breaking in the new pair of flats Elena brought the other day.

No doubt, Alex has people watching me, so any moment now, someone will come for me. And what will they find? Me, sitting on a bench in a downtown park awaiting their arrival.

So it's unsurprising when the figure cuts in from the right.

"Willow."

That voice is much different than any I imagined because it's my angel's voice. The very one who awoke me from my nightmare, and who talks to me through a bedroom door, aware I won't open it myself.

Hawke drops onto the bench beside me, keeping a couple inches space between us. His legs spread wide and his elbows rest on the bench's backing. Despite his relaxed position, my shoulders lower, shame settling heavy that he's found me, all for me to send him away.

The sun glints off his piercings and he pushes his hair behind an ear as he twists to face me. His expression is neutral, calm, and not indicative of being angry.

"I'll admit I'm a bit hurt you wouldn't come down to spend time with me but you're willing to leave the house entirely. I hadn't realized you're an all-or-nothing girl."

He *is* irate. My breaths stall, my arms and legs stiffening as my mind searches for the words to speak. But then his eyes glint, a grin tugging on his mouth.

"You're not mad?"

You won't hit me? You won't tie me up and leave me hanging for hours?

"Because you left the house? Fuck, no. Worried, yes, and confused, for sure, because you didn't come across as wanting to leave. But not mad, so don't let your mind go there, Willow."

The tightness eases from my muscles again and I lean back, attention falling to my clenched fists.

"I didn't want to leave," I admit. "Elena came to talk with me. She gave me her number." I watch him, gauging how my words affect him because I don't want him to be angry at her. "In case I need anything, but I realized then how you're all being so kind to me, and it's foolish because you'll only get hurt."

Confusion deepens the skin between his eyes. "How so?"

"Alex is coming back," I explain. "The courts won't care what those pictures show. He'll win, and then he'll return. He said he would, and when he does, he'll kill anyone between us. Elena, Ryker… you."

"Ah." Hawke twists his body, keeping more of me in his sight. "Willow, that's not happening."

"You can't know that," I shoot back, panic making

my heartbeat increase. "Not for sure. You *can't* guarantee my protection."

He says nothing, but his eyes bounce around my face and after the longest moment, he sighs, leaning back too. "Willow, I said I wouldn't push you, but maybe you should contact one of the clinics from the psychologist's list. This—for good reason, yes—is twisting your mind. You're worried. First, not leaving your room, and now wanting to protect us all. Your symptoms—"

"No. Therapy will make me face this, will want me to be normal again, and *if* Alex goes away, then I'll consider it, but I'm not allowing a stranger to give me a sliver of hope, only for the courts to release him."

Again, Hawke doesn't push the subject, but he does slide across the bench until there's hardly any space between us. My mind blanks with his nearness, my senses filling with all of him.

When I inhale, I'm breathing in the same air he is. My eyes collide with his, a strange sensation shooting up my chest until it wraps around my heart and tries to tell me something I don't quite understand yet.

Then his hand lifts slowly, tentatively, and he tucks stray strands of my hair behind my ear, and my body reacts in a foreign way. A way that has me curling into his touch, my eyes shutting as my body and mind drifts to a place that decides having such a response to a guy is normal.

When I open my eyes, his are glowing brighter than I've ever seen, with a new shade of a familiar colour I recognize.

Lust.

I've encountered it so many times. Every time Alex was near me, every man he's forced me to be with—they all watched me with the black, shadowy, twisted look of lust and I learned quickly, it's a colour that results in pain.

But on Hawke, it's not black. It's white and bright, a

colour that compels me closer and leaves my poor, traumatized mind behind. For a moment, I *want* to be the girl who accepts his colour, like I'm ordinary and able to.

Hawke's hand falls away from my face and back into his lap. "Sorry, I guess I wasn't able to stop myself."

"No, it's okay."

Then I cry. The tears swarm to the top before I can process what the hell is happening and then, it's too late. They block my vision, blurring his shock behind a wall of tears. Emotions are a bitch, and when they all come at once…

"I don't know what to do," I whisper harshly, hand pushing at my cheeks and forcing the tears back into place, but it doesn't work. "I wish I knew how to handle this, Hawke. I'm… lost. I feel *lost*. I don't know who I am anymore. I certainly don't feel free. Instead, I'm more scared now than when I was in Alex's basement. At least, down there, I knew what to expect, but now I spend every moment of the day sleeping, recalling his touch, and believing he'll return for me because I don't know what else I can do. I don't know how to move on, like how everyone seems to want me to."

Hawke remains silent and still, and I'd kill to know what's running through his mind. Until finally, he states, "I get it. I do. Not to your extent, but I know about the memories. The self-doubt. The disbelief that life will ever be normal again, and it's why I'm here." Hawke's hand slides across his leg until his palm is flat, his fingers straining and scarcely touching the edge of my jeans; a barely-there touch telling me he's trying, while also keeping his distance. "But you need to believe I'm fighting for you. We all are, and Alex *will* get what's coming to him. If you don't believe me, it's okay. It happens, but I do ask for one thing."

"What's that?" My lips hardly move with my response.

"Let me help you. When you feel like you're scared,

I'll be by your side. When you want to run away, I'll be there to hold you back from doing so."

I nod slowly, giving him the response he wants and the one I want to give. "How long does this go on for?"

Hawke shrugs. "Everyone is different. I think when you realize you're truly safe and Alex isn't coming back, it'll push you in a more positive direction."

He's still so certain about that, but my doubtful hasn't dissipated.

"When does that happen?"

Hawke blows out a breath and sits straighter. "Honestly, I am trying to expedite it, but I'd prefer if Teagan was out of the hospital first. Both your testimonies will help a lot."

His specific wording doesn't go unnoticed. "I'm not testifying."

"You'll get the chance to tell your story."

I picture it. Imagine what I've seen on TV; the room full of people making silent judgements, the jury who will need to choose to believe me or not, and the judge who will look at me with contempt or pity.

"No." I shake my head, letting my hair hit him in the shoulder. "It's not happening." Because it's more than the judgement. It'll be Alex who is sitting in the courtroom, staring me down and expecting a certain response. His face, his evil grin as I'm forced to recount everything he's done.

I can't do it.

If Hawke thinks I'm broken now, I'll be shattered then.

I'll be—

Warmth covers my hand, yanking me from my thoughts and I whip my gaze down, spotting his hand over mine. His thumb strokes back and forth until my heart returns to its normal rate.

"Sorry."

"First off, *never* apologize, Willow. I won't deal with that shit, you hear me? We'll get through this, and I don't want you feeling bad for anything. If you don't want to testify, you won't do it."

I watch him, search for the lie in his gaze, finding only honesty. "Seriously?"

"Yes. I promise I won't force you. From now on, Willow, *you* make the decisions. Everything is your call."

Everything is my decision. The last time I had such control was when I chose my job at Miller Inc., a judgement that has me questioning my own ability to make important choices. Hawke's attentiveness as he hands me a piece of his power—his power over my life—makes me soften. My heart beats again as I return to life and accept the gift he's offering.

"Thank you, Hawke. Seriously. I'm still trying to figure out why you're doing this for me. Dealing with me, I mean, on such a personal level."

His thumb picks up its pace while his other lifts, this time coming to hover over my cheek. He doesn't quite touch me, but I shut my eyes and imagine his soft, tattooed touch as he brands my skin with new empowerment.

"Because there's something more to you, Willow, and it's my mission to help you become *you* again."

Still doesn't answer the *why* completely, but I nod. My teeth fold over my lip and I pull my face away an inch, creating more distance between him and my useless, unstable heart, which is, once again, adding extra meaning to his words.

My gaze falls to his lips, to the ring, and I visualize what it'd feel like against mine.

"You're already healing," he murmurs. "Your bruises are fading quickly. That makes me pleased because soon, he won't be as much of a physical presence."

I'm healing because you took me from him.

"We should get home," he declares suddenly and stands, his attention on the phone I didn't notice him retrieving. "According to Ryker, Elena is still freaking out."

I follow him up. "I didn't mean to scare her. I was simply trying to protect all of you. Sorry."

"That word," he growls his reminder.

Right. It won't be an easy thing to stop, but considering all Hawke has sacrificed for me, I'll try.

"Besides," he continues, walking toward the sidewalk, "you'll learn real fast you won't have to protect me."

"Why's that?"

He turns his head, catching me in his gaze. "Because I'm not going anywhere."

Hawke walks a short distance away, and I spot the car he drove us home in the other day. The shiny, black car stands out amongst the older, faded ones it sits beside.

Hawke opens the passenger door and gestures inside the cabin. "Your seat, milady."

His odd words wipe away my worries and I laugh, stepping into the car, being enveloped with the light sensation he's building between us. Like, we're two normal people and he's taking me out for a date.

Not that I would know what that's like.

Hawke shuts the door behind me and walks around the front before taking his spot. Confidence exudes from him, and when he smiles before starting the car and pulling away from the curb, I wonder how many other women he's smiled at like this, after shutting the car door for them. How many women have sat where I am and watched as he drove them around? How many admired him and knew, at least for the night, he was theirs?

Why do these reflections knot my insides and have my throat clogging with a silent sob?

I was someone's and it wasn't pleasant. I don't want

to be again.

    Only… what if the someone was different?

Seventeen

HAWKE

Elena and Ryker leap to their feet the moment Willow and I enter my house. Elena's frantic energy bombards us at the door as she stops short, her brows dropping overtop concerned eyes as she focuses on Willow. "I'm *so* sorry if I freaked you out with my rambles. It's an issue I seem to have."

Willow pauses for a moment, but I can tell by the way she munches on her lip, causing blood to swell, negative thoughts are coursing through her mind. My hand twitches with the need to touch her back, anything to soothe the concern from her frazzled mind, but she needs to do this alone. Willow wants to grow past her own fears. Talking to someone else can be the first step.

Elena, ever patient, simply watches and waits, but it's Ryker who glances at me, his dark eyes filled with so many unspoken words. He shifts behind Elena, glancing at Willow briefly before focusing on me again, his brows dipping between his eyes.

I shake my head slightly, hoping he comprehends the necessity to drop the subject.

After a long pause, Willow finally mutters, "It's fine. I

guess, things just hit me and I got scared."

Thankfully, Elena only smiles it off at the same time Ryker mutters, "Come on, Dolly. Hawke found her, so we need to be leaving." He steps around her, edging to the door, but still keeping his eyes on mine. The tip of his head is so subtle, but I understand the meaning.

Follow me.

Elena moves by, to follow him out, but at the last moment, she turns to face Willow. "Remember what I said earlier? I mean it, Willow."

When she walks out onto the entranceway, I shut the door, waiting for Willow to indicate her next step. If she wishes to remain down here, then Ryker won't get the conversation he's asking for, which doesn't bother me.

She scans the entranceway and the hallway, toward the kitchen. By her sides, her hands come together, fingers clenching. I'm about to ask if she's hungry again or would like to fucking watch a movie—anything to encourage her to remain down here with me—but instead, she inches toward the staircase.

"I would like to go lie down again."

I open my mouth, maybe to protest, but she's already gone, disappearing up the stairs quickly and slamming my bedroom door. Sighing, I turn for the outdoors.

Elena stands on my pathway while Ryker leans against the house, by my mailbox, his arms crossed. The moment I step out and shut the door, he's on me.

"What the fuck, man? *That*," his arm darts out, finger jabbing toward the door, "is *not* normal."

"Obviously." I pace to the side, getting closer to Elena, so he and I don't end up knocking each other off the small front porch. "But Ryker, what the fuck do you expect? She's traumatized. So much of her life has been flipped upside down."

"She's scared of her own shadow," he growls. "Even

Teagan wasn't like that."

He's referencing how she acted when Brent had her down in the basement. Even when he trapped her down there, she never lost her shit, always arguing her way out until finally admitting what she knew.

"Everyone experiences trauma differently, dick. She isn't Teagan."

"Clearly."

Elena speaks up, "I don't agree with how Ryker's talking to you, but I do agree with what he's attempting to say." She glances up the side of the house, toward the upper windows. "I know she's been through hell, but being scared of everything, including herself, and then running away from the people who are trying to help her," her expression pinches, "is difficult to manage. Maybe she shouldn't have been taken from the hospital so soon. She needs help."

They don't get it. They've never *had* to understand it. While people always encourage others to get help after they experience such a life, that's where their empathy ends. They don't grasp how difficult accepting help is, or even that changes don't occur until the person wants the assistance. Which is why, while I encourage therapy, Willow will make the ultimate call.

"She should be where they moved Teagan," Ryker declares. "You can't be taking all this on, on top of the trial."

"I am," I shoot back right away. "I am, and I'm managing. I do agree though." My sigh lowers my shoulders a fraction, easing some of the tension in my shoulders. "I've suggested therapy, but she's not interested."

Ryker sends me a bored look. "She's like, what, a hundred pounds? We can get her to a counsellor easily."

A growl climbs my throat, readying to tell him where he can shove that idea when Elena speaks up, "Ryker, no, that's not how you go about getting someone help." To me, she turns and lays her hand on my arm. "You're trying, Hawke, and if you need help, you know where to find me."

"Thanks."

She jerks her head toward her boyfriend, taking a step away. "Come on, Ryker. We've bothered them enough."

Ryker stalks by me, giving me a long look. "If she doesn't process that grief and trauma, Hawke, imagine how well court will go. Just think about that part. I'm not trying to be an asshole, but it's really unhealthy for her."

"Like you two are the definition of healthy?" Bullying Elena in high school and then again after getting released from prison, until he finally broke her down enough for them to each admit their feelings for each other isn't exactly healthy either.

He glowers before stalking off, following Elena down the road and out of sight.

They're right, you know.

They are. But Willow needs to come to this conclusion herself or else therapy will only go sideways and will increase her fear. She needs to welcome the help.

Should you have left her in the hospital? In the moment, I wanted to do what she asked of me. I hoped being away from the hospital and alone with only me, she'd improve, like I had. But perhaps it's what I've been relaying: all trauma is experienced differently, and for Willow, the additional help would have been healthier for her, even if she didn't feel that way at the time.

Lowering myself to the front porch, I take in the surroundings, breathing in the afternoon air.

Hawke, how the fuck did your life become this?

Some days, I wonder why I chose this career. Wanting to help, not to be my family—sure, it's worth it. Then there's others, where I'm thrown right into what I was born into, and this case is too close to the shit I might have once witnessed in person.

Either way, I found myself surrounded by crime, even if I am on the other side this time.

My arms hang limp between my legs, my phone slipping from my fingers to fall the two inches to the cement step. Exhaustion tears at me—mental exhaustion more than anything—but I've been pushing on. For Willow, for me, for Teagan. For the world to be fucking rid of Alex Miller.

I'm scanning the quiet neighbourhood I picked out a couple years ago to settle down in, glancing over at the nearby houses, the few cars scattered along the road, not parked in driveways, and the couple of kids shooting a basketball down the road. Its *thump, thump, thump* makes me chuckle. Such a regular outdoor activity, a mere six houses down from a woman who's experienced real-life nightmares. But that's why I chose a house here. I wanted normality; somewhere where the greatest drama is someone's home garden not producing vegetables in the quality they were expecting, or for someone not to mow their lawn for a couple weeks past when the grass needed it. Average has its benefits at times.

I'm so busy watching the kids, I miss the complete flash, only catching it in my peripheral vision, and by the time I turn again, all looks still and silent.

I stand, scanning the area, pausing on each of the cars. Because I swear, that flash, was from a camera…

Not spotting anything though, I return inside and lock the door for good measure before heading straight downstairs, retrieving the gun stored there.

Just in case.

Eighteen

WILLOW

"Come on, you fucking cunt. Kneel before your master."

Kneeling is Alex's new preferred activity. After he forced me to kneel unmoving for six hours yesterday, bruises have formed on my knees. The only mercy is now we're in his carpeted office and the material may soften the pain.

We're not in here often, since he favours keeping me below, but when we do, it's never for a good reason.

It means I have a visitor.

The first time, I was dumb enough to run. It was shortly after my second month here, and I believed being in his office to be a sign. I took off, only to be stopped by his guest at the door.

For the rest of the day, I prayed they'd kill me. They used me in ways I was sure they would, but my stupid body continued to hold on.

So, I kneel as he commands. The carpet scratches and burns at my bruises and sharp pains shoots up my thighs, but I bite down on the inside of my mouth to prevent showing Alex how much I ache. He likes my pain, so I'd rather not show it.

"Ah, just in time."

Footsteps approach the door, but I don't look up, even if my instincts are crying for me to do so. Alex prefers when my head is *down, and I think it's so he can have the pleasure of ripping out my hair when he shows his guest my face.*

"Fuck, Miller, you weren't lying." The steps advance and my eyes flick up and down so quick, I'm hoping they don't notice.

Leather shoes approach. Of course he's another rich fucker. They're always rich. Rich with their own secrets, which is why they're approving of this.

"Told you." I hate the smugness in Alex's tone, but I despise the feeling of his hand fisting around my hair more. He yanks the strands, forcing my head back and bowing my naked breasts.

The man licks his lips as he studies my face, my chest, before dropping his slimy gaze to my core.

"Come here, girl. Come stand in front of me so I can feel your wet pussy for myself. Alex sure has spoken greatly about it."

Alex releases me with a shove, throwing my face forward, toward the carpet, but I catch myself and stand to walk with wobbling, resisting legs toward the man.

His eyes glow brighter as they lock on my core. When I'm within distance, his hand reaches out and—

"Willow!" I'm jerked awake, being yanked from the dark memory before the real nightmare begins. It was always worse with a stranger because they were unfamiliar to me. At least Alex was predictable for my insides.

This time, there's relief not fear when I open my eyes and find my angel hanging above me. Catching my attention, he moves away, standing by the bed. The bedside light he presumably switched on earlier casts across the bare skin of his chest.

My dry mouth parts, while my insides throb with a need I've never felt before. His chest is decorated in more of the same tattoos that are on his arms. Flames lick down his sides, disappearing into the edges of his pants and—

"Sorry," he murmurs, pulling my attention upwards. "You were screaming again, and it was louder than last night. Bad one?"

"Yeah." In some ways worse, because it involved more than Alex.

Hawke grunts, a frown lining his mouth. It's obvious he wants to say more but doesn't know what. "All right. Well, I'll leave now. Hopefully, the nightmare remains gone for the night."

When Hawke moves toward the door, I swear my heart slams against my chest and a silent *No* screeches from my frightened silence.

Don't be scared.

"Wait." The word slips out past numb lips, but with every passing second it takes until he faces me again, feeling returns to my skin. "Stay?"

He freezes, as do I, while I wait for the inevitable to come. No doubt he's determining the best way to deny my wish.

Despite the possibility of rejection, I add, "Please. It might help, you being here."

What are you doing, dumbass? Asking Hawke to *stay*. To stay *here*. With me. There's no logic in it.

Something passes in his expression, and I wish I could identify it. Rather, I pull the blanket over my chest, covering the plain tank I've been sleeping in. Not for protection, but to hide the blush I'm sure is expanding on my chest.

"Yeah, okay," he replies in a thick voice. "I'll sleep on the floor."

I glance at the floor, head already shaking. "No, that's absurd. Sleep in the bed with me."

Did I just offer him to come to bed with me?

He relocates to his previous spot, by the bed, but based on his expectant expression, it's obvious he's waiting for me to change my mind.

I don't, instead shifting over a few inches to make

room. My rationality screeches at me, calling me witless for willingly getting into a bed with a man who's a near-stranger. Feeding me, protecting me—that's one thing. Sleeping with him is a whole other matter.

I lift the blanket, gesturing for him to claim the spot. His knee lands on the bed as he slowly lowers himself onto the mattress, still watching me, waiting for when I freak out and push him away.

The light catches on his skin again, and with his attention on my sanity, I unabashedly stare at him, following the marks on his skin, up his chest and over his shoulders.

Hawke follows my gaze. "I can put on a shirt if it'll make you feel more comfortable."

Not that I plan on touching Hawke, but the possibility that I'll feel the heat from his direct skin as he lies beside me is unnerving. But also, I'm curious. As in, I don't want him to put on a shirt because I'm curious to know what a man's natural body heat feels like.

The last man I've ever touched was Alex, and for as long as I was down there, I believed he'd be the final one: that'd I'd never have an opportunity like this.

"No," I whisper. "It's okay."

With my permission, he finishes getting into bed. The large mattress suddenly seems too small, too suffocating, as he claims one of the pillows, keeping to the far-left side of the bed. He may be maintaining space between us, but it feels as though he's touching me.

My body heats, my skin feeling itchy, and I rub at my arms. Fingers find the blanket again and I twist it. But none of this is in fear. No. In fact, as he settles beside me, a new sense of ease lowers my stress.

Rather, I'm anxious because I *should* be fearing this. Not Hawke, but the basic act of willingly lying beside a man in bed.

"Is this okay?" Hawke turns his head to peer at me, but I lock my gaze to the painted white ceiling.

It shouldn't be okay, but it is. I'm fine with this. It's wrong for me to be feeling good about such an act, like a normal person would be, but I am.

You're not normal.

No, I agree with my inner voice. *I'm not.* I'm not normal because a normal woman's insides wouldn't be twisting, turning, and pulling by a simple, basic act. They'd be cool and collected, having done this before.

"Am I fucked up, Hawke? Answer me honestly."

"No," he responds right away, a bit louder than I assume he was going for. "You're not fucked up. Cracked, but not broken. Repairable."

"Am I though?" I turn onto my side, the blanket bunching at my waist. My arm hooks beneath my head and I peer at him in the low light that the bedside lamp emits. "Because right now, I'm nervous as all hell."

Hawke mistakes my words for worse and his brows drop at the same time he begins lifting the blanket. "I'll sleep on the floor. I'd rather you be comfortable."

Without thinking, my hand darts out, landing on his bicep. A part of him that doesn't look as muscular as it feels, but the hard muscle melds beneath my palm. Hawke freezes, his attention dropping to where mine is.

Before this goes too haywire, I quickly correct myself. "No, I'm not nervous because you're in bed. Rather, because I'm *not* scared that you are." My hand slides from his arm and onto the bed between us. I stare at it, rather than him, so I won't need to see his reaction to my next words. "This—you—don't scare me, but it should."

Hawke rolls onto his side as well, and the jostling forces my eyes up to his face. What I see in his expression has a soft gasp escaping. I recognize his look. It's the same one from the bench earlier.

Lust.

"I'm scared," I continue, "because I'm not sure I can ever be touched again, and that makes me fucked up. I'll forever be feeling Alex instead. I'm scared because I want you"—*whatever that looks like*— "but we haven't known each other for long. Most of our days together have been spent with me passed-out in a hospital bed or hiding up here, and that's not ordinary."

Hawke's eyes fill with emotion, and his arm lifts, hand slowly coming to my face. So slow, the pace one would approach a deer they didn't want to spook. I lock my muscles, right down to my jaw, to soothe his own hesitation. His hand lands on my jaw before slowly sliding to the back of my neck.

"What's normal, Willow? Normal is whatever people make it be. You haven't lived a typical life since last year, so it's fine for you to feel what you do, whether it's fear or otherwise."

His words sound pleasant, but there's a deeper meaning beneath them. A meaning he may not even realize is there.

It's okay to be abnormal. Maybe to him, but the world and their perceptions don't believe that.

His thumb strokes a patch of my skin. His gentle touch is so nice, for a moment, I shut my eyes and just *feel*.

"You make me feel safe," I admit without opening my eyes. "Like, it's okay to be with you."

Hawke's hand leaves my neck, and I'm about to demand he return his touch, when he weaves his fingers into the hand I have resting between us. He lifts it, bringing our joined hands toward his bare chest. His eyes bounce around my face, checking my reaction, but I'm too busy staring at the sight of us joined together to care what he may find.

He rests my palm on his smooth chest, overtop more

tattoos. My fingers press lightly into his skin as I flex my hand, feeling complete and utter smoothness. Alex is the opposite, having hair on his chest, and I dislike how it felt when he took me from behind.

Hawke's breath hikes and his body stops moving, but his heart continues to beat rhythmically, indicating he's not dead inside like the men from my previous experiences. His hand releases mine and lowers to the bed, allowing me to explore him unaided. I slide my hand around his pecs and dip close to his stomach.

He watches me, his bright eyes tracking my every movement. I don't return it, focusing on feeling every single one of his visible tattoos. Meeting his gaze will bring me back to the moment, which will remind me of how wrong this is. How I'm touching an angel with dirtied hands when I should return to my shell.

After another moment, Hawke reclaims control and guides my hand to his heart.

"You feel that?"

I nod, and finally lift my eyes to his.

"For a long time, its beats were irregular. It took me a while to accept what had happened and to move on and live. My goal is to make sure you live again and your heart beats."

"Does this beat for someone specifically?" The question slips out before I stop it. He's yet to mention another woman in his life, but it's now an answer my heart craves to know.

"I think it's starting to."

Fireworks shoot off in my stomach and I rip my hand away, tucking it beneath my head again.

"This feels quick," I admit.

Hawke leans back, putting more space between us. "That was—"

"I was about to say how I don't mind. I-I…"

When my verbal pain goes unspoken, he picks up the silence. "I refuse to rush you, Willow. I'd hate myself if I hurt you."

Idiot. You're so worried about yourself, but there's another person here affected by your selfish decisions.

Once again, my inner voice is correct. He's so worried about hurting me, and I continue to say the wrong things.

"You're not hurting me," I murmur. "None of this is—You're not hurting me," I repeat, instead of stuttering through whatever I was about to. "You want to help me, and this is what I need. I want to touch you without fear."

Hawke stares for the longest beat, and just when I think he'll deny me, a breath whooshes from his lips and he readjusts until he's lying on his back again. He pushes the blanket aside, baring his entire body. His hands go behind his head, adopting a position of ease.

"Touch me then. Any way you want, until you feel comfortable. My hands won't move from their spot."

Then he closes his eyes, shutting off his bright blue hues and his form goes still, awaiting my touch. He's giving me control, allowing me to have command over his body.

I push myself up onto my knees and shuffle closer, until I'm able to trail my fingers up and down his chest and over his heart again. I follow a path of images, noting the torn-up flowers and flames scattered on his lower stomach.

"A lot of tattoos," I comment.

"They represent my journey."

"A journey similar to mine," I clarify, recalling his note.

"Yes. Worse in one way, but better in so many others. The flowers represent that notion of being better. That it gave me the relief I later realized I required. The flames embody my memories because they burned away the past."

"How'd you get over it?"

"I never did."

The starkness in his words have me pausing. The bit I've witnessed and come to know about him doesn't indicate he's over his past. In fact, he seems fine. Ordinary.

Lucky.

"Do you have nightmares too?" *Are you still fucked up like I am?*

"Occasionally. Usually around the anniversary of the event."

Occasionally. Which means Alex will forever plague my mind. There will always be a part of him inside me.

"Get out of your mind," he murmurs, still without opening his eyes. Of course Hawke knows where my thoughts went to; he seems to read me in unique ways that should frighten me. He continues, "Miller has no place here. In this bed, it's you and me. You're regaining control and he won't take that from you."

My mouth parts, a rebuttal prepared, but his words chime through my mind. *"In this bed, it's you and me."* So I obey his previous command and push Alex away in favour of touching Hawke.

My fingers glide down the expanse of his stomach and trace the waistband of his black sports shorts. His breath hitches and his eyes scrunch quickly before evening out again. If Hawke experienced something similar to what I had, perhaps this area of his body is too sensitive. I know what it's like to be triggered, so I move my hand away.

"Too much?"

"No," he rasps, "this feels really fucking good, Willow."

Thankful his eyes are still shut, I smile wide and

unabashed as fearless adrenaline makes my head go fuzzy. He's doing more than letting me freely touch him; he's empowering me. With that empowerment, I do something I've wanted to since he first bent over me in the cage.

My hand continues upward, past his chest, over his collarbone, until I find his cheek. My thumb strokes over his full flips, once again imagining them against mine. I push the thought away to lightly trace his piercing.

"Did this hurt?"

"No more than what happened to me in the past."

"Can I tell you a secret?"

"Only if I can keep it."

His bewildering response has me blinking once, twice, before I can speak again. "I've been wondering what it would be like to kiss you."

His eyes shoot open and find mine, softening. "I've been thinking about kissing you too. Since the moment I first saw you."

When I was a naked, torn mess. Now, I'm simply a mess.

My attention flicks to his lips again, and I shift, aware my awkwardness is killing the mood. I've kissed guys in the past, before Alex, but other than that, Alex and his friends are my only experience sex and related acts.

"I want…"

My sentence hangs, but it's all right because Hawke pushes himself to a sitting position, his body approaching mine. Without hesitation, his hands move up to my cheeks, one angling my head while the other cups the back of my neck.

"Willow," he groans, his eyes flicking to my lips, "if you are uncomfortable at any time, push at my arm and this stops."

I won't. I think. I hope.

The inch between us is packed full of an anxious energy. Mine, I think. And the longer he hesitates, the more my unease heightens.

"Willow."

His soft murmur, the slight concern clouding his eyes, has me realizing he's waiting for me to make the first move. Or to give him blatant permission.

My mouth barely moves, but he hears my whispered, "Kiss me."

His lips descend on mine. I wish I could say this kiss created insane sensations within my stomach, but it didn't. It didn't because my mind shuts down. My body freezes, my heart slows to a pitter-patter, and I die inside.

It's been so long since I felt anything more than pain.

The smack is so sudden, I don't feel it at first. Not until the metallic taste of my blood seeps between shocked, parted lips.

"You're bleeding? Fucking useless. Now when you suck me off, I'll have blood on my cock. Disgusting."

Except blood is fine when he's inside me. Then he doesn't care about it.

"Get out of your mind," Hawke murmurs. He pulls back to look me in the eyes. "I won't let him ruin this."

He kisses me again, and this time, I kiss him back. My mouth moves under his and—

Alex dissipates. The memory of him. Every touch, every hit, every crude word. My past doesn't matter, nor does the unknown future. Only the present. Only Hawke. Only this.

I awaken. My heart flies, butterflies finally taking flight in my stomach. They go, lifting my body with their rising height, until instinct has me rising on my knees to get closer to Hawke, our hearts lining up. My arms wrap around his neck to ensure this never ends.

This is passion.

This is fire.

This is *mine*.

Alex won't steal this from me.

Hawke kisses me harder, and by instinct, my lips part, my tongue seeking his. He meets the kiss, a low moan in the back of his throat, indicating his surprise with my forwardness.

But this feels right. *He* feels right.

It should be like this, but I no longer care. Not as I tilt my head into the kiss and my hands rove over his back, his neck, his shoulders, keeping his chest pinned to mine. His strength wins out though, and he manages to break the kiss and put space between us. Our heavy pants mingle and join.

"Willow," he whispers.

It's a pained beg, like he's craving more but doesn't want to go there.

It's a yearning request, seeking permission for what he covets.

I pull him back toward me, deepening our kiss and taking control, letting instinct and lust rule my actions. For once, I don't mind one bit. I don't think, only feel. I long for more—for him.

"Harder," I murmur against his lips. "You won't hurt me. I want this."

Thankfully, he doesn't fight my request, and it's clear he was holding back earlier. His tongue duels with mine, his hands gripping my face tighter. His arm goes around my waist, and he pins my body against his.

A sound escapes my throat; it's a combined moan and sigh that isn't at all enough to describe—to prove to him—what sensations he's creating inside me. Lust drips through my core and instinct drives me to move my hips against him, seeking more, unwilling to even consider that I should *not* be wanting *that*.

The kiss goes on for a moment, or an hour; I'm uncertain how long exactly. When Hawke pulls back again, my lips feel swollen and full of blood.

His eyes flick around my face, and I watch, fascinated, how his mouth forms a single word: "Fuck."

This time, I don't hide my happiness. I smile so wide, my cheeks pinch.

"You're fucking delicious, Willow. We need to stop or else I'll be tempted to learn what you taste like in other places too."

Other places? Oh! My cheeks heat and my thighs clench together, picturing him kissing me *there*. No one's ever done that. No one prior to Alex, and definitely not him either. He only used my body for his own pleasure.

I stare at Hawke, imagining it. Envisioning those tattooed shoulders between my legs while his dark bangs skirt the base of my stomach as he—

"I'm freaking you out."

You're being selfish again. I shake my head wildly, waving my hand in the air to reassure him. "No, you're not freaking me out. I was—I, um… I'm surprised at myself. To want you like this after—"

Understanding flashes through Hawke's eyes and he links his fingers with my own, bringing our joined hands to his chest.

"Willow, the fact you want me at all is everything. It means you trust me."

Trust him? I do, even if it's idiotic to place my trust in another man so soon.

"Intimacy," he continues, "is different when there's trust. Alex took sex and twisted it. You want me because I'm not him and you trust me." His fingers flex around mine. "The fact that your instincts are able to make the distinction is a beautiful beginning."

"A beginning to what?"

"To your future."

Nineteen

WILLOW

My upper teeth munch on my lip as I stare at him, the memory of what we did heavy over the room. "What now?"

"Now," he drops back to his pillow, his hands releasing me, "we sleep. I'll be here all night, keeping away your nightmares."

Seems so natural, but there's nothing conventional about this entire thing. There's no way to avoid the awkwardness, so after inhaling a sharp breath, I fall onto the pillow beside him, pushing to the farthest edge of the bed to keep the maximum amount of space between us. Despite what we shared a moment ago, sleeping arrangements are an entirely different thing.

"Thank you, Hawke. I know I repeat that a lot, but still."

"Don't thank me yet. I've tasted you, so now, you're inside me."

The possessiveness of his words sends shivers down my spine. They should spike my anxiety, but instead, they ease my tight muscles and I breathe deeply.

You're inside me too.

Hawke flicks off the light, bathing the room in darkness, giving me the space to smile freely, without him seeing it.

"Goodnight," I whisper. "Thanks for being here."

"I told you, Willow. We'll get you better and I won't stop until you believe in yourself again."

With his words floating around me, I have a nightmare-free sleep.

A heated, heavy weight rests on my centre, and as awareness comes, I flinch but don't fight back. When Alex is on me, I'm too weak to combat his strength, so it's easier to let him finish and get off me when he feels ready to.

When I open my eyes, I expect to be watching myself in a reflection as Alex forces himself in me, but instead, only white fills my gaze. I blink, lifting my head slowly, spotting the spongy pillow my head is on.

Every morning when I awake, it takes a bit for my brain to catch up and realize I'm no longer in Alex's basement, but rather in a comfortable bed, safe for now. This time though, the weight doesn't go away as I wake. I scan myself, seeking it, catching the flash of skin over my waist.

At the same time, he stretches behind me before his arm tightens, pulling me closer into his body.

I'm cuddling with Hawke.

I should be panicking. My feet should be kicking out and working to get his weight off me, so I can rush away from this room and him and everything we're doing… Yet, I don't. I think I even close my eyes, even while my brain continues to question my sanity.

By the time I smile into the pillow, shamelessly blissed, he's woken himself up and jerks away from me. "Shit!"

The bed jostles with his quick movements. "Fuck, I'm sorry, Willow. I didn't mean to touch you. I guess while I was sleeping, I didn't know and——"

He cuts off his ramblings and I roll over in time to watch him rub a hand down his face. It does nothing but highlight his agony and his sexy morning look.

The knots in my throat tighten, removing the ability for me to speak clearly, so my next words are whispered. "Hawke, it's fine. It felt nice. I think I liked it."

His hand falls to the mattress as he tilts his head and catches my eye. "Yeah?"

"Yeah." A slow smile creeps on my face, and once I realize it's there, I let it go: let it expand to ensure he sees it entirely. "Everything with you feels wonderful. Stop apologizing." Then my smile shifts into a light giggle, as I recall the same request he had yesterday. "Sorry I was such a bitch to you. You did a good thing, taking me in, giving up your room."

Hawke shoves an elbow under his body and hoists himself into an upright position. His bangs fall over his forehead as piercing eyes lock on me. "I definitely don't want an apology for *that*. You had every excuse to be frightened. I'm simply pleased you responded to my notes."

"I enjoyed them, to be honest." The various words he wrote to me roll through my mind, landing on a particular set. "You mentioned something like this happening to you. You also alluded to it last night."

Hawke's eyes darken and all playfulness drops from his expression. A breath slowly seeps out; his billowed cheeks depleting gradually.

"You don't need to tell me." *I'm an idiot to bring it up.* My teeth sink into the inside of my cheek. It makes sense he's uncomfortable, as I'm uncertain if I could detail everything done to me——even to him.

"No, it's——" His lips pull up on one side. "It's a dark

past I pretend to have buried, but it'll never be gone. It's forever a shadow. A single event that ripped me from my family."

"Your family?"

"Yeah." He sits up, leaning against the dark headboard. His knees bend, blanket lightly draped over top, and his arms hang, creating an eased position. I sit up too, turning to face him with my legs crossing.

Hawke watches me for a moment, his lip ring disappearing in his mouth.

"No one knows what I'm about to tell you. Not Ryker, Tristan, Brent, or even Jason, my partner at the firm."

My ears perk and I nod, indicating I'm intently listening.

"My real name is Hawke Corsetti. I'm the firstborn son of Lorenzo Corsetti, of the mafia family based in Montreal, Quebec."

"Mafia?" I squeak, eyes bulging. That's something of fiction.

His lips twitch. "Yeah, it's a bit odd to even admit out loud. I had my last name legally changed on my eighteenth birthday to cut affiliation with them. That way, I'm able to live an ordinary, boring life."

I scan Hawke, noting his goth-like appearance, various tattoos, and piercings. Nothing about him is *boring*, and he is unlike how I imagined someone from the mafia appearing. Not that I exactly have a concept, but I imagine ruthless businessmen who will murder, lie, and steal as they desire. Blood and loyalty are said to their strongest traits, and yet, one of their own blood relations is sitting here with me, in a small town far away from Quebec, working as a lawyer.

"I broke ties with them when I was a teenager."

"With your parents?"

Hawke licks his lips, catching my gaze. "Yeah. Parents, siblings, cousins. All of them. I want nothing to do with that lifestyle."

"Why? Isn't the mafia, like, super powerful? You'd be more commanding than being a lawyer allows you to be."

He scoffs, shaking his head. "That's the problem. They're *too* powerful, which makes members of the Family constant targets. Even," his voice drops, bitterness filling his tone, "if it means dragging someone in between the fight."

Oh. I think I see now.

He continues, "I'm the oldest son. I should have been Capo, like my father was before he was promoted. I'd be that now, if I never left. Instead, my brother, the second oldest is."

It's hard to imagine him in Montreal, leading a mafia, of all things. He wouldn't be here with me. Our lives would be totally different. I'd likely be dead by now, having never been saved.

"I was fourteen and out with friends when they took me. I don't know who they were, but they certainly knew who I was. They revelled in having found my father's heir because they wanted land or weapons. Or money. Honestly," he scoffs, "I don't know why they captured me, because in the end, it doesn't really matter. Either way, they wanted something my family had, and used me to get it."

My hand flies to my mouth, shutting in the millions of questions demanding answers.

Hawke shrugs, and with his simple, blasé action, I notice this is bothering him. His eyes darken with sadness as they stare at his clasped hands, and it's the same sadness lowering his shoulders.

"They were a small group of men who determined capturing me wasn't enough. Not when I had more they could take. So, they did. All of them, one after another, over and over, while they filmed it to send to my parents.

Motivation for them to find me, they said."

Oh my God. All those times Hawke referenced knowing how I felt was because he lived a comparable experience. He lived and survived it, and is now recounting it.

"It worked, of course, and my family came, bringing with them an army larger than the group of men ever imagined. They were all slaughtered, but it was too late. I was in captivity for three days, and after the first video, they never stopped. Said I felt too good." His voice turns bitter. "I was raped by all five of them multiple times. Forced to touch and suck them for their own sick pleasures.

"Though I enjoyed seeing every single one of them get their hearts yanked out by my father, the harm was done, permanently etched into my soul. Three days resulted in a lifetime of memories and self-hate." His fingers skirt alongside his arm, over a tattoo of a flame.

Ordinary people would sympathize. They would try to empathize with him, but it'd be pointless because the past can't change. I understand that.

"Hawke…"

He smiles crookedly, but it doesn't meet his eyes.

"After that, I was in the hospital for a while. I turned them away, even when they paid off the staff. My father may not be directly at fault, but his insane fucking lifestyle is. He only saved me because I was his heir and he needed me."

"Hawke." I know what having a shit family is like, but an assumption like that is, well, only an assumption. Parents wouldn't choose to leave their child in such a situation.

"Once the hospital discharged me, I marched straight home, packed a bag, and announced I was done. With them, with the Family, with everything. It was a fight that went on for a while. I have younger brothers, you see, who could become the next heir, but that's not how it's done, and my father would lose face when everyone learned his heir abandoned him in favour of a civilian lifestyle. Finally, they conceded and left my credit cards active and accounts topped up, because they were so sure I would return. They believed it was simply a mental breakdown.

"But that's the thing." His agonized eyes slash toward me. "They believe it was a temporary mental state, and I'd be fine with time. Because they didn't know—didn't *understand* how something like that felt. How, at fourteen, being raped, feeling as though your body and soul are being torn from you is more than a *breakdown*. It's life-changing and permanent, as you well know."

I do. He was correct when he said in some ways, his experience was worse. Fourteen-years-old… I picture Alex and everything he did to me being done to a girl, hardly a teenager and—My thoughts cut off, bile rising in my throat. I won't imagine it.

"You never returned, did you?"

He shakes his head once, then offers a sharp nod. "No. Once they realized I was telling the truth, there was nothing they could do. Usually when a Made Man abandons the Family, he'd be branded as a traitor and killed. You see, there is *no* leaving. Once you're sworn in, it's for life." Hawke pauses before murmuring, "*Unisciti a leale. Muori leale.* Join loyal. Die loyal. It's the Corsetti motto, and what saved me. I was still a year away from being formally inducted, so it's more difficult holding me to the mantra."

The unusual language flows so easily from him. Italian, I believe. The words he first spoke to me echo in my mind, and I must ask him their meaning.

First I point out, "And since your father was in charge, it'd be different."

Hawke's brows lift. "Maybe. He would do what he needed to, son or not. At that time, I was in such a dark place, I didn't care if they did kill me. Instead, I was branded as an outsider, and I left. I believe my father always hoped I'd return and reclaim my rightful place," he rolls his eyes, "but I've never contacted them. A few years ago, my brother found and phoned me. We spoke briefly then, long enough for me to tell him to fuck off." Hawke glances away quickly. "Until recently."

Why do I sense where this is going?

"I don't have arresting capabilities and Tristan, even being a cop, would be questioned as to why he was in Miller's basement without a warrant. The RCMP has national arresting power, even if they also have rules they need to follow. The mafia pays them well, to bend some of those rules, to ensure none of their members see the inside of a jail cell, considering all the illegal shit they do. The entire system is so corrupt, and I hate it, but I reached out to my brother because this time, I had to break the rules a bit to win."

"You..." If I could shrink into the bed, I would. He contacted his family—the past he left behind—to arrest Alex.

"Yeah," he agrees with my unspoken statement. His throat bobs with his swallow. "I had to. There's only so much I, as one person, could have done, and I needed to ensure Alex was taken away and you could be saved."

"The others don't know any of this?"

He shakes his head, smiling gently. "They suspect there's things from my past I'm not admitting, but they're happy that it's all over and won't ask those questions."

Maybe over.

Hawke falls silent but keeps his eyes on me, as though he's waiting for a reaction. It takes a while to collect my thoughts though, because his life is something from TV. Hawke, a seemingly average guy—if average means breaking into a villain's basement and saving the victim—is born of the *mafia*.

"I'd appreciate it if the truth remains here, Willow."

"Of course," I respond instantly. As if I'd give his past away. "Thank you, Hawke, for contacting your family for me."

"A necessary evil I have no regrets doing. At least now, you understand why I recognize what you're feeling." His hand slides across the bed, lightly touching the edge of my foot. "It was a long time before I would let anyone go near me. My teenage life was spent on the run, avoiding anyone who looked at me twice. There was no one I trusted, believing they knew who I was and would use me exactly as those men did."

Instead of responding with words, I lean forward and kiss him. What begins gentle soon turns heated and his arms come around my body, hoisting me over his lap, and that's when I feel it.

Feel *everything*.

Our bodies lined up together, his lap hard beneath my core. Hawke clasps my hand, and he takes me away from his world and into a better one. I sigh into his mouth, which seemingly shatters the spell over us.

Hawke pulls back, his lips lifting on one side. "Well, I feel infinitely better now."

I giggle, my chest expanding with every laugh it takes. "Good. It's how you make me feel." Returning to my previous thought, I ask, "The language you spoke earlier, when repeating your family's motto—that's Italian, right?"

"Correct. My family's French-Italian. I try not to speak Italian, especially in front of others, but old habits sometimes break through. It's natural to do."

"Like when you spoke to me in the cage. You called me something. *Bella*-something."

"*Bella ragazza.*" Hawke blinks, folding his lips together, his brows lowering over troubled eyes. "Huh. I don't recall doing that. Must have slipped out."

"What's it mean?"

Holding my gaze, his fingers trail the side of my face, lingering as he replies, "Beautiful girl. It's the first thing I thought when I saw you."

Is it possible for one's heart to swell? Because I swear mine does. Even then, he shared a piece of his history with me, which makes the nickname all the more meaningful.

Repeating himself, he murmurs, *"Il mio bella ragazza. My beautiful girl."*

The addition of 'my' does curious things to my insides. "It's strange to hear you speak it," I admit, "but I enjoy it so much. It's lovely, Hawke."

"As are you." Hawke's arms tighten around me again, and just when I think he'll kiss me, he releases me with a deep, longing sigh. "I should get to my laptop and do some work. Unfortunately, I do have other clients still. Would you like to come downstairs?"

Suddenly, a bucket of cold water drenches me, wrenching me back to the present. To when I'm hiding inside his room, and we're not cuddling like a couple. To where being in here means I won't need to *be* for the time being. Kissing him is one thing but living… living is another.

He flicks strands of hair off my face as he studies me. "Willow, you don't have to if you don't want to."

He recognizes my expressions so well. It pains my insides to be so blatantly obvious to another person.

"I'll stay up here."

Hawke nods, and it's so simple, so accepting. He gets out of bed before striding to the closet and pulling on a shirt, covering up his bare abs. I frown, watching him, already missing his body.

"Want me to send up food?"

Because I'm so useless I can't even walk downstairs to get a tray of food myself. With real life resuming, disappointment and self-hate lowers my shoulders, shattering the joy I felt moments ago.

"Please," I whisper through a clogged throat.

Hawke smiles, unseeing—or uncaring—where my thoughts are. "Give me ten."

Then he's gone, leaving me alone, staring after him.

Twenty

WILLOW

For the first time in six months, I've had the sense of a busy day. While I laid in bed for most of it, my mind continued playing out every scenario of what not stopping at only a kiss would look like.

When Hawke returns to the room that night, he immediately yanks off his shirt before his arms find my waist and he pulls me in for a kiss. The fact he did so without checking, by only assuming I'd want this, brings a smile to my face because it means he'll soon finish treating me as though I'll break.

"Stop me if you don't want this, Willow, and I'm serious."

I shake away his silliness. "It's fine. It's perfect," I correct before adding, for good measure, "I want this."

"Good." He kisses me again before leading me by the hand to the bed. He slips in and I lie beside him, adopting a similar position as we did last night. "I missed you today."

When I refused to leave the room.

When I was staring at the door all day, realizing I'm frightened of living because all I've done was survive these past few months.

Hawke switches off the light, which I appreciate because, in the dark, everything is different. Without being able to clearly see him and his expressions, I find myself asking, "How did you get over it?"

"I told you, I never did."

"I mean, you're living. Going to work."

"Ah." As the realization of my actual question settles, he replies, "It wasn't instant. I wandered around for a long time, living off my parents' money until I was able to get my own job and I built myself from there. Got my GED. I suppose to answer your question, it was necessity rather than want."

Necessity. Eventually, I'll need to move on from Hawke's house. If Alex is truly being sent to prison, this can't be my future: hiding inside his bedroom, frightened of the world.

"It's the same for me then," I murmur, twisting my fingers in the blanket. "Eventually I'll need to leave here."

Hawke's silent for a moment, and the pause is deafening and heavy. Finally, he speaks, "I agree you'll need to leave this room, yes, but you're to be here as long as you want."

"You're kind, but—"

"But nothing," he interrupts. "It's my own selfishness driving me to say those words."

My heart thumps loudly, but overtop the increasing sound, I manage to whisper, "I don't fully know what that means."

The bed shifts as he rolls over and through the dark, the moon catches on the metal in his brow, nose, and lip. His penetrating blue eyes pin me. They glint and a shadow moves—his arm—as his fingers wrap around mine. I allow him the control as he brings my hand to his beating heart.

"From the moment I saw you in that basement, this started to beat differently. Its pattern was altered, matched to your breaths. If you don't want me, then once you're the person you wish to be, I'll step aside. But," his hand grows heavy over mine, "if you like me—if there's a small fragment of your desire—I won't handle you leaving this room all to leave me too."

Another man wanting to possess me. But no—I shake my head—Hawke doesn't want to possess me. He wants to *be* with me, and the distinction is hugely different.

And it aligns with the emotions I've been dueling with all day.

I lean forward, using his chest to steady myself when I kiss him, but this time, my tongue dances along his lips, begging him to take this deeper. He does instantly, and my tongue sweeps his as my body pushes itself across the bed. He makes a surprised sound in the back of his throat.

Another kiss is my response. My hands land on his shoulders to steady myself as I lift myself overtop his lap, aware my core rubs right over his cock. I don't know what's driving my body to react like this, but I don't want it to stop.

"I want you. Show me everything I've been missing. Help me move on from *his* touch."

"Willow." This time it's guttural—animalistic—and his kisses get rougher. Rougher than they've ever been before, but I appreciate that he's no longer treating me like a fragile doll who'll break. "Only if you're sure."

"I am."

"If it's too much, stop me at any time. I will make this good for you, I promise."

I know it will be.

Hawke kisses me again, but this time, his hands rove over my hips before stopping and knotting in my shirt. Slowly, he lifts it, baring my skin inch-by-inch, and with it, I swear he finds my heart too.

"Gimme a sec." He lets me go to root around for

something to the side. Through the dark, my eyes make out him reaching for the lamp. It flicks on, casting the room in light again. "I want to see you, but more so, you need to know who's touching you. That it's me with you here and not *him*."

Gratefulness squeezes at my heart.

I nearly expect him to yank at my clothes and get on with this, but I should know better, considering who I'm dealing with. He rears back, scanning my form before taking my arms and legs in hand and positioning them in a way he likes.

"Your hands are by your side, if you need to push me off you."

Won't happen.

Next, he returns to my shirt and finishes dragging it up my chest. I try to sit forward, to allow him the space to remove it, but he nudges me back down and instead lowers himself to my body.

"You have marks." His fingers trail the multitude of old scars and bruises on my body, tracing them around the lines of my stomach. "But they're getting better day by day, just like you."

I flinch, even wishing I could shrink into the bed and hide away from this. Not from his touch, but from the clarity he sees me with.

"Shh." Then, his lips replace his fingers. Soft kisses re-trace the lines he first took with his fingers. "Survivor's marks, Willow, that's all they are."

"They're ugly."

"I won't stand for that, baby. Nothing on your sexy form is ugly. Not the scars, not the bruises, nothing."

My core clenches in response. Words like *baby* and *sexy* seem so foreign to me.

He pushes the shirt up my chest and this time, allows me to lift my head. The shirt is removed and my breasts are revealed to yet another man. Even with a bra on though, this is the only one I've wanted to see me, and I curse the cloth blocking me from his gaze.

Despite the bra, he devours me, eyes trailing the curve of each breast. His bright, unusual eyes get brighter, eager, and for the first time ever, a man's excitement doesn't have me wanting to hide.

He reaches for me, his fingers softly touching my skin. I know it's not my breasts he's touching though, but rather the scars as well. Alex enjoyed hurting me here.

"Shame for one to think himself worthy of marking these as his."

"You're worthy," I find myself replying.

He scoffs, but still a small smirk tugs at his mouth. "Believe me, I'm not. No one is."

I lift my hands, only to trace the scars left behind by Alex's blades. Whenever he sliced at my breasts, the pain was so much more intensified. I hate them even more now though, because while Hawke may not see them as ugly, I do. No doubt, he's been with flawless women in the past and I am far from flawless. I'm flawed in every way possible.

"Willow, no." Taking my hands in his, he places them onto the side of my body. "You're not allowed to think of yourself as such."

"How'd you know?"

With one finger, he spins it in front of my face. "This right here tells all."

My responding sigh wracks my body, but I don't fight, instead watching where his exploration will take him next.

His hands grasp at my pants and he slowly tugs them down my legs. With every inch, he stares into my eyes, forever ensuring I'm okay with his actions. I am, even if I don't breathe through any of it.

This part is simple. After the initial time of Alex ripping off my clothing, I was naked for the remaining months. Hawke undressing me is the furthest thing possible from being triggering, as this is absolute paradise.

Once my pants are off, Hawke gains access to the worst parts of me—my thighs, where Alex scratched our timeline into my skin. Hawke saw them briefly in the hospital when I showed him, but he didn't have the chance to fully study them.

"Six," he murmurs, his finger tracing each one before looking me in the eyes.

"Six months of captivity. One mark for each passing month."

His jaw ticks, but he remains silent, instead retracing them with his fingers before lowering himself over my legs until his coasts over Alex's ticks.

"Each one is a story of what you've lived through."

"Like your tattoos."

"Yes. Six months of captivity, but I also see it as being six months of empowerment. Every scar here is a testament to what you've lived through. Who you are now. Your qualities. You're strong." His tongue traces one, gently, teasingly, drawing a shiver from me, before moving onto another. "You're powerful." Another lick, another scar. "You're courageous. You're beautiful. You're amazing. You're a motherfucking queen." Six licks, six qualities.

"Hawke." But it comes out weak, wanting.

"That's right, baby," he purrs. "Say my name."

I do, unable to bite down the lustful, "Hawke."

He makes a sound in the back of his throat, his hands drifting back up my body. His fingers hook around my panties for the briefest moment before continuing upward and doing the same to my bra, as though testing me.

Everything he's doing sends fireworks off in my body. To be touched in such a soft, caring way is unknown to me, but I fucking love it. I want to be touched everywhere. After today, I don't want to ever associate Alex with my body.

"You're shivering."

"For good reasons, Hawke. Don't you dare stop."

He chuckles, his lips following the line his hands are taking, pressing soft kisses all the way up my body.

"Touch me. Touch me how you've touched other women you've been with."

It makes me infuriated to even consider Hawke doing this with another, but it's a shitty fact to come to terms with. He's experienced, and I want that experience to be used on me.

Hawke's hands mold my breasts, massaging them through the cloth. My nipples bud, responding to his call.

"More," I beg. "Please."

"Please what?"

"I want you to touch me."

He pulls my bra down, his fingers finding my stiff nipples. He rubs his hands in circles on them, and by the time his mouth finishes its journey up my body, I'm ready for him. Maintaining eye contact, his tongue flicks out at one.

I moan, back arching into him. So opposite from how Alex would yank at my nipples until I believed they would tear off. Hawke is revering them.

He finishes with one and then the other, going back and forth until I think I might die from pleasure right here, right now. A man's never had his mouth on my nipples before, but I see what I was missing.

"That's it," he murmurs. "Feel what I'm doing. I'm in love with your sounds."

I'm in love that I can give them to you.

"Tell me what you like, Willow, so I can be sure to give it. Before Alex, what would guys do that brought you pleasure?"

All the warmth is instantly sucked from the room with his question and I freeze, mind whirling to form the next part of my story. How could I admit this to him? What guy would want to deal with me after this?

Hawke leans away, his body stiffening and his brows dipping low. "Willow?"

Alex stole my autonomy, never giving me the opportunity to discover what sexual acts I do and don't enjoy.

"Willow," he probes, voice hardening, "what aren't you telling me?"

Ten seconds. Ten beats of my heart pass before I open my eyes again. "Alex was my first." Emotion clogs my throat, so my words are nothing more than a pained whisper.

"No."

Hawke releases me, stealing with him all his warmth as he flies off the bed, his hands going straight for his long hair. He backs up a few steps, pushing his back to the nearest wall as he watches me through horror-filled, pinched eyes. It's a look I've never seen on him, not even when he first saw me in the basement.

"No, no, no, no… No! You were a fucking *virgin* when he took you?"

I nod.

I've only ever known Hawke to be rational and calm, but what happens next comes from an entirely new place.

Hawke spins and his fist crashes against the wall behind him. Before I can blink, he does it again. And again. And again.

Until the wall is marked and his hand is red.

I lift from the bed, hating how my own horror has affected him so badly. It shouldn't. Hawke's too superior of a person to be dragged into my darkness, considering all he's also endured. My hand lifts to his back, hovering over a shoulder blade, not quite touching as his body moves with heaving breaths.

"Hawke?"

"That motherfucking bastard! That scum of the earth took your innocence—took what was *yours* to give away. I-I assumed you gave it up in the past, like when you were a teenager, but he… *Fuck*."

Hawke spins, the redness in his face fading until he's pale again, but it doesn't hide his wrath.

So much emotion.

So much care.

"Hawke, it's o—"

"*Don't* say it's okay. It's fucking not. It's wrong you've only experienced Alex and the moment I stop seeing red, I'll be treating you like a goddamn queen. You deserve your first time—your *proper* first time—and I'll give you what that cunt never did." He shakes his head roughly, more of a jerk than anything. "It fucking hurts knowing what he's done, but I'm so damned honoured you've chosen me to be your second. We'll wipe away every touch he's ever laid on your body."

The next words slip out before logic can impede them. "You're my seventh."

"What?"

"You're my seventh," I repeat, crossing my arms over my chest, suddenly feeling as though I need to block myself from his scrutinizing view. "There were five others. Five men he forced me to—"

He explodes again, but this time, not with violence.

Twenty-One

HAWKE

I get it now.

I fucking *get* it.

The moment Ryker told me how he ended up in jail, I couldn't understand how a girl could affect him so much, he accidentally gave up his own freedom in rage.

The moment Tristan didn't leave Natalie alone, even after getting what we needed from her, I couldn't understand how a girl could make someone so obsessed.

The moment Brent took off after being unable to see Teagan in the hospital, I couldn't understand how a girl could wipe away one's logic.

But now, I understand. I understand because Miller got off too easily. The guys wanted to take him down and I don't doubt they could have killed him, but that's the exact lifestyle I left behind. I may have gotten to Miller illegally by bending the rules, but I was determined for every moment following his arrest to abide by them.

Now, I question my own sanity. It'd be so easy to gather the three of them up, call up my contact, and get Alex released into our custody. He either wouldn't make it the hour, or we'd relish in drawing out his pain, the same way he did to Willow.

"There were five others. Five men he forced me to——"

Five. Fucking. Men.

He *forced* her to be with others; as if what he was doing to her each day wasn't enough, he just had to take it the extra fucking step.

"Hawke."

Her soft voice cuts through the red cloud of fury hovering over my head, but it doesn't cool it. I wish she could, but this beast within me—this anger—this... *everything* inside me is begging to be released. I know how to fight. I know how to handle a weapon. I may never have finished my induction into the Family, but I learned plenty as a child. I learned that when a man fights, a primal side of him awakens and it can take a while until that primal beast is tamed and put back into its cage.

"Hawke," she repeats. I hear her feet drag across the floor as she tentatively approaches. Her small hand presses into my bicep.

I force a deep breath, taking in as much air as I can, pushing it through my lungs and body, and exhaling. Three times I do it, letting the fog clear.

"Hawke, look at me please." Fear tinges her words, and I realize then, what a moron I am. Of course she'd fear any show of strength or rage.

I turn, continuing my deep breaths until my fists finally unclench and the tick in my shoulders slightly unknots.

Until I see her fucking demure face, her half-lidded eyes as she tentatively peers up at me, and the feelings return. She's like a goddamn deer, timid and afraid, waiting for anyone to jump out at her, all because of what *he* did.

When the fury returns, and I feel that need to kill something—some*one*—again, I channel it in other ways, ignoring how the shred of logic getting buried beneath emotion screams at me to not.

But she needs me. *I* need her.

Without thinking it through, without anything other than feeling, I grasp her upper arms, turning us both until her back is against the wall for leverage and I'm on her, taking her mouth in a bruising kiss.

You won't ever have this part of her, fucker. She'll never moan into your mouth or beg you for more.

I wait for her to realize what's happening and panic, but it never comes. Or she pushes it down because, instead of fighting back, she arches her back and parts her lips, allowing me to take. To consume. To claim.

I kiss down her neck, stopping to lick the skin where her pulse beats rapidly, enjoying the evidence of her life, before I continue downward. Her breasts heave with her heavy breaths and I take them in hand, bringing her nipples once again to my mouth.

She responded so well earlier, it pained me because it's obvious now, she's never experienced pleasure from any act. I lightly pull on her nipples with my teeth, letting my lip ring drag around the skin before kissing down her stomach.

I lower myself to my knees for her, an act contrary to all my preferences, but for her, I'll get on my knees anytime. My lips trail down her stomach and over all the markings *he* left behind. A sinful act alone, for her creamy, pale skin should never be scarred by anyone or anything she hasn't requested.

Her panty-covered pussy is right in front of my face, but instead of gazing upon it, I look up the length of her body, seeking permission before continuing. She nods slightly, a tip of her head, granting me the permission I crave before my fingers hook in the cloth and I slowly pull them down her skin, waiting for the moment this all hits her and becomes too much.

Until then, my lips follow her panties all the way down

her leg, unhooking them and tossing them to the side. I look up, past her core, back into her eyes.

"Do you want to lie on the bed?"

Surprisingly, she shakes her head, so I grasp her ankle and slowly lift her leg up, drawing it over my shoulder, completely baring her pretty pussy. A small tuft of hair sits on her mound, and it's obvious there was some grooming that occurred.

The last person here never deserved her. The five others dared to take this without permission. Instead of reacting on the rage, I place a finger on her, testing her reaction, but she continues to openly watch me.

"Stop me any time, Willow." It'd be a shame to end once I get even a drop of her on my tongue, but for the sake of her mental well-being, I'd do it.

"I will."

I move my finger lightly over her core, brushing my thumb against her swollen clit. First, a barely-there stroke, and then again, harder.

She gasps and her arms hit the wall by her side, her fingers scratching at it.

I smile with dumb male pride, knowing it's *my* touch bringing her pleasure.

"Hawke…"

"Tell me, baby."

When my finger prods lightly at her core, not entering, but simply feeling, she gasps again.

"Hawke."

"I'm going to taste you here, Willow."

"*Yes.*"

Again, I smile, but it quickly fades when the realization of her past returns. Six men, and I fucking doubt any one of the pricks ever touched her here for her pleasure only. I don't want to ask the question I'm sure I know the answer to, but there's a need in me urging the question past my lips.

"Has a man ever had his mouth on you?"

The muscles in her thighs tighten, telling me all I need, even before she responds with, "No."

I smooth my hands over her thighs, the one over my shoulder and the one keeping her upright, not using words to respond. While I'm pissed at her past, I'm also fucking thrilled because it means I'll be the first one to grant her the pleasure she deserves. I'll be the only man on this planet to have tasted her, leaving my mark in a way no one has before.

"Just remember who's down here, Willow. Don't let the bastard take this from you."

Before she can respond, I lick her core to clit, sparking an instant gasp from her. I circle her clit twice before sinking my tongue inside her, tasting her sweet juices.

"Oh, my god," she cries. Her hands dive into my hair, pulling on the strands, but thankfully, not away from her. She clenches tightly, pushing my face deeper into her.

Obeying her wordless command, I bring her other leg up over my shoulder, positioning my hands behind her, keeping her steady for my mouth so with the assistance of the wall, she's poised in the air.

"Hawke. What—"

"Enjoy this," I murmur against her thigh before returning to heaven. "You taste like you were made for me."

"Maybe I was. Maybe I was put through Hell specifically so you could find me."

"That's a price you should never have had to pay."

Before the conversation goes any darker, I return my attention to licking at her clit, sparking gasps, then probing her core and causing her to groan. Her hips move slowly and I position my hands in a way to return that control. Her fingers tighten in my hair as she rides my face, taking what she needs from me.

It's sexy.

"Hawke, I feel…"

That's all I need. I pull her clit in my mouth, using suction to finish her off and her responding cries fill the room—and my heart. She chases her orgasm, rocking her hips against my face, uncaring about the mess she makes on my face. By the time her orgasm ends and she slows her movements, her fingers lightly unhook from my hair, and through heavy pants, she giggles.

I love it.

Twenty-Two

WILLOW

Seven men in total have seen that part of me. Each one memorable in their own way, but none more so than Hawke is quickly becoming. Alex may have raped me over and over, using my body as his personal playground. He may have loaned me out to five others who did the same, seeing me as a fun time to work out some horrific fantasies on, knowing at the end, when they go back home, I return to a cage, unable to tell anyone what occurred. But nothing in my past leaves a mark on my soul in the same way Hawke does.

I thought my first orgasm would be fucking terrifying, knowing I've never had one before that I hadn't given to myself. I believed allowing a man to see that part of me so soon would be unimaginable and I'd break down.

Even when Hawke was pissed off, either at me or what I said, he never lifted a hand to me. He never harmed me. He was mad, and I didn't get hurt, making it an entirely other first.

I'm sticky and wrought out, balancing my body on the wall with my legs over Hawke's shoulders. It leaves me so open and yet, I don't mind. I revel in how unabashed he is with me actually. How, despite treating me so delicately for the past few days, this was a moment he unleashed many pent-up emotions.

He lowers my wobbly legs back to the floor, officially ending the moment, but not for long since he stands, taking my face in his large, tattooed hands. I scan my angel's beautiful face, his piercings, his bright eyes, and his honest soul.

"I'm sorry for reacting how I did earlier."

"How's your hand?"

Hawke scoffs. "That's not what I meant. My hand is the least of my worries, and honestly, I don't really notice it. I mean for grabbing you how I did."

I could see why he's concerned, but apologizing for the highlight of today is laughable at best. Instead of laughing though, I lay my hands overtop his, shaking my head lightly.

"Don't apologize, please. You didn't scare me."

"You sure?" He drops his head onto mine, our foreheads pressing together, and he still manages to maintain eye contact.

"Positive. I didn't mean to tell you like that." Or at all, if I'm being honest with myself.

"I'm glad you did, Willow. It's important to get everything out, so we're aware of boundaries."

"Do you have any?"

"Yeah, but we won't discuss those right now." He pulls back, lifting his forehead from mine. "How do you feel with—" Instead of finishing his question, he moves one hand down to my thigh, stroking a patch of skin there, leaving me to finish his unspoken words.

"Amazing," I breathe. "Tired." Tired in a way much different than the past six months. My body has been happily used and is asking me to lie down, but I don't dare stop this moment.

Hawke steps back, dropping both hands from my body making space for me to walk by. "Then you should sleep."

He's actually ending this now? Sure, my head demands me to get rest, but the lust coursing through my body is demanding we continue. I follow Hawke, pressing my body against him and feel—*Oh*.

Obviously, I know what a man's erection feels like. Too well, in fact. But never has a man's hardness made *me* want him too. Usually, it only makes me want to vomit and hide away.

Hawke coughs and paces away again, angling his body away. "Sorry."

"No." I reach for him. "You're…"

"Hard," he supplies, taking his lip ring into his mouth. He's nervous; I recognize that reaction. "It happens. Get into bed though, and I'll be back shortly."

"But—"

Hawke shakes his head, his small smile letting me know he's not upset. "I think we should be careful how fast we rush you, Willow. Trust me, the last thing I want to do is take this too quickly and ruin your progress."

"I guess…" At this point, he might very well know me better than myself, given what he's gone through as well.

Hawke strides out of the room, leaving me alone. I scan the messy bed and finish at the wall that changed a lot. How was it, only days ago, I was in the hospital unable to deal with everything and now I'm… rejuvenated.

I slip my damp panties back on, unable to bite down the grin as memories of him removing them bombard me. Nothing was ripped off, nothing was rushed or rough, despite what he thinks. Everything Hawke did was perfect.

Lost in my thoughts, I don't hear him return until his hands slip around my waist, and he kisses my shoulder blade, grinning into my skin.

"I like that look on you."

"Which look?"

"The one that conveys you're happy." He moves away, getting into bed, and holds the blanket up for me.

I am happy. Happier than I've ever been before at least, and Hawke has a lot to do with it.

But as I slip into bed beside him, where even he can't keep the memories away, I know I'm not perfect.

Twenty-Three

HAWKE

My jeans are yanked from my legs, leaving me bared to the five men's leering gazes. They already removed my shirt by cutting it off and leaving knife slashes in my skin. Blood seeps from the faint marks, and I'm thankful they're not deeper.

It's the only thing I'm thankful for.

They chortle, all scanning me as I'm forced to stand in front of them, hands tied behind my back and a cloth shoved in my mouth. It doesn't stop my eyes from cursing them.

Dad began my training a couple years ago, but we haven't gotten anywhere close to how to get myself out of situations like this one. So far, all my kicks and fighting have gotten me are return punches.

"Well, his cock ain't that big, but his tight little ass will make up for it." The one directly in front of me drops his attention to my dick, and while my legs clench together, I can't hide from them.

"Remember his age," the one beside him murmurs. His balding head shines the dim lighting back at me. "It'll grow."

"Get the camera set-up," another one orders, flicking his fingers toward the one who just spoke.

That's when their plan dawns on me. The first man marches forward, his large feet deafening against the silence of the cold base-

ment floor. I swear only my rapid breathing can be heard.

He stops short, looking down at me without tilting his head. "Hear that, boy? We're gonna take turns breaking you in while we record it. Then, your dear old dad will realize how much of a mistake it was to refuse us the money we were promised."

"Nugh!" My yell is muffled against the cloth, and I skitter back a few steps, even knowing it's pointless. I won't make it to the door before they're on me.

"Aww," another voice coos. "Look at him trying to run." I don't hear him, but suddenly, my back slams into a body behind me, the cold leather of his jacket pressing into my skin. His hands land on my waist and he spins me around to face him. "So cute. So fucking young." His tongue shoots out to lick his lips. "I like 'em young, and boy, you're exactly my type."

Bile rises in my throat, but I swallow it back, aware it has nowhere to go anyway. He's serious. They're all serious.

"Go on, go bend over the table." He gestures to the right and I rake my eyes to that side of the room, unwillingly finding a table.

"Boss, you're up first, man. Enjoy."

I gasp, opening my eyes to the darkness, heart pounding stronger than it has in years. Sweat clings to my body, making it all too easy to slip from bed silently and get away from Willow's sleeping form, so I don't disturb her with my own darkness. She has enough to deal with.

Rubbing my hand across my face, I attempt to wipe away the nightmare as I approach the window, looking into the houses beyond.

Normally, the nightmares don't impact me like this anymore. Not to the point they wake me up, and usually not for a few more months. Perhaps it was the recent conversation or perhaps it's simply Willow dredging up a whole lot of my own past.

Not that I would ever let her know that.

I still recall exactly what the man said to the camera as it streamed the encounter live to him.

"We have your son here, Corsetti. All because you refused to pay us. Now, you get to watch what your stupidity has cost you. Consider it a tax."

A fucking *tax* is what they referred to me as.

I remember staring into the red light, knowing my father was watching me be taken roughly, but almost *wanting* him to see as I had my childhood ripped away from me.

How many times had I asked to simply hang out with friends instead of having shooting practice? Or learning how to dismember a body. Or how to fight. Skills that were all useless when my hands were bound, and I was weaponless.

I would have killed to be Aurora then, to be protected by guards simply because of her gender. As a girl, she was kept away from the training and killing, taught instead how to be demure and what my parents would eventually expect of her.

"Look at this. Look what we've done to your little boy. Pay up, or it happens again. Price just doubled. Get on it."

The red light goes away, and the men fade in the background as I'm left bent over the table.

Dead.

His voice echoes in my ears and I blink tightly, willing him to go back into the past.

I wasn't dead at that time, but how I wanted to be. They all took me that night. Their leader and all of his men. Over and over.

It was an entire day later when I finally heard the familiar gunshots and knew my father came for me.

Staring blankly outside, I nearly miss when the bush in my backyard moves. I peek up, toward the trees, finding every leaf still. There's no breeze, and yet, something in the bush moves…

It's an animal. Relax.

"Relax," I whisper, this time aloud, as I swipe at my

face again and fix the curtain to block the outdoors. Obviously, the nightmare has stirred up my paranoia.

I turn back from the bed, expecting Willow to still be asleep, but do a double take at finding her eyes open and staring at me through the dark room.

"You're awake."

"You were thrashing in your sleep and woke me up."

The bed dips as I kneel beside her, slipping beneath the covers again and keeping the inches of space between us as I stare at the floor, wondering if I should deny her insistence to remain in bed and sleep there; that way, I don't interrupt her with anymore possible nightmares.

"Sorry."

"Nightmare?" She tucks her arms beneath her head, propping herself up to peer at me.

"Yeah," I reply, voice thick, not willing to allow my mind to return there. "They happen occasionally."

"You've mentioned before. Is it nearing the anniversary?"

She remembers when I have them too. I find myself responding with the truth though, not caring if she probes deeper. "No. I suppose lately things have been bringing it all back to light."

Her hand reaches over and she rests it on my forearm. Her heat sears me, ridding away previous concerns, and I find myself leaning into her touch.

"I should apologize, but in truth, it's nice to see it's not only me."

"Told you."

But then, I don't despise the fact that the nightmare hit or even that I was woken from it. If it helps Willow move on, then I'll experience a million nightmares with gratitude. If seeing how memories can plague any trauma victim helps her, so be it.

"I know," she says with a breathless chuckle. "It's one

thing to tell me though and another to show me."

I lie down and roll to face her, my hand resting on top of hers so she can't move it.

"I'm glad something came from this then."

"Did you want to talk about it?"

And that's when I don't even pretend to hide my emotions regarding this beautiful girl because despite all the shit she's dealing with, it's *me* she checks in with. It's *my* nightmare she asks to discuss. For all her own bad memories, she offers to listen to mine.

My hand tightens over hers, showing what my throat becomes too clogged to verbalize. "It's okay, Willow, but thank you. It wasn't anything new—just the same one I always have in which *it* happened." I don't elaborate on *it*.

"I see. I'm sorry for what they did to you."

In a way, I'm not. Had I never been taken, I wouldn't have found the strength to leave my family, and if I never left them, I wouldn't be here with Willow right now. I'd be Capo and an entirely different person. It's a lot of 'what ifs' and 'maybes' to even get her and me both in this bed, but I don't fucking care. Not that I'd ever say what they did to me was good, but if there is a positive in all this, it's lying beside the sweet girl in my bed.

To not freak her out with those dangerous thoughts, I simply murmur, "Thanks, Willow. We should get back to sleep though."

Through the darkness, I watch her bite her lip, and while I want nothing more than to reach over and take her mouth, I don't. I let her sleep, and with her hand on my arm and my hand holding her there, we both return to a nightmare-free sleep.

Twenty-Four

WILLOW

The morning sun peeks through the curtains, waking me naturally. I stretch, feeling Hawke's arm around my centre. I like that we naturally adopted a sleeping position in which I'm curled into him and neither of us questioned it last night.

I like all of this more than I should.

I liked last night. Being able to discover an entirely new layer to Hawke—and his trauma—was somehow comforting to me.

Sitting up, I take some of the blanket with me, which pulls it a bit off Hawke, revealing his chest of tattoos. I recall what he said about them, about the flames and flowers, each representing a part of his journey.

What symbols would represent my journey? A cage, indicating my entrapment, and a bird, I think. A bird takes flight, escaping from the cage trapping it, exactly as I'm trying to do. I glance at my wrist, imagining blank ink there. I could match Hawke in another way.

Idiot, stop planning the future.

My mind's right. Alex will come back, no matter what Hawke is claiming, and my flight will be interrupted. He'll clip my wings, ensuring I'll die in his cage, unable to try flying away again, even if the slimmest opportunity presented itself.

I scan Hawke's sleeping form. Yesterday, he said everything is up to me now, but before it no longer isn't—before my wings are clipped—there's more I wish to experience.

My hand hovers over his chest, unsure how even to begin. Living as a virgin until six months ago hadn't provided me with all the necessary experiences, like how to properly touch a man.

I picture Hawke's blue eyes watching me figure this out, silently urging me on, and it's the knowledge that he'll be supportive, no matter what, that has my hand lowering to his sculpted abs.

I trace the petals of a flower and he sighs, still asleep. I follow a flame down his stomach, to the waistband of his pants. Unknown warmth heats my insides as my fingers dance over the edging of his pants.

"That's a nice way to wake up."

He's watching me touch him, a sleepy smirk lining his mouth.

"Morning."

"Morning," he replies, glancing down again. "I wouldn't go much further if I were you."

"What if I want to?"

He matches my challenge with his own brow lift. "I would ask if you're ready because as much as I want you, this is going quick."

It has to be though, or else there might not be another chance.

I shrug. "You said everything's up to me now, right? And I want this. I don't feel it's too soon."

Hawke's heavy hand lands on top of mine and he sits up, coming closer, until our faces are lined up. His lips cover mine and he kisses me.

"If you're sure."

"I wouldn't ask if I wasn't. You also said we need to remove the past, and this is it."

Doubt clouds the blues of his eyes briefly, and I can see the pending argument in there, but I kiss him before he can object further.

"Why can't I deny you anything?" he asks with a groan in between kisses.

"Because you're you, and—" I stop, curling my fingers into the hard muscle beneath my palm. "I-I want to touch you, but you may need to show me how."

How does one touch a man without the demand to do it a certain way? Alex always ensured I followed his exact direction, but with Hawke, I suspect there will be no direction. I'll be left to explore how I want.

He reclines, keeping one hand on my neck and bringing me forward with him as we fall back against the pillow. Against my lips, he whispers, "Pull my shorts down."

My fingers go cold against his waist, but I force them to unfreeze and do as he instructs. He's thickening, and I feel it from where I'm brushing over his lap. Hawke's kisses grow more intense, more desperate. His tongue flicks against mine, making my head go light—and me to forget about what else I'm doing.

"Keep going, *il mio bella ragazza*. You're doing great."

"Am I?" I don't feel like I am. I feel like a child as I slowly tug his waistband down. Even his use of the nickname does little to settle me.

"Breathe, Willow."

In. Out. Air exits my lungs, but it does little to settle my nerves, especially when the pants get farther down and his partially-erect cock is revealed. Six men prior to Hawke and I've *never* seen one that looks like his.

Because this one has three piercings in it. One in the head, one at the base of the head, and one halfway down his shaft.

Holy. Fuck. My mouth goes dry, and I swallow once, twice, three times, but nothing's enough to rid the parchedness in my mouth. It's… different. Different, but beautiful.

"Fuck," Hawke curses, shifting his hips away, "I've had them so long, I honestly forget—"

"It's okay." I press weight into his hip, encouraging him back to his previous position. We've swapped roles, with me having to reassure him now. "It's okay," I repeat. "Will it…will it hurt?"

Even if it will, I think I'd be able to handle the pain. After all, what's a piercing compared to anything else that's been done to me?

"It'll intensify the feeling for both of us."

I nod, still staring dumbstruck at the unique adornments. I've learned what it's like to kiss a guy with a piercing in his lip, and now I'll know what they feel like when inside me. "All right."

Now what? Why am I so useless at this?

Hawke watches me, his mouth folding into a frown. He sits up again, gesturing to the spot of the bed he vacated. "Why don't you lie down?"

Because I'm fucking this up. Because I'm—

My hair is swept aside, baring my shoulder, which he kisses. "Out of your head, baby. You're not doing anything wrong, but I think this might be a bit easier if you can simply enjoy and not think about every move?"

"What about you?" Sex is all about give and take, even if I've had to give in all my experiences as the men take.

"Believe me," he smiles crookedly, repositioning the blanket to make room for me to settle, "this will be as much for me as it will be for you. Seeing you undone, getting to experience this part of you as you ask for it, willingly take it, is enough."

Okay. I don't speak the words, simply move my lips, but Hawke's rapt attention reads me. He must also read the nerves because he climbs overtop me, keeping his weight off me.

"Touch any part of me you feel comfortable with. I won't rush this. The moment you say stop, this ends. This will be the first time you should have had."

Sweet but also pointless, since we're so past my first time that it won't make a difference, but I don't deny him what he seems to be needing as well.

Hawke kisses my neck and then up to my face. One hand cups my chin, angling my head to kiss me deeper until I'm panting into his mouth. He rips his mouth away, trailing his lips back down my body, over my breasts. I'm still in my bra and panties from last night, but he undoes the bra, slowly pulling it from my arms.

I lift them to make it easier. The moment the garment disappears, he presses his chest to mine and I feel him *everywhere*. He takes my mouth again, obviously waiting for me to relax into the state he needs me to be.

It seems so impossible to get to such a place though, because my mind whirls, my vision going hazy with stress. *What if I don't like it? What if my body is trained to expect pain? What if, even during all the horror, Alex recoded my body for him alone, and I'll never be able to have sex with Hawke?*

Forcing myself back to the present, I place my hands on his shoulders, holding Hawke to me. Something must flick on inside me because my hips begin to rock, arching against his hardness, asking for him to continue.

He reads me and moves down my body, his hands skating the length of me until they get to my panties. *It'll be just like last night*, I tell myself, *when he undressed me before giving me the only pleasure I've ever known*. It's the memory of the orgasm that allows my leg muscles to remain lax.

When the panties are tossed to the side, he asks, "Do

you recall my mouth on you? How you came after a short while?"

"Yeah."

He reaches out, a single finger lightly stroking my opening until my legs fall open and the flush spreads.

"It's like that. I'll put my fingers inside you first, and then my cock, okay?"

"Okay," I whisper, unable to look at him. Instead, I fix my vision to the ceiling. I want to watch him, to see my awakening, and yet, looking might remind me of everything I should be fearing—namely a man's touch. *This* act.

He continues to play with me until his single finger is wet and—

Alex shoves three fingers inside me, pumping them rough and fast. "Come on, cunt. If you don't get wet, this is going to hurt."

I get wet. I force myself into thinking he's being rough with me because he's passionate, and this is his love language.

"Willow."

It's not Alex. It's Hawke.

Stay in the present.

"Eyes on me, baby. Remember who's here with you. Who *I* am."

Hawke. My blue-eyed angel. My saviour. My—

His finger dips inside, curling and rubbing on a spot that instantly makes my legs fall open wider and a groan to release.

"That's it," he murmurs. "You feel amazing, Willow. Like you're mine."

I want to be yours. If this is what being his is like, then Hawke can lock me in his cage forever and I won't care.

"I'm going to go deeper, okay?"

He does, and the pleasure is all-consuming, but so are the memories of Alex. So is—

Alex slams me from behind, shoving my face into the desk as his associate watches me from the leather desk chair, his angry, red cock gripped in his hand. He strokes himself quickly, eyes rapt on my pain.

"You see? The whore loves when you give it to her rough."

"How's she like it from both ends?"

"Does it matter?" Alex chortles and shoves into me again.

My nails scrape against the smooth wood as I watch the man stand, his cock bobbing in front of my face. I'm numb though. This isn't the first time I've been tag-teamed like this before, and it likely won't be the last.

Alex's hand wraps around my throat, and he yanks my head backward, arching my back in a painful angle that also cuts off my air supply.

"You bite him, and you know the pain you will receive."

I do because I bit the first man he ever let use me. I made him bleed, and hopefully scar. My body paid for it though, reminding me the fight isn't worth it.

Alex releases my head in time for the man to shove his cock down my throat, taking no time to prepare me. I gag, but he bucks in deeper, uncaring about my reflexes.

"Take me. All of me, whore."

They always get off on the names.

Alex's hand tightens in my hair and he yanks my head back, forcing my throat wider for his friend. "Look at you. Ours for the night, and mine forever."

"Willow!"

That's not Alex's voice.

"Willow!"

Hands tighten around my upper arms as they're pinned to the bed. I'm held down, expected to obey, and like the trained animal I am, I do, letting him control me because fighting back only earns me hours of pain.

I can't do pain again. I won't survive it this time.

"Willow!" the voice repeats.

That's not Alex.

I open my eyes. Shaggy black hair falls close to my face due to his proximity as ice eyes study me before going wide with relief. "You've returned to me."

He falls back onto his heels, providing me space to sit up. His hard, pierced cock bobs between us, the reminder of what *I* just fucked up.

Shame settles on my shoulders, and although I glance away in an attempt to bite down on the tears, it doesn't work.

Useless.

Alex found his way into my head, like he will every. Single. Time.

"I'm sorry."

And then I burst into tears.

Twenty-Five

WILLOW

Sex and I will never get along. In hindsight, there is no other practical outcome for what occurred. My body doesn't know *how* to have sex properly.

I'm not sure how long I cry in Hawke's arms, but it's enough to make overwhelming self-hate creep up. I should pull away from him and let him go his own way, but I selfishly cling to him, unabashed in wiping my tears on his chest. No matter how many times I wipe though, more seem to come.

At some point, he pulls away, finally realizing what I've already come to comprehend—that he deserves more. He leaves the bedroom without a word and wanders down the hallway. The moment he's gone, the tears come fresh, my sobs not as quiet as I wish they'd be. Even biting my hand does nothing to hold back the constant cries; all that does is make a mess of my hand.

He returns a moment later, and though I don't meet his gaze, he takes one of my hands, pulling me from the bed. Of course, now that he understands I'm unsavable, he'll send me on my way. I'd do the same if I were in his place.

Instead of releasing me though, he pulls me down the hallway, toward the bathroom. The door is open and a cloud of steam drifts from the shower that's presently running. This must have been where he disappeared to.

Wordlessly, he ushers me toward the shower and opens the glass door, gesturing me to enter. I step under the hot water, letting it mix with the tears continuing to stream from my eyes. They mix together and fall into the drain at my feet. My arms grow heavy as I watch them go with longing, wishing I could be sucked away so easily.

Hawke climbs in behind me and I hear him shut the glass door, but I don't turn around. Don't do anything other than stare at my feet and wait for the self-hate to dissipate.

I should have fucking known. Alex will always find a way to hold my mind; there's no getting away from him.

Even through the numbness, I feel Hawke wipe a loofah against my back, leaving behind suds. He washes my back, ass, and legs before turning me to face him.

Beneath my eyelashes, I manage to peek at him, but he's so focused on his task, I don't think he notices. I study him, seeking a set jaw or hard eyes that will provide any indication of his anger, but I find nothing. Perhaps he's good at hiding his emotions though, considering his chosen career.

He finishes with my body before quickly doing his own. I watch him, not really seeing or taking in what he does. He finishes, reaches past me to switch off the water, and then opens the glass door, retrieving two towels hanging up I hadn't noticed earlier.

He grabs one and brings it into the shower with us, wrapping my body up before doing his own and leading me from the shower. Like a doll, I let him direct me to the bedroom.

This is it. He'll have me get dressed and then kick me

out.

From the bag Elena brought the other day on the floor, he rummages through until finding clothing for me, which he lays on the bed. I watch as he goes to his closet and dresses in jeans and a plain black shirt that complements his hair way too much. Even the jeans hug his ass nicely, and I take in everything Hawke is before he'll end this.

Hawke faces me again, and for the first time since I began crying, I find emotion in his own expression. His mouth folds into a frown and his ice eyes freeze with sadness.

He leans forward until his face is aligned with mine. With two fingers, he flicks wet strands of my hair behind an ear, clearing the way for whatever he wants to tell me. Instead of looking into his obvious disappointment, I shut my eyes. The darkness is always safer.

Instead of speaking though, I feel his lips press into my forehead.

"I'll get you breakfast," he murmurs against the skin there.

And then he's gone, shutting the door behind him.

I stare at the door. At the simple wood, the metal handle—it'd be so simple to leave. I already did it once before, so what's the difference in going downstairs with him?

For Hawke, I have to *be* more.

I get dressed in the clothes he laid out for me and tie up my hair, getting the wet strands off my neck, so they won't be a bother.

Then I do it. The doorknob is weighted in my palm, but I slowly twist it open. I may have been in the hallway moments ago, but this time, it's different because I'm the one making the decision to leave my self-imposed cell. My safety barriers shatter with every step down the stairs I take.

One.

Two.

Three…

… Twelve.

Then down the hallway, toward the kitchen. I count those steps as well, reaching fifteen by the time I broach the doorway and watch as Hawke moves through his kitchen, pouring coffee and popping a bagel in the toaster.

"Hawke," I mumble softly, just loud enough he can apparently hear me over the coffee machine's gurgling, for he twists right around, his eyes widening.

"Willow. This is—You're…"

"Yeah." I step deeper into the room, stopping by the table where I grasp the back of a chair.

I hadn't given much thought to the kitchen when he first showed me the other day, but now I'm able to take a good scan of it. It's so *normal*; it makes me nearly laugh. I used to have a kitchen. Hell, I used to have an entire apartment, but Alex was very open in telling me he cancelled my lease and got rid of everything I owned. He couldn't risk leaving behind evidence of my old life.

"You can sit if you'd like." He gestures to the chair I'm holding. "I'm finishing up your coffee. Also making bagels, if you want one?"

"Please."

I sit and watch him finish the task. Within minutes, he has two bagels with cream cheese on the table, and a coffee in front of me, made to my exact specifications. The first morning, he brought up cream and sugar for me to make it how I prefer, and the smart guy he is figured out which I used and hadn't, so the next morning, my coffee was made exactly how I enjoy.

Days later and I still groan as I take that first sip. I hadn't realized how much I've missed coffee during my entrapment.

"Well, that was hot." Hawke's lips twitch, but he soon

masks his smirk by claiming his seat.

"Me drinking coffee?"

"Witnessing your happiness."

So different from earlier are is unspoken words. My teeth chew on the inside of my mouth as I wait for my apology to form.

"I'm really sorry, Hawke. I know you're mad—"

"I don't want your apology," he interrupts, his tone cold. "I don't want it because you shouldn't be the one having to give it. I am mad, but certainly not at you."

"Then at who?"

"Who do you think?" His jaw ticks. "Miller, for being in your head. He took *our* moment. No—he took *your* moment *again*. That's why I'm pissed, but not at you." His brows lower over sad eyes. "Never fucking at you, Willow. You could rip my heart out and stomp on it repeatedly and I'd still beg you to put it back inside my chest and move on with a smile."

Still… I fiddle with the edge of the bagel, unable to meet his eyes. "I should have fought him though. You deserve better than some broken girl."

Hawke shoves his plate aside to stretch his arm across the table. I give him my hand, letting him wrap it up in his much-larger one. "Don't you dare think that. Believing that allows *him* to win, and I refuse to let that happen. I deserve you, and that's all I'll say on the matter." He pauses, his expression turning thoughtful. "You seemed to be doing fine up to a certain point."

"I was. You were tender and everything Alex never was, but thoughts of him still consumed me. Maybe because I'm not used to such kindness?"

His musing expression deepens. "How much do you trust me, Willow?"

"With everything I am. One hundred percent."

"I have a theory, and it won't work unless you trust

me. If you do, take my hand." He stands and stretches out a hand toward me, his body already angled toward the doorway.

I have no idea what he's planning, but still, I lay my hand in his and hand myself over to him.

More than I already am.

Twenty-Six

WILLOW

Hawke shuts his bedroom door behind us and scans me up and down. Something passes over his expression. Not anger, but an emotion I don't recognize.

"Strip." His voice is distant, if not a bit cold.

I blink, surprised by his blatant command. Downstairs, he asked for my trust, so I do as he commands without question.

Once I'm naked, slow, easy steps bring him to my side. He circles me, like I'm prey, and instead of fear, I shiver in desire. He stops in front of me, a slow grin stretching his mouth, which lessens some of the anxiety coursing through my veins.

"Sit on the bed."

When I'm seated, Hawke drops to his knees in front of me, resting his palms on mine. It's such a contrast to what Alex would force me to do.

"I mentioned that it took a long time before a woman could touch me, and even then, I had my limits. Still do, I suppose. The older I got, the more sexual encounters I had, but I struggled to get off with every woman."

"How old *are* you?" A ridiculous thing to not know

about a person at this point.

"Twenty-seven. When I was nineteen, I spoke with my therapist about my issues, and she went on about the relationship trust and trauma have with each other, and how both notions link into sex. I thought it so strange, considering who she was to me, but she suggested a BDSM club." He pauses, searching my face. "Do you know what BDSM is?"

When I shake my head, he continues, "It's an acronym for bondage and discipline, domination and submission, sadism and masochism. It's a way some people prefer to express their sexual interests. Often, it does involve domination and submission, as the name implied, which means one partner takes on the dominant role where they'll use authority and skill to dominate the submissive partner, whose role is to give their body and mind over to their partner."

So factual, and yet, my heart hammers inside my chest. Dominant, submissive... *This* is what he's suggesting?

"It was suggested I go to one, and at first, I had no clue what I was doing there, but with time, it allowed me to work through my trauma."

He's insane to think anything having to do with control will make me forget Alex's treachery.

His thumbs stroke my skin again. "I'm asking you to trust me, Willow. BDSM is all about trust and consent between partners. Often, these acts will involve items of control, like restraints, *but* we can make it our own. Desires and boundaries are key here."

"Are you a submissive?" The question nearly gets lodged in my throat because I'm not certain I wish to know the response.

"No," he replies softly. "I enjoy taking charge of a woman's pleasure."

I think about yesterday, against the wall. I may have been the one standing and he the one on his knees, but it was obvious he was in complete control of it all. Then this morning, when he let me undress him before he took over when I got stressed about what I found beneath his shorts.

"You tried this morning to let me take charge."

"I did. While it's not my preferred role, I will take it on if it's what my partner needs from me, but more often, I'd choose a different partner because we clearly won't be suited. If they need a submissive, even me taking on the role won't be natural or true to both of us. But for you, I'll be anything you need me to be."

"You think having *that*," my face scrunches, "kind of sex will fix me?"

"I think this morning, he found his way back in your mind. Perhaps it's like you said, and gentle isn't it for you. Maybe that's when he can find his way back in. Or maybe—"

"Makes no sense," I interrupt. "Why would doing things similar to what he did be better for my mind?"

Hawke shakes his head. "Willow, that's the difference. What he did to you was *not* any act of BDSM. It was torture. At least for me, BDSM gave me a space to work out my anger and be free of the bounds I was placing myself in. I'm simply suggesting we try with you." His shoulders lower a fraction with his heavy sigh. "When I ordered you to strip, you did so without a thought. How did that feel?"

"Natural."

"Natural," he repeats. "You trust me, which means we're already halfway there. What you experienced with Miller is *not* what we will be doing. When you give yourself to me, I'll only show you pleasure."

"You mentioned punishment."

Hawke glances at his hands for a second, collecting his thoughts. "I did, but not all acts need to involve it. Like

I said, it's a method where we can be our true selves. If you choose to disobey something I command, then that's the end of it. I refuse to go *there* with you until you're ready, and if that's never," he shrugs, "then so be it."

If I disobeyed Alex, it wasn't the end of it.

"Bend over."

"Hands up."

"Whore, make noises for me."

"Walk faster. You have a visitor."

"Come here."

"Put your hands here."

"Stay."

So many orders, all with cruel intentions.

"When I disobeyed Alex, I paid for it."

He winces, pressing his lips together for a moment before responding in a tight voice, "If I command something of you and your body, it's for your own pleasure. You listen, you'll be rewarded with the act. As I've said, trust is a huge factor, and we'll have a safe word. The moment it leaves your lips, I stop."

"Stop."

"Alex, please, no more."

"Alex, I can't any longer."

Nothing I said to Alex got him to cease his actions, but a single word will end whatever Hawke is doing?

I stare into pure, honest eyes and find my answer. Yes, that's exactly the case. He won't push me.

"Willow, I want your consent before we try this."

Consent. A key to this, according to Hawke. Certainly something Alex never received from me.

"Yes."

Hawke stands, towering over me, still dressed. He flicks his hand to the headboard. "Move up to the pillow."

As I'm doing that, he retrieves something from his nightstand drawer and lays it on the bed, facing him. I wait as his fingers fly over the keyboard of a laptop. He pauses, seemingly scrolling through a webpage before his eyes alight and he clicks something.

He slides it across the bed, still facing away before positioning himself behind me, so his legs cage my body in.

"Lean against me."

When I do, Hawke drags the laptop over, spins it to face us, and presses the space bar to start what he's loaded.

A movie plays.

Of a man and a woman, both without clothes. The man circles her, a rope and blindfold in his palm. She stands, waiting and watching him stalk her, a grin lining her lips.

Porn.

I twist to face him. "What—?"

"Before we do anything, I want you to see what consent looks like. She'll give herself to him willingly, and he'll tie her up, but it won't be for the reasons Alex did. Before they fuck, he'll check in with her."

"We're watching porn together."

"We are starting here, yes."

"Okay." I turn back to face the video.

"Get on the bed," the man orders and she responds instantly, lying down with her arms and legs spread as though she already knows what he expects. I study the woman's expression, seeking the fear and agony I always felt, and finding none. Instead, she watches him with pure want igniting in her eyes.

He walks around the bed, stopping by her head. "Arms up."

Well-practiced, she links her fingers together and lifts them above her head. He wraps the rope around her hands and wrists. She continues observing him, almost fascinated, and I lean forward, peering closer to the laptop, examining her curious, anxious expression.

That's when I feel it.

Hawke's lips descend on my neck, licking softly at the base of my ear.

By now, the man has the woman's hands completely wrapped. "Keep them above your head. You know what happens when you move them."

"Yes, Sir," the girl responds almost breathily.

All the pleasure Hawke is sparking within my body goes away with her response. It's a term used to show rank: to mean he is truly in control of her.

"I'm your fucking master and you need to learn that real quick."

Hawke senses—or feels—my panic and rubs at the sides of my arms. "I don't want you to refer to me as such. If you ever choose to, that's your prerogative, but I don't expect it, nor want you to."

Good, because I'm not sure my sanity could handle it.

The man climbs overtop the woman and straddles her stomach. His cock bobs hard against her breasts. They have such an easy time touching one another. No part of them is hidden from the other. It's exhilarating.

The blindfold is laid over her eyes, cutting off her vision. He immediately asks, "Are you okay? Binds not too tight?"

"You see how he checks with her before they get into anything?" Hawke whispers against my skin. "You see how she ultimately has all the control here? If she were uncomfortable at all, she could speak up and he would fix it before continuing."

The woman declares everything is fine, but I almost wish something wasn't, so I could witness what Hawke claims. Even so, I *do* see it because if she had no sway, then he wouldn't check with her at all. The basic question shows me all I need to know.

"Has Alex ever blindfolded you before?"

"No. He enjoyed when I had to witness everything."

"Good," Hawke purrs, his tongue circling the skin beneath my ear. "That'll be something you and I get to experience together. You'll be gorgeous, unable to see where I first choose to give you pleasure."

I groan, visualizing Hawke and me in place of this couple. A blindfold over my eyes, blocking my vision, while I wait for him to touch me. I imagine his mouth on me, like he did yesterday, but unable to see his eyes as he eats me.

On the video, the man reaches down and pinches the woman's nipples. They bud bright red, all the blood rushing to them.

She gasps—and so do I.

"Oh!" One of Hawke's hands latches onto my nipple, twisting and pinching in time with the man. My low cries mingle with the woman's.

"Feel good?"

"Yeah," I breathe

His pinch gets harder and I yelp, before relaxing because I know Hawke isn't doing it to injure me.

"Too much?"

"No."

"Good girl."

"Good girl," Alex says, gazing down at me.

How many times has he said those words to me? And though my back tenses and Hawke loosens his grip, my mind once again recalls that Hawke and Alex are not the same person. I'm *not* Hawke's pet or possession, but rather his partner. Calling me a good girl isn't meant to be derogatory.

"God, you're sexy," the man on the video says, yanking my attention back to the computer. "Do you remember your safe word?"

"Red."

"Good. And if you are unable to speak?"

"Three taps on the bed."

The man shifts forward on his knees until his cock comes dangerously close to her mouth, but he doesn't stop until he brushes her lips. Despite the blindfold, she responds, parting her lips and he slides inside effortlessly, moaning as she swallows every inch.

Moaning.

Alex always forced himself down my throat.

But the guy goes slow, allowing her throat to adapt before pushing more of him inside.

"Take me in your mouth. Swallow your master's cock and show me what a good girl you are. Show me how skilled you are at swallowing my cum."

My thighs clench, but it does no good against the liquid that just graced my insides. When Hawke pinches my nipple, I have to bite down on my lip to resist from throwing my head back and getting distracted from the riveting video.

"You see how she takes him into her willingly? How he went slow and ensured she's not in pain? Again, he may be dominating her body, but in a way, she holds power equal to his. It's because they trust each other."

"I trust you," I remind him. What I'm actually expressing is, *I think I want to take you in my mouth like that.*

What would his piercings feel like against my tongue?

He whispers, "Tell me what this video is making you feel."

"It's making me hot. My neck is warm."

"And?"

"And I'm wet."

"And?"

"And I think I like watching them. I like how gentle he's being with her. How he isn't hurting her. I think I want to do that for you."

Breaking my gaze with the laptop for the first time since Hawke started the video, I twist my head until he's in my line of sight, so I can catch his reaction. Instead, he captures my lips, his tongue probing my mouth as his hand slides down my stomach and finds my core. His fingers slip over my clit.

"Mm, you are *very* wet. You're loving this."

"Yes." There's no denying the truth.

And then he does something I've never imagined. He lifts his fingers to his nose, inhaling that part of *me*.

"I'll never tire of your scent."

A shuffle from the video captures my attention. The man stands from the bed, reaches over, and grabs something out of camera view, returning with a flogger.

I stiffen. Alex called a flogger child's play. It was too merciful a method, being often confused with concepts of pleasure. Instead, I was hit with worser items.

"We won't do that," Hawke states. "If you're okay, I want you to still watch, to understand and witness how, even when he whips her, trust is present. How she never uses her safe word because she knows he won't go that far, because he's aware of her limits. Limits, Willow, are key."

Limits. Sexual limits to ensure neither party ever goes too far.

Alex ignored my limits. Shattered them and the wall I attempted to build. Limit one was taking my virginity. Limit two was simply anything else he ever did. I'm uncertain of my limits now because I was never allowed to have any.

Hawke's fingers find my slit again, and he strokes two fingers through lazily, rubbing me agonizingly slow.

Due to our conversation, I missed the first few times he whipped her, but her stomach is now red, and he's moving onto her legs. The man lifts the leather and slashes it across her thighs, ripping a gentle cry from my throat. I look away to avoid watching more.

"Willow." Hawke shifts the hair off my shoulder to press a single kiss there. "Willow, watch the woman's expression."

Trust. So far, Hawke's never led me astray, so with great discomfort, I face the screen once more, this time ignoring the flogger in favour of the woman.

Even with the blindfold on, a face can convey a million things. Her mouth parts in obvious enjoyment, a low cry coming from her. Her wrists and ankles thrash against the bindings as she fights off the building sensations.

Through all of it, she never cries though. Doesn't scream or beg for mercy. Instead, as he pulls the flogger back, her breath catches and her bottom lip curls under her teeth as she anxiously waits for the hit to come again.

And then it does, and she moans.

"So fucking wet," Hawke growls in my ear. Two fingers continue to slide through my folds until they find my core and slip easily inside. "Tell me what you're thinking right now."

That you're inside me. That we've made it further than this morning.

"I'm thinking about how much she's enjoying this. I see what you mean now, in how BDSM is all about trust."

His fingers curl, finding that sweet spot inside me and I jerk, my motion rolling the laptop over. Neither he nor I go for it, even as the couple's cries provide a backdrop for my own noises.

Instead, I lean back against his chest, giving him more space to pump his fingers, while his other hand finds my breast. His lips land on my neck and I'm taken to the clouds.

Alex depicted Hell, but my blue-eyed angel flies me straight to Heaven.

I come, my cry covering over the woman's moans, my hands fisting the blanket. Hawke palms my breast and doesn't slow his speed until my body slumps, spent and pleased.

"Wow."

Hawke's fingers slip out of me, leaving me empty and wanting more. He reaches past me and shuts the video off. "'Wow' is one way to put it."

"That was—Thank you," I say instead. "Seriously, you're so damn patient and—"

He cuts me off with a hard kiss. "You're fucking worth it, Willow. Never think otherwise."

I state my previous thought aloud. "We did what I failed to do this morning."

He lifts up his hand, fingers still shiny from my release. "I'd say it's a positive start. Simply watching the video allowed your mind to go to another place, where you were able to accept the pleasure and not be lost to the past."

"Thank you."

Hawke opens his mouth to respond, interrupted by the shrill sound of his cell phone coming from beyond the bed.

"I'll ignore it. They can call back."

"No, no." I lift off his chest, and then the bed, swaying before settling on steady legs. "Go work. I think I need to shower again after that." If anything, to wash the sweat from the rest of my body.

Hawke follows me up, immediately reaching for me. He kisses my lips, my nose, and then my forehead where he pauses and breathes in. "I take it you're interested?"

"Very interested."

When his cell rings again, Hawke sighs with a deep longing present in his gaze. "All right, work calls, I suppose. Enjoy your shower. Will I be seeing you downstairs afterwards?"

Meaning, *are you hiding up here again?*

"You will."

Twenty-Seven

HAWKE
Seven Years Ago

BDSM. My therapist must be fucking whack, but holy hell, as I stare up at the club's dark doors, I think I am too. Since, after all, I'm here on my own accord.

Despite five years having passed since *it* happened and I left the Family, I'm not healed. At nearly twenty, I still can't completely relax with a woman. Not enough to have an orgasm.

My therapist suggested something stronger and more intense. Something that may, at times, remind me of my capture, but she said trust is the main factor in situations like this one.

Here I go.

Dozens of people swarm the main room. Men and women in all varying states of undress, and those that are dressed, their outfits seem to be mostly leather contraptions, leaving little to the imagination.

A blonde woman walks by me, smirking, and I note the collar around her neck. The guy with her scans me, his eyes ablaze and interested, but then they land on my right wrist, on the red and green bracelets indicating I'm free and only attracted to women, and he frowns, continuing behind her. I watch them walk toward the velvet curtains at the back of the room.

Couples or small groups are intertwined with one another, most choosing to escape into back rooms to continue what they've started. Some remain here, openly fucking one another.

Cries pierce the heady air, pulling most of the room's attention toward a woman. She has her hands bound behind her back while another woman braces above her mouth.

I turn, attention narrowing on them, and take a step closer for a better view. Inside my jeans, I thicken.

The woman continues to ride the other woman's mouth, her hands finding her own breasts and pulling at her nipples. From the shadows, another figure approaches the duo. A man, and he wraps his hand around the girl's upper arm, stealing her from the bound girl before forcing her to her knees.

I step forward, prepared to stop him as he shoves his cock into the girl's mouth before a small hand wraps my bicep, nails digging into the flesh. "Slow it down there. Don't interrupt unless you want your ass kicked."

I glance to the left, to the thin, naked woman standing there in nothing but heels. I scan her, eyes stopping briefly on her breasts and the landing strip of hair on her mound.

Her brows lift, a smirk showing me she's aware of me checking her out.

"Why would I get my ass kicked?"

"Because he's their dominant, and he gave them strict orders not to play with one another. And, well, they disobeyed." She leans in close, her hand still on my arm, and I feel her perky nipples brush my arm. In my ear, she whispers, "It's hot though, isn't it? Watching him command the two of them like that. So, tell me, you a Dom or a sub?"

Was I supposed to already know that? "Um, I don't

know."

Luckily, she pieces things together, and her lips part in an O. "Oh, first time, huh?"

"Yeah." My hands fist by my side, hating the feeling of being powerless. "It was recommended I come here since regular sex isn't doing it for me."

"Everyone here," she gestures around the space, "would agree with you there. Vanilla sex is boring. We do get some couples who come looking for more excitement, but most here are singles searching for someone to share the lifestyle with."

"Right."

The woman continues, her knowing eyes studying me. "You're a young one. You're legal, right? They checked your papers, I assume."

"Yeah, I'm nineteen."

Her full lips drop into a pout. "Well, why don't we move this to a back room and get to discovering if you're a Dom or a sub. I'm a Dom, so we'll begin with that. If you find yourself hating it, I'll let you sub with me, after you see how it's done. We'll go our separate ways, and you can call yourself enlightened and all that shit."

When my therapist first mentioned this plan, I assumed these clubs were pure sex, in which people would begin pulling at me at first chance. But it's clear after speaking with this woman, consent and agreement is important here. Everything is agreed to by both parties.

"Thanks. Why are you being nice to me?"

Her finger wiggles by my face. "Because this pretty little face with these gorgeous blue eyes looks so fucking lost. About to fight with someone over controlling his women." She laughs. "You would have made a few dozen enemies for that alone. It's a balance between respect and boundaries here. They explained the wristband colours, I assume?"

"Yeah."

She points to the trio's wrists, to the blue bracelets indicating they are unavailable to be played with. "Unless they invite you in, you don't go near those girls, understand? Even if what you think you're doing is noble, it's not. Okay? Let's go." She links her hand with mine and begins tugging me in the same direction I saw the other couple disappear earlier.

"What's your name?"

Before she lets the black curtains swallow us whole, she winks. "Does it matter?"

Then she shows me who I am. Everything I like, what I don't, and what I need.

Twenty-Eight

WILLOW

With damp hair tied up and dressed in my final set of clothes, I find Hawke in the kitchen, exactly where he was earlier, like everything we just did hadn't occurred.

He glances up from his laptop, his blue eyes going molten. Dressed or undressed, he still has my thighs clenching in desire. I sit, focusing on his laptop, recalling what we recently used it for.

"Working?"

"Unfortunately. Gotta pay the bills somehow."

"When will the trial be?"

His shoulders lift and drop quickly, a frown soon overtaking his mouth. "Sooner than later. Given the evidence, the judge is working to get this expedited, but they're also waiting for Teagan to be released from the hospital."

My ears perk at her name. Being here with Hawke has made it easy to forget the other shit happening around us, and the fact that there's more to this whole thing than just Alex. There's another girl who experienced things as well, and she's now healing from those.

"She's still in the hospital? I was only there a few days."

"Well, the mental health department—" He stops, glancing up from his laptop, his brow furrowing. "You don't remember?"

"Remember what?"

"Fuck," he curses, falling back against his chair.

"What?"

"Willow, I don't think I can. I don't want you to recall what your mind clearly blocked out."

I think back to the day Hawke found me. So much of that event is fuzzy because my broken, confused mind believed it was a dream, but I focus on the moment the group entered the basement. Who moved where, what Alex said…

"Teagan," Alex purrs. "Babe, look at me. Kill her."

I recall thanking him for granting me the moment I've been begging for and welcoming her grip, aware it would soon bring me to peace.

"She tried to kill me."

Hawke stills, watching me over his laptop. "You remember?"

"I thought it was all a dream. The entire event, right up until you got me away from the basement. The first time he ever took me out, I counted the steps I'd be required to take. I hoped one day I could escape and knowing how far of a run it would be helped me plan. I counted the steps you took, and it was only when you went over the amount, when you made it to the staircase, that I realized it was real."

"Fuck," he curses again. "That entire time, you believed it a dream?"

One shoulder lifts in a half-hearted shrug. "I had no reason to believe otherwise."

"You're very matter-of-fact about all this." Hawke leans forward slightly. "Willow, it might be a good idea for you to speak to someone."

"A therapist, you mean. I'm fine." He's helping me so what do I need someone else for? But getting back to the subject, I ask, "Teagan's still in there because she tried to kill me?"

Hawke slowly nods. "He conditioned her. But she's seen everything he's done over the years and I need her testimony. It'll work in our favour if the jury hears it. After her story, and the evidence and—" He stops, his lips slamming shut, and when he speaks again, they're with different words. "After that, I doubt anyone will find him innocent."

"You want me to testify too," I state, not forming it as a question.

His lips roll and the drumming of his fingers stop. The silence between us pulses—or is that my heartbeat as I wait for his response? "I do. Because as the victim, you hold so much power."

Victim. I *am* a victim, and it's exactly what the judge and jury will view me as.

I've seen trials on TV and in movies. It'll involve dozens upon dozens of people watching, forcing me to recount everything I lived through in front of Alex. He'll stare me down with his knowing smirk, right before the jury finds him innocent. He'll take me from that stand, away from Hawke, and back to a place where I'll never see my angel again. Every second I'm there, I'll beg Alex to kill me because now that I've tasted freedom, I won't accept anything less.

"I can't," I whisper around a tight throat. No tighter than it'll be when Alex strangles me. "Besides, it's useless. He'll pay everyone off and it'll be over before it begins."

Hawke leans forward, his tattooed arm cutting into my vision and breaking my stare with his table. "Willow, not this again." He sighs, exhaustion dragging down his words. "He's unable to because he's under close surveillance."

"It's his name. The Miller name carries a lot of weight and fear with it. That'll be enough to switch the jury's decision."

"Not this time."

He's so certain. We've been down this path countless times before and it always ends with us going nowhere. So, we'll return to that peace. The peace in which Hawke believes he'll win, and I'll spend the rest of my days happy before Alex returns.

But he doesn't drop it. Instead, his chair scrapes against the tiled flooring as he comes closer, deleting the few inches between us. His hand remains on the table, but his other one finds mine and grips tightly.

"After everything happened to me, I told you I took off. Lived on my own for a bit and worked odd jobs. It killed me to use my parents' money, but I wasn't stupid. I knew it was either take their help or be homeless. I emptied my account, and when they added more, I withdrew that money too and lived a cash-only life, so they couldn't track me. Finally, when I was old enough, I got a job at a grocery store.

"One day, a man came in. He was so frazzled, so obviously exhausted, his fancy suit amuck, and he bought half an aisle's worth of junk food." Hawke chuckles, his eyes shifting to the side and into the past. "I was his cashier, and he explained he was a lawyer and was working a case involving child abuse. He was up all hours of the day building this case because he was so determined to win. The food was fuel, you see."

I do see. I see more than he's admitted to already. It was a single man's busy schedule that changed Hawke's path.

"You followed his footsteps."

Hawke nods, his lips pulling up on one side in a fond smile. "I never saw him again. This was in a different town, one many hours from here, and while I've searched the law firms in that area, hoping to thank him all these years later, I didn't find him. But I won't ever forget him because once he cashed out, I spent the entire night thinking about what it would feel like to help children—people in general, really—who are in situations like mine. How, if only, there was someone to help me." He pauses, his eyes flicking to me again and scanning my face. "And you.

"After that, I started compiling all my family's money. To this day, I hate it was their lifestyle *still*, even after I left, that helped me become who I am, but we all need a bit of help sometimes, right?" One shoulder lifts in a half-heart-ed shrug. "I saved and saved and saved everything they gave me and everything I made from working, until I could afford university. First, my undergraduate degree, and then law school."

All because he met a man. One lawyer who needed late-night fuel to continue working. A single man changed Hawke's life, and in turn, affected mine.

I wonder who he'd be today if that one lawyer never went to that grocery store. He wouldn't be Hawke Black-wood, attorney-at-law and my angelic saviour. He would never have found me, and I wouldn't be here. I'd be in the basement with Alex. Perhaps by now, I'd be a corpse.

Whose life could you affect? If I testify, it ensures this dom-ino effect continues. Alex will go away, and more women will remain safe and alive. Saving them means they'll con-tinue their lives, have great careers, families, and futures, forever shaping the years beyond us.

Because one single man bought junk food.

Because one single man decided to be a psycho and play with women's lives. I'm here, not only because a man bought junk food, but because another one thought it was fun to torture innocents. Whatever he did to the first wom-an he kidnapped must have satisfied his cravings, and he continued the pattern. He took her life, and the next girl's, and the next girl's… all of them, until finding me. Because I answered an online job posting and got what I believed would be a fancy job as a CEO's secretary.

Fate, life, whatever the fuck you want to call it, is obviously decided by so many factors. Hawke and I are here because he admired a stranger, and because Alex chose me. Otherwise, our paths would never have crossed.

Alex made his decisions. Hawke made his. And I need to make mine.

Will my story be the determining factor in Alex's imprisonment or not? Hawke mentioned being certain Alex would be put away regardless.

But what if he doesn't, and it's your story that ensures he does.

There's no way to know that.

Both voices battle it out under Hawke's scrutiny. Maybe he's spoken already and is waiting for a reply, or maybe he hasn't. Either way, I'm lost in the maze of my mind, tortured by the unknowns and the fears of simply opening my mouth.

"I-I don't know if I can, Hawke."

A thumb strokes over my palm, pulling me back to the present and centring me. I glance at my lap, to where he's holding my hand, almost fascinated by the way a simple touch can affect me.

It's *him*. Hawke Blackwood has something magical within him. It's why his eyes are so bright, I'm certain. It's the magic buried within.

"It's okay, Willow. You know why I had to ask."

I do, but I don't tell him that. Don't tell him how my decision has my throat tightening and hands going numb. For once, not in fear, but rather self-hate because who else have I condemned by denying Hawke? Because I'm too fearful to do it? Who'll pay when we lose this?

Hawke and his hard work.

Other women—future victims.

Teagan.

Myself.

That's when the shame hits strongly. The fact that I'm too fucking weak to protect even myself.

I'm lost again. I'm a lost little girl, the very one Hawke had to search for the other day. As though nothing in the past two days matters. How despite his kisses and touches, I'm still broken.

I'm.

Still.

Broken.

Twenty-Nine

HAWKE

I watch her breakdown even before it begins. I see when the light fades from her eyes, and when calling her name three times does nothing. If I knew where she went off to, I'd follow her down into wherever her mind brought her to.

She fought it. I watched the glint in her eyes, felt the stiffening of her hands before she succumbed completely. Wherever her mind took her to, she nearly managed to stay.

My thumb strokes over her hand and I call her name yet again, knowing it won't do anything, but hoping it will. That it'll be the moment she blinks and comes back.

I shouldn't have asked her, but fuck, I need her to testify. Not for the case, and definitely not for me, but for her. She deserves what I never got the chance to do—to watch her rapist burn.

When my father rescued me, he ensured the men never left that basement, but in Willow's case, her assaulter will be right there, presumably in a suit and a cocky smirk as his fate is decided. She *needs* to be there—to be the one to give the executioner's orders on the jury's decision—to see him get carted off to prison. It'll do her good.

"Broken."

Her lips move, but I'm not sure she even realizes she's spoken.

Broken. She believes she's broken.

My stomach drops, knowing we're back here again, when in a few short days, her growth has been exponential. She's left the room, we've shared pasts, and she's allowed me to touch her. The damned angel she is let *me*—someone scarred and broken—touch her. Her, who only deserves gentleness and love.

I think about the revelation we made earlier and how she responds to me, *wants* to be ordered around. That video had her panting, and I can't wait to be the one who makes her do it again. It's what I'll give her, what I'll show her. How, when being tied up can lead to pleasure and not pain. How, when I wrap the rope around her wrists, it'll be with the complete intention to undo them.

I'll undo her bindings, but it'll be me who's undone.

I'm halfway there. This strange, broken, beautiful girl could stomp on my already-fragile heart and I wouldn't care.

I don't love. I don't know *how* to love. I certainly never received it from my money-hungry, power-driven, political-playing mafia family, nor any other woman I've ever been with. Willow makes me want to try to figure it out. As we work on her healing, she's building a bridge from her heart to my own.

It's quick perhaps, and even a little abnormal, but normality isn't made for people like us. What we've seen and experienced, other people couldn't dream of.

While she believes she's broken, she's actually healing. She's so fucking strong to have made it through six months with Miller. Illness makes my throat full and I wonder how long she would have had left if we hadn't found her. Would she be dead by now?

The phrase, *it gets worse before it gets better*—this is it getting worse. Willow will lose herself in her mind, her self-misery, and her self-hate, but when she awakens, she'll be better.

How do I know? Because I know her. She's the same as me.

And she's mine.

She'll return to me.

Thirty

WILLOW

Broken.

So damn broken.

And then I laugh. Possibly only in my head, or perhaps out loud; I don't really know. I laugh because Alex got his wish. I'm broken. Shattered. He's not even here to toss the pieces of me away. Either way, when he's found innocent and comes for me, he'll only find a shell.

I blink and focus on the face in front of me. On the hair I've enjoyed rubbing my hands through. On the tattoos sketched up his arms, toward his neck, and down his chest. On his facial adornments.

So patient. So beautiful. Everything I want.

Want. Not wanted. I want Hawke still, now more than ever. Now, before he goes to trial and loses and Alex returns. Now, while there's still a piece of me to give.

He won't want me like this. Hell, *I* wouldn't want me like this. But Alex will. Alex will enjoy this new version of me.

Unless he never returns. Unless I disclose the truth and ensure he doesn't come back.

But—

I blink, and the room around me returns to focus. Hawke's hair is black against his forehead, the bangs falling over his eyes, which shine blue again. The chill in my hand dissipates with the feeling of his thumb stroking my palm.

Realization crashes over me like a rough wave, drowning me until I gasp. "Oh my God, I'm sorry."

Hawke says nothing but continues to study me. Muscles tick in his jaw, and just when I think he's angry, he pushes away from the table and reaches for me.

"Come on. Let's go somewhere."

Somewhere? As in… outside. I don't move and bring my hands closer to my body, away from his reach. "Where?"

"Out. You haven't left this house. You went from one cage to a hospital to another."

"I was out the other day," I state, recalling my other breakdown.

The skin around his eyes crinkle, but not with amusement, based on the rest of his expression. This time, he reaches for me.

"Let's find your shoes and go for a drive."

"Where?"

"Anywhere that isn't here."

He truly has no path or plan laid out, other than driving around aimlessly. At first, I hated it because I'm out in the open for anyone to see, but after a while, I took the deep inhale he suggested and let the spring air fill my lungs. Hawke is correct. Other than leaving the hospital and when I escaped his room the other day, I haven't been outdoors, which my body desperately needs.

As Hawke drives around town, all four windows are down. For the briefest second, I push aside the fact that

Alex probably has someone stalking me, and simply enjoyed being outdoors. Enjoyed the warm, crisp air and let it stitch me back together.

I glance over, noting how relaxed Hawke appears. How his arm rests on the centre console, his long fingers dangling limply while his other hand is draped over the steering wheel as he maneuvers his expensive car through the town's streets.

"You look relaxed," I comment.

"I was going to say the same about you."

I settle deeper against the leather seat. "I suppose you were right. This feels good. I'm sorry for earlier."

Warmth spreads on my leg, and I realize it's him. He's touching me like we're a regular couple, and I rest my hand over his.

"I shouldn't have asked, Willow. I'm sorry too."

Except he has no reason to be. He was trying to do his job and I'm the one who stuck a roadblock in his way.

"He's going to jail either way," he continues, but I know his words are simply to ease me. "You said no the other day and I need to respect your decision." His fingers flex, but they don't dig in, merely remind me his hand is on my leg. "The first time I had to work a rape case, I broke down when my past hit so hard.

"I was still in law school at the time but completing my internship. I was lucky enough to get one in a prestigious firm alongside Jason. I think it's why we are who we are today. Our reputation was born within that internship."

Jason. He's mentioned him before. My mind scrolls through our conversations. "The guy you work with?"

"Yeah. We were friends since school. Anyway, the case they gave me was to help on a child rape case and I… I couldn't. I freaked out. All I remember was reading the report and running out of the room. It was the first time I had to deal with something like that since my own experience, and I apparently didn't handle it well.

"Jason found me, and though he didn't know the story—still doesn't—I think he pieced enough of it together. Somehow, having him not know the truth helped. He talked me down, got me back to the office, and sat me down to explain to my supervisor." His lips lift into a shadowed smile. "Law is a firm profession. There's little emotion in the workplace, whether you're still training or not. They don't care about that stuff, but my supervisor offered me a different case."

At a red light, his eyes cut to me. "I almost took the deal, but the suggestion to remove myself from it somehow built me up. I didn't want to fail the child, but more so, I wanted to prove to myself I could do it. I made it through my hell, but I now had children to save." He sighs in time for the light to flick green and the car moves again. "I did the case, and I won. I owe Jason for encouraging me to speak with our supervisor because if she didn't offer to remove me from the case, I don't think I would have found the strength to finish it."

Tears swell in my eyes, but I look away, using the sun to burn them away. He did the exact opposite I am. He fought back against his own self-hate and completed the case, so clearly, he's stronger than I am. I can't do that. I can't fight the past. I can't get up on the stand.

"Jason seems like a good friend," I manage, hoping the broken sadness isn't seeping through.

"He is."

When I feel as though all evidence of crying is gone, I face him again, and a question breaks from my lips. A question I didn't think I would ever ask.

"Can you show me your office?"

Thirty-One

WILLOW

Everything is white, shiny, and clean. If Alex's basement has an opposite, this is it.

My angel's heaven to my devil's hell.

Hawke steps by me and shuts the door, but the names on the wall steal my attention. *Adler & Blackwood.* To have your name on something that brings positive change for so many people is amazing.

"Well," a dry, feminine voice begins, "I hadn't thought we'd ever see you back in here, considering the way you took off the other day."

A middle-aged woman emerges from a hallway and takes a seat at the tidy, unoccupied front desk. Her tight bun doesn't move as her brows lift, but her smirk tells me she's not upset.

"Hey, Marge," Hawke calls. "How are things around here?"

"Have you been answering my emails?"

"Of course."

"Then you know how things are around here." She slips on a small pair of spectacles; the kind I'd imagine someone like her wearing.

I chuckle at their easy banter, unable to help the light feeling blooming in my chest. My noise gains Marge's attention and she glances up, past Hawke, spotting me. Her eyes widen and she pulls off the glasses as quickly as she put them on.

"My apologies, Mr. Blackwood. I didn't realize you had a client with you."

He waves her off. "This is Willow."

Her eyes bulge and her hand goes to her chest. "As in *the* Willow?"

With Hawke's nod, she rushes around the other side of the desk, her hands reaching toward me. Hawke, ever the saviour, side-steps and deftly blocks her.

"She asked to see my office, and who am I to deny her what she wants?" His eyes blaze deeper. It's a mixture of lust and something else, but either way, my stomach knots in desire.

"Would you like water, hon?" Marge's voice cuts through the electricity in the air.

"No, thanks."

She nods and glances at Hawke. "Mr. Adler is in his office, if you're wanting to see him."

"Want to meet Jason?"

Do I want to meet more strangers? No, but I am curious about the guy who's seemingly—and unknowingly—supported Hawke through the darkness in his life.

My hands fist behind my back, as I aim for ease, working to not show the rocks of anxiety tumbling through my body when I nod.

Hawke breaks into an easy smile, telling me I made the correct decision. Of course he wants to introduce me to his friend, a person who's been a part of so much of his life. His hand finds mine behind my back and uncurls my fingers.

"It'll be okay," he whispers. "I'll be with you the entire

time." His lips land on my brow, pressing a kiss there and he inhales sharply.

"I know."

He pulls me past Marge, who's staring at us with an open-mouthed, gaping expression, out of the waiting room, and to a short hallway, lined with various shut doors.

"Meeting rooms," he comments. "I can show you, but they're literally rooms with a table and chairs. It's where we host our clients."

"Ah," I grunt.

The end of the hallway breaks into two sections, like a Y. To the right, there's a single frosted glass door leading to another room. In front of it is a small desk with a pretty redhead working at a laptop.

"Hey, Brittany," Hawke calls. "Jason in there?"

The girl jerks upright, obviously surprised by Hawke's sudden arrival. "Um, y-yes, Mr. Blackwood. Go right in."

He already has his hand on the doorknob, pushing the frosted door open. I meet the girl's curious eyes tracking us. Over six months ago, I was her.

Before long, she's gone, shut behind a door as Hawke brings me into the office. Everything I imagined inside a lawyer's office is here. Wall-to-wall shelving filled with nondescript books. His desk is a mess of papers and files, some even strewn on the carpet by the ornate, wooden desk. Behind it, a man stands with our arrival.

I stiffen, puke rising in my throat. He's beautiful in a classically handsome way. His blond hair is pushed behind his ears, clearing the way for his dark eyes to study me. Clean-shaven, dressed impeccably in a suit, and the way his eyes flick over my form, as though he's studying me, memorizing me for his later use... he reminds me of Alex.

Hawke doesn't notice. Instead, his arm whips out toward the man. "Willow, Jason. Jason, this is Willow."

"And the reason you're never around anymore. Working from home," he scoffs. "We're way too busy for that."

Hawke's voice goes deeper. "Willow, he's clearly in a mood, but this grump has been my best friend for ages."

I'm not sure what Hawke has in his expression that has Jason backing down, but his hands lift and his mouth cracks in an easy smile before he drops back into his leather chair.

It doesn't relax me. It reminds me of when Alex would smile. Easy, pleasant—his business smile, as I referred to it. The smile he'd give me every morning, evening, and each time he passed by my desk. Little did I know, beneath his smile, he was scheming.

I think of the girl out there, beyond this door, and what her life might be like. My feet inch toward the door, but Hawke's hand tightens on mine, his eyes cutting to me, a question swirling in those blue irises.

Jason doesn't notice. "Sorry, sorry. I suppose I'm a bit frazzled. I know you have your hands full with the Miller case, but I've been working to keep up with the rest." He looks me over again. "Willow, huh. You're quite popular around these parts."

I swallow past the lump forming in my throat because this is Hawke's friend. Not a villain. Rather a lawyer, set out to assist people.

Alex is a trusted CEO within business circles.

Instead, I force logic away and plaster on a smile. I asked to come here, so I should try to enjoy it.

"I've heard. I suppose with Hawke being home all the time, for me. Sorry."

Jason watches me for another second, his head tilting to the side. No doubt, in this field, he's used to people being much more articulate. "I was kidding. It's good he's with you. How have you been managing?"

I shrug because I truly don't know how to answer that. One day, I believe I'm making great progress, and the next, a simple question tosses me into self-doubt.

Instead, Hawke supplies, "She's doing great. We figured it was time to get out of the house and she wanted to see the office."

Jason grunts, but his attention drops to our clasped hands. He stares at them for a long while, and his head finally straightens in time to say, "Welcome then. I'm sure you're anxious for all this to be over. Blackwood will get Miller put away soon, don't you worry."

So I keep hearing.

"Anyway, I'm going to take her to my office now. I'll text you later, okay?" Hawke says, already walking us backward.

Jason makes a gesture with his hand, but it's so quick I don't quite catch it. "You got it. Have fun, kiddos."

When we leave his office, the tension in my shoulders lessens slightly, but I can't look toward the girl, knowing what her outcome would be, had she been working for a different boss. When we exit that section of the building, it's as though I walked through a gate and the other side is freedom. Breath returns to my lungs, and I force it to the depths of my toes.

We head toward the left side of the Y hallway, to the alcove identical to what Jason's setup is like, only the desk here is bare.

"You don't have a secretary?"

Hawke shrugs and pulls out keys from his pocket. As he unlocks his office, he replies, "No one's job application really spoke to me, so no. Eventually, I will get someone, but for now, I manage my own appointments."

"Isn't that a lot?"

Hawke shrugs again, and I get the sense he doesn't want to talk about this. He pushes open his door and stands aside, letting me enter.

Hawke's office is nearly identical to Jason's with bookshelves surrounding the walls. Same ornate desk, same leather chair, and same computer. The biggest difference is the cleanliness. Unlike Jason's office, papers and files are stacked nicely on the corner of his desk. Everything is orderly and *clean*.

The other notable difference is the vibe. This room—it's pure Hawke. I *feel* it, like I sense him. The essence within the space wraps around me until it's impossible to ignore, weaves between my senses, my soul.

I stride forward and drop into his chair, spinning around once for fun before facing his desk to scan everything there. Then I look toward him and his strange expression. It's one that has my heart beating faster.

"What?"

Suddenly, Hawke's by my side, lifting me from his seat to slide himself underneath. Once I'm settled on his lap, he yanks me to his mouth.

I fall into the kiss, sighing, as all previous worries melt away. I find the plain cotton of his shirt and picture him in a fancy suit. Even in one, he'd look so different than Alex. The tattoos and piercings and unique eyes set him apart, and that's not even considering his personality, his empathy, and his patience.

Hawke runs his tongue along my lips, silently requesting more. I part my lips and let him slip inside as easily as he's slipped inside the rest of me. Kissing Hawke… there's nothing better.

When he tries to pull back, I hold him tighter. My teeth nip at his lips and he groans in the back of his throat.

"Willow."

He wants to end this, but I'm feeling more human now than I have in hours.

I want him. I want him in all the ways he's shown me this morning. I want to use my mouth on him, like he did for me, and as the woman did in the porn video. For the first time ever, I want to pleasure a man with my mouth because I *want* to, not because he demands me to do it.

I reposition, lifting myself and throwing my leg over his lap, straddling him. The wide executive chair makes this possible and I'm thankful for it. My core lands right over his jean-covered cock.

Hawke pulls from my mouth, his breaths coming quicker. "Willow?"

"Kiss me," I urge, and take his mouth again. "Show me how you'd like to control me."

With Hawke, I *want* to be controlled, I realize. The thought of being tied up and teased for my pleasure is a sweet torture I'll gladly accept from him, because he'll never go far enough to hurt me.

Hawke's eyes darken. "Put your hands on the back of my chair."

I remove them from his body and place them where he's instructed. A shiver wracks my spine, but I force myself steady, hoping he won't mistake the shiver as fear.

He collects my hair in one hand, keeping a firm but painless hold. "Tell me what you want. You decide. I'm ordering you to."

"I want to taste you."

Hawke leans forward and takes my mouth, his tongue stroking against mine, stoking the heat in my core again, but I soon end it.

I grind on his thickening erection. "No, I want to *taste* you." Hopefully, the emphasis on my words will make him understand their actual meaning.

Shock makes his expression slack. "Willow, no—"

I kiss him again, shutting him up. "I *want* to, Hawke. I want this. You. To make you feel good, like you make me."

Pain etches his face, his brows dropping over pinched eyes. He's scared but also wants what I'm offering. There's no denying the way his cock twitched beneath me at the mention of the act.

"Willow…"

"I want to, Hawke. I want to feel you in my mouth, filling it up with your cum. Make it so Alex will never again be able to come near me."

He growls—literally *growls*—and it does something to my insides. The grip he has on my hair tightens past the point of pain and his ice eyes glow, crazed with a brand-new emotion.

"Before you, my task involved keeping the other guys in line. They all wanted to kill him, but I insisted on going about this legally, to cover all our bases. I didn't understand them then, but I do now. I'll kill him if he even looks at you twice. I'll kill him in every way he deserves, before I fuck you on top of his ashes. You're mine now, Willow. The *only* person allowed to bind you is yourself. Not him. Never him."

Mine. Hawke's been so careful not to use that word, but something within him obviously woke up. Instead of fearing the concept, I like it. A few months ago, I vowed that had I gotten free, I'd never allow myself to be anyone's again, but with Hawke, he broke that promise, exactly as he's shattered my rationality, one word at a time… one touch at a time.

Now, here we are.

Mine. His.

"Yours."

His nostrils flare and the grip on my hair goes away. "Kneel in front of me."

I scramble from his lap as he readjusts the chair. His hands undo the belt on his jeans and he pulls them down, repositioning them at his ankles. His pierced cock bobs up, and it's so damned delicious looking.

"Fuck, Willow, the way you're looking at me…"

"Like I want to lick?"

He groans, and though my hands itch to touch, I wait for his command. I sit nicely, hands on my lap, waiting for the order, aware I sat in an identical position once for another man.

"What are you waiting for?" Hawke's grin is mocking, but beneath it, his breath catches. He's still nervous, likely pondering if I'll snap.

I lean forward, positioning my hands on his thighs. That's when the nerves decide to make my stomach flip. Not due to the act, but more the outcome. What if he's right and this is too soon? What if I have a breakdown? What if my mind believes he's Alex and I react?

You won't.

I won't. I need to believe it. So, before I second guess myself more, I wrap my lips around his head and flick my tongue, being sure to hit the piercing.

"Fuck."

At least he's reacting how he should. Alex often came in my mouth, but I'm sure it had more to do with his power trip than my skills.

I slide my mouth down his cock, swallowing as much as I can, inch by inch, passing the piercings until he hits the back of my throat.

"Don't hurt yourself," he commands in his soft tone.

Alex would always jam himself in my throat. More than once, I've thrown up on him, and all it's done is make him angrier. I always tried to relax my throat, to ensure giving him head wouldn't result in getting beat, but it never happened. Unfortunately, he was too large and unforgiving.

I drag my mouth back up to Hawke's cockhead slowly, stopping briefly to play with the piercings. My teeth catch on one and I tug lightly, playfully, instincts driving me. I'm not sure what instincts have me being playful during such an act, but when Hawke groans again, I decide not to question it.

"Willow, that's—" He never finishes his sentence, so I'm left to only guess.

I swirl my tongue around his head before pulling tight and flicking his underside. Hawke's hips lift from the chair, his cock slipping deeper into my throat before he stiffens and forces himself back down.

"Fuck, sorry."

I'm not delicate and he needs to comprehend that. I moan my approval along his length, and his hands whack the leather chair armrests, his groan soon following.

"I'm going to come soon."

I swallow him deeper, tightening my lips, and keep a steady sucking pace. My tongue continues to work his underside, pausing at each piercing.

"Are you wet? Touch yourself and tell me."

I immediately slide my hand into my pants, finding my damp core. Removing my fingers, I lift them, showing him what I've found.

"I want us to come together, Willow. Bring yourself to orgasm."

I haven't done that since before Alex, and while I'd much rather he do it, I wonder if this is yet another step I need to work through. Touching myself after everything would mean to accept what had occurred and love myself for it.

Maintaining my pressure and speed, I slip my hand back into my pants, playing with my clit, rubbing it back and forth.

"One day soon, I'll be watching you do that. I want to see you bring yourself pleasure, *il mio bella ragazza.*"

You can witness it now.

"You're making dreams I hadn't realized I had come true."

You too.

"Put your fingers inside yourself, baby. Feel the inside of your pretty pussy."

I groan around his length, his words spurring me on. I do as he commands and push one of my fingers up inside me. It's not nearly as nice as his, but I still rock myself against my hand.

Hawke moves my hair to the side, keeping my face bare. Our eyes lock and it's the very look of adoration he's giving me that finishes me off.

As the orgasm hits, I stiffen, my nerves tightening as pleasure tightens my core around my fingers. His own orgasm explodes in my mouth, hot liquid shooting to the back of my throat.

"That was fucking hot," he pants between breaths. "Let me get you a cloth to spit into."

I swallow, and the movement of my throat pauses his actions. His lips form one word: *Fuck*.

"Let me see your fingers."

Despite everything we just did, heat splashes my cheeks and neck as I lift my hand. Evidence of my orgasm is still coated on me. Hawke grasps my hand and brings the fingers to his mouth, licking every inch of them.

"Delicious," he moans. "I'll never tire of this." When he thoroughly has my fingers clean and my insides throbbing for more, he lifts me back onto his lap. "You know, now when I work in here, all I'll picture is you on your knees. I don't want to think about where those skills came from, but damn, Willow, you have them."

I doubt that, but then, there's something between us. Something I know I've never felt with another man and something I hope he hasn't with another woman—at least not to this extent.

"Trust."

A satisfied grin settles on his lips, and he leans back into the chair. "Yes. I trust myself with you more than anyone in the past."

Exactly what I wished to hear.

My hands land on his chest, sliding up to his neck. "That was only supposed to be for you, you know."

"Believe me, your orgasm was for me too."

Silence befalls us, and I stare at him—stare *into* him.

"Yours," I repeat his earlier word.

"Mine." His hand brings mine to his chest, right over his beating heart, still rapidly thumping from his orgasm. "The first moment I saw you, I knew you'd always be in here."

I love you. That's what he's telling me, without speaking the precise words. They're words I'm uncertain I wish to hear right now.

"When we get home, I want you to make me yours in all the other ways too."

Hawke pulls me to my feet. "Then let's get the fuck out of here."

Thirty-Two

WILLOW

Hawke throws his bedroom door shut behind us and tosses me against it, his mouth crashing onto mine. My hands fist in his shirt, drinking up everything, but before long, he's stepping away, leaving me panting with desire.

"Pick a safe word."

I think about any word that makes sense for us and come up with, "Angel."

"Say it."

"Angel."

"Be comfortable with that word, Willow, and I fucking mean it." His hand juts out, finger gesturing to the bed behind us. "I'm not Alex, and this bedroom is not his basement. You don't like what I'm doing, you put a stop to it *right away*. Not after the fact. *In the moment*." His hand grasps my chin, not roughly, but firm, and his body eats up any space between us. "The moment you even whisper that word, I stop what I'm doing. This entire thing means nothing if your comfort—your *trust*—isn't here. I'll tie you up and blindfold you like we watched in the movie, but nothing further than that this time. Tonight is about trust only, and I refuse to have it shattered."

Shattered. His use of that word is so appropriate for what's happening to my sanity. It's breaking—shattering— but in the sweetest way possible. He's smashing my walls down.

"I understand, Hawke." My hand stretches toward him, but he moves back, his nose lifting in the air.

"Say your safe word one more time. I need to hear it."

"Angel."

The fire in his eyes blazes brighter. "Then remove your clothing and go lie on the bed, arms and legs spread."

I strip under his focused stare, struggling to ignore the way he makes me want to beg for him to fuck me. With gentle, long breaths, I stride to the bed, aiming not to see it as a death-march.

I can do this. He isn't Alex.

Perhaps that's why this feels kind of worse. Like, so much more is on the line here, and I've already fucked this up once. What if I do it again? What would that mean for us?

As I position my body into an X, Hawke strides to- ward his closet, returning a moment later with a black blindfold and thin, red rope dangling from one hand. He sets them beside me, purposely letting me see them first.

"I'm going to bind your ankles and wrists to the bed- frame, maintaining this position. If you hate it, or feel yourself slipping away, say the word and you'll be untied instantly. Okay?"

"Okay," I whisper.

Hawke's fingers slide up one leg, moving past my knee, and with his simple touch, all my worries go away. His touch is soft, gentle, urging me to follow it. He con- tinues until meeting my core. His thumb pushes aside my lips, so he's able to brush his fingers over my clit before continuing on.

His movements may be quick, but it doesn't stop my

body from reacting—from jerking into his touch, silently begging him to come back and do it again. A whimper breaks from my lips. So, I guess not silent enough.

"You're already wet, Willow. How is that?"

"Because I want you," I respond boldly, not recognizing the girl speaking those words.

He hums again, but I'm distracted by the gentleness of the rope he places over my ankle, winding around once, twice, three times before looping it to the bedframe. He pulls tight, keeping my leg taut before tying it off and walking the base of the bed.

"Good?"

"Yes."

He repeats the same with the other ankle before heading for my wrists. This time, knowing what to expect, I stop breathing, anticipation making the air heady. Hawke stops by the bedside and glances down at me.

"Laid out like a feast for me to enjoy." He reaches down and flicks at a budded nipple. With how stiff it is, the flick slightly stings, but nothing remotely close to the pain I used to feel regularly. "You're pink, wet… wanting."

I bite down on my lip and continue to eye-stalk him as he moves past my head and grasps a wrist. His thumb strokes over the centre of my palm before looping a rope around my wrist a few times and grabbing my other and repeating the same. When they're both bound, he ties them together, linking it with the headboard.

"Tug on them," he orders, and I do. The ropes stay firm. "Does it hurt?"

I shake my head.

"Remember what I said about your word?"

Oh my God! "Yes! Hawke, just get on with this." My exasperation has turned into a hurried exclamation, to which he merely steps back and raises a brow.

"You need to recall who's in charge here."

Me. Because I hold the control with the single word, but I do comprehend what he means. He's speaking of the sexual power dynamic between us.

"You speak when I tell you to." His hand finds my nipple again and he pinches tightly, making me yelp. "I will deem when we begin. You speak out again, and I'll have to punish you."

Punish you. I feel the moment everything crashes around me and every muscle and nerve inside me go tense. He said we wouldn't be doing *that.* He said—

That's when realization hits him and Hawke releases my nipple, swallowing tightly. With his eyes on mine, he touches my cheek softly.

"I'm sorry, sweet girl, that's not what I meant. Punishment can be delivered in a multitude of ways, such as orgasm denial. Just when you're on the brink, I'll pull back. No physical pain, but your insides will be a sopping mess, crying for me to allow you to come. *That's* the punishment I speak of, and believe me, it's the sweetest most frustrating torture." His thumb touches my lip for the briefest second and he murmurs, "Willow, I promise you. I won't raise my hand against you. We'll use no whips, floggers, or anything of that capacity until you ask me to. And if that's never," he shrugs, "then it's never. You're worth more to me than those acts." His hand moves from my face and touches my breast, right over my thumping heart. "Hard or soft—*we're* what matters."

Shattering. It's the word that comes to mind again, because when my rationality was about to shatter again and toss me into that dark hole, he, once again, yanked me from it and shattered my heart. Shattered it by snatching it from my chest to steal for himself.

I think I love him too.

Words I'm unsure I'll ever be able to tell him, but I'll show him in my actions. I'll show him how he makes me feel every time he understands my horrors.

"So, yes," his voice hardens, becoming silky, "you do not make the demands here. I do. And I'll decide when you come."

I squeak. "When I come?"

His lips pull into a cocky, knowing smirk. "You've heard me, baby. You don't come until I tell you to."

As if I can control that. I suppose he'll be punishing—I swallow again—me, but then I consider his earlier words, and compared to what Alex used to do, Hawke's punishment will be nothing.

"For now, I'm going to blindfold you." He reaches over my body and grabs the scrap of black. "This will be for your pleasure only, so every touch I give you, every lick, will be a surprise. You won't know it's happening until I do it."

Shivers wrack my spine, followed by a flush of heat I know goes straight to my core, because, damn, his words make me want it. For once, I won't know what's happening to me. I'll be able to lie back and allow Hawke to fly me to paradise himself.

Trust.

I'll leave my body and pleasure in his hands for him to decide how and when to extract it.

I nod, showing I've heard him. The moment I do, my vision is stolen, blocked by the scrap of black he puts over my eyes.

"Lift your head a bit."

My neck strains with the effort to keep it upright, but he manages to tie the cloth around the back of my head quickly and I lower it back to the pillow, seeing only black. No shapes. No nothing.

"Fucking beautiful."

His feet scrape against the floor, and my ears perk. Having no ability to touch or see, my hearing is becoming heightened. There's silence for a moment, and then the clink of his belt—a sound I'm now attuned to—and the shucking of clothing landing on the floor.

More silence. Then the sound of skin on skin, and he groans.

He's touching himself.

My insides clench and my thighs pull together, stopped only by the rope tying them apart. He's touching himself, and I want to see. Want to watch his large hand slip over himself, over his piercings. Watch his speed and how tight of a grip he uses, watch how he brings himself to the edge.

But I remain silent. My lips part, taking in as much of the lust-filled air around me as I can and use it to fuel my silence. If I speak, I don't know how he'll respond, and I won't allow this to end so quickly.

Then the noise stops and I strain, listening for his next move. A step. The dip of the bed. Anything.

But there's nothing.

Nothing, and then—

His tongue licks me from my core to the top of my clit and back down, dragging through my folds over and over. Fireworks shoot off, and my hips rock against his mouth. Unashamed cries echo around the room, as I don't hold back, chasing the orgasm he's creating.

My arms yank against the bindings but go nowhere. I want to touch him. To weave my hands in his hair and ensure he remains there until I come over and over and over.

His tongue spears me and his hands go to the insides of my thighs, forcing weight upon my body and making it so my hips can no longer follow the path he's forging. His fingers pull my folds apart, keeping me open for his continuing licks, sucks, and nips. Heat continues building, the bubble being blown up more and more until—

"I'm going to come, Hawke."

"Don't."

A simple command, but it slams into me and I don't. My orgasm remains locked away; the bubble waiting to burst, but it never does. I feel as though I could cry with how badly I wish to come.

His mouth pulls away, and I think I understand what he means by orgasm denial now. To be there, but not quite—to be stopped so abruptly. And when I believe he's done, the feeling returns. His tongue finds my clit and his lips pull tight, using suction to continue the build. But then I get full as two fingers slip inside, pumping alongside his licks.

"Damn, you're so wet," he murmurs against the inside of my leg. "Dripping for me. I think I could fit three fingers in. Should we try?"

My whimper is all the agreement he needs before my core stretches, accommodating another finger. There's little burn, but it only lasts a brief second, the pain a fraction of what I've felt in the past.

"Mm, how do you feel?"

"Like I'm going to explode."

"Not yet. I'm not quite done."

His licks turn ravenous, ferocious. His teeth get involved and he tugs on my clit as his fingers continue their agonizing pace, somehow getting deeper with every pump.

I tighten around him, the build-up being too much to handle and I'm nearly about to demand he allows me to come—punishment be damned—when he gives me the delicious relief.

"Come for me, Willow."

I do, the explosion inside me greater than I've ever felt before. His fingers and tongue both increase their speed, pumping faster, and chasing my orgasm alongside me. I scream, wanton and uncaring if his neighbours hear me.

After a long moment, my breaths die down to heavy pants and Hawke easily slides his fingers from me.

"You've soaked my bed, baby."

"Worth it." I sigh.

Hawke's body shifts over mine, and his hair drags along the skin of my stomach right before his lips trails up my inner thigh, pausing at my hip.

"How do you feel?"

I feel like rolling my eyes, but I don't tell him that since I know his question is coming from a place of care. "Fantastic."

His kisses continue, soft and barely-there. He kisses from the scars on my thighs to my hip then up to my stomach, pausing to circle my belly button before continuing straight between my breasts.

I bide my breath, hoping he'll spend some time there, and am relieved when he does. When his head shifts to the side and his lips latch onto a nipple, my shoulders roll into his touch, pushing my breast even closer; at my movement, he chuckles against my skin, casting a warm path down my body.

"If you're able to do that, I didn't tie the rope tight enough."

He trails his lips up toward my neck and stops there, licking and sucking the slope until reaching my ear where his teeth nibble lightly.

"I'm going to take the blindfold off you now. I want you to see who's inside you."

He sits up, straddling my body. His heavy cock rests on my chest as he leans in close to me to undo the bindings behind my head. I let him, but just as he begins to pull the black from my eyes, with as much neck strength I can muster, I reach for him to lick his head, collecting the salty precum on my tongue before resting on the pillow again.

His eyes blaze as he throws the blindfold to the side. "Careful how much you touch, or I might find it in me to have you suck me again."

"Please." I flutter my eyelashes and smile, thinking of the movie and how much pleasure the man had gotten from the act while the woman was at his mercy.

"That isn't smart, Willow." Hawke frowns, playfulness leaving his expression as fast as it appeared. "When I'm in your mouth, I want you to have complete control. I don't want to go too deep or too fast and be more than you can handle. We won't until your hands are untied again."

"I trust you."

He groans, aware I'm tossing his own words back at him. "Willow."

I lift my head again and manage a quick kiss on his head before my neck muscles give up and I drop back to the bed.

He groans, shifting forward on his knees, and my mouth waters with the knowledge I won. He takes himself in his hand and angles his cock at my mouth. My lips part, letting him fill it.

"I'm not sure if I'm the dominant one anymore," he mutters, "since I can't resist anything you demand." After a beat, he states, "I'll stop here. If you can take more, hold up a finger. If you want me to stop, flick your hand, and if you need me to pull back, make a fist."

I hold up a finger and he gives me another inch. When he hits the back of my throat, I flick my hand, and he pauses.

"God, you look so pretty with my dick in your mouth, Willow. So perfect."

So yours.

I moan, knowing my sounds will vibrate against him. With the angle, I'm able to feel his piercings in a new way. They scrape against my tongue, and I hollow my cheeks, gaining deeper suction.

His hips flex once before he curses and aims to pull back. Instead, I press my teeth lightly into his shaft, ensuring if he pulls away, it'll only hurt.

"It's harder," he pants, "to not move. And I refuse to choke you, especially when you're like this."

I suck harder, earning a louder moan from him, until he pulls back, completely removing himself from my mouth. I watch him, noting the drool coating his cock, and knowing I'm the one who put it there gives me a high, makes me feel powerful.

Hawke pants, his hand resting over his beating heart. "God, Willow, you're way too good at that."

"It's the first time I've ever enjoyed it." Words I believe will make him happy, but instead, the core of his eyes expands, nostrils flare, and he looks away. I suppose the reminder only does more harm than good, and disappointment lands on my chest, right over the spot he was recently kneeling over.

"I'll make sure this is the first time you'll enjoy sex too. If it becomes a repeat of last night, then we'll handle that."

He's referencing when I freaked out, but I'm determined not to this time. Alex won't ruin this more than he already has. Still, I nod, because it's the response he'll expect.

Hawke slides down my body and positions his cock at my entrance.

Remain in the present. It's Hawke. Hawke. Hawke. I repeat his name over and over until it imprints on my mind. My eyes drift close, determination making me focus harder. *Hawke. Hawke. Hawke.*

With my eyes shut, his hurried breaths are all I hear; my anxious heartbeats all I feel.

"Willow, open your eyes."

Following his command, I do, finding him braced above me. "We're not doing this unless I can stare into your gorgeous eyes. You'll see who's inside you; you'll know it's not him. You'll come with *my* cock inside you, *my* rope around your body, and *my* name on your lips. He won't weasel his way into your mind because I'll be there instead, filling every gap. I swear to fucking God, remember your safe word because I won't forgive myself if this goes badly and you don't tell me."

"I will," I whisper. "I'm scared of a repeat."

He stares at me for a second before reaching up and untying my wrists, giving me free rein of my hands again. He positions one on his shoulder while linking his hand with my other one, grasping tight.

"Hold onto me. When you feel yourself slipping, remember whose hand you're holding."

And then his hips surge forward and he enters me in one swift movement, my wetness acting as lubricant, and our shared pleasure mingles in the air.

My insides quiver, accepting his girth, his depth—*him*—and despite his order to keep my eyes open, I don't. I close them and let myself *feel*.

Feel how different this is from when Alex would rape me. Feel how my arms go slack, the one draped over Hawke falling toward the bed to grasp the blanket. Feel how when Hawke pulls back and enters me again, a moan climbs my throat because even when Hawke's claiming to be rough, it'll be impossible for him to be as rough as I'm used to.

And that's when I open my eyes.

Because Alex is gone. He's not in this bed with me. When he tied me up, it was to ensure I wouldn't run away, but with Hawke, I'm not going anywhere. Alex hated when I dug my nails into him, aware I was doing it out of spite, but with Hawke, I want to leave my mark on him as deep as the one he's leaving on me.

My mouth parts and I'm trying to tell him all this, but the only sounds I can manage are sighs and moans as Hawke moves in and out of me. I lift my hips as much as I can with my ankles tied, trying to rock with him.

"You feel me, baby? You know who's inside of you?"

"I feel *everything*." Everything—my body flexes, my heart expands, and my soul sews itself back up. My hand tightens in his, but not in doubt or fear, rather in my desire to hold on tight and never let him go.

Hawke's pace increases to a speed I never thought he'd be capable of, and my orgasm builds. Though it's hard and fast, and I yank on the ropes, my legs straining, it doesn't hurt. It doesn't burn.

When Hawke grips the strands of my hair and smashes his mouth to mine, it's not in cruelty. It's in love. I feel it. I revel in it.

I love it.

I come around his cock, crying out both my orgasm and my happiness while my pussy milks him. He doesn't slow when I'm done, continuing to pound into me and confusing my insides as the spark begins to reignite.

"You didn't come."

"Because I'm not done with you." His accompanying cocky grin heats my core all over.

He moves faster, rebuilding the fire, and just when I believe I'm going to orgasm again, he pauses, leaving me to pant in frustration. Without removing his cock from me, he manages to twist around. After a second, my ankles are untied, and I'm free to move.

"I want to feel your legs around me."

He doesn't need to order me at all; I instantly weave around his waist, ankles hooking at the small of his back, and this time, I'm able to better participate.

Participate. What a strange notion. With Alex, I remained as dead as possible, in hopes he would eventually leave me alone. Never did I lift my hips to meet his. Never did I tighten my legs around his waist to ensure he never leaves me.

That's how I know this is different. My *body* knows this

is different. It trusts Hawke.

"I won't be able to hold back this time, baby."

He takes us up the mountain together, and this time, when I orgasm, he does too, following me into the depths below.

Thirty-Three

HAWKE

Instead of falling on top of her, I immediately rub feeling back into her wrists. Even though I may have untied her for some of it, I still ensure the rope didn't leave any lasting marks. A piece of me may want to eventually see *my* marks on her, masking the scars from Alex, but not now. My goal is to never harm her, physically or mentally.

"Are you okay? Was that okay?"

Instead of answering, I see the ghost of a smile grace her mouth. *She's not mad. That's positive.* She slides over the bed and slips into my lap, settling her bare ass against my pleased cock, and I have to bite into my tongue to resist reacting to her heat.

Her arm loops around my neck and she stares at me, amusement lighting her eyes. She seems happier than she's ever been before, and that makes me fucking ecstatic. So much happened today alone and I feel as though we've climbed a damn mountain to get her to where she is now.

"Hawke, that was better than okay, but thank you for being concerned."

I'm more than concerned. "I… I'm so worried you're going to see me as him and—"

"Stop," she demands, shoving her hand over my mouth to halt my words. "Stop, Hawke. You are *nothing* like Alex, and we both know that. That," she gestures to the bed beneath us, "was nothing remotely close to what Alex would do with me. When he tied me up, it was to keep me docile, but with you, it was pure pleasure. There was never a moment of pain. I was concerned being rougher would spark something, but it didn't. Because your rough and his rough are so different; they exist on opposite planes."

I hate when she speaks of the bastard, though I know as well as anyone, it's part of her healing. She needs to discuss it, to rationalize his reasoning, and see how I'm different from him. But hearing everything he did to her makes me murderous.

Before breaking into his house, I instructed Ryker, Brent, and Tristan not to kill him. To do it the legal way, and right now, I'm pleased he's locked securely behind the walls of the RCMP because if he was still walking free, I'd give up everything to slaughter him. My career, my reputation, and even my freedom if it meant I could rid her of him.

Instead, I focus on her last words. "Good, because I wasn't all that rough. Instinct, fear, something still made me hold back."

"I'm not breakable," she shoots back, though we both know she is. She *was*. This morning, at the table, her breakdown wasn't random. It was because his evil seeped into her mental state once again.

Until now. She's healing. She's becoming mine.

"I know," I murmur, and from my heart, the next words pour out. "But maybe I am. Maybe, I finally found something—someone—I care about, and it fucking terrifies me that he'll steal you away. Not physically, but mentally." I lift my hand and brush strands of her hair off her face, clearing her flawlessness for my eyes to soak in.

"He can't anymore," she whispers, then grabs my hand. So many times, I've taken hers and laid it on my chest, but this time, it's mine she takes and covers her right breast, directly over her heart. "He can't because you put yourself in here."

"I'll kill him," I vow. "If there's the slightest chance he'll be near you again, I won't hold back."

She smiles crookedly and drops her head onto my shoulder, exhaustion starting to weigh on her. "I like the sound of that, but for now, go the legal route. I saw evidence of your successful career. You can't be losing that."

She's correct, and the reminder of today sends my stomach into happy knots. It felt natural to share a piece of myself with her like that, but it reminds me of a previous question.

"When you met Jason, you stiffened right up. Why?"

She lifts her head to look me in the eyes. "Because he reminds me of Alex. The suit, the flawless features. He's beautiful and handsome, and that's what Alex is on the outside."

Her compliment of both Jason and Alex has my hands fisting behind her back, and though I understand the point she's making, it still makes jealousy eat at my sanity, which is a new feeling. I've never had that before, and I don't quite care for it.

"I've learned with Alex that just because someone looks like that, it doesn't mean what's on the inside is evil. I know Jason isn't Alex, and that you trust him, but for me, my first instinct is to fear people who resemble him."

"I get it," I reply thickly. I do. I can spot the correlation. "When you first saw me, what did you think?"

Her eyes land on my neck before shifting to my arms and chest. Then she studies my face and based on where her eyes pause, I know she's studying my piercings.

"You're beautiful in a different way. People like Alex

are hiding an inner beast, but you don't hide who you are." Her fingers trace a black-and-white rose tattoo. "You convey yourself through art and body jewellery. When I saw you, I nicknamed you my blue-eyed angel, because that's who you are to me, Hawke. An angel who came to save me from Hell."

Blood pounds in my ears, happiness filling up the edges of my heart as she officially claims ownership over all of me.

I want to respond. Want to say pretty words to her, words only her "blue-eyed angel" would tell her, but instead, I kiss her. I convey everything to her through that kiss, and as my hand finds the back of her head, she turns in my lap, rubbing her core on me.

My cock responds to her instantly, somehow readying to go again. It's her. She brings a part of me back to life.

I believed I was healed from my own trauma, but I see now there was always a part of me waiting to be fixed by Willow. I once made fun of Ryker's ruthlessness for Elena, and Tristan's obsession with Natalie, and even Brent's vicious love for Teagan, but I get it now. I do. Because I fucking burn for Willow.

I burn for her, and I'll burn anything *for* her. Alex, this world… whatever it takes to make her happy.

Her hips rock against me, and of course, I thicken. How can I not when it's Willow who's driving lust into my body at such a rate? She moans in the back of her throat, a sound quickly becoming my favourite.

"Can you go again?" I ask her.

She nods, lifting herself on her knees to position her pussy over me. Cute. But my submissive has another thing coming if she believes she's topping me today.

With an arm around her back, I flip us until she's beneath me, her face in the bed. But I pause, waiting for her to react. Fucking a woman from behind is hot as hell and one of my favourite positions, but there's a weird feeling in my gut that senses Alex felt the same, and I'll put preferences aside for her comfort.

She twists her head to the side, catching me in her gaze, with a sly, sexy smirk. "Well?"

My hand twitches, the skin of her ass right there against my body, all but begging me to smack for that cocky comment, but I was serious earlier when I told her we won't go there. Either yet or ever, because I'm certain that'll make the memories resurface.

Instead, I shove my cock against her ass, careful not to accidentally slip in yet. "Don't forget your safe word. Angel." *Oh.* It dawns on me why she's chosen that one specifically, and it brings a smile to my face.

"I won't," she whispers then wiggles her ass, tempting me once more to leave my mark on her pale, perfect skin.

"If this is too much, you know what to do."

"I do." She sighs. She's annoyed me with me, but she's too important to lose due to miscommunication.

I mount her, stroking my cock up and down her wetness before using it to push my head inside her pussy. I pull out halfway before pushing back inside, getting deeper. She cries out instantly. I prefer this position because it allows my piercings to hit all the correct areas, and it's clear, as I gain another inch, Willow is also discovering its benefits.

"Fuck," she moans, the word being dragged out.

I smile at her inhibitions and take a hold of her hair to pull her head back. I know this won't hurt her, I pause though, listening for the safe word, but she doesn't use it. Instead, she cries out at the pressure arching her back puts on her pussy.

I speed up, hammering into her until I feel her tightening and rippling from the inside. Until her cries grow louder, and I know she's on the edge. I won't come again so soon, but this is all for her.

My free hand goes beneath her body and I find her clit and pinch it. She jerks, her hips lowering to meet my touch but then I push into her harder. My fingers stroke her back and forth, pausing to feel myself inside her, and I fucking love it more than I ever thought possible.

She's mine.

I won't keep her in a cage, or a basement, or remove her freedom. But I will damn well make sure she has everything she'll ever want or need. I'll give her the love, care, and protection she's always deserved. I'll return her independence and I'll be by her side, observing her reclaim her life like the fucking survivor she is.

It's with my last push inside her, she cries out, her sounds music in the otherwise quiet bedroom. She tightens, but I still move, dragging out her pleasure as long as possible, and only when her pants subside, do I release her hair and slide out of her.

"Well, that was nice." She laughs, slumping onto the bed, her eyes drifting shut.

"More than nice, I'd say." I drag a finger up her thigh, readying to ask her about the position, simply because I need to ensure she's fine now that the moment has passed, but then a soft snore drifts from her.

Passed out. I suppose after the emotional roller-coaster of the day, plus the number of orgasms she's had, it only makes sense. I tug the blanket over her, stepping back to clear off the rope and blindfold from earlier and simply gaze upon her.

I should go downstairs and get my work done, but that's not what's calling to me. Instead, I position myself behind her and wrap my arm around her waist.

We sleep.

Thirty-Four

WILLOW

Everything is different when I awake the next day. I feel altered. I feel human.

I feel like living and not hiding beneath a rock.

The spot on the bed beside me is empty, the sheets cool, indicating he's been up for a while. He's likely returned to work because that seems to be all he does when he's not with me.

Putting Alex away.

Sometime between the moment Hawke's cock was inside me and my orgasm, I realized it doesn't matter if Alex is found innocent. I'll kill him myself before he comes for me, even if I die in the process. Anything is better than returning to that monster.

I've wasted days being frightened, fearing every second of the day he would come for me. Fearing he'll hurt Hawke and his friends and will fuck up the little progress I've made.

None of that matters anymore. I feel *happy* for the first time in months. I feel like showering and dressing with care for once, before pouring coffee and having a regular morning discussion with the man I care for.

I'm done stressing over Alex. He's not coming back. I *must* have faith in Hawke and his plan or else I'll go nuts for the days, or weeks, until the trial. I don't want to live like this any longer.

Within a day, it feels like so much of the old me has returned, but no—not the old me. The old-new me. Because the old me was a scared little girl, determined to work and make something of herself, away from her parents. There are elements of her that have come back though, such as the willingness to leave the bedroom I've been trapping myself in out of fear.

There's still so much more of me I need to reclaim though. So much of Alex and what he did to me that I need to process. With that thought, I slide from the bed, feeling evidence of Hawke's claim on every inch of my body, and go toward the bag Elena gave me, retrieving the paper I stashed there.

The list of therapy clinics the doctor wrote out.

Hawke has suggested it a few times, and every time, I denied the idea because it'd mean speaking about what occurred to a stranger, but I think I need to. I think it'll be a final step in moving forward. Even if I hate every moment of it, I want to do this for myself and for Hawke.

First though, a shower. The air reeks of sweat and sex, and I'm sure I'm not much better.

The bedsheets could benefit from being washed, so I strip the bed and add them to the pile of dirty clothing, which presents itself as an issue. I have nothing to wear, having used my final pieces of clothing yesterday.

After a quick shower, Hawke's shirts prove useful, and I pull one over my head and tie up my wet hair before rolling all my dirty clothes inside the sheets and going to find him, which isn't challenging. The strong scent of coffee leads me into the kitchen, where I drop the bundle. The whack it makes with its weight garners Hawke's attention, taking him from his laptop.

"Morning." His eyes scan my outfit as he approaches.

I gesture to the pile at my feet, explaining, "I have no more clean clothes. The sheets will also benefit from a wash and—"

He steals my words, shoving me against the wall as he takes my breath, swapping mine for his. His hands go to my hips and he pushes the shirt up, finding me bare of panties, since they're all in the bundle at my feet as well.

"Willow, you look so delectable in my clothing. New standard. If I didn't have to work on other cases, before Jason has my head, we'd be having another round."

Probably a good thing because my insides need a break. Muscles in my stomach ache with the workout they received last night.

"How do you feel?" he checks, seriousness masking his previous humour. "After yesterday."

"Alive," I start, licking my dried lips. "I woke up feeling different than I did yesterday. Hawke, I have so much to thank you for, truly. You've brought me back and reminded me what it feels like to be normal. To be happy and not scared of everything."

"You did it yourself, Willow. Not me."

He doesn't understand. I place my hand over his heart. "You taught me to trust again. When I woke up this morning, I realized I don't care if Alex does walk free and comes for me, because I'm not going back to that hell. I'll fight him with everything I have, and if it means killing him, then so be it. If I die in the process, it's okay because it'll mean I'm free. Spending the rest of my days until the trial in fear are useless if I'm not actually *living*."

Peace consumes Hawke's expression. His shoulders untense, his eyes growing brighter, and he smiles, wider and more pleased than I've ever seen. He kisses me again, this time a quick peck.

"I'm so fucking proud of you. You fought your demons and won."

"Not completely." I pause, preparing for my next words. "I want to go to therapy. I think it'll be the final step."

"Okay." His head moves up and down quickly, if not a tad cartoony. "Would you like me to call and set you up somewhere, or we can drop by somewhere, or you can call, or—?"

I push my hand against his mouth, stopping his rambles. "How about, we first check out the list and Google the places. We'll go from there. Okay?" Without waiting for his approval, I move onto the next topic, bending for the pile of laundry at our feet. "For now, I need clean clothes because I can't wear yours forever."

"Why not?"

My eyes roll. "Funny. Where's your washer and dryer?"

Hawke gestures to the door under the stairs. "Basement. Back corner, there's a side room. In there."

It's interesting how the mere sight of the door terrified me the other day, but now, I'm not. I know what's in Hawke's basement, or more like, what isn't down there. Approaching the door without an ounce of fear, I twist the knob and enter.

I make it three stairs down before I hear, "Wait!" Hawke's footsteps thunder after me, but I continue, seeing no reason to randomly stop on the staircase.

Until I make it to the bottom and wish I had listened to him. Because I see *everything.*

Whiteboards filled with notes, lines drawn every which way, but I can't determine what they say. Notes, files, and pictures strewn across a table. Headshots of Alex—obvious even from my distance—and photos of red.

Of blood.

"Oh my God."

"Willow," Hawke utters from behind me, his anxious voice blowing over the back of my neck.

"What the fuck is all this?"

"Something I forgot about." Regret is heavy in his tone when he adds, "Something I never wanted you to see."

I stride forward, abandoning the pile of laundry at our feet and head for the table, eyes immediately taking in the images. The blood. The broken bodies.

Bile rises to the top of my throat, the excessive saliva requiring to be held in by my hand that goes to my mouth. I can't look and yet, I'm unable to look away.

"This is what he would have done," I whisper, the heavy realization crashing down on me. The picture drops from my numb fingers and I lift another one. This one depicts a woman with blonde hair. Her head is—I shut my eyes, unable to even formulate words.

Hawke's heat pounds through my back as he approaches, reaching past me and sliding the image away. He places it face down and slips between the table and me, his hands going to my shoulders, no doubt waiting for the breakdown.

Hell, *I'm* ready for it. It's bound to occur any second because this is too overwhelming to handle.

But never does. Instead, as my heart beats and blood pounds in my ears, I feel uncontrollable rage. More than I've ever felt, even when Alex tricked me into his basement, because it's the first time I feel the electricity coursing over my fingertips; the muscles clenching in my back as I imagine Alex's smug face, telling me of my future fate, but never quite understanding what he meant.

"He's a monster." More than I ever fathomed.

"He is. That's what all this is." His arm sweeps in an arc. "We've been hunting Alex for a long time. I had been following his victims for years until meeting Ryker Ames."

The familiar name of his friend momentarily stalls my flurried emotions. "Ryker?"

Hawke folds his lips before leaping into an entirely new chapter of this fucked-up story. "You probably don't remember everyone, but there's Ryker, Tristan, and Brent. Ryker was here the other day with Elena. Tristan and Brent were also in the basement when we found you. Brent was in the cage with me, in fact."

I recall people being there but not their faces.

"The three of them went to high school with Alex. So did Elena and Teagan. Once, right before graduation, Alex made a comment about Elena, causing Ryker to go apeshit on him. The abuse was bad enough to send Ryker to prison for assault.

"Alex wasn't as smart with his first victim. She had a family, and it was her family who came to me. Detectives stopped searching, but they wanted to file a civil suit against him, suing Miller Inc. for damages. By then, more previous staff had also disappeared, and I began picking up on patterns. Eventually, my search led me to Ryker."

"You didn't have detectives look into any of this?" Becoming a lawyer to help is one thing, but Hawke went full-on superhero mode.

He shrugs, glancing at the images again. "I wasn't foolish. Alex controlled a lot of the local police force, so I needed to be careful how much digging I did. After getting in touch with Ryker, he mentioned what his friends, Brent and Tristan, had also pieced together. At that point, it made sense for us to work together." His lips pull up on one side. "Common enemy and all that.

"I got Ryker released from prison earlier than he should have been and a plan we were formulating took off. Elena's friend, Natalie, we learned was Alex's recently-discovered sister, so Tristan's task was to get close to her and see if she knew anything. Brent and Teagan had history in high school, so he wanted to track her down because she and Alex dated in high school and he thought she might know shit about him—"

My brows lift.

"Long story short, Elena linked us to Natalie. Natalie led us to Teagan, who as it turned out, was still with him. Once Brent got the truth out of Teagan, she led us to you. We wouldn't have gotten to you as quick as we did if it wasn't for her."

Meaning, I owe Teagan for my freedom. I wasn't privy to their relationship, but the bit I saw showed me she was trapped exactly as I was. In some ways, worse, because her cage was larger but still as restrictive.

I owe her everything.

I owe them *all* something.

Seven people. Seven people who had a successful master plan. Ryker, Tristan, Brent, and Hawke did more than save me. They saved them *all*. Elena in the past, Natalie from whatever it would mean to be Alex's sister, Teagan from a lifetime of torture, and me from—I glance past him, toward the pile of images—death. Death in the worst form.

"You did so much."

"Yeah." He glances down at his feet before meeting my gaze again. "I didn't tell you sooner, because, well, how do you tell a person all this? I never wanted you to see what your fate could have been."

"No," I whisper, lightly rubbing my head in an attempt prevent from swaying. "No, it's fine." Because it is. "I think... I guess, I'm surprised. Shocked. Horrified. All that, but mostly, I'm angry. Angry because that was nearly me." I stab a finger toward the images. "But you all saved me from it. *Teagan* saved me."

"She did," he agrees softly. "Without her—"

Without her, you'd still be there, are his unspoken words.

Would I be? Perhaps I'd be in a dumpster or left in a forest. Perhaps I'd be just another image on Hawke's table.

They all had a part to play, and now I have mine. I see it now. I'm the final piece to the grand plan to ensure Alex does not win.

"Hawke," I murmur, finally blinking and seeing him rather than looking through him. "Hawke, I know what I need to do. I'll testify against Alex."

Thirty-Five

WILLOW

It's been three days since I told Hawke I'd testify, and he's been on the phone for most of it, though I'm not entirely sure what for. Sometimes, I hear Ryker's name being thrown around, sometimes Jason, and sometimes Teagan's.

Hawke told me earlier that she's in the hospital, healing from Alex's mental torture, and then I think about what he told me in the basement the other day, about her being his girlfriend in high school. She likely had no idea the monster she was getting into bed with.

Alex has negatively affected so many lives. An inappropriate joke back in high school—except it wasn't really a joke—landed a man in prison. Alex's evilness made him turn on his own sister. His villainous nature created a "girlfriend" persona of Teagan for the rest of the world, while behind closed doors, he was the man I knew him to be.

I was a mere piece of his crime, which is why, three days later, I'm firm in my decision, and even a bit regretful I didn't make it sooner. If other people found strength—Teagan included—to fight back, then I should be able to as well.

"Ready?"

Hawke's question pulls me from my musings and I blink at the building we've stopped in front of.

Bridgetown Trauma Centre.

Of the list, a trauma centre seemed the most appropriate, if not a bit more terrifying than the rest. Hopefully, my story fits along with the others told within those four walls and I won't stand out too much.

We phoned yesterday and got an appointment set right up. Apparently, the hospital forwarded a referral to each of the places and they've been waiting for me to call, so it expedited the process. Something I'm both thrilled and anxious about.

"Want me to come in with you? I can wait in the waiting room, if you'd like."

Yesterday, I asked if he could come right into the therapy room with me, and for the first time ever, Hawke turned down one of my requests, claiming therapy would be better experienced if I were alone. That way, I could speak about anything, even things I haven't described to him.

At first, I hated his decision, but as I sit in the passenger seat today, staring at the pretty, brick building, I realize it's the correct decision. He's helped me through so much of my healing, but this next part, I need to do alone.

"No, I'm good."

When I lean over the console to kiss him goodbye, his smile is blinding, but his eyes are a mix of pride and concern. I understand his apprehension though, but I don't think he needs to worry.

I will be fine.

I can do this.

"Text me when you're done and I'll be here. I'm going to the office and it's only a couple blocks away."

Yesterday, Hawke also surprised me with a phone. I'm honest enough to admit I wept over the small piece of technology. I hadn't realized how much I missed possessing one. Not having the access to social media never bothered me, since I didn't care much for it, but the simple act of owning a device that everyone else does signifies I'm *back*.

Striding from the car takes a lot of strength, but I climb the couple of steps and open the centre's front door. Before entering, I wave goodbye, ensuring I'm smiling, so when he drives away, he's confident in my ability to handle this.

I head straight into the waiting room, a small-ish room with a couple of padded chairs and a front desk; a woman sits behind it, tapping on a computer.

She smiles as I enter, emitting only warmth. "Hello, how may I help you?"

"I-I have an appointment. With a therapist." *Idiot. What else would you be here for?*

The receptionist doesn't seem to notice or care about my blunder, and checks the computer screen, "Willow Avery?"

"That's me."

From her drawer, she retrieves a small packet of paperwork and slips it onto a clipboard before sliding it over the desk to me. A pen soon follows, and she gestures to the empty chairs behind me. "Please fill out this paperwork, answering to the best of your ability. The key form is the first one, your consent to receive counselling. I'll let your therapist know you've arrived, so when you're finished with the paperwork, you can go right in."

I nod and take the packet she's holding out to me, finding the nearest chair to fill it out in. The pen is hefty in my hand, reminding me of when I'd write notes to Hawke and send them under the door.

Signing my consent is easier than I initially thought, and the other forms are pretty standard. Name, address, stuff like that. The line asking for my phone number brings a smile to my face as I jot down my new one. The spot requesting my email I leave blank. No doubt, Alex deactivated my previous email account, and really, anything in there is from my old life, which I no longer want.

I fill them out quickly and return them to reception. The moment I do, an older lady appears at the entrance of the attached hallway, a gentle, easing smile calling to me.

"Willow? I'm Brenda, if you'd follow me, please."

She leads me down a short hallway and into the second office on the right, closing the door behind us.

"Please take a seat."

I choose the couch closest to the door, which will allow for a quick escape, should I want to flee.

Brenda tracks me before claiming the seat across from me. Her brows are lifted slightly and I have no doubt, she's mentally noting my actions. Seems like the place where they'd do that.

"Hi, Willow. As mentioned, my name is Brenda. I'm very happy you've come today. You've made a very brave choice, and we strive to make this a welcoming environment where you'll feel comfortable with sharing your story. This first session is really so I can gather your information and why you've come. Feel free to share as much or as little as you wish to, though. The key here is there is no pressure to talk. If you wish to spend the next few sessions chatting about animals until you feel okay enough to open a bit more, so be it. That's what we'll do. Everything said in this room remains between you and me. I do have to report to the appropriate channels if you admit to harming yourself, others, children, or pets."

At the end of her spiel, the tension in my stomach unknots the slightest fraction. She reminds me a bit of Hawke, like she could be his mother. It's in how she claims to not want to rush things.

Given what this centre does, I'm sure many people

come in not wanting to speak, and while that might be me too, to a degree, I'm ready. I'm here for a reason, and if I wasn't open to talking, I would never have made the appointment.

"Before we get started, there's always something I like to tell people who come through here. Often, we see trauma in one way and one way only, as though there's a correct way to experience it. But that's not the case. Trauma affects us all differently, and how you experience it doesn't make you weak in any way. When you feel as though you're not making the progress you should be, shove that thought aside. Move on when *you're* ready to, not when you think you have to."

I ponder her words for a moment, linking them to how I was able to be physical with Hawke, even after some trial and error. And how I'm here, ready to admit my story.

"That's helpful," I tell her softly. "Thank you." Straightening, I begin, "I don't know what kinds of stories you get here, so maybe mine isn't that different. Maybe it's not as bad, or maybe it's worse, but I am ready to tell it, and tell it all. Up until three days ago, I fought against the concept of therapy, figuring I wouldn't want to discuss it with a stranger, but after recent events, I think I need to. For myself, for my future, and for what will be soon coming when the trial begins."

At my mention of a trial, her brows lift slightly, but she doesn't say anything, giving me the floor to continue.

Then I tell her everything. My past, my job at Miller Inc., the day Alex invited me to his house and how that ended, the first rape, the first time he shared me, all the way to the final rape, right before Hawke and his friends discovered me. I admit believing that moment was a dream, even though I was nearly strangled. I talk about the hospital and how I didn't wish to speak with even the doctors, how I believe Alex will return for me, and the journey I took from fearing that outcome to nearly wanting it—if only to end it all. I spoke about Elena's visit, and the moment I ran away. I tell her everything about Hawke. From when he lifted me in his arms, the ambulance and then the hospital, and taking me home, giving me his room, space, friendship, and later love. I discussed the moment we first kissed, the first time we did anything sexual, and our initial attempt at sex. With a hot blush, I recounted his idea of porn and the other sexual practices he suggested, and the next successful attempt. I discussed visiting his office and meeting Jason and Brittany, and the emotions they dragged up. And finally, I spoke about waking the other day, wanting to come here before I found the basement and Hawke admitted how long he has been trying to nail Alex. I told her about the moment it all hit, how everyone played their part, and I'm ready for mine. How coming here today was another step for me, but also for everyone else. Finally, I told her how I wanted to get this all out to a single person before an entire courtroom.

And when I finish, Brenda speaks one word: "Wow."

There's a dried tear line down her cheek, evidence my story does carry a lot of weight and power with it. Evidence that even while I'm at a trauma clinic, the counsellors are mere humans, who choose to listen to other's horrors and take it all home with them, knowing what kind of evil exists in the world.

It makes me feel a bit better.

Even just disclosing it all lifts a weight off my shoulders and I breathe easier than I have in six months. I see now that for all Hawke's done for me, this step was impossible for me to achieve with him. I *needed* this—to admit everything to a stranger and let them process it alongside me. Simply speaking it aloud, sharing my horrors outside the closed circle of people who presently know, is empowering.

It happened to me. It's in the past, but I'm ready for

the future.

Brenda sits forward, her face pinched with discomfort and pain. She wipes at her cheek, removing yet another tear before saying, "You started that by wondering what kinds of stories I've heard before. Nothing like that. All clients' pasts are theirs—their horrors—but you've been carrying so much, so much more. You—he—wow." She coughs lightly. "Sorry, you've rendered me a bit speechless for the moment, but I need to ask you something. A few times, you've mentioned needing to recount your story to someone, and now that you have, how do you feel?"

"Relieved."

"You've made more progress in a day than some clients make in months." She smiles gently, glancing at the empty pad in her hand. I can't even imagine what she'll attempt to make her notes about. "But I can see there's still a lot to work through, and I'm very pleased you've chosen us to help you. We can continue today, or you can go. I think, considering everything you've unleashed, you deserve a break."

Somehow, I feel more energized than ever. I suppose it's the outcome of lifting so much weight off my shoulders, but I appreciate her understanding of everything.

"All right. Sorry for saying all that."

She chuckles. "Willow, please do *not* apologize. What you've survived is heartbreaking and amazing all at the same time. It's a testament to your strength, and while I shouldn't admit this—professional and all," she rolls her eyes, "I will. When the trial begins, we can discuss anything leading up to it and after it, but for your sake and the sake of everyone else, I better see the news reporting his imprisonment."

For some reason, that makes me laugh. Perhaps because I was expecting strict professionalism when I arrived here, not a sympathetic human being. Maybe that's also how I was able to reveal all I did. Brenda's a person like the rest of us, with the same emotions.

"Thank you. Nice to know more people are on our side."

Her eyes get this faraway look when she murmurs, "Had more people known the truth about Alex Miller, I think you'd have more support than you believe you do."

"I hope you're right because now there's a jury to appeal to."

"They'll make the correct decision."

She can't know that for certain, but again, her words are appreciated.

"Can I come back next week?" I pull out my phone to bring up the calendar. Not that I have such a busy life I couldn't remember my one and only appointment, but simply adding it in makes me feel alive.

She stands and goes to the small desk in the corner, bringing up her own schedule. She clicks through a few pages before replying, "I have the same time available next week, if you'd like."

"That'd be great." I stand, after adding the appointment to my calendar. "Thank you so much."

I exit her office and bring up my messaging app. There are only two numbers in my phone, Elena's and Hawke's, and I click Hawke's name.

Me: *Done.*

But before shutting the app and going outside, I study Elena's name.

Thirty-Six

HAWKE

"Is it weird that I've never seen this place?" Tristan scans my office as he leans back in one of the two chairs that are placed on the other side of my desk.

Ryker reaches over and shoves at him. "Next time, you be the one to get arrested and maybe you could have."

After Ryker was released, there were times I had him down here for paperwork purposes.

I observe the banter between these two, frowning with the knowledge I'm about to break up their cheeriness.

After dropping Willow off at the counselling clinic, I hadn't lied when I said I'd be coming to my office. I simply left out a key part—that I'd be meeting Tristan and Ryker here as well. I invited them earlier after finding something that could change everything.

Before starting, I take a final pointless glance toward my phone, seeking the response I'd hoped I'd get after messaging Brent earlier.

Me: *Hey, there's something you may want to see if you'd like to come home.*

No response.

Reaching inside my desk drawer, I retrieve the note I

found taped to my front door this morning. Thank fucking Christ, I found it and not Willow. I toss it onto the desk, interrupting their banter.

Two sets of eyes zero in on it.

"What's that?" Tristan asks, leaning forward.

"Read it."

He picks it up, unfolds the paper and quickly scans the words, his eyes bulging with every pass before flipping it so Ryker can read it too. Ryker takes it but skims it slower, actually reading each individual word.

Mr. Blackwood,

Seems like we have a common interest. I've been made aware my girl is in your care. I feel as though I should thank you for healing her. She'll be so much stronger for when I come for her, I'll be able to begin the process all over. As for you, I'll see you in court, I suppose. I'll enjoy watching you be shredded apart and forced to stand aside as I reclaim her. You come for us, you die. You show this to <u>anyone</u> in the system and I'll have a bullet put in Teagan's forehead. Don't think about submitting this into evidence.

A.M.

Ryker's eyes slide up to me. "Fuck."

"Yeah." My lips press together. "That was taped to my door this morning."

"Fuck," Tristan echoes, snatching the note back. "*Fuck.* So, he knows then. He knows about you, who you are, where you live, and where Willow is. How?"

"The other day, I saw something outside my house. A brief flash, like from a camera, but I thought I was imagining it honestly." Beneath the desk, hidden from them, I fist my hands, fuming that I've ignored signs I shouldn't have.

"He has eyes on Teagan too," Ryker murmurs. "Brent can never know this, or else he'll lose his shit. Teagan either, I think. We need to warn the hospital."

"We do nothing," I decide firmly, hating every word I speak, knowing that right now, Alex continues to maintain a hold on the authority he wields. "I refuse to call his bluff and risk Teagan. We say nothing, we do nothing." I stare at both of them, eyes bouncing between them. "Hear me? Natalie and Elena will not know about this because we can't risk them doing something. Alex clearly has people on the inside, so I'm not risking her life."

Tristan tosses the note back on my desk, leaving it among the three of us, none of us willing to look at it again. "You're not telling Willow then, I assume."

"You assume correctly. I won't let her know she's being watched." It's the *exact* fucking fear she's had from the very beginning. The fear I've been reassuring her that she doesn't need to have. This entire time, she's been right; someone has been watching her.

"She'd lose herself again," Ryker mutters, crossing his large arms.

I want to deny his words, to yell at him for daring to be negative about her, but he's telling the truth, and I know it. If Willow learned that Alex knows where she is, she'll be swept away by her anxieties and horrors.

And I'd lose her.

I refuse to allow that to happen.

"Yeah," I finally agree. "That's why this stays between us. We continue moving toward the trial as though nothing is amiss. Pretend this note doesn't exist. Keep your eyes open though. He still holds power here, and one step out of line, we risk both girls—at minimum." I won't verbalize that at any point he can come after Elena and Natalie, but I'm sure they understand my implication. "It's a price not worth paying. He'll lose in court, he'll get locked away, and then we won't have to worry about this shit again."

I grasp the note, shoving it in a desk drawer, and by the time the drawer shuts again, Tristan and Ryker are both nodding their agreement.

Thirty-Seven

The morning after counselling, I sip my second coffee as I watch Hawke at his laptop. I need a hobby because, while Hawke is working, I'm left to my own devices. It reminds me of being upstairs, hiding alone in his bedroom; except now, I wander the house, talk a bit at the table with him, and just recount my life leading up to my job at Miller Inc. Things I wanted, goals I had because now they're all possible again.

I study Hawke, watching as his eyes flick around his laptop screen, and fall for him all over again. Because of his appearance, society would deem him an outcast, lazy, and unmotivated to do anything else than work a dead-end job, but he's amazing. He puts so much attention onto his cases. He becomes a whole other person in the way his eyes darken with an intense concentration. The pen in his hand is almost always tapping against his lip ring, and I've taken to understanding it means he's thinking intensely.

For the millionth time since yesterday, I glance at my phone, considering the other person's number programmed in there. It seems like such an excellent idea, one I believe Brenda would approve of. It almost feels as though I'm working off some imaginary list.

The How-To Have A Life Again list.

Still, I lift the phone, tap Elena's number, and wait as it brings up the messaging app.

You're insane to do this.

Me: *Hi. It's Willow. This is my number. Hawke got me a phone.*

Elena: *Hi! I've been thinking about you. How are you?*

Me: *Alive… thanks to you. I was thinking about your offer.*

Oh, my fuck, this is so awkward. How do people make friends? Reaching out randomly to them isn't the way. She has her own life, and never wanted me to be a part of it. No doubt, her words the other day were out of loyalty to Hawke and she never meant them.

Elena: *Say no more! I'm kicking Ryker out. You can come over right now, if you'd like.*

Glancing up from the phone, I slide my chair closer to Hawke, getting his attention without directly interrupting his process.

"Hi." He smirks. "Your expression says you want something."

"A ride." I press my lips together, wondering how to formulate the randomness of my next statement. "I texted Elena."

That pulls his attention completely away from his laptop. He drops the pen to ask, "Oh yeah?" He acts blasé in how his expression remains flat, but I know him well enough to recognize his excited energy.

"Yeah." I feel like a teenager asking her parents to go out with friends, and I wish we were more normal, and that it'd be as simple as tossing a quick, *"Hey, I'm going over to Elena's."*

Hawke shuts his laptop. "Absolutely. Let's go."

I message Elena back right away. **Me:** *We'll be right over. Thank you.*

The drive over is short and Hawke pulls into a pleasant neighbourhood, similar to the one we left behind and stops in front of an even nicer house.

"Elena's?" I check.

"Ryker's officially. They moved in together a month back, or so." Before exiting, he reaches for my hand, clasping it tight and pressing a soft kiss to my palm that has my insides heating for entirely other reasons. "You're living again, *il mio bella ragazza*. It makes me delighted."

I touch his cheek, wading through the deep emotion in his eyes. "I have you to thank for restarting my heart, my sanity… my soul."

After another deep kiss, packed full of longing, and a promise he'll be back later tonight, we exit the car at the exact moment the front door slams shut and feet pound on the cement pathway.

Elena pulls to a stop, her eyes flicking between the two of us, her hands barely contained by her side. "I'm really ecstatic you took me up on my offer, and I hope you don't mind, but I also invited Natalie over." Her thumb looks over her shoulder and I follow her gesture toward the house, noticing the other woman standing in front of the door.

Natalie. Alex's sister.

Dark hair falls halfway down her back, but it's the only feature I can make out from over here. With her slow wave, my heart rockets against my chest.

Will she remind me of Alex? Hawke and Elena trust her, and she helped them take down her own brother but—

"It's fine," I push out, biting down on the fear.

"And Ryker?" Hawke rumbles.

"Left with Tristan. I think they're going to continue trying Brent's phone till he picks up."

"It won't work," Hawke comments.

Elena shrugs. "We both know that, and I think they

do too, but they're trying."

My gaze snowballs between them, trying to decipher what they're discussing. Seems Hawke left something out about one of his friends, but I guess, there are so many details, it'd be difficult for him to recount them all, especially when they're about people I've only heard of in passing.

Whatever the situation is gets pushed aside when Hawke presses a kiss to my forehead. Heat spreads across my cheeks and down my chest with Elena's scrutinizing look.

"Remember what I said?" When I nod, he flicks his eyes to Elena. "The moment she decides she wants out, you stop the conversation and call me."

Her arms cross over her chest, and for a moment, I think she's offended, but then a smile breaks out and she laughs. "You're hilarious, Hawke, after all the shit you gave us all about getting together. And here you are with Willow."

"Guess I needed to find the right person." But he doesn't say it to her. Rather, his eyes are locked on me.

Fire blazes between us, and my lips part. The world falls away in favour of Hawke and I reach for him.

Elena's cough interrupts the fog, and she sidles closer. "Not to break that up or anything, but…"

Hawke glances at Elena and then me before his head jerks in a rapid nod. "Right then. I'll leave. Have fun."

He climbs back into his car but waits while Elena leads me up the path and past Natalie, who's holding open the front door. I pause at the entranceway, glancing back. He won't leave until the door's shut, and he definitely won't go if he sees anxiety on my face, so I school my features and give a quick wave before letting Natalie close the door.

Once the door shuts, it's as though all my anxiety is left at the door because there's no way I can be stressed now. There's a vibe in this house that indicates trust, so I breathe deeply, taking the scent into my lungs.

It's a simple entranceway, much like Hawke's, connecting to a hallway that leads to the rest of the house.

Then I notice how I'm being stared at through two sets of eyes, watching me like I'm a ticking bomb and they're the ones who'll determine if I blow or not.

"Hey, um," Elena steps forward, "sorry for inviting Natalie. I wasn't trying to stress you out, but I thought maybe two girls might be better than one. Less focus on you and all that, but she can go and—"

"No," I interrupt quickly, glancing at the second girl. "No, I was telling the truth. It's fine."

Natalie is extremely pretty. Her dark hair is the exact shade of Alex's, and their eyes are nearly identical. It's easy to see the similarities in the siblings, but there's one obvious difference between them.

While Natalie's eyes may be the same shade as her brother's, they aren't packed with a dark evil indicating treacherous plans. Rather, the brown is a soft, natural colour, warm and inviting, filled with only an obvious goodness.

I make that next large step and stick my hand out for Natalie to shake. She takes it, but the spiked brows and wide eyes tell me she's surprised. She slowly shakes it before releasing me.

"I never realized Alex had a sister."

Her gaze goes to the floor and she shifts her feet. "I hadn't known him for long, and it wasn't until very recently, I learned about his... habits." Slowly, her eyes lift to mine, mouth pressing together in discomfort. "I know I had no part, but I'm sorry for what my brother did. I believe he was a product of our father's training—not that I ever knew the man. I'm suspecting a psycho sired another psycho."

"But we're ending that line, right? It won't matter

soon."

"We're?" she squeaks.

I open my mouth, but Elena interrupts, gesturing to the house beyond. "Why don't we take a seat in the living room. It's much more comfortable for a conversation like this one." She spins on her heel and I follow her and Natalie into a small living room, with a couch and TV. Pop and crackers are set out on the coffee table in the centre of the room.

Elena's cheeks bloom pink. "Sorry, I wasn't sure if you'd be hungry or not. Sometimes having a drink gives your hands something to do."

"Thank you." I take a can and lower myself onto one side of the couch, pressing as close as I can to the arm. Natalie takes the other end and Elena plops on the floor, facing us, and crosses her legs before relaxing backward on her arms.

"I just want to say," she starts, "how happy I was when you reached out. When I left you my number, I didn't think you'd want to use it, but you're here. Second, we don't have to talk about what happened to you if you don't want to. We're here to do whatever you want."

My lips curl in a faint smile to show my gratitude. "Thanks, but I think I need to talk about it. I won't be able to get through today unless I say something. Elephant in the room and all that." I flick my gaze toward both of them before focusing on the snack tray, talking to it instead of them. "Hawke told me everything you all went through to get me. How Alex has been an issue in your lives since high school. It's what made me decide to testify."

I straighten, even setting the canned drink on the floor at my feet. "I don't want to hide away my entire life, fearing the jury will find him innocent and he'll take me again. I'll go on that stand and recount everything needed to convict him, because what he did to me is unimaginable."

Elena lowers her eyes, focusing on my feet rather than my face. "Teagan told us what she went through. How she lived through every woman he dragged down there."

I nod, hearing her but also not hearing the exact words. "In some ways, Teagan had it worse than me—than we all did—because she had to witness everything and couldn't help. In other ways, he only harmed her when he was angry. I was—" Tears prick my eyes, stinging them, and I swallow, my throat making a vicious gulp. "—I was his fucking game. His toy for whenever he wanted. If he was angry, I paid the price in blood. Choking, cutting, starvation, beating… If he was horny, I was raped in the vilest ways. If he was in a good mood, he treated me like a pet, touching me gently and saying pretty words to me before he claimed parts of my body that were never his to take."

Elena's eyes swell, growing wide with emotion, and Natalie's drops to her fisted hands, but I see the tears falling down her cheeks too. Only for a moment because then my own blur my gaze.

I don't wipe them away. I don't stop talking. I don't because I realize I haven't had a solid cry yet. Even yesterday, with Brenda, I somehow managed to tell her everything without a single tear being shed.

I need this.

"Hawke doesn't know any of these details, only what I've chosen to tell him. I've been limiting the descriptions, so please don't tell him. Don't tell him how I was lured to Alex's house with the promise of a drink after a job well done, and then his basement to get another bottle of wine. Once we hit those bottom steps, he dragged me past the wine cellar and locked me into that glass cage. He took the clothes I was wearing, ripped them off me, and burned them." I huff at the old memories and what they meant then. "He burned them to represent how I'd wear nothing ever again. It was cold in that basement. Twice over the six months, I got sick and both times were in the beginning. He didn't let up ever. He—"

I stop talking, opting to skip over the parts when he made me choke on his cock with a congested nose and nearly killed me from lack of oxygen. Or when my head was pounding, he yelled at me and tossed me around, uncaring about the agonizing pain.

"After that, being sick wasn't an option, but I was lucky because my body had been trained then to deal with the cold and starvation. He fed me once a day, since he didn't like his women too skinny or malnourished." Again, I snort. "I suppose I *am* lucky because I did get food. It wasn't great, but it was food nonetheless. There was no part of me he didn't touch. Inside, outside, it didn't matter. He stole my virginity and reveled in it. He raped my ass, used every sort of toy, tool, and weapon imaginable on my body. For hours at a time, he'd hang me up, leaving me to dangle. What he did to me... I wouldn't wish on the worst person in the world, besides him. There were no acts of humanity. Alex isn't *human*." My hands tighten on my lap with the word, and I wish for that pop can again, for something to clench. Instead, with my thumb, I brush over old, fading markings on my wrists, drawing upon the scars to continue.

"Just when I thought it couldn't get worse, it did. He dragged me upstairs, and I was so relieved with the warmth. He brought me into his office. I was foolish though. I tried to run but didn't get far. His friend caught me at the door, and then..." I pause, swallowing to wet my dry throat. "Then they both punished me. When his friend left, I was brutally beaten for trying to get free. So," I shrug, lost in old memories, "it's the last time I tried to run. After that, there were four other instances he brought me to his office. Each time, I was shared.

"Alex was very open in telling me he only keeps women for six months. On the day of my sixth month, I was so hopeful it would be over. I no longer feared death since it would be an escape. No matter how painful he'd make it, it would be worth it, knowing after the pain, it'd be over. Then he claimed I wasn't broken yet and he'd be keeping me alive for another six months. *God*," I groan the word, "I felt broken. Elena. Natalie." Finally, I focus my eyes on them, but still, they're a blur behind a mask of tears. "I wanted to *die*. I begged him to let me go, but instead, he raped me. Cut me. And just when he was going to do more, the doorbell rang, and my life changed."

"We showed up," Natalie murmurs, wiping at her eyes.

My dry lips crack with my smile. "Yeah. You all showed up, and somehow, stopped him. Saved me. Took me from captivity and put me in a new form of hell. Hell, because suddenly I had to live. Society would expect me to return to work. Hawke wanted me to leave his room. You offered me friendship. But how could I do any of that, after what I lived through? I didn't want to leave the room, didn't let Hawke inside until I had a nightmare and he entered on his own accord."

I stop talking, thinking about that night. And then the other nightmare, which resulted in him staying the night.

"Hawke's helped me so much. I *feel* again. I want to live and not be scared about Alex's possible return. If it happens, I refuse to return to Hell after I've seen what else this world has to offer. I won't lose Hawke, or my freedom, or even… you."

Out of the corner of my eye, I see two figures move. Two blurs approach me on the couch and wrap their arms around my body: one at my waist and the other around my neck. Their eyes are wet against my heated skin.

Together, we cry.

Together, we forge a bond.

Two strangers become the other piece I'm missing.

Thirty-Eight

I don't know how much time passes before they release me. Or I release them, I'm not entirely certain.

"I'm sorry, I wasn't planning on releasing all that."

"We heard a lot from Teagan, but your story…" Elena trails off, wiping at her eyes. "I'm so damn sorry that happened to you, but thank you for telling us. We won't say anything to Hawke." She and Natalie share a look, a smirk growing on both their faces. "We saw you two outside. No doubt he'd go apeshit."

"And we need his head straight for the trial," Natalie comments.

"He knows about the other men and didn't react well. He's been so good to me. He's patient, and kind, and… everything."

Elena gives me a knowing look. "You love him."

I do love him. I haven't loved anyone ever. My family was shit, I had no one in my life, and I most definitely never loved Alex. But with Hawke, it's as if my heart expanded and every time we're together, it only gets bigger. He understands me.

"I do," I whisper, my hands knotting again. "I think

I do."

"Have you told him?" Natalie asks.

My hand goes to my chest, over my heart. "I think he feels it, but I haven't said the words yet."

Elena takes up a position on the couch beside me, putting inches of space between us again. "We'll keep your secret then, for now."

"Thank you."

Two strangers and they know more than Hawke does after weeks in his house, but this feels right. It's nice to have girlfriends to tell our secrets to, knowing they will remain undisclosed.

"Thank you," I repeat, this time for a different reason. "For hearing me out. For keeping my secrets. For welcoming me." I gesture toward the food, a chuckle rising past the previous misery. "For welcoming me with food."

Elena twists to look at Natalie briefly before they both face me. When Elena speaks, it's a quiet murmur. "This might seem weird, and perhaps a bit forward, but we want you here with us. Consider us friends, if you will. I-I don't do the friend thing really. In high school, I had one close one—Teagan—and now, in university, Natalie. I've always been content with one person to be semi-close to. I've never been that girl who needed a group, but," she shrugs, "maybe it's because I never found my group. I have Teagan again, and Nat… and you."

I'm still processing her flurry of words when Natalie leans closer and picks up the mantle. "Other than Elena, I don't do friends either. When Tristan dragged me into this, I realized bigger things were going on. Things I was linked to based on genes alone. I want to know Teagan eventually, and you." She lays her hand over my clenched ones, right overtop scars, but I don't pull away. Instead, the heat of her palm relaxes the tight muscles.

"Basically," Elena starts again, "what we're trying and

failing to say is we're here for you. If you need to talk or want a damned sleepover, you're not alone. You're not in that cage."

I'm learning that. Every day, a new element is freed from Alex's hold, and now, with Elena and Natalie, Alex's hold loosens even more.

"So, Hawke mentioned how all this came to pass, and that a bunch of you went to high school, but what's the exact stories of how you and Ryker came to be, and," I glance at Natalie, "you and Tristan?"

They laugh and jump into some crazy-ass, hilarious stories.

The door crashes open and there's a thundering of feet echoing down the hall. Elena straightens from where she's leaning against the far wall, surrounded by a wall of snack foods and pop cans. Given the hours that have passed, she's been binge eating.

At the entrance of the living room, a large figure moves, his eyes locked on Elena. Ryker swipes aside a bunch of the packaging and drops beside her, instantly pulling her on his lap.

I watch them, recalling everything Elena told me about their situation. A story she believes is fucked up, considering how she enjoyed his attention, but it's theirs. I mean, getting his friend to date her is a bit messed up, but even as I watch them now, it's easy to see why he did it; why he was frightened of losing her while he was locked up. When Ryker stares into her eyes, I spot their love.

I'm so distracted watching them, I miss the tall dark-haired guy stride by me and drop in the seat between Natalie and me, pushing himself close to her. His arm goes around the back of the couch, cradling her into his chest, and he kisses her long and deep.

Another unique situation, where she fell in love with her stalker—both versions. During the daytime, when he was simply Tristan, the cop and her protector, and also when he was her "nighttime visitor," as she referred to him. Messed up, but all in all, a brilliant plan that worked out for them both. Natalie pulls back from the kiss, her cheeks pink, and like Elena and Ryker, there's only love in her gaze.

More steps continue and Hawke approaches the couch by my side, propping himself on the arm. His hand finds the back of my neck and he lightly strokes the skin in a way meant to be calming.

Our eyes collide. In their bright depths, a familiar look enters them. One I just watched inside Ryker and Tristan's eyes. Love. He loves me, but like me, hasn't said the words aloud.

"How many hours have passed?"

"A few," Hawke responds, smirking. He glances at the other girls. "I get the sense they tortured you to keep you here."

"Did not." Elena sticks out her tongue. "We had a lot to talk about."

"It's true," I mutter, so quiet only Hawke can hear me.

His hand shifts from my neck to my hair, where he lightly plays with the strands. Not in a way like Alex would when he pet me, but rather like he can't help but touch me in some way.

"This is nice," Natalie comments, scanning the room. "Us all together like this. I suppose I have Alex to thank for one thing."

"Not all of us," Ryker rumbles from beneath Elena. "Can't find Brent."

"And Teagan's in the hospital," Elena chimes in. "But

soon. Soon, we'll all be together." She looks toward me, a question in her gaze.

Together. I know what she's asking. If, after Brent and Teagan return to them—to us—if I'll still be willing to come around.

"Together," I agree, and lift my pop can to my mouth.

She smiles, understanding my message, and from the corner of my eye, I spot Natalie winking over Tristan's shoulder.

"For now," Hawke starts, "we finish this thing and get that bastard sent to prison."

Thirty-Nine

WILLOW

One Month Later

Moron, this is a horrible idea. Why would you do this to yourself?

The brush drags roughly through my strands, once, twice, and again until I'm satisfied it's smooth enough. I tie it up, then instantly yank the band out and let the strands fall down my back.

It's too much hair.

I swoop it in a bun, clearing my face. Clean and honest. The jury will appreciate that.

But now I can't use it to hide.

I remove the bun and the hair tumbles over my shoulders again.

All the movement from doing and redoing my hair causes the simple dress Elena and Natalie suggested I buy for today to hike up. Growling, I readjust it and rub my hands down my sides a few times as I scan myself. High-necked with a collar to not show any skin and cause the jury to believe shit like that I asked for it—a disgusting possibility we all agreed it best to prevent—but now the collar feels stifling and I tug on it, wishing I could stretch the material.

The makeup isn't right.

With the eyeliner pencil in hand, I draw over the faint line already there, making it bolder. I do the same with the other before huffing. *Now I look like I'm ready for a club.* The makeup is too forward and I need to—

Two hands wrap around my wrists, long fingers tugging the pencil away from me. In the mirror, I watch as Hawke approaches me from behind, his sad but knowing eyes meeting mine through the reflection. He shakes his head, his styled long strands skirting his brows.

"You're stressing, baby. You look perfect."

"The jury will—"

"Will nothing, *il mio bella ragazza,*" he cuts in smoothly, before grasping my hips and turning me to face him. "You're perfect and the jury will see that. Their judgement will not be based on what you look like. Trust me."

"But—"

This time he kisses me, his soft lips molding over my lipstick, and I groan, partially frustrated with his insistence to shut me up and partly with the lust travelling to my core.

"None of that. Not right now." He pulls back, smiling, and his brows slowly lift as his eyes bounce over my face. I notice the lack of piercings, not only in his brow, but his nose and lips too. The suit he wears is immaculate and covers most of his tattoos. With his high collar and long sleeves, only hints of the lines can be seen.

"Tonight, it'll be you and me only," he adds.

"All night long?"

"All fucking night long," he agrees. "For now, we need to get to the courthouse."

The courthouse where Alex will be. And the judge and jury, who will make the ultimate decision I've been fearing. Alex's lawyers will stare me down as I recount my story.

Brenda and I have been discussing today for some time, and yesterday, I left her office feeling completely prepared, but now that the day has come, I'm not.

In the audience, behind Hawke will be everyone else—Ryker and Elena, Tristan and Natalie, and Brent and Teagan—both of who returned only a couple days ago. Barely enough time to settle before Hawke was yanking them away for this trial.

I haven't seen Teagan yet, even if I want to, but until the trial passes, I'd prefer not to be distracted. Although the weeks have been great, the closer we've come to today, the more scattered-brained I've been.

"You remember how this will go? Tell me, so I know you know."

Protective as always. "You'll do your stuff, present the evidence and such, and then you'll bring me out to speak to the jury."

He nods, his hands finding my biceps. "Yes, and then you can let me know if you want to stay and watch the verdict."

I already have my answer. As gratifying as it would be to watch, I can't. What if Alex does indeed remain free? I'll have to witness what he threatened when getting carted by us—to steal me away again.

Hawke tilts his head toward the door. "Let's go."

I'm waiting in a fancy room, and I've been here for nearly an hour. Hawke's showing the evidence to the courtroom, and the judge would prefer Teagan and me, as witnesses, not be in the courtroom during that time.

The door clicks as it unlocks, the heavy maple wood falling open, and Hawke's distinct black hair is the first thing I see.

I rush him, needing to feel his body against mine. If

he's here, it means it's nearly my turn to take the stand and the thought has my insides doing somersaults, in fear, anxiety, and excitement.

As I loosen my grip, I notice how hollow his eyes are, how frazzled his normally perfect hair is, and my stomach drops alongside my smile.

"It's not going well," I deduce, barely louder than a whisper.

"No, it's not that, it's just," he sighs, "a lot. Alex's lawyer isn't countering much, which tells me it's because they have nothing to counter with. Which is a good thing."

"So why do you look like hell?"

"Because there's so much on the line. Like, if I get this wrong, it'll all go south."

I don't tell him it'll be okay or that I believe in him because I'm having the same concerns. My mind's been stewing for the past hour. If I say the wrong thing, or make the jury believe otherwise, it could result in Alex's freedom.

"I'm up next."

Hawke takes my face between his hands. "Yes, but I believe in you. Burn the fucker alive, baby. I must ask you a series of questions. Answer them honestly and with as much detail as you can." The skin between his eyes crinkles and the grip on my face grows tighter. "I know you haven't told me everything but please don't let that hinder you. The judge and jury need to hear the disgusting, gritty details—even if they'll make me want to lose my fucking mind."

My lips barely form the word, my heart pounding so hard against my chest at his words. "Okay."

Hawke releases me, but before he gets too far away, I grasp his wrist. Maybe it's not the most ideal time to tell him, but I need to in case today doesn't end how we plan.

"Hawke, I love you. I love everything you've done for me, the person you've been for me, and the person you made me again."

Instead of that movie moment, I get blankness. Complete blankness, in which not even his eyes move, or blink, for that matter. And then—

He throws me against the long, gleaming table and shoves himself between my legs. He grabs the strands of hair, bringing my face toward his as he kisses me ruthlessly, obsessively, and viciously, shooting burning flames straight to my core. Against my chest, his own heart thumps.

"I fucking love you too, Willow. I think I have for a while now, but I didn't want to frighten you."

"Your love would never frighten me." Even as I speak the words, I recognize the lie within them. A month ago, it might have. It'd been too much.

Blue flames blaze between us, and I'm lost in them until he blinks and glances at his phone, muttering, "We still have five minutes."

"For?"

My back meets the table, and by the time I catch my bearings, he's tugging off my panties and positions my heels on the table.

My breath catches. "What are you—?"

His mouth covers my core and he licks rapidly. My body responds instantly, chasing that feeling already clenching my inner muscles. Unable to help myself, I push his head down, ensuring he doesn't think about ending what he began.

His shoulders shift, fighting back against my control. His mouth abandons me to speak. "Hands up."

Without thought, I obey him. Once my arms are positioned above me, he continues his torture. Licking and sucking, expanding the flames. My hips move, rocking against the table, only to be pinned into position and to lose all control. Moans break through my mouth, and as the feeling intensifies, my noises increase until—

Hawke shoves his hand against my mouth. "Bite me. We can't have people overhearing you."

I do, sinking my teeth into the side of his hand at the precise moment the feeling explodes in my core. Although, I remind myself not to bite down overly hard, the orgasm wracking my body is too intense to ignore.

The feeling breaks, fades, and my teeth unhook from his skin as I lower my head to the table. Panting, I stare at the perfectly painted white ceiling, affixed with fancy, decorative lighting. So representative of the world we see, covering the ugly reality.

"Still alive?"

Hawke moves into my view, wiping at his mouth with a devious smirk. He helps me off the table, my legs trembling as I re-ground myself to continue.

He watches as I straighten my dress once more, but before my thighs are completely covered, he moves closer, reaching for my leg. Without hesitation, I allow him to touch me, half curious of his next move.

His fingers stroke lightly over the six scars, a hardness covering his gaze. "*This* is what he did to you, Willow. The physical marks he dared to leave on your skin. Don't allow him to get any deeper."

Immediately, I comprehend his words. Don't allow Alex to get into my head today; beneath my skin. Rationality is key. Brenda even suggested that when things get tough, I rub my palm over those scars, as a physical reminder to continue even when I believe I cannot.

"I won't," I promise.

My words seem to reduce some of his anxiety, as he leans away and holds up his hand, the light catching on the distinct set of teeth imprints I left there when he instructed me to bite him.

"Damn, baby."

I can't help but giggle, the previous conversation

about scars now gone entirely. "If that's what I would have gotten for telling you I love you, I'd have done it a while ago." My hand lands on his chest, over his heart, as I repeat the words that are becoming much easier to say. "I love you, Hawke."

This time his hands weave in my hair and he yanks my face to his, pressing another hard but chaste kiss upon my lips. "I love you too, Willow. When you go in there and recount everything the bastard did to you, remember it'll be me you're going home with and there's a lot more of *that* to be had." He indicates to the table.

His words hit my brain, lodging themselves there. When I'm staring at Alex, it'll be Hawke I think about.

"Same with you. When you're thinking about hurting him, remember I'm yours. You're the one whose mouth just fucked me into bliss."

Hawke drops his forehead to mine, sighing as he lifts his phone to check the time. "Recess is nearly done. We need to go."

We need to end this, are his unspoken words.

Forty

WILLOW

The world I enter and the one I've left behind in that meeting room couldn't be more different.

Two dozen people sit in the stands, all turning to watch as I enter the courtroom. I have no idea if two-dozen viewers are average for a case like this one, but either way, it's more people than I've been around in a long time.

Hawke leads me down the aisle and toward the prosecution's table, which is situated in front of the row where Elena and Natalie are seated with Ryker, Tristan, and Brent.

Elena leans over until she's close enough that I can hear her. "We're here for you, girl. When you think you're freaking out, look at us and remember what you're doing and why you're doing it. Don't look at *him*."

When the door opens again, the air changes. I don't need to turn around to watch as *he* strides confidently through the courtroom. He has a smirk on his face; I know it even without peeking over.

Sweaty droplets drip down my neck and no amount of deep breathing—a strategy Brenda told me about—helps as my body realizes its captor is *right here*. A month and a half since the last time I saw him, and while so much has changed in my life, none of it matters the moment he takes his seat.

"You are nothing. You're mine. Mine to take how I goddamn please."

Why did I think this was a smart plan? I could easily slip away now and return to the safety of Hawke's bed.

Stop it, my mind chides, while the reminder Brenda made me recite comes to the top. I'm not his anymore. *I control my life.*

Beneath the table, Hawke grasps my hand and squeezes. His eyes cut briefly to mine, letting me see the agony present. I know him well enough to know he's also thinking about how this is a bad idea, and for him, I must prove otherwise.

A man in a long, black robe enters from a door in the corner of the courthouse and everyone stands, waiting for the man to take his seat. Upon standing, Hawke releases my hand, and although I know he must, I feel cold again without his touch. Once the judge sits, his eyes sweep the room, momentarily pausing on me as the newcomer. Everyone also follows suit and sits.

A moment later, a stream of people file into the side stands, and I know they're the jury. A group of strangers who'll look upon me, judge me, and ultimately will be the deciding factor on whether Alex captures me again.

"Court is assembled again. Prosecutor, rise and call your first witness please."

Hawke stands again, positioning his hands on the table. "I would like to call Willow Avery to the stand, Your Honour."

This is real. This is happening. Which means, now isn't the time to chicken out. I need to get my ass to the stand and follow through with what Hawke and Brenda have been preparing me to do.

I need to fight and win against Alex. This time, there are no chains holding me down. No cage trapping me inside. Only the blatant truth I get to share.

The march toward the stand is agonizing, but nothing's worse than leaving Hawke's side and putting all that distance between us. The look he sends with me is meaningful and packed with longing; a look I want to wrap into my heart and use throughout this entire ordeal, but it's the weight of another man's stare making it more difficult.

Alex stalks me as I walk across the room. His stare is hot, heavy, and dangerous. Knowing I soon need to face him—face my past—has the door off to the side looking all the more tempting. I'll be far away before anyone catches up to me...

Alex needs to be put away.

It's that reminder that forces my feet toward the stand.

I can do this. Breathe.

One. Two. Three. And out.

My palms rub on my thighs, right over my scars. An action everyone else will assume is due to stress.

I can't do this.

The moment I sit, I look straight. Every nerve in me urges me to hide, to not look at him, but the only way I'll be able to testify, without breaking down two minutes in, is to get the worst of it over.

Cold, dark eyes, the very ones I still sometimes see in my nightmares, stare me down with the same expression he'd wear as he tortured me, causing me to scream in pain, to cry for it to end, all while he ignored me.

He fucks me harder, rougher, and my broken nails scrape uselessly against the glass as I take it. His teeth clamp down on my shoulder, his bite hard, breaking the skin. I flinch as I release yet another traitorous wail. After a moment, his head lifts again; I don't need to look in the mirror to feel the hot, wet liquid sliding down the side of my neck and onto my breasts.

Blood.

The memory is sudden, sparking a light gasp from me. My breath comes out staggered, my heart skipping beats before determining it'll hang onto life for a bit longer. Brenda warned me about the trauma flashbacks.

When our eyes meet, he smirks. It's the grin he'd use as he sliced my skin and stole my innocence, sanity, and peace. Even now, even in court, he doesn't appear fearful whatsoever. Instead, he leans back in his chair, his eyes getting brighter with excitement. This is all some game to him. His lawyer whispers something in his ear, but Alex shows no sign of hearing the man.

"You are nothing. You're mine."

Hawke steps out from behind his table, his shiny shoes loud against the marble flooring. Yet again, my blue-eyed angel saves me because his approach interrupts the stare down I'm having with Alex. He watches me, a million emotions swirling in his gaze, and I'm pleased his back is to Alex because I can't imagine Alex knowing the truth about Hawke.

I recall what he said this morning: *Look only at me. Keep your eyes on mine and don't look to the left. Don't let him win, and don't torture yourself. You can do this.*

Hawke blinks and when his eyes reopen, gone is the love he has for me. A professional lawyer replaces the man I know and his initial words come out cold and detached, so unlike everything I've heard from him before.

"Please state your full name to the court."

Inhaling the largest breath I'll ever take, I respond, "Willow Avery."

Hawke gestures toward Alex. "Do you know who this man is?"

"Alex Miller."

"Can you tell the court of your affiliation with Mr. Miller?"

"About seven months ago, I was hired to work at his company."

"Please tell us the name of this company."

"Miller Inc."

"What was your position there?"

"Alex's secretary."

"His personal secretary," Hawke muses, his fingers knotting in front. "Do you have any experience or formal training in office management or secretarial work?"

Alex's lawyer stands. "Relevance."

"Overruled," the judge announces, briefly glancing at me. "Miss Avery, please answer the question."

"None."

"Did you find it strange to have been hired when you have no training or experience in that field?"

"Leading," the argumentative voice chimes again.

"Overruled."

"Yes." I swallow, allowing my gaze to dart to the jury watching intently. With Alex's lawyer objecting so often, my brain is struggling to remain in the present and not return to that dark place again. "Yes, but I applied because I was desperate for work, and thought, what the hell. Worse they can tell me is no. When I got the position, I vowed they wouldn't regret hiring me. That I'd become good at my job."

"Did you feel as though you did?" Hawke's brows rise with his question.

"Question calls for speculation, Your Honour," Alex's lawyer interrupts my response.

This time, Hawke argues before the judge can make his call. "This is leading somewhere, Your Honour."

The judge ponders for a moment before waving his hand. "Go on. I'll allow it."

"Did you feel you did a good job, Miss Avery?" Hawke asks again.

This is the question leading toward the truth. Barreling toward it, is more like it. It's why Hawke fought to keep this question in.

"Alex told me I was doing a good job. He invited me over."

"Non-responsive," the other lawyer calls out.

Beneath the stand, my hands fist in annoyance. Of course, Alex would find himself a lawyer as equally horrible as he is.

"Answer the question directly, Miss Avery," the judge orders.

"Yes, I think I did a good job."

"Did you get recognized for your time with Miller Inc.?"

Ah. No matter the objection tossed out, Hawke knows how to swing this around to where we need it to be.

"Alex spoke to me directly, to compliment me. Then he invited me to his home."

Unable to help myself, I glance behind Hawke, toward Alex's lawyer, unable to bite down on a smirk at seeing the man's eyes narrowed.

"Did you accept the invitation?"

"Yes."

"Can you tell the court what happened when you arrived at Mr. Miller's house?"

I nod, but before I start what'll lead us to the grand finale, I look toward Alex. Some of his cockiness has slipped off and I spot something new in his dark gaze—something I've *never* seen before.

Fear.

"Alex led me to his kitchen and poured me a glass of wine, but the bottle was nearing completion, so he asked me to come with him to the wine cellar to retrieve another. Then…" I swallow and let my mind drift toward the past, to the place I've been struggling to escape from. "He grabbed my hand and yanked me away from the wine bottles and down a cement hallway."

"What was at the end of the hallway?" Hawke prods.

"A cell," I whisper, before forcing my tone louder to ensure the jury hears all the gritty details they'll need to convict him. "A glass cage. I tried to fight him, but he shoved me inside and locked the door."

I blink, returning from the past and seek Elena and Natalie in the crowd, needing someone else's support after speaking those heavy words. Natalie nods, urging me to continue and Elena shoots a quick thumbs up.

"What happened after that?"

"I was his prisoner. He took my clothes, forcing me to be naked. He fed me enough to keep me supple but not enough to provide much nutrition. When I got sick, he made it worse." I shut my eyes and let the rest fly, as I feel the tears poking at the edges of my eyes, demanding me to release them. "He r-raped me. Every day for six months, sometimes multiple times a day. He forced me into every sexual experience, even when I begged him to stop. He used things on me, inside me. He tortured me, cut me, tied me up… He shared me with five different men on separate occasions over the six months."

I stop, and my teeth sink into my tongue. Tears swell again, but I blink them back. The jury will have to deal with me not crying—not falling that far into victimland—because I refuse to allow Alex the satisfaction of any more of my tears.

Hawke treads closer and his eyes briefly shut. His chest expands with air, and I know he's breathing deeply before his next question.

"To clarify, did you tell him no explicitly when he attempted any sexual acts with you?"

I flinch. His question is pure idiocy, though understandable. Hawke needs to ensure the jury is aware my claims are truly rape. "Explicitly. Multiple times."

"And he ignored you?"

"Yes," I whisper.

"Miss Avery, I know this is difficult, but could you tell the court what Mr. Miller planned for you?"

I swallow, imagining the images of the other girls. The images I know the court has seen by now. "After six months, he would kill me." My daze darts to the jury and I speak off script, "Alex is a psychopath. It was more than sexual abuse. It was mental… physical. The death he often spoke of wouldn't be granted in a peaceful, gentle way."

The jury shifts, some looking away entirely and others glancing at each other. Hawke's lips twitch, as though he's fighting a smile at their reaction, and my spine compresses in relaxation. From the corner of my eye, I spot Alex fuming. His arms cross over his chest, but then his lawyer whispers in his ear and his arms drop to his side, his expression smoothing out again, adopting the easy façade once more.

"Miss Avery," Hawke brings the attention back to him, "if my math is correct, by the time you were removed from Mr. Miller's home, the six months had passed, had they not? By your statement, you should be dead, no?"

I nod, shoving my hands under my thighs to keep myself steady. "Yes, I believed the same, but on the six-month anniversary, Alex told me he wanted to keep me alive for a bit longer because my mind wasn't broken yet."

Though I don't want to, my eyes drift toward Alex again. He leans back in his chair, even crossing his legs. His chin tilts in a manner to hide his growing smirk. Of course the asshole revelled in my crushing mental state.

"Thank you, Miss Avery. No more questions."

Hawke walks to his table, stretching the space between us. I crave to follow—to breathe again—but he warned me in advance of the process, so I focus my attention straight, directly at Alex's lawyer for his cross-examination.

The man stands slowly and adjusts his suit jacket, as he heads for the spot Hawke recently vacated.

"Miss Avery, you mentioned willingly going with my client to his basement. Correct?"

"Y-yes," I respond, eyes darting to the jury. A couple write in their notebooks, but most watch me.

"So would you agree, you willingly went into my client's cage?"

I jerk back. *How did he come to that conclusion?* I willingly went for a *drink*, not to be dragged down the hallway and have my life ripped away. And he's totally skipping over the fact Alex *owns* a cage.

"No. The deal was a new bottle of wine. That's why I went down there." My eyes cut to the jury, who scribbles more notes, but I hope they're in my favour.

"But you went willingly."

"Badgering the witness, Your Honour," Hawke's smooth voice comes from behind.

"Agreed. Defence, new question."

The man visibly huffs but asks an even worse question: "Did you deny my client from completing sexual acts *every* time?"

I gape. *He's playing* that *card?* "Well, maybe. Yes. No. I don't know." My hands rake over my hair, messing up what I spent so much of my morning attempting to make perfect. I may have been locked away for a while, but I know how the world works. Since there wasn't a denial each time, all those situations wouldn't be counted as rape.

But even one time is enough to convict him… right?

"Pick an answer, Miss Avery, or the court may be inclined to scratch everything you've stated thus far from the record."

Again, my mouth falls open. Worse, because Alex and his lawyer both wear identical expressions of pleasure, as though they're winning.

They can't win. He can't go free.

Hawke chooses then to intercept. He leaps to his feet, dragging the court's attention toward him and stalks straight toward the judge, a document in his hand.

"Objection. May I remind the court of evidence I submitted just earlier?" He lays the paper on the judge's stand. "This is the doctor's and psychologist's medical files regarding Miss Avery's mental and physical state. If I must remind the court, the report states that given the length of time Miss Avery was in his captivity and what had occurred there, it's only natural she stopped denying him. She became his captive in every sense of the word and feared what denying him would lead to. Remaining silent ensured her a moment of safety." His eyes flick to me, a furious fire burning between them before he faces Alex's lawyer. "Rape is rape unless Miss Avery explicitly gave her verbal permission."

"Did you ever give permission, Miss Avery?" the judge asks, not looking away from the document in his hand. I hadn't even realized Hawke possessed them, but then, I get the sense there's a lot of this case's process Hawke never revealed to me.

"No," I state, loudly and firmly. "Never. Mr. Blackwood is correct. I stopped denying him because he ignored me."

The judge nods slowly and returns the document to Hawke. "Defence, you're overruled. The question will be removed from the record."

Alex's lawyer huffs again but smooths his features quickly as his hands brush away invisible dirt on his jacket. "Very well then. No more questions."

It seemed too easy, which means, there's bound to be more to this.

"You may step down, Miss Avery. Thank you for your cooperation." The judge swings his arm in an arc and lifts his gavel before whacking it on his desk. "We will take twenty."

The bailiff gets to assisting me from the stand and the moment my feet touch the courtroom's floor again, Hawke is right there, grasping my hand and pulling me away from the courtroom and Alex. He leads me to the room he had me in earlier, immediately shutting the door.

"That wasn't fucking easy, but you did amazing, baby. Absolutely amazing."

"Do you think it's enough?"

"I think they're scrambling, so yes. The evidence is too strong. There's no denying your story, and soon, Teagan will be up there. This is nearly over."

Over.

Hawke glances at his phone. "I want to stay, but I need to go debrief Teagan. She should be here soon." The door opens and shuts in a blink, leaving me alone in the conference room. He's so frazzled, he forgot to kiss me goodbye.

With nothing else to do, I wander to the long table, hand brushing the spot he had me on earlier. It wasn't that long ago, yet also feels like a lifetime has passed.

So many lifetimes have passed. My old life, working at Miller Inc., even being saved from Alex's basement. It's up to the jury to ensure I get the one I'm growing now.

The door opens, and I glance over my shoulder, expecting to see Hawke returning. Instead, two faces peek in.

Natalie and Elena.

There's no words. No explanation. Only a hug I hadn't realized I needed.

Forty-One

HAWKE

"All rise." The judge enters the courtroom and retakes his seat on his bench.

I can't think of a time when I've battled through a more stressful case, but knowing the end is near—that I *will* win—makes it incredibly difficult to remain still.

My gaze darts beside me quickly, catching Teagan's eye, but her attention is completely on the judge. Ryker and Tristan each crack a grin, and Brent nods. For years, we've been a team, and all our work has led up to this moment.

"Have you elected a foreperson?" the judge asks.

An elderly jury member lifts to his feet, nodding as he goes. "We have."

Instead of watching the typical court process, in which the jury foreperson will hand their verdict to the bailiff, who'll then give it over to the judge to be checked, I can't help but glance over to the defence table, toward Miller.

Guilty people often have a tell, indicating when they're lying or not, but Alex is too good at pretending. He's leaning back in the chair, his chin propped up by his hand, while he watches the process with a smirk. Guilty people sometimes stare down the jury, silently threatening them, but not Alex. He merely watches the procession, and when the judge has the documents, his smile grows.

Beside him, his lawyer's leg is bouncing beneath the table, and I silently chuckle at the obvious nerves he emits. Lawyer 101: never let your opponent see when you're anxious because that's the moment they can strike. With that single leg bounce, I catch all I need to—Alex is guilty and even his shitty lawyer knows there's nothing more that'll save him.

"The defendant will rise and face the jury."

Alex stands, straightening from a lazy slouch. Fuckers like him always ensure they go down looking good, and I have to hand it to him, he's maintaining the same attitude the entire way through this process.

"As to the first count of the eight known instances of murder, we the jury find Alex Miller… guilty."

Carmen's parents sit at the back of the room, at the insistence on my part, because this is the moment I wanted them to witness. The closure they'll receive knowing their daughter is finally avenged.

"As to the second count of the nine known instances of kidnapping, we the jury find Alex Miller… guilty."

On and on it goes. Alex is found guilty for every charge—the captivity and torture of Willow and the deceased women, the psychological torture and conditioning of Teagan, the multiple rape counts

When the judge lowers the papers, he glances toward the jury, asking his customary, "Is there anyone who does not agree with the verdicts just read?"

A resounding, "No," echoes through the jury box.

Professionalism be damned, because I smirk and don't care who sees it. Years of work and research is all made worth it with that single word.

The judge stands, delivering his final statement. "Alex

Miller, the jury has found you guilty of the listed crimes. You will be sentenced to nine consecutive life sentences in a maximum-security prison, without parole. You will be remanded into the custody of the province immediately. Bailiff, take him into processing, please."

Prison will never be enough for Miller, but it's a start.

You have another option. If devils on shoulders were real, mine just whispered to me. I won't go down that road though, or else I'll be no better than the family I've left behind.

Willow is free and there's nothing more I wish to do than go deliver the news, but I remain still, forced to finish the trial to the bitter end. The habitual need to chew on my piercing while I await the rest of this slow-ass process to occur is strong, and I can't wait to get it back in my lip.

When the judge whacks his gavel, it signals the end, and needing this over with soon, I immediately go to the other side of the room, hand out toward Alex's idiot lawyer to finish all the niceties. He begrudgingly takes it with a frown.

He immediately releases me, looking toward his client, in time for the handcuffs to get slapped on his wrist. There's never been a more agreeable sight.

In the back of the room, Carmen's parents move into the aisle, their red-rimmed eyes locked on the scene. I give them a head nod, letting them know I see them, and Carmen's mother smiles back, mouthing words so impactful, I catch them from here. *Thank you.*

My pleasure, I mouth back.

Behind me, Ryker and Elena approach slowly. Tristan has his arm around Natalie, who's eyes are also red from crying. I can't pretend to understand the emotions ravaging her body. From what we gathered, she hadn't known him for long, but for a woman with little family, learning about another one was horrifying and thrilling all at the same time. To lose him so soon, for reasons so horrid… I feel for her.

As the bailiff brings Alex around his table, Teagan comes closer, her watery eyes locked on her captor. I move my body, blocking her as much I can from his sight, but it doesn't stop his next words.

"It's been fun, Teagan. I'm sorry we couldn't have forever."

"Don't respond to him." He's aiming to get a rise out of her.

Alex's attention whips to me, his lip curling as he scans me head to toe. "Say goodbye to Willow for me. Can't wait to visit her dreams each night."

"Go to hell," Teagan spits from behind my shoulder. My hand goes to her arm, putting a bit of pressure to ensure she doesn't leap toward him or do any of the insane shit I've gathered Teagan would do if provoked.

Just when I'm about to share impatient words with the bailiff for the speed he's removing Miller from the courtroom, they finally pull him toward the backdoor. Alex's heels dig into the smooth ground and his head twists as much as it can, still determined to have his final words.

"Ames." He nudges his chin at Ryker. "Guess it's my turn to experience prison." Alex's attention shifts a fraction. "Elena, too bad you didn't take me up on my job offer."

As if this whole nightmare can't worsen, Natalie pushes past us all, approaching at such a speed the bailiff holds up a hand, warning her to remain back. "Why?" Her sorrow-laden voice is no higher than a whisper. "Why try to be a family to me at all?"

The speed at which his idiot lawyer nearly flies across the room is laughable. "Say nothing more, Alex."

But Alex doesn't listen, and he shrugs lazily, scanning his sister. "Women are good for one thing, Nat, and only one thing. Why would I not capitalize on that?"

Tristan practically lunges from his spot, but Ryker throws his body in front of him. I meet Ryker's eyes, silently thanking him, because the last thing we need is to reconvene because Tristan attacked someone—convict or not. Alex is spewing his hate, but very soon, this won't matter, because he'll be gone from our lives.

Finally, the bailiff moves Alex toward the door, but somehow still, he manages to turn, his eyes locking on the woman beside me.

"Goodbye, Teagan. Just remember, your life will always be mine. No one you care for will be safe."

The moment they're gone, I grasp Teagan's hand, dragging her past everyone and out of the courtroom. Chaos will ensure that Brent will be on her, and I know it's not what she wants.

"I have a few more battles to fight with his lawyer," I mutter, already dreading the fight over the late Miller's will, and hoping Jason got something completed on that front. "I need to get Willow home. I assume you're good to get yourself out of here?"

Pushing through crowds beyond the door—interested reporters that somehow made it inside and other people milling around—I lead her toward a quiet area in the hallway, close to the front of the courthouse.

"Yeah." Red hair falls around her face as she tilts her head up. More openness, more vulnerability than I've ever seen reflects in her expression. "Thanks, Hawke. For everything. Seriously."

So final, and yet, so obvious. Teagan is a runner, and already, she's inching herself toward the doorway, eager to rush away from the shit life she's had thus far.

I wink, letting her know I'm on to her and her secret plans. "My pleasure. Good luck, Teagan. I hope to see you around." Perhaps my words will tie something down in that brain of hers and urge her to remain, because the moment she takes off, Brent's going to lose his mind.

A problem for another day, because Willow is the only thing on my mind now.

With a final wave, I back deeper into the courthouse, heading straight for the room I've left her in. If there's anyone else who deserves to hear the verdict, it's her.

You're free, Willow. He's not coming back for you. He'll be locked away in federal prison behind gates and guards and he'll have no way to get out.

The irresponsible devil on my shoulder returns to wonder, *What if he does?*

He won't. I won't let it happen.

For now, I have two final tasks to complete today.

First: finding my girl.

Second: fucking her into oblivion.

Forty-Two

WILLOW

Five minutes have passed since Hawke gave the news, and still, my mind can't stop whirling, repeating his words over and over.

Guilty.

Guilty.

Guilty.

Alex is gone. Truly gone. He's not coming back. He won't take me from Hawke.

Free. I'm free.

"Let's go." I yank his arm, propelling him to the door. "We need to get home and celebrate."

His eyes ignite and he takes over, now pulling me along, clearly in agreement. I stare at his suit-covered back, imagining it bare as he climbs overtop me before tying my hands.

Maybe today we'll try more. There's a world of possibilities now. Everything seems brighter, more expansive and limitless. I'll *live*, and fear will never hold me down again.

The moment we're out the room, Hawke stops short and I crash into his back. His arms shoot out to the side, blocking my view, but I lean to the right, determined to see what's going on.

"He shouldn't be out here," he snarls, the vibration casting down his spine and into my body.

"Who?" As quick as I ask the question, I see it. See *him*.

Alex. Two cops surround him as they walk him through the bustling hallway. Everyone stops, staring, mouths agape as the city's newest and richest convict is marched out the front doors.

"They have a backdoor for this shit," Hawke rumbles.

I'm not listening. I can't focus on Hawke when all I'm contemplating about is how the Alex I'm watching stride by is a totally different version than the one who was in court earlier. For the first time ever, his shoulders are caved in, his head lowered, like all his energy is depleted. He's lost and the comprehension of that finally hits me.

That is, until his eye catches on something.

Me.

"You'll never forget me, Willow. I'll forever be in your head, a part of your life."

One of the cops pushes on Alex's shoulder, urging him faster and then the crowd swallows him up and he disappears from view.

Without another second, Hawke faces me, his arms circling my waist. "Don't think about it, Willow. Your mind is your own, and only yours."

I know. The moment Hawke repeated the jury's verdict, my mind became my own. It's as though a light flicked on or a candle got lit within me. New meaning blossomed. New desires and dreams burned away old fears and anxieties.

Alex won't steal it away because I won't allow him.

Rising on my toes, I begin the kiss. One packed with so much emotion and feeling, it's as though my heart will burst. I begin the kiss, but I let him end it.

In our bed. At home.

Together.

Twice, our celebration is interrupted. The first time, Brent shows up and begs Hawke for his car, to which the keys were practically tossed out the bedroom window before he continued going down on me.

And now, by phone. After it rings three times, Hawke groans and reaches over me toward his nightstand where he retrieves his cell.

"What, Ryker?" he growls. "You have *no* fucking idea what you're insisting on interrupting."

The voice on the other end is too muffled for me to catch the conversation, but Hawke's face blanches white and his previous annoyance manifests into fear.

"We'll be right there." He hangs up and tosses the phone to the side before slipping out of me. "Sorry, *il mio bella ragazza*, but we need to go."

On and off for the next month, Hawke visits the hospital often. Sometimes I go with him, but other times, he goes alone. The day of the trial, Brent was in an accident, wrecking Hawke's car in the process. The accident was bad enough that doctors induced a coma to allow Brent the space to heal.

Most of the group has been lingering around the hospital in that time, but the most noticeable person is Teagan.

It's obvious she loves him. Although we haven't spoken much in all the weeks I've been here, we don't need to. The people we were weeks ago are much different than the people we are now. She's not the woman I witnessed being raped against the glass walls of my captivity, and I'm no longer the broken girl who she had to pretend wasn't trapped down there.

The one time we did speak was after Elena finally got a hold of her, and she returned to Brent's side. I went into the room with Ryker when he announced the rest of us would be leaving. I'm not entirely sure why I had gone; maybe because I knew she'd need my words as she sat by Brent's bedside, looking entirely lost and out of place.

Broken. Just like I was.

"Teagan—"

"Stop. Don't speak. Willow, I have so much to say—"

"No, we don't need to do this now. It's not why I'm here. I just… Hawke told me why you left. It's hard, and I know it's worse for you, but it's okay to love him. Don't spend the rest of your freedom allowing Alex to still control your life. Because when you run away, when you hide from your memories and don't have your happy ending with the man who loves you, then he wins." My lips curl in a frown. *"And that's depressing. And not fair to either of you. You want Alex to go away forever—to never be a bother to you again? Don't leave."*

Since then, for the month he's in a coma, she hasn't left his side, even when Natalie and Elena dragged her away to shower and change her clothes. Finally though, when weeks have passed, Brent wakes and, days later, is released from the hospital.

The second time we speak is a few weeks later, when I asked her over to finally address the past.

I'm just finishing dressing after an intense round with Hawke when the knock comes.

"Willow? I'm here. Can we talk?"

Why did I think this was a good idea? I should get rid of her, cast her away from the house, refusing to have this conversation. Brenda appreciates my willingness to speak with Teagan and address the fact that we were both in horrid situations.

With a heavy hand, I manage to open the door, even if I don't meet her eyes right away.

Teagan slowly enters and gets no farther than that when her legs seemingly give out and she slides to the floor, her back pressing the door shut. Seeing her shattered like this hurts my insides because Alex doesn't deserve any more of our emotions. I crouch by her, maintaining a few inches of space. "Willow, I'm so sorry. I wanted to help you every single day you were in his cage. Trust me, I did."

As quick as a reply is there, it's gone, and I close my mouth. This occurs twice before I manage, "You couldn't. I'm not mad."

Inside that prison, I was never irate at her because I knew the man Alex is and how much she'd have to fight him. And knowing everything I do now only strengthens previous feelings. She couldn't win against the man who conditioned her.

"You should be. You should hate me," she mutters harshly, her eyes narrowing on the floor between her feet. "I did it once. I tried to save a girl. Got her nearly out of the basement when he found us. Her death was harsher, swifter, because *I* tried to help. She paid the price of my idiocy, and I was forced to watch every brutal moment of it. So I stopped and turned a blind eye to every one of them." When she lifts her head, her eyes are a curtain of tears streaming down her cheeks. "To you. Your life would have been worse and ended sooner had I tried."

Knowing the photos that were once in Hawke's basement—now cleaned out and burned—her words hit differently. All because she tried to save a girl, she would have had to witness the process he took to get the girl to that point. I may have lived similar shit, but witnessing it would be almost worse.

"I understand."

"I *hated* knowing what he did to you, Willow. Hated it with every fiber of my being, but I turned it off, you know? Pretended I was okay with it since there was no way out."

"And for you too. You lived through hell." Having to pretend would be the cruelest part. Going each day, disregarding one's knowledge of what he's doing to others.

She shakes her head roughly, strands of her red hair coming loose. "Not like you. My cage was large, gilded and all that. He controlled me in other ways, but at least I didn't have to see him—endure him—every day."

When leading up to today, at therapy, we last spoke about guilt and all the ways that can look for a person, and how, sometimes, no matter what another says, the guilt will never go away. With time, maybe Teagan will see I'm not upset.

For now, though, I shuffle closer and wrap my arms tightly around her neck. Two survivors who've made it through the darkness and we can be here together.

"You survived, Teagan. We both did what we had to do. Besides, Hawke told me what you did. How you led them all to Alex's basement. *You're* the reason I'm alive and having this conversation. I owe you my life. You gave me my freedom, Hawke, and a future. You've paid your dues, so please, Teagan, don't beat yourself up about this any longer." I get to my feet, bringing her with me in order to get her out of the ball she's placed her body in. "Alex is gone and locked behind bars forever. We both need to move on with Hawke and Brent and live our best lives. He'll always be a part of our pasts, but one we shouldn't focus on any longer."

My words must penetrate some small piece of her guilt because she smiles, glancing at the unmade bed behind me. "Hawke, huh? How'd you move on so easily and *want* a relationship with him?"

Exactly like that, we each say, *I understand and agree to move on*, switching topics abruptly.

"He's good for me. I'd still be shivering in the corner if it wasn't for his help. I… It wasn't easy. Or instant. The thought of another person ever touching me—and yet, there was something else—a connection. The moment he lifted me out of Alex's cage, I *felt* something." My cheeks heat with admission. "I suppose it sounds dumb."

"No. No, it's… inspiring."

"Hawke encouraged counselling. I didn't think it was required until I went, and everything just came out. My therapist helped me process so much of the abuse and torture, but she also told me that healing from trauma looks differently for everyone." Hopefully, she understands what I'm also attempting to express within my words. "I know you had also gone to therapy around the same time, and yet, you're wondering how I got into a relationship with Hawke so quickly. Trauma affects us all differently, and it doesn't make you weaker in any way, Teagan. You lived it for longer, so wanting to be with Brent is a change for you, which makes sense. Move on when *you're* ready to, not when you think you have to. That was probably the most important lesson I took from my sessions."

For a long beat, she doesn't look at me, simply stares at the floor, but it's okay. She doesn't need to respond; she just has to have heard me. My words will stick or they won't, but that's on her now.

"Tell me about you and Brent."

She smiles and travels down memory lane, going all the way back to childhood and a heartbreaking story which, thankfully, ends in a happily-ever-after.

Forty-Three

HAWKE

One Month Later

Willow rolls over in her sleep, whimpering as her arms thrash. She moans, more of a shout though, before settling back to sleep.

I sigh, fixing the blanket over her shoulders again and stand from bed, rubbing at my chest as I wander to the window to look out at the street beyond.

Almost two months since the trial, and she's still having nightmares. I know better than anyone, that nightmares linger, sometimes never going away, but I really fucking hoped, for her sake, they would upon realizing he is too.

He's not gone though. He's out there still, alive and able to get to her.

Often, I think about the fact that my rapists were slaughtered and wondered if that's the reason I was able to go on. With Willow, her nightmare lives.

I've failed her. If only I let the guys have their shot at him, then he wouldn't still be breathing. He shouldn't be here…

Before I rationally think it through, my phone is in my hand and I'm dialling *his* number again.

"Big brother, you realize it's nearing two in the morning, right?"

My teeth grit because even the simple reminder of what I am to him makes me question my fucking sanity. "Yet you're awake." With no sleep roughing up his voice.

He grunts. "You know us. The work doesn't end. For you either, it seems like. Two calls in one year. What do I owe this pleasure?"

"I need a favour." The words are bitter on my tongue, but this task is something I know he can handle. The unfortunate truth, but for Willow, I'll pay the price of this conversation.

The judge didn't state it, but I know where Alex is located. The nearest maximum-level federal prison is the Sainte-Anne-des-Plaines' Regional Reception Centre in Quebec, only a few hours away from here. It's built to hold sick fuckers like Miller.

I don't have contacts within it, but my brother does.

"Another one?" he murmurs, his voice dripping with interest. "I've seen the news. The verdict is all over TV. I'm pleased to see the RCMP came through for you after all. What could you possibly need from me now?"

"I know you have men in the Sainte-Anne-des-Plaines' Regional Reception Centre." No matter how tight my family is with the RCMP, sometimes local jurisdiction wins out, and a few men find their way inside.

"Fun place." Amusement lightens his tone.

"Get rid of him," I growl.

"Hawke…" All amusement leaves his voice, and the brother I remember from childhood returns. "This isn't you, brother."

"The RCMP was the worst plan I had. The legal route was the biggest mistake I've made, and I didn't completely understand how much until the verdict was read. Prison isn't enough for what he's done to those women. To my girl."

"Your girl," he repeats, his voice oddly calm, but equally fearful. "I see. It'll be done. I'll text you. I kind of don't want to do this, though, since then you'll return to not speaking to me."

"You know why I don't."

Before he says more, I hang up and delete the call history from my phone, effectively also deleting it from my memory. Tomorrow is Ryker and Elena's wedding—my new family—and my past won't overshadow that.

I toss the phone on the charger again and slip in behind Willow. My hand winds around her wrist, over the fresh tattoo she got earlier that day.

A birdcage wrapped in flames.

Her own version of my flowers and flames, representing that she's burned through her captivity and gotten freed. The other day when she approached me, inquiring about tattoos, I knew with clarity that she's the woman for me.

Soon, the final flame will extinguish, and Alex will be no more.

I'm impressed. Elena and Ryker managed to pull together a wedding fairly quickly, and not a half-assed one at that.

The venue is draped in white chiffon—at least that's what Willow's referring to it as. The guests' chairs, the walls, even the fucking ceiling to create some sense of a "heaven" theme, whatever that means. Either way, the place is full of the material, making the entire place look like a cloud threw up in here.

In the end, the setting doesn't matter; the guests do. After leaving my own family, I never believed I'd want to surround myself with another group of people, but Elena and Ryker, Natalie and Tristan, and Teagan and Brent have become just that. I left a fucked-up lifestyle and found one more suited for me.

That fucked-up lifestyle is the reason you're watching Willow stride down the aisle. The reason Alex won't be breathing after this week.

She's so fucking beautiful, it physically makes my heart ache. Her blonde hair tumbles over her shoulders, immaculately curled, framing her flawless face. The pale blue dress falls in waves around her body, brushing the floor. It's impossible to imagine her as the naked, bruised, scarred girl from the basement I found months ago when she appears like this.

Brent nudges my shoulder, grinning. I shove him back, annoyed he disrupted the moment, but my attention refocuses in time for her to shoot me a sly smile before taking her spot by Elena's side.

Teagan appears next, in a dress identical to Willow's, but in my opinion, it looks sexier on Willow.

Brent whispers under his breath, "Fuck if I can't wait to get home later."

Home? Cute. If I manage to make it to my new car, Willow and I are winners. Chances are, I'm fucking her in a bathroom.

When Natalie appears, Tristan shifts, his anxious energy consuming the wedding party. Dressed like the others, her dark hair is swept to the side, giving her a more edgy look. She's grinning from ear to ear, her eyes bouncing over the small group of guests made up of Elena's, Ryker's, and Brent's parents.

Last week, Natalie found herself heir of the entire Miller fortune, including the mansion. Turns out, for all Miller Senior's faults, he left the mansion to her and not Alex. She sold it, only after Tristan talked her off the ledge when she threatened to burn it to the ground. I wouldn't have minded if she had. It sold quickly though, adding to her fortune, and she used a fraction of it to pay toward her aunt's care, which Alex was once managing. Jason's pretty thrilled with himself for getting through the complication of the will, adding Alex's imprisonment into it.

When the bridal precession tune comes on, I know it's Elena's turn, but instead of watching her, I glance at Ryker. The large fucker adjusts his tie three times within a second before wiping at his face. Once, I teased him for his ruthlessness toward Elena, unable to understand how someone could care that much for another. Now, I appreciate his nerves because that'll be me on the day I marry Willow.

Elena's made it halfway down the aisle by the time I look toward her. Her gown is slim and feminine and the veil covering her face does nothing to hold back her eagerness. She walks alone, despite her father sitting in the crowd, but to my understanding, they have a rocky relationship.

When she arrives at Ryker's side, he grasps her hand, and the minister begins. I pay the man's words little attention until it's time for the vows.

"Dolly, you're fucking mine. Deal with it, or I'm hunting your ass down and dragging you back home."

Her responding chuckle is pure music. "I won't be going anywhere, trust me. I know what it means to go against your wishes. Ryker, I've always loved you and always will. I have no purpose in running away. We're endgame."

Endgame.

I glance at the other guys, and then at their girls.

Four women. Four men. All brought together through the fucked-up games of one man, but we found something in the fight.

Love.

Ryker found his always.

Tristan found his obsession.

Brent found his family.

And I found my future.

But more than that, we became each other's families, filling in the gaps for what we're all missing.

I'm so lost in thought I miss when the minister pronounces them as married, but suddenly, Elena is bent over backwards, Ryker fiercely kissing her.

The crowd starts clapping and I join in as Brent leans into me. "Can't wait for that to be us."

I agree but don't respond, eyes falling on Willow again. One day. Maybe sooner than later.

For the rest of the night, we dance, we drink, we laugh. We live.

Forty-Four

WILLOW

With my arms woven around Hawke's neck and my head on his shoulder, we spin, taking an entire circle around the dance floor. It's now I choose to say what's been nagging at me for the past few days.

"You know I love you. You've helped me heal, gave me a home, but I can't continue doing nothing."

Beneath me, his muscles tense. "Why can't you? You're not leaving me, Willow."

"Normalcy, remember? You said so yourself. It's not good for me to be a housewife who lounges at home while you're at work, especially when you seem to be missing a personal secretary." Beneath my lashes, I peer at him. "If you recall, I now have a background in that role and would like to apply, if you're fine with my lack of a degree."

Our dancing momentarily pauses as he takes in my words. "You're serious. You'd want to work for me?"

"Why not? At least I know my boss won't kidnap me."

A shadow passes over his face at the dark memories. "Oh, I'll most definitely be kidnapping you, but you'll like it."

"Exactly. Think about all the fun we can have at your

office."

He presses close to me, his hard body aligning with mine in all the right places. The material of the dress is flimsy and so easily removable.

"I might have to set ground rules or else we'll never get any work done."

"Sounds like a sweet deal to me."

"Fuck, Willow, you really know how to make me go insane. I mean," his eyes skate my frame, "fucking *look* at you. I can't wait until I can rip this dress from you." His hand travels the length of my back, stopping right above my ass where he gathers the fabric and fists it. "Such a nice material. So perfect for tying you to the bed later."

Beneath the fabric, I feel my nipples strain in response. Lips parted and throat dry, I push out, "Yeah?"

"Unless," he lowers his head, his lips kissing my neck as he whispers, "you're up for a little exhibitionism. There's bound to be a closet nearby."

A whimper breaks through my tight lips at the simple thought of what that could mean. In the past month, I've been opening up and stretching my limits bit by bit, always remaining in the realm of what is comfortable. We've fucked in more places than the bed, but never outside the house.

"Closets have coat racks where I can bind your arms to. Remember the first time you rode my face? Seems appropriate if we aim for a repeat of that moment, hmm?" He releases the dress to follow the line down to my skin, lifting the dress inch by inch as his hand disappears beneath it.

My legs part on instinct, and I lift onto my toes, creating a path for what he offers. Our dance all but stops as I cling to him, letting him take me to another place where we're alone.

"Think everyone here will understand you're mine

when you're screaming my name? Or would you rather I bind your mouth too, so your moans are mine and mine alone?"

I whimper. Exhibition sounds thrilling, but right now, I want it to be only him and me, alone in our bed, where he can unleash everything he's offering without the fear of getting kicked out.

I open my mouth to tell him this, but his finger skirts the side of my pussy, finding the building moisture and suddenly, that closet concept sounds really good.

"You two done fucking on the dance floor yet?" Ryker's loud voice cuts into the slice of heaven we've created. I break apart from Hawke, making it so my dress falls back into place. Elena and Ryker waggle their brows. "Isn't it the bride and groom who are supposed to be on the verge of tearing each other's clothes off? You're making us look bad."

Elena laughs, pressing her hand into her new husband's chest. The diamond glints from her hand. "Leave them alone, Ryker. It's nice to see Hawke so happy. After all," she flicks her teasing eyes toward him, "the rest of our relationships were such an ick factor for him. How's your words taste?" Playing on the reference of *eat your words*.

Hawke fake licks his lips. "Delicious, Elena, exactly as Willow's—"

"Don't need to hear it!" Her hands fly up to cover her ears. "Thanks though but I don't need to know that about my friend."

"So, I take it you don't want to hear her moaning from a closet as I—"

"Nope!"

The whole interaction has me shaking in laughter, bringing a few people's attention toward us, but I don't care. For the first time, attention isn't a thing to fear, but something to revel in.

"She's right, Hawke," I start, my ability to speak slowly returning, "why don't we go home?"

"Spoilsport," he mutters at Elena, but to me declares, "I'll get the car and will meet you out front."

Elena waves goodbye as she and Ryker return to dancing. I turn toward the tables, spotting Tristan, Natalie, Brent, and Teagan all in their own world. Natalie and Tristan sit so close, their heads bent together, talking rapidly. Meanwhile, Brent is reclined in his chair, an arm thrown over the back of the chair adjacent to him, where Teagan sits, silently scanning the room.

"You know what's the best," Tristan announces loudly as I reach their table, "that a few short months ago, Hawke bitched and whined about the fact that I fucked Natalie in his bedroom, but all of a sudden, since he found his own person, now it's completely fine for him to fuck her in public at a friend's wedding." Focusing on me, his brows lift and he grins. "You be sure to tell him that too."

Natalie slaps at his chest. "I think it's sweet. Leave them alone."

"Fucking on a dance floor is sweet?"

The two go back and forth in their banter, so I simply wave goodbye at them before murmuring to Brent and Teagan, "Hawke and I are headed home. See you two around."

As I back away, Teagan calls out, "You two won't even make it down the road before pulling over!"

"Maybe!" I shout back.

By the time I make it to the front of the building, Hawke still isn't there, which I find strange, considering the parking lot is only around the side. The evening air is chilly in my thin dress, but even so, it feels different than normal. Not colder, but pricklier.

Headlights swing around the building, so I walk down the two small steps of the venue's front, halting at the edge of the driveway and leaving plenty of room for Hawke to stop the car. His black car pulls to a stop and—

I don't hear the footsteps, or feel him until it's too late. Until my nightmare is birthed again, brought back from the dead and beyond—from fucking prison—to haunt me all over. Until it's too late for me to fight back.

Heavy arms wrap around my front, a large hand covering my mouth at the same moment, blocking the jaw from opening more than an inch. A body lines with mine, unbreakable, and a painful reminder of all the hellish things in life.

"I'm back, bitch. You and I need to have a talk."

A voice from my past. A voice I believed I heard for the final time as the officers took him away. A voice I still hear, deep in the nighttime, when even Hawke can't keep the trauma away.

Alex.

There isn't even time to ponder *how* he's here, out of jail, and able to touch me again. There isn't time to curse his very existence, or even revel in the fact that all my old fears were not misplaced, no matter how many times Hawke and Elena said otherwise.

How many times have I been a doll for him to control, to rape—to break. How many times have I wished I could fight him? But he destroyed me. Distorted who I once was to be meek.

But not this time.

Not. This. Time.

He may have my mouth covered and my arms pinned, but my legs have free rein, and all I need to do is hold on long enough for Hawke to arrive. It's obvious now, the black car in front of me, driver unrecognizable in the dark, isn't who I was waiting for.

With Alex keeping control of my body's upper half, I use the leverage and lift, kicking my heeled feet out at his shins, knees, thighs, anywhere I can reach.

He grunts, shifting himself to the side, but he doesn't release me, not even an inch. It matters little though, with how I continue to kick out, shaking my head from side to side to smash his face, swinging my arms any way I can to challenge his hold—*anything* that'll give me the tiniest bit of leverage.

"Fuck," he curses, bending forward, pushing his weight into my back. The new position removes my ability to kick, so I dangle my legs, making it so he's holding my entire weight. "Fuck," he repeats, but this time, the sound of a car door follows.

Alex grasps my neck and shoves it to the side, pushing my curls over my head until the night air brushes my neck. Although I continue to fight with everything I have, it's not enough as the prick of a needle pierces my skin and everything goes black.

Forty-Five

HAWKE

Unhurriedly, I retrieve my car, giving Willow a few extra moments to say goodbye to everyone, and also, so I can calm my dick down and not be on Willow the moment she gets in the vehicle. Maybe we'll make it all the way home, but I doubt it.

After a few minutes, I take the car to the front of the building, expecting to find her waiting. She's not, so I park and wait.

Minutes pass and still nothing.

Me: *Get stuck talking?*

After a minute of no response, my stomach twists with unease. Her remaining behind with friends is nothing to feel alarmed about, and yet, I am because something about this entire thing feels amiss.

I rush back inside the venue, passing Ryker and Brent's parents lounging at a table with a bottle of wine between them. I continue on to Natalie and Tristan, sitting at a table, talking to one another. My sudden intrusion halts the conversation. I wouldn't doubt if they can hear the blood coursing through my body with how quickly my heart is beating.

Natalie glances up, her brows dipping instantly. "Hey, Hawke... You're still here?"

"Willow talk to you?" I ask, urgency causing my voice to harden.

"Yeah," she replies, glancing behind me, "like, a while ago. She said you two were leaving."

Fear pounds at my sanity, but before I jump to conclusions— "And then?" I demand.

"She left," Tristan responds slowly. He stands, abandoning his amber drink, staring at me as his eyebrows draw together.

Elena's voice chimes in then, as she and Ryker approach. "Hey, I thought you and Willow would be gone already. Didn't expect to see you two until tomorrow, at the earliest." But as she glances at me, her perky smile slowly fades.

Instead, it's Ryker who voices her question, his attention bouncing between Tristan and me. "Where is she then?"

"Bathroom?" Natalie unhelpfully suggests.

Brent and Teagan come from the side, his arm around her shoulders. His grin lowers at the somberness, his eyes sweeping the group. "You're still around? Willow said you were leaving for the night."

"Fuck."

Fuck.

Elena grasps the side of her veil, twisting it in her fingers. "Did you text her?"

"She didn't answer." My teeth press together to resist from yelling because while I'm aware they're trying to help, they're not. Until she's *here*, no one is. "Unless she can't respond."

I release my phone, letting it thump onto the table, as my muscles lose any and all energy. If she can't respond, it means—

"Hawke, no," Ryker exclaims, knowing where my mind is. "It's *impossible*. He's locked up."

"Is he though?" I glance at Brent. "He was and still managed to harm you." After my call to my brother last night, I hadn't heard anything back, and now, the words from the note still buried in my desk drawer burn into my brain, mentally re-reading them, seeking something—*anything*—indicative of his abilities.

"You're assuming," Elena murmurs, pushing between the bodies, so she's closer to me. Her hands come up to my shoulders and she stares into my eyes. "We'll find her. Maybe she walked somewhere."

I'm so busy listening to Elena's pointless words, I don't hear my phone vibrating. Not until Tristan reaches over and hands it to me. "Hey, um, your phone is going off."

Willow. It better fucking be Willow because, if it's not, I can feel my mind slipping away. I can feel my stability snapping. I can feel myself fucking *losing* it.

When Willow was merely a stranger who needed saving, she was a task. But when she placed her arms around my neck, she became so much more.

She became *mine*. Mine to fucking love, mine to hold, and mine to kill for.

The longer I remain here with her whereabouts unknown, the quicker I feel the past returning. I may not have been inducted completely, but I was my father's son. He trained me to kill. When I was five, I was gifted a knife. When I was six, I knew how to use it as well as anyone else. When I was ten, I was handed a gun for the first time and taught to shoot.

I'm a trained killer and if that's who I need to be tonight to get her back, so fucking be it.

It isn't difficult to recall the feel of a gun or the trajectory it needs until it executes. Or the grip of a man's throat between my hands as I ensure he'll never come for her again.

When I turn my phone over, it isn't Willow's name flashing on my screen.

N: *Miller has escaped.*

N: *My men finally had access to him, but he was gone by the time they arrived.*

N: *Say the word and I'll send my men to you.*

My hand tightens around my phone and the urge to throw it away, far away, pulses through my arm. I nearly do too, if only to watch it hit the wall and smash, but I know my brother. If I don't message him back, he'll follow through.

Me: *No.*

Instead, I reach for the nearest thing, which happens to be Tristan's drink. I don't think twice, don't see through the red haze covering my eyes as I stand here *talking* when Miller is free and in the world again and Willow is missing.

"FUCK!"

The glass smashes across the room, narrowly missing wedding guests, but I can't care. Won't care. Cuts from glass are *nothing* compared to what Willow could be experiencing this very moment. She may have worked through much of her trauma, but what the fuck happens when the source of her nightmares is back?

"Miller's escaped."

Sounds of surprise echo through the group, and finally, Tristan asks, "How do you know for certain? Who was that?" He nudges his chin toward my phone.

"My brother," I grit between clenched teeth, already turning for the door

"Your brother?" Ryker repeats. "Man, you have a past you're not letting onto. What the fuck are you hiding?"

Now isn't the time. With quick fingers, I bring up the device tracking app built into her phone. When I gave it to her, did I set us up under one family account that way

I could track her, if the worst-case scenario was to arise? Yep, and now, I have zero fucking regrets because it's the only thing that'll lead me to her.

I make it to the front door by the time the dot, indicating her phone's location, flashes. Now, I need to hope the fucker didn't toss her phone away.

Feet quickly follow me, and by the time I make it to my car, Ryker's sliding into the passenger seat, Brent and Tristan in the back. To my left, Elena stands in her wedding dress, Natalie and Teagan each holding her hand as they observe the silent departure.

I throw the car into drive and get away from the venue so quickly, my tires skid in the pebbled driveway, kicking up rocks to mark our exit.

"Your wedding," is all I manage, cutting my eyes quickly to the right, toward Ryker.

He shrugs, looking grim. "Willow matters more, man. She's one of us, and so are you. You won't lose her."

"I'm killing him," I state. "The feds can charge me all they want, I don't fucking care. She'll be safe, alive, and he'll be six feet under by the time I'm done with him."

"Where does he have her?" Brent asks.

I turn down the next road, taking the only path out of the city I know, following the direction the dot indicates on the map. Without turning around, I toss my phone in the back seat.

"She's there."

"Where's there?" Brent voices my previous inner question.

"That's an abandoned airfield," Tristan states, meeting my eyes in the rear-view mirror. "We get calls pretty often, down at the station, usually about dumbass kids getting stoned there, believing it to be an easy place to hide from us."

"Fuck." An airfield. Which means Miller has a plane.

He's likely been planning this for a while.

I press the gas harder.

"Beneath my seat, there's a gun. Get it."

Behind me, Brent retrieves it, sliding it onto the console between Ryker and me.

"I wish I had mine on me," Tristan mutters. "Two weapons are better than one."

"I'll only need one."

Long, country roads eventually lead me to the airfield, and as we approach, a small private plane sits, lit by its own lights. I stomp on the brake, throwing us all forward with the quick arrival, but it doesn't hurt. The only thing that can injure me now is finding Willow, heart stopped and soul gone to the heavens.

Forty-Six

WILLOW

Things slowly begin to make sense again, as I come to, but only for a short time as I wake in the back of a car.

Hawke really fucked me senseless, it seems.

I move, and my neck aches, cramping as I straighten it. My lips feel cracked and my mouth dry, and that's when it all comes back.

Getting grabbed, the stab in the neck… Alex.

I blink, but don't indicate I'm awake as I take in the back seat of the dark car. Two figures in the front, and due to the light of the dashboard's buttons, Alex's face is lit up.

A whimper escapes me, but I quickly bite down on any sound that'll give me away. Instead, keeping my head still, I scan what I can see, catching sight of the door and the lock. How quickly can I sit up, unlock the back door, and throw myself from the car before he'd notice? How far would I get before he caught up to me?

I manage to scan around me, seeking my clutch. If Alex has any brain, he would have gotten rid of it, but then, he also may have been so focused on stealing me, that he didn't check. I don't see it, but I can only hope it's nearby and accessible for when we stop because my phone is in there.

"Ah," Alex grunts, seemingly to himself. "Finally."

Finally. I shut my eyes, faking sleep, until the moment we stop. Two doors immediately open and close before mine is opened, a fresh wave of cool, night air gusting over my form.

I kick out, throwing any and all strength into my lower calves as I manage to hit whoever is there—ideally Alex. I hear the familiar voice curse, telling me that's indeed who it is. In the same instance, I throw my body from the vehicle, not even making it two feet before Alex's arms wrap around my waist.

"You're not going anywhere, cunt. You and I have a trip to take." He turns us around, one hand cupping my chin to force me in a particular direction.

There's a plane, readying to take off, made apparent by the few men standing around, ignoring the obvious kidnapping occurring right in front of them.

Still, I shout, "Help!" on the off-chance one of them doesn't realize I'm an unwilling traveller.

When no one responds, or even turns to peek, Alex snarls, "Real cute, pet. No one here will help you." He shoves me in the direction of the plane's staircase, but I throw my heels into old, cracked cement, hoping for some resistance.

"Alex," I protest. "Fuck, stop!"

His evil laugh throws me straight into that basement again. This whole scenario isn't the same though, and while my insides wish to curl up and avoid his wrath, I've *never* fought back before, making this instance so different than any other experience we've shared.

"Little Willow gained some fight," he murmurs. "I kinda like it. It'll make what I do to you all the better."

But the comments. Those are the same. He'd always talk through his torture. For a half second, I freeze, letting him push me around.

"You've always been such a meek, little slave. Always taking me how I wanted and never complaining one bit. Maybe it's the time apart, but I think I might prefer you like this. Believing you have a shot is really cute, and I'll enjoy breaking you all the more as you fight for your life." He pauses, letting his last words sink in. "Because this time, you won't make it out alive. You and I will be taking a small trip, and when I finish with you, I'm returning for Teagan. The two of you *stole*," his hand tightens around my throat, "my life. Made me the bad guy in all this, instead of owning up to being whores." His face rubs against the side of mine, bringing bile to the top of my throat. He does another pass, and then I feel something wet—his tongue, I think—lick at the side of my face. "When you're dead and gone, I'll make her pay worse than I ever have before. What I do to you will be *nothing* compared to her. I'll finalize my revenge by returning for Hawke Blackwood. If you're a good girl, maybe I'll bury your bodies together."

It's not the thought of him taking my own life, or even Teagan's. It's Hawke. For all the shit that's happened in the past few months, Alex will *not* touch Hawke.

I screech, kicking my feet out, scratching at his arms, and doing anything to be free of his arms. One loosens the slightest bit, and I throw my body forward, breaking his hard hold entirely.

Yes. Victory pushes me forward, and I run in a circle, doubling back to go the opposite way from the observing men. I'm sure they're only paid to be here for the plane, but I can't risk one catching me and handing me back over to the villain of my story.

Feet pound behind me, getting closer with every step, but I don't dare look. Instead, I push on, pumping my arms and legs in an attempt to increase my speed, even by the slimmest chance.

Alex growls before his body tackles me to the ground. My hands reach out to catch me, but it's useless as Alex's arm wraps around my body and twists.

In the last second, before I end up on my back, I spot lights in the distance. Like a car's headlights, but I can't focus on the fact that Alex likely called backup and they're just now arriving, which makes this even more impossible.

"Bitch," he curses, forcing my arms above my head. He climbs over me, pinning my legs down. "I wanted to wait until the ship, but you seem to think you can win."

With his free hand, he reaches out and slaps the side of my face, hard enough I can't ignore the pain, and blood pools in my mouth. I spit it out, revelling when light pink lands on his white shirt.

He clutches my throat, removing any chance of air, and all my energy goes into getting my throat freed. My mouth parts, welcoming any remaining air in, but his grip tightens, making breathing nearly impossible.

Maybe he'll kill me here and now. Maybe he'll end this before he gets me to wherever his final destination is.

Maybe, in the last second that I still have air, I can reimagine this night's ending. Picture Hawke getting to me before Alex, and the fact that we'd be home now, and I'd be passed out from the numerous orgasms he'd given me.

Maybe, just maybe, I'm not imagining the body slamming into Alex, throwing him to the side, and returning my breath.

Forty-Seven

She's *right* there. Right. Fucking. There.

With a roar, I leap from the car, pushing my body as quick as it'll go until I reach her side.

He's pinning her to the airstrip's cement, one hand at her throat and the other holding her hands above her head.

Everything around me blurs. Everything but her. But him.

But the red haze of death filling my eyes.

I lunge, throwing myself into him and forcing him off her. The moment she's freed, I slam Alex onto his back and land on top of him, pinning him the same way he did her.

Brent should still have the gun I asked him to retrieve, but a gun is too quick, too painless for what Alex deserves. Arresting him those couple months back was too clean an ending, and that's why this is happening. I've dedicated my life to the law, to not being my family, but sometimes, it's the rougher lifestyles that have it right. The legal route will still allow Alex to live, which only grants him the ability to try this all again.

My way ends this. Alex won't have another chance.

I smash my fist into his face, recalling the way Ryker once told me he hurt Alex enough that it got him sent to prison. Back then, Tristan pulled him off Alex to avoid killing him. This time, I know, even without looking up, no one will stop me. They all want the same thing.

"You'll never fucking touch her again."

With two fists, I wail on him, each one taking its turn. His blocks are weak—as is the rest of him. Only a weak man would prey on a woman like that.

"You'll never think of her again."

I take a break from punching, grasping his shirt, only to lift his head and smash it down on the cement. It makes a loud crack, telling me it's over.

But it's not over. It'll never be over. Not until *I'm* satisfied the fucker is dealing with the devil.

I lift him again and throw his head down, the skin making a squelching noise as the cement completely breaks through.

And again.

And again.

No one stops me. No one dares interrupt what I've finally ended. I should have allowed them to do this in the basement. This would have been over months ago, and Willow saved, having never experienced hell all over again.

I take penance from him. Hitting his head onto the ground, punching his face, anything I can take—any ounce of blood I can claim. An apology to Willow for not doing right by her.

His face is mangled, the back of his head a mess I can't make out anymore. I've long since killed him, I know it, and finally, my strength does too as it's zapped out of me.

I lift my head, scanning the immediate area. The men that were here are now gone, clearly money only bought so much of their loyalty. Nearby, Tristan has my gun hovered in the air, but seeing me finished, lowers it to his side. Brent and Ryker share identical expressions of appreciation.

It's funny how a single man can make monsters of each one of us. I left the lifestyle to avoid being a killer with no morals, and yet, I didn't think twice when it came to murdering Alex tonight.

Behind the wall formed by them, Willow is still on the ground, staring blankly at me.

At me.

I glance down at the blood staining my hands and my suit. A suit that represented so much an hour ago; the opposite of what just happened here. Ryker's wedding day ended in a fucking murder that Willow was forced to witness.

I want to move, but I don't know how to. The only thing I need right now is to hold her, even if it means staining her pretty bridesmaid dress with *him*.

Finally, I do. The compulsion to hold her becoming too overwhelming to resist. I push past the guys, falling to my knees beside her. Still, she hasn't moved, scanning me silently with wide eyes.

I hold my hands out, now disgusted at what I'm about to touch her with, but hoping she'll accept me anyway.

"It's over, Willow. For real this time. All over. I'm so fucking sorry."

I don't know which of my words break her this time, but she falls into my arms, a sob sounding through the night air.

"I-I tried, Hawke. I *really* tried to fight back this time."

"You did, baby, and you did fucking amazing." Pulling back, I cup her cheeks, staring into her beautiful eyes. "You survived, Willow. You held on long enough for me to find you."

"I-I don't how-how you did, but… *thank you.*"

I stroke her face, staining her with the scum's blood.

"I'll always find you." I grasp her hand, sliding it down onto my chest and over my rapidly beating heart. "You're in here forever, which means there won't be anywhere you go, I can't find you."

My words seem to steal the last of her energy and she falls into me, her head landing on my shoulder as her grip tightens, holding on to me with every ounce of strength she has left. After a moment, the soft paces of the guys come closer.

"What do you want to do about Miller?" Brent asks.

"My phone." After a moment, he returns from my car, phone in hand.

I take it, opening up the most recent text thread.

Me: *Never mind. Send your men. There's a body they need to take care of.*

I add in the coordinates of the airfield's location, and wait for his response.

N: *You got it. I'm proud of you. Men will be there in an hour.*

Without responding, I close the app, dropping the phone onto the cement.

"An hour. People will be here in an hour for him."

Brent crouches, coming into my line of sight over Willow's shoulder. "Let's take her home, man."

I nod, unable to answer. By now, Willow's as stunned as when I first met her and carried her from the basement. Like that moment, I lift her into my arms and walk us to the car, overwhelmed by the shocking, painful similarities of both experiences. Yet, I'm thankful, as they now represent a new beginning.

Taking her from the basement was the beginning of us.

Taking her from the airfield is the beginning of our future.

Forty-Eight

This time when I awake, it's surrounded by Hawke's familiar scent, the feel of his bed, and the knowledge of safety. Hawke is lying on his side, facing me, and as my eyes peel open, he smiles.

"I should be creeped out you're watching me sleep."

"But?"

"But I'm not." I shrug one shoulder. "I like it. Makes me feel safe."

Hawke reaches out and grabs my hand, pressing his lips to it in a gentle kiss. The touch is a reminder of his own knuckles, stained red the last time I saw him.

Last night.

When Alex found me.

When Hawke killed—

"Oh my god."

He spots the moment the realization hits me, and sits up, bringing me along with him. His eyes follow me, waiting for me to react however he believes I will.

But I don't. With a calm voice, I state, "You killed Alex."

"I did."

"He took me. You found me."

"Always."

"I'm safe now." I scan his room. "Home."

"It was an inner battle to take you to the hospital or not."

"I'm fine," I state, even without checking myself. I know I am though, because I don't feel bruised like any of the other times Alex would get a hold of me. "I don't want to be anywhere but here, with you."

"How do you feel?"

In his eyes, I see the hidden question. "I'm fine, Hawke."

"Him capturing you again… I was worried it'd be so much of a reminder of—" he cuts himself off, shaking his head and adds, "And then seeing what I did…"

Again, I repeat, "I'm fine. I'm better than fine. I won't allow Alex to kidnap my mental state forever. Besides," my attention lands on my lap, "I think some part of me appreciated your actions last night. As in, I needed to see him, like that, *gone*, for the processing to continue. I can't be traumatized over someone that isn't here any longer, you know?"

"Not sure it works like that," he crooks a smile, "but I get what you mean."

"You protected me." I reach for his hand. "For that, I'll never fear you. I'm just sorry you had to kill him. I know that kind of lifestyle is what you avoid."

"I wish I found you sooner," he whispers, eyes landing on my neck, where Alex strangled me. "I could have prevented so much if I was ten minutes quicker."

I shake off his self-hatred, brushing a hand down his cheek, thumb pausing over the piercing in his brow. "You got to me. It's all that matters. You found me quickly."

"For a while, I wasn't certain… what… I'd find." He shuts his eyes and his throat bobs with the difficult words.

I slide myself into his lap, wrapping my arms around his neck. "I fought him, Hawke. I did something I never did in the past, and I believe the only way I was able to, was because of *you*. These months with you, loving you, it empowers me in a way I never felt before. All those times, I let myself be attacked. Being trained by him to not even try. Last night, none of that mattered. The past didn't come up, and I think that's because of *you*. I love you, Hawke, so fucking much."

Without waiting for him to say more, I press my lips to his, letting the sheet between us fall so that my bare breasts press against his chest. He kisses me back, softly at first, and then rougher, his hand weaving between my hair as he tilts my head this way and that, controlling my body as well as the kiss.

I shift from his lap and pull him down with me, his lips moving down the column of my throat.

"I love you too, Willow. I've claimed you as mine, and you know what happens when a mafia man claims a woman as theirs?"

Giggling, I move my head until I can see his face. "Except you said so yourself, you've left that lifestyle."

"I temporarily adopted it back last night. On an as-needed basis."

"Then what happens when a mafia man claims a woman?"

"They become ours. It means their happiness becomes our greatest priority. Their pleasure," he strokes his hand down my bare side, "our every thought. Their safety comes before our own life. Their body is ours to enjoy. And when we say 'I do,' it's forever." With his eyes on mine, he repeats, "Forever."

"Forever," I agree, accepting all he's giving. "Forever and always, Hawke. Now, show me what a mafia man is like when he's pleasuring his woman."

Hawke chuckles darkly, making my core clench. He shifts his body down mine, his lips following his path until he makes it to my chest, stopping once to suck at each nipple individually before continuing downward.

"I'll never lose you," he murmurs into my skin, tattooing his promise to my stomach. "I'll never trap you though. As long as you'll have me, as long as you'll want me, I'm yours, and you're," his mouth continues down, hovering over my core, "mine."

With his final word, his tongue claims my pussy.

He parts my lips, keeping me spread for his unforgiving tongue. Ensuring he won't go anywhere, my legs bind his head, locking around it tightly.

Until he chuckles against my thigh and pulls away, breaking my hold. With my ankles in his hand, he pins them to the side of his body. "Keep these here."

"Or?" I challenge.

"Or pay the price."

His price is always worth the outcome though, so the moment his tongue spears me again, I move my legs, replacing them by his head, daring him to follow through.

Much to my disappointment, he does nothing, but instead of dwelling on it, my head falls to the pillow beneath me and I let him pleasure my insides with every flick of his tongue. It doesn't take long until the heat blooms within my core. I arch off the bed, following the sensation and then—

He pulls back, his grin a delicious coating of my essence. "Ah, ah, baby. I told you there'd be a price to pay."

"*That's* your price?"

"Precisely." His finger dips knuckle-deep inside me. "You don't listen, you don't get to come."

His finger crooks, pressing the invisible button inside me that makes me moan. He taps it once, twice, and when I lift my hips and press myself onto his hand, he pulls back again.

My responding moan is low and dragged-out, full of annoyance. *"Hawke."*

He chuckles but lifts entirely from the bed, going for the nightstand. I watch with rapt attention, biting down on my smile because I know what's there.

He returns a moment later with a blindfold and rope, gesturing for me to lie flat. Eager, I do, positioning my hands and legs in the places he needs them. Hawke binds me quickly, a well-practiced maneuver we've done many times.

When I'm tied and unable to move, he covers my eyes with the blindfold, removing my sight and then asks his usual, "What's your safe word?"

"Angel."

"Good girl."

I hear him move around the bed, but impatience has my thighs rubbing together, damp from what he started.

"You look so hungry for more."

"I am," I cry, a slight whine to my tone.

"Your punishment hasn't even begun, Willow. You won't make it very long."

"Please."

He chuckles. "You trust me?"

Taken out of the moment for a second, I reply, "You know I do."

"I want today to be about new things, Willow."

I can't imagine what these "new things" are, but a thrill goes through me with unknown possibilities.

The air prickles in anticipation, charged energy surrounding us. I move in any way I can, conveying my impatience, even knowing it's not what he told me to do.

"So greedy," he purrs, his voice sounding closer. "So mine. Mine to love."

His finger strokes my neck, and I bend it, giving him

more space.

"Mine to have."

The finger traces my nipples before dipping toward my stomach.

"Mine to hold."

It continues over my mound.

"Mine to set free."

He enters me, adding a second finger to stretch my pussy. I whimper, back arching off the bed, but as fast as my body registered the pleasure, he's removing it.

"Mine to play with."

"Hawke…"

"You know how to stop this if you really want to. One word and this all ends."

I don't want this to end though.

His touch goes away all together, leaving me to lie on the bed and contemplate all the ways I can convince him to let me come.

The bed dips and—

Vvvvvvv.

I cry out, my arms and legs yanking on the bounds with the new sensation.

"Wh-what?"

He drags the vibrator around my hip and up to my breasts. The quick motion of the rubber is tingling against my straining nipples, but thankfully, he doesn't remain there for long before dipping back toward my core.

He's going to let me come. This is it.

The vibrator dances over my clit, re-sparking what was already there, the need to come so strong I—

He pulls it away, drifting it down the skin of my leg.

"Hawke!" I cry out, feeling on the verge of sobbing. "This is *cruel.*"

"You didn't listen. This is your punishment."

A punishment kinder than any in the past, and yet

somehow, much crueler. With Hawke, I don't want to curl up and die but rather spread my wings and live and embrace his concept of punishment.

The vibrator returns, and even though I know it'll be taken away before I'm given what I need, I still can't help but rock my hips and attempt to orgasm in the seconds the sensation remains.

When it's stolen away, this time, the sob cannot be contained. The feeling too intense to hold back, I yank on my bindings, suddenly *needing* them gone.

"Hawke… I can't…" Can't keep this up. Can't survive without orgasming.

"Oh, you can, and you will."

He presses the vibrator back to my core, but this time, his mouth accompanies it. His tongue flicks at my clit, and the vibrator is moved toward my entrance. My muscles clench, my entire body freezing, the pending orgasm second to everything else.

"Just feel for a moment. I'm not putting it inside you."

His lips create suction on my clit, making it easy to relax my body again and forget about the earlier concern. He moves the vibrator in slow circles while his tongue attacks me.

This time, I finish the climb, and when I come, shouting into the room, he allows me, not stealing it away.

When I return to Earth, and my breathing evens out, I check, "You deemed punishment time over?"

"You know I can't deny you for long."

The vibrator is tossed off to the side, the blindfold being ripped from my eyes as well. Hawke climbs up my body, repositioning my bound legs in a way to accept him. His eyes lock with mine and his thick cock pushes inside easily, assisted by evidence of my orgasm.

I moan, eyes shutting as I let myself *feel*. Feel his piercings scrape at my inside, feel every inch of his body lined up with mine, and feel ultimate trust for the man who re-built me.

Our hips rock together, our motions hurried and messy, our moans mingling in the air. I'm still sensitive in-side and feel the moment I tighten around him. He clasps my face and takes my mouth in a bruising kiss, feeding me his moan as hot cum shoots off inside me.

He unhurriedly pulls back from my mouth as the or-gasm subsides for both of us. I'm breathless and limp.

Hawke quickly undoes my bindings, rubbing feeling back into my wrists and ankles. He's always so concerned, and I secretly love it.

"You okay?"

"Never better. I'd stop you if I wasn't."

"I know." He sighs, pressing a chaste kiss to my palm. "I'm always so worried you won't though."

"Don't be. You—"

A door slamming from downstairs interrupts my next words, as do the two bellows coming through the house.

"Get down here!" Ryker yells.

"Stop fucking!" Tristan adds.

"I really need to take my keys back," Hawke growls, pulling me from bed. "Before they wander up here though and I have to kill them too for daring to see you like this, you need to get dressed."

He opens our shared closet, half of it filled with my clothes. Mine. After the trial, Elena finally convinced me it was time for me to shop and I'll happily admit the girls' day I shared with her and Natalie was too fun to ever turn down another one.

Once we're both dressed, Hawke leads me down the stairs, finding everyone in the living room. Brent and Tea-gan are seated on the couch, Ryker and Elena beside them. Tristan leans against the far wall, while Natalie is sitting on the single-seater by his side.

"Don't you two have a honeymoon to get to or something?" I nod toward Elena.

Ryker cuts in, "Well, some asshole decided to fuck up my wedding by capturing one of our own, and even I can't ignore that. So we've postponed it for a little bit."

"Go," I urge, "I'm sorry for last night."

Elena waves her hand. "We discussed it, and honestly, it just seems strange to. In a month or so, when things settle down, we'll go. For now, we want to be here." She scans the room. "With everyone. This is our version of a vacation."

"*Well,*" Ryker emphasizes, rolling his eyes, "it's not, because we're not naked but close enough."

In the midst of laughter, Natalie asks me, "How do you feel?"

"All right," I reply honestly. "Bit tired."

This time, I glance toward Teagan, catching the secondary hidden question amidst her gaze. *Are you lying about that claim?* When I shake my head subtly, her lips twitch, informing me she gets my meaning.

"I've been trying to probe into how Miller escaped," Tristan announces. "I mean, I'm sure we can make our assumptions, but if we can track the exact fucker who was on the inside…" His threat trails off.

Money being the most likely motivator. No doubt, he paid guards off.

"I also have connections to the prison," Hawke says. "I'll see what I can discover."

They still won't give up, even with him gone. I scan the room, pausing on each of my new friends, and ending with Tristan and Hawke as they animatedly discuss yet another plan.

Laying my hand on Hawke's, I shake my head, ending the arrangement from going further. "Does it matter? Like you said, Tristan, we can make our assumptions—money being the driving force. The rest doesn't matter, and I don't want any of us living in the past. He's gone, therefore, we need to move on."

Hawke glances down, twisting his arm so he's clasping my hand rather than mine being overtop his. The corners of his eyes crinkle with pride as he smiles wide, nodding slowly, silently agreeing with me.

"She's right, Tristan," he murmurs, still holding my gaze, "I think we did what we need to, and the rest can disappear. The how isn't important any longer."

Tristan's lips curl in a frown, obviously dismayed at not getting the complete truth, but even he tilts his head in acceptance.

"Well—" But whatever Brent is about to say is cut off, as he stands, attention focused outside. "Dude, why is there a fancy ass car parked outside your house, with a fancy ass scary-looking guy staring at the house?"

Forty-Nine

HAWKE

As Brent stated, there's a black car parked by my curb. Its windows are tinted black, making it impossible for anyone to see inside. For certain, there's a driver in the front seat because the owner of this car doesn't drive himself.

"Stay here," I mutter to everyone and rush outside, coming face to face with the man I haven't seen since I left home, when his much-younger face watched with agony from the stairwell.

My brother, Nico Corsetti, is leaning against the car, his arms crossed. Sunglasses perch on his head, not at all hiding his watchful eyes. He's so much larger than the kid I remember, and yet, still so much the same.

He's identical to our father.

"Why are you here?"

Nico spreads his arms wide. "A brother can't come visit?"

"We're no longer family," I remark coldly, "Blackwood, remember?"

"Oh, I recall." His arms lower back to his side. "But I also remember how last names no longer mattered when it came to your goal. It was all too easy for you to reach out for help. Not just once, but three times."

I flinch with the reminder of the desperate decisions I made—and the mistake. I should never have asked for RCMP assistance. Should have just killed Alex myself in the moment and saved so much trouble.

"That why you're here? To gloat."

"Not at all." Nico kicks off the car, taking a few strides closer. "I sent my men last night to clean up your mess, but came as well to see you. And to apologize."

Surprise has my eyes widening. "For?"

"You asked for a simple favour. To kill Miller when he was in prison, but because my men were unable to complete the task in time, he escaped, forcing you to revisit your past last night." He pauses, scanning me knowingly. "I saw the body. You did good, Hawke."

"It's fine. I should never have asked you to complete a task that was always mine."

Nico's head tilts to the side as he gives me another one of his studying stares. I imagine him now, in Dad's office, giving others the same knowing scan. "You've grown, Hawke, for the better. Life away from the Family looks good on you."

"Life within the Family looks good on you," I shoot back. "Capo suits you."

He chuckles, rubbing a hand over his head. "I still think you would have been better at it. Natural leadership qualities and all that. You already have your girl." He jerks his chin behind me. "I feel as though I'm stumbling through the role. Father's hounding me to take a wife, but I haven't found my future queen yet."

I glance behind me, spotting Willow standing in the doorway. I don't need to look to know six other faces are plastered to my window.

"That her?"

"Yeah," I admit, turning back to face him. "Yes, that's

her." There's an edge to my tone; I need him to know not to touch her. Brother or not, he's seen Alex—seen the outcome of my protection.

"She'll never be harmed, brother. Relax."

"I know the family's tendencies," I mutter, still an edge to my tone. My spine straightens, reclaiming the piece of myself I've forgotten in this conversation. "Dad know you're here?"

"No. I haven't told him or Mother. Aurora or Rafael either."

Hearing my siblings' names—names I haven't heard or even thought about in a *long* time hits my gut in a funny, discerning way.

"You have a decent group of friends, it seems," he continues, now staring at my window. "You made your own little mafia."

"Yep." He's learning too much, so my answers grow shorter. He's not a dumb Capo, I'm sure, so soon, he'll pick up on the reason.

"Hm," he grunts, doing exactly as I guessed, "I suppose this is it then."

"Bye."

Nico smirks, stepping closer again. He lifts his hand, leaving me the opportunity to accept or decline it. Instead, I stare.

"Be happy with your girl, Hawke. This is the last time you will see or hear from me, if you wish. Regardless of the past, or even present choices, you're still my brother. You're still a Corsetti. You need anything, I'm here."

Truth is sketched all over his face; no hidden meaning in his words, so I step closer and accept his handshake.

"Thank you, Nico. For the assistance, and everything. And… the visit." The admittance is rough on my throat, even as I add, "But we need to return to what we were last year. I'm a Blackwood and you're a Corsetti. Our lives don't intersect for the safety of everyone involved." Alex was enough to last a lifetime, and fuck if I'd ever place Willow in harm's way because who knows what a rival family would do to her, if they got wind of who I truly am.

Nico returns the shake and quickly releases me, stepping back until he's pressed against his vehicle again. "Understood, brother. I am sorry for the past, even if Father never said it. This family owes you more than I can verbalize, but if it's silence you want from us, so be it."

"Thank you," is all I reply with, continuing to keep my responses short.

With another nod, he glances behind me. I know he's looking at Willow and it takes every nerve in my body not to shove her inside the house and keep her safe from his examination.

"You may call yourself Blackwood, but deep down, you're a Corsetti. I wonder how long you'll continue to run from that fact, when I saw the truth of who you are last night."

With that, Nico climbs into the car and it pulls away from the curb in time for his words to echo through my entire body, impacting the little nerves within my brain that have me wanting to chase after him and prove him wrong.

Problem is, he might not be too far off. Last night was from a place I was bred from. Not everyone could kill a man the way I did so effortlessly.

Small steps pad down the pathway and Willow links her hand in mine, laying her head on my shoulder. She doesn't speak, just lets us be.

"That was my brother," I finally confess.

"I figured. I also heard almost everything." She moves in front of me. "You know, he's wrong, right? You're not who he claims you are. You're who you *choose* to be."

I kiss her forehead. The fact she believes that is the reason I love her, even if she's incorrect, because there's a chance that Nico could be right.

Either way, I take her hand and walk back into the house, shutting the door behind us, and even locking it for extra measure. The moment the door is closed, six people are on us, with Ryker pushing to the front, gesturing toward the door at my back.

"Are we ever going to get to know who that is?"

"No." I slide past him and into the living room.

Brent's staring out the front window still, but he turns at my entrance. "Can I take a wild guess and say he has something to do with your connection to the RCMP?"

"You could guess that and I'll admit you're correct."

"Can I take another guess and say he's the brother you mentioned last night?" Tristan chimes.

"You could guess that and I'll admit you're correct," I repeat, giving them that much.

After a beat of silence, Brent shakes his head. "No more than that though, huh? Nothing to expand on?"

"Right again. It's all that matters, we'll leave it at that. That guy, he's a person from my past."

Willow meets my eye, and when I stretch out a hand to her, she takes it and sits on my lap.

"The past no longer affects us," she states, loud enough for the entire room.

"That's very true. We fight for what we want, for who we wish to be, and—"

"And who we wish to be with," she fills in.

"That's you," I whisper, this time only for her.

Her response is to touch the spot over my heart.

It wasn't an easy journey for any of us, but we made it.

Ryker and Elena fought their history, moving beyond old mistakes and irrational games.

Tristan and Natalie fought against family, making the ultimate decision of which side to choose.

Brent and Teagan fought themselves, becoming who they've always wanted to be.

And Willow and me, we fought trauma. Each other. The possibility of a future. It was a hellish fight, and one I'm happy to have won.

I won her.

Willow and me… we're endgame.

What's Next?

Remember Nico Corsetti, Hawke's brother? Nico begins Fractured Ever Afters, a fairy tale inspired mafia romance series.

Book 1, The Hunt in Elusion, is up for preorder on all ebook retailers. Releasing January 10, 2023. It's Cinderella inspired involving primal play, fake identity, and Capo & maid romance.

Get The Desire in Deception, a prequel to the Fractured Ever Afters series in the Heartless Heroes Anthology. Read all about Hawke and Nico's parents dark beginning.

More Books

Dark Romance

CAPTIVE WRITINGS
Ruthless Letters
Obsessive Messages
Vicious Texts
Burning Notes

FRACTURED EVER AFTERS
The Hunt in Elusion
The Craving in Slumber
The Beauty in Scars

STANDALONES
Heartless Heroes Anthology

Paranormal Romance

THE WITCHES BIND TRILOGY
Cure Bound
Moon Bound
Union Bound
Fate's Binding: The Witches' Bind Trilogy Complete
Collection

SHADOW TRIALS
Princess of Ruin

Cala Griffin

Interested in contemporary romance? I now have
an alter ego specific to that genre.

Check out calagriffin.com to learn more.

Acknowledgements

I can't believe this series is over! Thank you to all the readers who stuck by me with this series! You are all the best!!

I can't thank my PA, Megan, enough. She was a trooper as I worked through this book (and series) and took on so many roles for me - beta reader, assistant, and part of my PR team.

And then, thank you to my other beta, Colleen! Your words are invaluable.

Rebecca Barney from Fairest Reviews Editing Services gets huge thanks for all the edits she did on this book. Love working with you!

Thank you to The Next Step PR. Colleen, Jill, Megan, Anna, and of course, Kiki - you're all amazing. Thank you for everything you do. You're the best team to have!

Thank you to Cat Imb of TRC Designs for giving Hawke his cover! I love it so much!

Thank you to Yorkville University for the Counselling degree. This book had such interesting moments to write, to pull on that piece of my education.

Thank you to all the bloggers, booktokers, and bookstagrammers who helped with the release of this book. Your help doesn't go unnoticed. Thank you for continuing on this insane trip with me, and I hope you're ready for more.

About the Author

M.L. Philpitt is Canadian-born and raised, and enjoys representing Canada within her novels. As a Ravenclaw, she loves education, having undergraduate degrees in English Literature and Sociology, a certificate in Autism and Behavioural Sciences, and a MA in Counselling Psychology.

She writes in various romance new adult genres including paranormal, fantasy, and dark romance. She has lots of crazy trapped in her head for readers to enjoy. M.L. Philpitt writes contemporary romance through her alter ego, Cala Griffin.

When M.L. Philpitt isn't making up stories, she's devouring those imagined by other authors. Her love of reading began when she was a young child and only grew with age. She enjoys many genres, as reflected in her writing preferences.

Visit mlphilpitt.com for all the important links and to sign up for her newsletter.

Join *M.L. Philpitt's Minions* on Facebook for sneak peeks, book news, and fun.